THE ITALIAN LOVER

The Italian Lover

A NOVEL

Robert Hellenga

LITTLE, BROWN AND COMPANY

NEW YORK   BOSTON   LONDON

Little, Brown and Company
Hachette Book Group USA
237 Park Avenue, New York, NY 10017

Visit our Web site at www.HachetteBookGroupUSA.com

First Edition: September 2007

Map by George W. Ward

Library of Congress Cataloging-in-Publication Data

Hellenga, Robert.
    The Italian lover : a novel / Robert Hellenga. — 1st ed.
        p. cm.
    ISBN-10: 0-316-11763-3
    ISBN-13: 978-0-316-11763-0
    1. Motion picture authorship — Fiction.   2. Motion pictures — Fiction.   3. Americans —
Italy — Fiction.   4. Florence (Italy) — Fiction.   I. Title.
PS3558.E4753I84   2007
813'.54 — dc22   2007008716

10 9 8 7 6 5 4 3 2 1

Q-MART

TO BILL AND SYDNEY

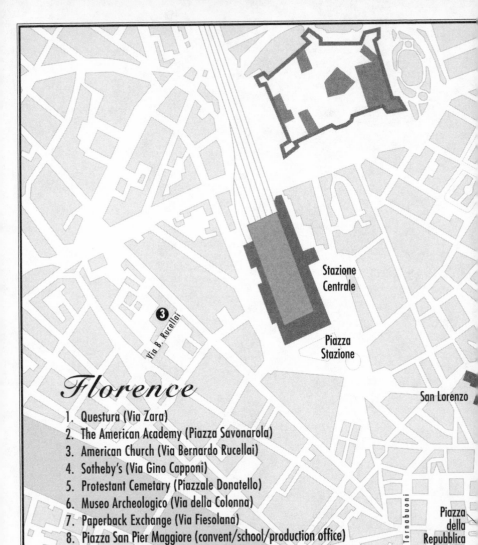

Florence

1. Questura (Via Zara)
2. The American Academy (Piazza Savonarola)
3. American Church (Via Bernardo Rucellai)
4. Sotheby's (Via Gino Capponi)
5. Protestant Cemetary (Piazzale Donatello)
6. Museo Archeologico (Via della Colonna)
7. Paperback Exchange (Via Fiesolana)
8. Piazza San Pier Maggiore (convent/school/production office)
9. Michael and Beryl's apartment (Via Pietrapiana)
10. Woody's apartment (Piazza Tasso)
11. Margot's studio (Lungarno Guicciardini)
12. Albergo Porta Rossa (Via Porta Rossa)
13. Tribunale (Via Magazzini)
14. Enoteca Pinchiorri (Via Ghibellina)
15. Margot's apartment (Piazza Santa Croce)

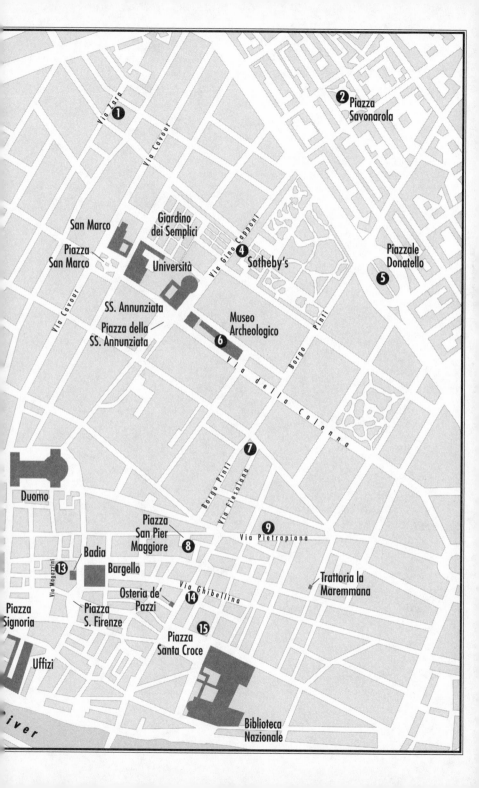

PART I

Preproduction

The Bebop Club

Saturday night. End of September. Florence, Italy. Margot Harrington excused herself from a table at Il Fiasco in Via dei Servi, saying that if she had another grappa she'd be too tired to walk home and that if she drank another espresso she'd never get to sleep.

It had been a long week of endless meetings, and she was tired of talking, almost sorry she'd brought up the subject of the film, which she wouldn't have done except that everyone was sick of talking shop, and the conversation had slowed to a trickle. Besides, she was excited about it, so why not talk about it? A film about her. It *was* exciting.

She offered to pay for her share of the dinner, but Signor Alberti waved her away, inclining his head ever so slightly toward Mr. Bancroft, one of the sponsors of the conference, as if to say, *Let the Americans pay.* Margot said her ciaos and her good-byes and stepped out into the street. She could take a bus (too complicated), or a cab (too expensive), or she could walk. It was a lovely fall evening, almost crisp, almost midwestern.

The sidewalk in front of the Bebop Club on the other side of Via dei Servi was crowded with young people who were making so much noise that she almost didn't recognize the song that was being piped out into the street:

> *Oh, baby don't you want to go*
> *Oh, baby don't you want to go*
> *Back to the land of California*
> *to my sweet home Chicago*

It was a song her father had sung, and now, on this cool September evening, it overwhelmed her, as if someone had stuck a knife in her ribs.

She'd lived in Italy for almost twenty-four years. She missed her parents, but they were dead, so she might as well miss them in Italy as in the States. She missed her sisters too, but one lived in California and one in Florida, so living in Florence she probably saw more of them than if she'd been living at home. In Chicago, that is. And they thought nothing of sending a niece or a nephew to spend a month or two or three with their aunt Margot in Italy; Aunt Margot, who taught them things that they hadn't been taught at home. So what? If they wanted to know why she wasn't married, she told them. Why not? She liked living in a big apartment in Piazza Santa Croce and running her own book conservation workshop, or *studio,* on Lungarno Guicciardini, between the Chiesa Presbiteriana and the British Institute.

MARGOT HARRINGTON
RESTAURAZIONE DEI LIBRI ANTICHI

And she didn't want to live or work anywhere else, not London, not New York, not even Rome.

She got lonely from time to time, but she'd had a string of lovers, most of them married. Well, why not? That's why she was so beautiful. She hadn't been beautiful when she first came to Italy, after the big flood in 1966. She'd been mousy. Then for a while she'd been spunky, and then for a while she was handsome, and finally she became beautiful. If enough Italian men tell you you're beautiful, you become beautiful. That's why you see so many beautiful women in Italy. If they—her nieces and nephews—wanted to know why she had so many friends, she explained that too. In Italian. *Chi ha l'amor nel petto, ha lo spron ne' fianchi.* A spur in the loins. Let them figure it out. They were going to have to learn about these things sometime. It might as well be in Italy, where human nature can be accommodated more easily than in the United States.

She pushed her way through the crowd on the narrow sidewalk, paid the ten thousand lire cover charge, and squeezed through the door. The Bebop Club wasn't one of her favorite places. It was too noisy, too crowded, too big, like an enormous cave that opened up into other caves, like the Carlsbad Caverns in New Mexico. She had no idea how deep you could go and had no intention of finding out. She wanted to sit at a table in the main cavern so she could see the singer, who was still singing "Sweet Home, Chicago," really belting it out, playing an astonishing guitar—silver or chrome, light reflecting off it, blinding. A young woman joined in on the chorus: "Come on, Baby don't you want to go." The guitar had the funkiest sound Margot had ever heard.

The singer was a big rough-looking white man with a beard and a big rough Mississippi Delta voice. He looked familiar, like someone she'd known a long time ago, but she couldn't place him.

> *Now one and one is two*
> *two and two is four*
> *I'm heavy loaded baby*
> *I'm booked I gotta go*

And the girl joined in on the chorus.

> *Oh, baby don't you want to go*
> *Oh, baby don't you want to go*
> *Back to the land of California*
> *to my sweet home Chicago*

The man played a pretty fancy guitar break, and they sang the chorus once again, and when they came to the end they both started laughing.

The girl was Italian, Margot was sure of it. When he sang, the man sounded like someone from the Mississippi Delta, but he looked like a midwesterner. But then when he opened his mouth to introduce the next song, he spoke Italian with a Bolognese accent, and she thought she might be mistaken.

Margot would sometimes pick out someone on a bus and imagine this person, this face, these clothes, in an American context, and pretty soon she'd be convinced that whoever it was was a fellow American. Sometimes she'd say something in English and get a blank look. Not that Florence wasn't full of Americans. But Margot had lived her life outside the American community. She had Italian friends from way back, from her class at the Liceo Scientifico Morgagni when she'd spent a year in Florence with her mother; and she had friends she'd made through her work as a book conservator at the Biblioteca Nazionale and the Archivio di Stato. And she was still friends with some of her lovers. It was amazing to her when she thought of it, of them—so handsome, so suave, so full of tricks in bed—because she could still reach down inside herself and find an innocent girl from Illinois. And she could still remember that all she'd wanted to do was re-create the life her parents had led, the life they'd lived in the big house on Chambers Street in Chicago, where her father had been an avocado broker on the South Water Street Market, and her mother had taught art history at Edgar Lee Masters, a small liberal arts college on the north side.

Most of the time she thought in Italian and dreamed and fantasized in Italian, but sometimes when a new lover was caressing her breasts for the first time and whispering in her ear, she'd be thinking of Christmas morning in Chicago or of sitting in the car with her mother and her sisters while her father made a few phone calls at his office down on the market. And maybe when he was done, he'd pry open a flat of avocados and take out one for each of the girls—Margot and her two sisters—and peel them one by one with his pocket knife.

> *I'm going away, Baby,*
> *Cryin' won't make me stay,*
> *The more you cry,*
> *The more you drive me away.*

Margot, who hadn't found a seat yet, called out a request for a song, letting the singer hear her voice, letting him know that she was from the Midwest. "'Sittin' on Top of the World,'" she shouted. "Can you play 'Sittin' on Top of the World'?" And she saw him searching the audience for her. She waved.

"That's in open D," he said into the microphone, in English. "I'll have to retune my guitar." He said something to the vocalist while he retuned the guitar, and she nodded. *"C'è l'ultima canzone,"* the girl said, *"da Illinois Woody."* There was a round of applause and Illinois Woody began to sing.

Margot squeezed in at a table full of young people. Someone had gotten up to get a drink, and Margot took the chair despite some grumbling. The young people went back to their conversation, though why you'd try to have a serious conversation in the Bebop Club was beyond Margot.

> *'Twas in the spring*
> *One sunny day*
> *My sweetheart left me,*
> *Lord, she went away,*
> *But now she's gone gone gone*
> *And I don't worry,*
> *'Cause I'm sittin' on top of the world.*

All you had to do to pick up an Italian man, Margot had learned, was look at him. But she wasn't sure about a midwesterner. Illinois Woody. Besides, she didn't want to pick him up, for heaven's sake. She just wanted to talk to someone from the old country, to compare notes.

Illinois Woody finished the song and put his guitar in the case. He pushed his way through the crowd toward Margot, and as he approached she remembered where she'd seen him.

"I know where I've seen you," she said. "I saw you on Rai Due, on the anniversary of the bombing in Bologna, the *strage*. You were one of the speakers. You really gave the government hell. In fluent Italian too. Your daughter was killed in the bombing, wasn't she? I'm so sorry." She put her hand on his arm. "I didn't mean to blurt everything out like that."

"It's all right," he said. "It was a long time ago."

They ordered drinks. A beer for Illinois Woody, white wine for Margot.

What Woody told her about himself was that he'd come to Bologna in 1987 for the trial of the terrorists who'd put a bomb in the busiest train station in Italy on the busiest day of the year—the bomb that had killed his daughter; that he'd lived with an Italian woman in Bologna for a couple of years; that he'd taken a teaching job at the American Academy of Florence; and that he was hoping to go home at the end of the year. Back to Illinois. St. Clair.

Margot wasn't sure where it was.

"Between Moline and Peoria," he said.

Margot told Woody, making it sound more certain than it actually was, that a producer was interested in doing a film based on the book she'd written about her experiences when she first came to Italy after the big flood in 1966—her discovery, in the convent where she was working, of a unique copy of a book of Renaissance erotic drawings, Pietro Aretino's *I modi*, and her subsequent love affair with an Italian art conservator. It wasn't for sure, she said, which is why she probably shouldn't be talking about it, but you never knew, did you?

Woody said you didn't.

She was irritated with herself for bringing up the film because she knew she was doing it mainly to make herself interesting, as if she weren't interesting without the prospect of a film. She thought she was *very* interesting. In any case, the book had been optioned when it first came out, fifteen years ago, by MGM for Emma Thompson, and then by Esther and Harry Klein, and then by a string of other companies whose names she didn't remember, and she'd gotten quite a bit of money, but nothing had come of it, and by now her agent had retired. She didn't know if she should look for another agent or not. The woman who wanted to produce the film—the same Esther Klein who'd optioned it after MGM—was coming to Florence next week, so if she wanted an agent she'd have to do something right away.

He didn't ask her about the book. What he asked instead was if she ever thought about going home.

She shook her head.

"Ever get homesick?"

She shook her head again. "Never," she said. "Not till tonight." This was not strictly true, but it wasn't strictly a lie either.

"Really?"

She nodded her head yes.

"Why's that?"

"It just hit me, when I heard you singing 'Sweet Home, Chicago.'"

"It's a Robert Johnson song," he said, "but everybody's got a version—Johnny Shines, Elmore James, Taj Mahal."

"My father sang all those songs," she went on. "'Key to the Highway,' 'Sittin' on Top of the World,' 'Come Back, Baby.'"

"Is your father still living?"

She shook her head no. And then she laughed. "He died in India. My mother had been dead for years, and he fell in love with an Indian woman at my sister's wedding and moved to Assam. Up in the north."

"I know where it is," Woody said. "The Romans got silk from the Brahmaputra Valley, but they didn't have a name for Assam. That's where all the tea comes from."

"Right. Nandini—that's the woman he fell in love with— owned a big tea garden."

"So, things worked out for him."

"Yes. But I wish he'd lived longer . . ." She shrugged. "The sad thing is that I wish he could be buried next to my mom. She's all alone in Graceland Cemetery. I know it's a stupid thing, but he loved her so much . . ." She started to tear up, and then she started to laugh again. "It really is stupid, isn't it?"

The band started another blues song, "Vicksburg Is My Home," and the young woman sang, "I'm gonna leave Chicago, go back to Vicksburg, that's my home."

"She's pretty good," Margot said.

Woody nodded. "Her name's Marisa," he said. "She's one of my students. She doesn't speak English very well, but she sings like Ida Cox."

Margot was glad when it was time to go, which they both knew without either one of them having to say it. Woody helped her on with her coat. He got his guitar and said good-bye to the band members. Margot buttoned up her coat as they started down Via dei Servi toward Piazza Santissima Annunziata on the way to the bus stops at San Marco.

"I live in Piazza Santa Croce," she said as they entered the piazza. "You?"

"Other side of the river. Piazza Tasso."

"We could walk together," she said, knowing that if he walked her home she'd invite him to come up. "I could carry the guitar partway."

But what happened was that as they entered the piazza a car came out of a little side street with a dog tied behind it. The car turned into the piazza, which was used as a parking lot during the day, and began to circle Giambologna's statue of Grand Duke Ferdinand, going faster and faster till the dog, which was running for its life, lost its footing and was dragged on its side behind the car, which swerved to the right and stopped in front of the statue of the Grand Duke. A man and a young woman got out of the car, and the man started cursing the dog. "I hope this will teach you a lesson, you miserable piece of shit. You fucking lazy bitch."

"He's got a knife," Margot said. "Look." The blade of the knife gleamed in the streetlights. "Let's get out of here."

But Woody, his guitar still in his hand, was already running across the piazza. "What the fuck is the matter with you?" he shouted in Italian. "You stupid asshole."

The man with the knife turned to face Woody. Medium height, expensive jacket. He held the knife in both hands, held it low, with the point sticking up, moving it up and down in front of him, pulling it upward with all his might as Woody, using the guitar as a shield, crashed into him and knocked him over. The man tried to scramble to his feet and to hold onto the knife at the same time, but the knife was stuck in the guitar case, and he lost his footing when he tried to pull it out. Woody glanced at the young woman, who was keeping her distance, and then kicked the knife man in the head. The knife man fell back on the pavement. The woman screamed. Woody kicked the man again and then again. He kicked him in the ribs and in the head. Real kicks. Margot was afraid he'd kill him. She was tempted to run away, but at the same time she was excited. "Stop," she shouted. "Stop, you'll kill him." She could see that the dog was covered with blood. She couldn't tell if it was alive. It was a medium-size black Lab. She ran to Woody and grabbed his arm.

Woody knelt beside the dog. "Call one-one-three. Get an ambulance. There must be a vet clinic that's open all night. I'll stay with the dog."

"Let's get out of here."

"We can't leave the dog."

"What about the man? What if he dies?"

"He deserves to die. Get going."

Margot started to run toward San Marco, but Woody shouted at her and pointed toward the Hotel Le Due Fontane, on the other side of the piazza. She asked the man at the desk to call Pronto Secorso and then she sat down in a chair in the lobby and put her head in her hands. She was having trouble breathing and her fingers were cold. "You'd better call the police too," she said. She waited while he called the police.

The ambulance was already there by the time she went back into the piazza. Woody was arguing with the driver, who didn't want to take the dog in the ambulance.

"We can't take a dog," he was shouting, "it's not permitted. You should have called the Guardia Medica Veterinaria."

Woody was shouting back: "There's no time. You can see this is an emergency. Help me get the dog on the stretcher. There's a clinic on Via Masaccio. I walk past it every day. I think it's open till midnight."

The woman—knife man's girlfriend?—got into the car and slammed the door and started the engine.

"Jesus Christ," Woody shouted. The dog was still tied to the car. Woody had to put his foot on the guitar case to get enough leverage to pull the knife out. He fell back a step when the knife came free but managed to cut the rope as it was tightening around the dog's collar. The car screeched out of the piazza and disappeared down Via della Colonna.

"*Porcamadonna*," the ambulance driver said. "What about the man?"

"Call another ambulance."

The driver took a look at Woody and Woody's hands, which were covered with the dog's blood, and at the knife, and at the dog lying on the ground. He nodded to his assistant, who helped Woody get the dog on the stretcher. And then he radioed for another ambulance.

Margot watched Woody put his guitar in the back of the ambulance and climb in with the dog. The police arrived as the ambulance was pulling out of the piazza, lights flashing. It wasn't easy to explain what had happened without explaining why the man had been left lying in the piazza, but Margot did her best. There'd been a fight, she said. She'd been on her way to San Marco; she'd called the police from the hotel . . .

But why hadn't the ambulance taken the man who was lying on the pavement? That was the question.

"There was a fight," she said. "There were two of them. There wasn't room." A second ambulance arrived. The *poliziotto* took her name and address and phone number and went to assist the man on the ground.

Margot slipped away down Via dei Servi. She walked home to her apartment in Santa Croce. She walked down Via degli Alfani, past the Liceo Scientifico Morgagni, which she'd attended when she was living in Florence with her mother, and then down Borgo Pinti, past the apartment where they'd lived. She was ashamed of herself for everything: for boasting about the film; for planning to invite a man up to her apartment and into her bed—just because she was lonely and he was a midwesterner; for being afraid, and for being excited, and for wanting to run away instead of helping the dog. She thought of her old dog, Brownie, how brave he was when they took him to Dr. Vollman to have him put down because he couldn't walk and couldn't eat and couldn't drink. Not even a sip of water. And especially, she was ashamed for being homesick. She kept circling back to this point, like a hunter lost in the woods, each circle getting a little larger. Once every few months at first, and then once a year, and then once every two or three years, and so on, till she'd forget about the circle and think that she was walking in a straight line.

First Reconnaissance

Esther Klein made her first recce in Florence at the end of September 1990. She flew economy class to Rome and bought a second-class train ticket to Florence. She had no financing, no director, no actors, but she had a script, and when Harry—her husband and partner for the last thirty years—had dumped her back in March, left her for a woman her own age, she knew she had to make this film. It wasn't as if she'd never made a film before. It was just that she'd never done it without Harry to direct. *An Esther and Harry Klein Production.* That was their credit line.

The property she wanted was a book that had been knocking around for fifteen years. She'd picked it up cheap, years ago, after MGM had put it in turnaround, and she'd written a screenplay herself. Then Harry decided he didn't want to do a romantic comedy, and they went on to something else and the option had expired, but Esther'd kept an eye on it. It had been optioned several times since then, but nothing had come of it, and now that she was on her own, she was determined to make it. What she needed were the rights to the book. What she wanted was a free option. Once she had the rights she could write her own ticket.

On the train to Florence she'd tried to keep a lid on her feelings. She'd wanted to make this film for so many years that she'd started to think of Margot as her daughter, the daughter she'd never had. She always told herself that her films were her children. All fifteen of them, all made with Harry. But sometimes she longed for a flesh-and-blood daughter, like Margot. She wanted Margot to have a lover like Marcello Mastroianni. Which was out of the question, of course, but when she imagined Margot, she imagined Julia Roberts or Meg Ryan; and when she imagined Margot's Italian lover, she imagined Marcello Mastroianni: worldly, sophisticated, handsome, even in those big glasses he wore in $8^{1}/_{2}$. Or maybe Giovanni Cipriani, who would cover foreign sales and who had a significant American fan base, though he'd been denied a visa to enter the U.S. after making fun of President Bush and Dan Quayle in a skit he'd done at Harvard.

Esther had filmed in Italy before, but Harry had always been there to direct, and there'd always been people to look after the details, to take care of train tickets, to translate, to find bathrooms, restaurants, hotels. Everything had been first-class too. Now she had to settle for a two-star hotel near the station where the woman at the desk didn't speak English very well. It was four o'clock in the afternoon by the time she'd unpacked her suitcase. She lay down on the bed and slept for four hours, and then she went outside and followed a street till it came to the Arno, which didn't look like much — hard to believe it could have flooded the whole town — and ate at a place called Dante's Pizzeria. She asked for pepperoni on her pizza and got big chunks of green pepper, which she didn't care for. Dante Schmante.

In the morning Esther walked around the narrow streets of Florence. She was planning to do the interiors in Eastern Europe, but there was no way to fake the Duomo and Giotto's tower and the Palazzo Vecchio. Florence wasn't a city adapted for films — no room for the trucks, too crowded. Maybe it wouldn't be so bad in winter — February and March. She'd seen Mario Monicelli's *Amici miei* at Cannes, with Harry. She tried to remember other films shot in Florence but could come up with only a handful: William Dieterle's *September Affair,* Brian de Palma's *Obsession,* and, of course, *A Room with a View.* Ismail Merchant had told her once that he'd made *A Room with a View* for three million dollars. She hadn't known whether to believe him or not. Three million was nothing. Even in 1985. All that period stuff. Shooting in England too. Harry had a huge budget for the piece of schlock he was directing at Paramount.

But Esther was still a player, even without Harry, a player with a reputation for bringing in her films on time and under budget in spite of Harry, who didn't believe in budgets and time cards. She'd never be able to afford a flood, of course, but a broken pipe would get the job done, and they could dress up something to look like Sotheby's and shoot the auction scene right in Florence. She'd like to block off one of the big piazzas — Piazza Signoria or Piazza Santa Croce — but that could be a major headache. Permissions would be expensive — you rent the piazzas by the square meter — and you'd need plenty of extras too, but she wasn't going to do the flood, and she wasn't going to do the sixties, so she wouldn't have to worry about a sixties look. Just let the extras wear their own clothes. It wasn't rocket science, after all. It wasn't magic. You hired some actors, you filmed the script, you edited the footage, you put it up on a screen and invited people to watch.

Esther found herself in Via Tornabuoni, where Harry had

bought her an emerald broach at Cartier, but nothing appealed to her. Nothing. Just the opposite, in fact. Everything looked ridiculous. Gucci, Ferragamo, Bvlgari with the annoying *v,* Armani, Prada, Pucci, Louis Vuitton. She was looking at her reflection in the window at Louis Vuitton. She'd never paid much attention to clothes. That was her signature, her persona—a tough old broad who didn't give a damn what she looked like and who always told the truth, even when it made everyone squirm. That's the way she'd always played it, and that's the way Harry'd always liked it. At least that's what she'd thought. But now Harry was gone, and the figure in the window looked matronly rather than tough. It wasn't a good look, especially in Italy. The wardrobe consultant she'd hired after the divorce wouldn't like it at all. She'd come to the house in Santa Monica, with its polished fieldstone entryway and red Italian tiles in the kitchen, and thrown out most of Esther's clothes—lots of silk dresses and jackets with bulky shoulder pads, and *Dynasty-*inspired evening gowns that she'd bought on Rodeo Drive and never worn. She'd advised Esther to buy monochromatic outfits with diagonal lines and some texturing that would make her look slimmer and taller. She advised her to develop her clothing radar so she could zoom in on the things she really loved, but Esther hadn't had the heart for it. If only Harry had run off with a bimbo, some floozy half his age, everyone, including Esther herself, would have known what to think.

She was going to meet Margot at her *studio,* at one o'clock for lunch, and she was hungry, even though it was only twelve. She was walking up and down the Lungarno on the other side of the river from the *studio*—she didn't want Margot to see her—when her clothing radar registered a coat in a shop window, a coat made from different-colored leathers and trimmed with fur. It was really stunning. *Simple,* she thought, *and stunning.*

And something inside her said *Yes!* in a loud voice. A woman wearing a coat like that . . . She was trying to see the price, but the tag was turned the wrong way.

A man came out of the store and spoke to her in good English. He was very nice and seemed to understand exactly what she needed. They went inside and she tried on the coat. It felt fantastic. She could feel his eyes admiring her. A woman wearing this coat could not fail in any endeavor. You could wear a coat like this to the Oscars. It would be a little unconventional, but that didn't bother Esther. It was practical too. Lined with one of those new insulating materials. But the price. Horrendous. Over a million lire. Not that she was broke. But you needed a sense of proportion in these things. Harry would have told her to buy it. It's only money. That was all very well for Harry to say. He was directing Diana Giulia in a disgusting studio blockbuster. It wasn't the money that bothered her; it was the lack of integrity.

"It's lovely," she said, "but I'll have to think about it."

She went outside, walked up and down, and thought about it. She watched the river for a while. The next time she looked at her watch it was twenty minutes to one.

It made her angry to think about it. She didn't want a material possession to take hold of her like this, especially not a piece of clothing. She had an espresso at a bar, and the coffee made her feel better. She had a good feeling about the coat now. She knew that if she was wearing this coat when she went to see Margot, she'd get the free option. She couldn't afford *not* to get the coat.

She paid with a credit card and left her old coat in the shop. She'd pick it up later.

Margot was so exasperated with Rabbi Kors, who wouldn't stop talking at her in that raspy singsong voice of his, that she had no idea who this woman was, coming through the door in the ridiculous leather coat that she'd seen in the window of the Leather Factory near the Ponte alle Grazie—scraps of different-colored leather sewn together like a patchwork quilt. It wasn't a fashion statement, it was a fashion shout. "Get out of my way," it said, "I'm coming through." And it was at least a size too small! The shoulders were tight, the sleeves too short.

"Esther Klein," the woman said, holding out her hand. Margot shook her hand, trying not to stare at the coat.

Rabbi Kors, a small man with a king-size beard and a lot of energy in his eyes, kept right on talking. Margot motioned to him to be silent, but without success. Something had to be done immediately, he was saying, something had to be done by Margot. Other arrangements had to be made.

What had happened was this, as Margot tried to explain to Esther. There'd been a fire in the yeshiva library at the synagogue in Severiano, a small town south of Siena, in the province of Grosseto. The rabbi had called Margot, who'd done some work for him in the past, and Margot had arranged for the damaged books to be freeze-dried at a fast-food facility near the big wholesale market in Florence on the edge of town. But the only freeze-drying unit that was available had been used for pork sausage patties—*traef*—and the rabbi refused to use it for his precious books. Margot should never have mentioned the fact that there was a new freeze-drying unit—*liofilizzazione* was the Italian word—at the Biblioteca Nazionale's *laboratorio di restauro* in Piazza Sant'Ambrogio, because the compressor was down, and they wouldn't have been allowed to use it anyway. But Rabbi Kors had got the idea stuck between his teeth and couldn't stop worrying it.

"They're not going to *eat* the books, are they?" Esther asked.

"No," Margot said, looking at Esther. "The members of his congregation want to go ahead and freeze-dry the books, and I called Rabbi Levi at the synagogue here in Florence, and he said that kashruth doesn't apply in this case, but Rabbi Kors, here"—Margot put her hands together in a praying position, pointed them at the rabbi, and shook them up and down—"Rabbi Kors here wants me to make other arrangements."

Rabbi Kors started to appeal to Esther, first in Italian and then in Yiddish, which Esther recognized because her parents had spoken Yiddish when they hadn't wanted her to know what they were talking about. But she didn't speak it herself, and the rabbi didn't speak English, and after two minutes Margot stopped translating. Margot was tempted, in fact, to wash her hands of the whole business. She was the book conservator, the expert, the *perito*. The rabbi needed her help. She didn't need his.

But she knew that that wasn't quite true. Here was a man prepared to sacrifice the things most precious to him—his books, his library—for the sake of something more precious. She wanted to be close to that something because she wasn't sure that there was anything quite like it in her own life.

"Why don't you just kosher the freeze-drying unit at the market?" Esther asked, pulling on one of the buttons of her coat.

"I hadn't thought of that," Margot said. She translated for the rabbi. He hadn't thought of it either.

"You can get this kosher dishwashing liquid now," Esther said. "You don't even have to boil the water. Just wipe everything down with a sponge."

Margot and the rabbi both looked at Esther as if she were King Solomon.

That afternoon they koshered the freeze-drying unit with two bottles of special dishwashing liquid from a kosher restaurant next to the synagogue, where Margot sometimes ate lunch. Esther and Margot and two men from the synagogue in Severiano carried in the boxes of books from the back of a truck. In most fires the damage to the books is caused not by the fire itself but by the water from the fire hoses. If something isn't done within thirty-six hours, the books will start to mold. When a book is freeze-dried at −40 to −50 degrees Celsius, however, the microorganisms that cause the mold cease to proliferate, and when a freeze-dried book is allowed to thaw, it's dry. Just like coffee crystals or sausage patties. The ice vaporizes without passing through a liquid state.

Ideally they would have taken the books out of the boxes and opened them up, but there wasn't time for that now.

When they were done, Esther's coat was covered with soot and one of the buttons had come off, but she shrugged off the damage. Rabbi Kors thanked Esther profusely but refused to shake the hand she held out. "He's not supposed to touch a woman," Margot explained. He wanted to know when Margot would have the books ready for him to take back.

"Rabbi Kors," she said, resisting the temptation to put an arm around the old man, "I know you're not a patient man, but I have a lot of things on my plate right now, and you're just going to have to wait your turn."

"But Signora Harrington," the rabbi began to protest. Margot put her hands over her ears.

At dinner that night, at Trattoria la Maremmana near Piazza Santa Croce, Esther ordered *lasagna al forno* and then loaded up her plate at the buffet with octopus salad and crostini and slices of melon wrapped in prosciutto. They'd skipped lunch and she was hungry. She was happy too. This was the restaurant where Margot had eaten with Sandro, her lover, after the *strappo* in the Badia, and afterward, out in the street, Sandro had sung "The Flowers That Bloom in the Spring" from *The Mikado,* and she didn't see how Margot could say no to her, not after the work they'd done that afternoon, not after she, Esther Klein, had saved the day by suggesting that they kosher the freezer.

"Who would you like to see play you?" she asked, cutting a little octopus in half. "If you could have anyone you want. Anyone."

"Oh, I don't know," Margot said.

"Dream a little," Esther said. "Anyone you want."

"Jane Fonda?"

Esther put down her fork and stared. "Jane Fonda? You're kidding. She's over fifty."

"Well, she *looks* young."

Esther shook her head. "Julia Roberts?" she said. "*Pretty Woman*? Wouldn't that be a coup. Andie MacDowell? *Sex, Lies, and Videotape*? That won at Sundance. Nicole Kidman, *Days of Thunder*? But you know who I see? I see Meg Ryan or Debra Winger. They've both got spunk, and that's what you need for Margot, don't you think?"

"Why would they take this role if there's not a lot of money?"

"Because they're hungry for good roles. Debra Winger and Andie MacDowell are both over thirty. How many good roles are there for women over thirty? It's not about money." But Esther could see that Margot didn't know who these actresses were and hadn't seen any of the films she mentioned.

"You're not a film person, are you?" Esther said.

"I used to love to go to the movies."

"What was the last movie you saw?"

Margot stopped to think. "I saw *Coming Home* with my sister, in California."

"My God, that was over ten years ago."

"And I saw *Gone with the Wind* a few years ago. With my friend Francesca Postiglione."

"Francesca Postiglione. Wasn't that the name of your lover's wife? Sandro's wife? How did that happen?"

"It just happened. She owned the apartment in Santa Croce and kept trying to kick me out after Sandro died. Finally she gave up and we became friends."

"I'm sorry. You sound just like my daughter. I mean, I don't have a daughter. Just what I imagine my daughter would sound like. If she were you. You know, I've always imagined Margot—in the book—as my daughter. How I wanted her to be happy—that's how real she was to me. And now here you are about my age. It's hard to believe."

The waiter brought Esther's lasagna and Margot's risotto and took their orders for the second course.

"I could have been a mogul, you know," Esther went on. "I should have been. Like Dawn Steel or Sherry Lansing. I should be running a studio instead of running around begging for money. If it hadn't been for Harry . . . I was a D-girl at MGM. Harry was making a film about a friendship between a wise old man and a slum kid from the Lower East Side, and he was so out of control—Harry, not the kid—that they wanted to fire him, but they were afraid to tell him, so they sent me out to the back lot where he was shooting. I told him he was fired, and he asked me to have dinner with him. Just like that. We made the film two years later on our own, and we never worked for a studio again. *Atlantic Avenue* was the name. I don't suppose you saw it? Forget it, that's all right."

"Shouldn't I have an agent?"

"Agent smaygent. Why do you want to give your money to an agent?"

"What money? Isn't that the question?"

"Ten percent. That's what money."

"What do authors usually get?"

"It all depends. Look, this property's been knocking around for fifteen years . . . You're lucky to get an offer at all. But I've got to have the rights. You understand that? I can't do anything till I have the rights. I can't pay you up front, but I'll make it up to you on the back end."

"You paid for the rights the first time you optioned it," Margot said. "Everybody else paid."

Esther interrupted her. "I know the whole story, doll — MGM, New Line, TriStar, the Jersey Tomato Company. It's old news. But let me ask you this: do you have a movie?"

"No."

"Do you have any prospects for a movie?"

"No."

"You got anything coming up on the horizon?"

"No."

Esther spread her hands out, palms up. "I'll tell you what you got. You got me. You got Esther Klein, and Esther won't let you down. The big boys are all waiting to see what happens. This is my first film since Harry left me. Can she do it? they want to know. Can she pull it off without Harry? They should be asking, can Harry pull it off without me, without Esther? Harry's got a huge budget for a piece of schlock, but Harry doesn't believe in budgets. Ah, the hell with it. Do we have a deal? I'll give you ten dollars to make it legal."

"Okay, but I'll write the screenplay. I read the screenplay that MGM had. It was the stupidest thing I've ever seen. No wonder they couldn't get anyone to play the part. I could come up with something better than that in a weekend."

Esther started to say that she already had a screenplay but decided against it. She leaned forward. "Look, doll, do me a big favor. Leave the screenplay to a pro."

"How hard can it be? I wrote the book, didn't I? If I wrote the book, I ought to be able to write the screenplay." Now Margot leaned forward. Esther leaned back. She didn't want to get into a staring match.

The waiter brought their *secondi*.

"Give it a shot, why not? You do it on spec and we've got a deal."

"On spec. You mean for nothing?"

Esther sighed. "Not for nothing. When I get the funding, you'll get Writers Guild minimum for a high-budget screenplay, okay? You'll get paid on the first day of principal photography."

"Who's going to pay?"

"The production entity."

"How much?"

"Eighty-nine thousand dollars. Plus something for the book. Let me shop it around and see what I can do for you. Plus ten percent of the net. Don't say Esther Klein doesn't have a big heart."

"Ten percent of the net is zero, right? I read the papers."

Esther's shoulders sagged a little. "That's how we do it," she said, "because that's how it's done. But there are bonuses too, depending. It's complicated. Maybe a deferred fee after breakdown. For an Academy Award nomination. For a win. For Golden Globes. Leave it up to me. The main thing is, I can't make a movie until I get the rights."

"All right," Margot said. "It's a deal."

Esther signaled the waiter and ordered another bottle of expensive Chianti.

Margot walked Esther back to her hotel near the station and then, instead of going home, went to her *studio*. What she did when she was experiencing a nameless dread, as she was that night, was get her hand on a book or a manuscript. Like the Galileo codex she was planning to bid on. It had been rescued from the flood, at the very last moment, by Sterling Pears, one of the foremost authorities on the Galileo collection in the Biblioteca Nazionale. Pears had called her to say that the Biblioteca Nazionale was finally getting around to soliciting bids for the restoration work.

The manuscript on her desk right now, unfortunately, wasn't doing much for her nameless dread. It had been brought over by the chief of the music division at the Biblioteca Nazionale to see if she could do anything about it. Many of the pages had been stained a dark pink. It looked to Margot as if the whole book had been treated with calcium hydroxide and calcium bicarbonate, which had dissolved some editorial markings in the margins. There was nothing to be done. Some problems have no solution, and this was clearly one of them. She could accept that as a conservator but not in her own life.

Actually her nameless dread did have a name. It was home-sickness, nostalgia, the place she'd come back to on Saturday night. It was a kind of longing, a kind of ache, a kind of sadness, the kind of fear she'd felt when she'd heard Woody singing "Sweet Home, Chicago," the fear that her true home was elsewhere, that her real life—her true spiritual life—was not here in Italy, here at her workbench in her very own *studio* on Lungarno Guicciardini or in her very own apartment in Piazza Santa Croce, but waiting for her back home, back in Chicago, back in the big house on Chambers Street, waiting for her to take up where she'd left off.

On two occasions she'd come close to going home. Both times she'd changed her mind at the last minute. Not for the sake of an Italian lover, but because two powerful women had befriended her. The abbess at the convent where she'd stayed when she came to Florence after the flood, and where she'd discovered the Aretino, had helped her set up her own *studio* right in the convent; and Francesca Postiglione had given her a life interest in the big apartment in Santa Croce. The abbess had been her mother, and Francesca her sister. Both were dead. And now there was Esther Klein, who was going to make a movie about her.

She didn't know what to make of it. What she was hoping was that a movie would validate her life, would validate her decision to stay in Italy. Because she thought that maybe she had come back to this place—this longing, this ache, this fear—for the last time. She was fifty-three years old. It was time to settle things once and for all.

She put the book with the pink stains back in its solander box and put a note on the cover for one of her three assistants to return it to Signor Malfatti at the Biblioteca Nazionale, with a note inside to say that nothing could be done. She locked the door of the studio behind her, crossed the Ponte alle Grazie, and walked home along the river. The lights of Piazzale Michelangelo were reflected in the water. She thought about going to the Bebop Club, but it was too far away, and it was too late, and she was too tired.

Questura

The bidet in Woody's tiny bathroom reminded him, as it did every morning, that he didn't belong here. In Italy. His people were not bidet people. A couple of generations back they'd been outhouse people. Now they had indoor plumbing, of course. But no bidets. He didn't know anyone who had a bidet in St. Clair, Illinois, where he'd taught Latin and Greek for twenty-five years, before his daughter's death had torn his family apart, before Hannah's nervous breakdown, before she'd divorced him and entered a convent, before the scandal that had set the dean against him, before he'd come to Italy for the trial of the terrorists who'd bombed the station in Bologna. He knew what the bidet was for, and he had his own method of using it. But questions remained about bidet etiquette. Was it proper to use a bidet in someone else's house, for example? And if you did, was it proper to use the little towel, hanging on a metal ring, to wipe your ass? There was a bidet in the faculty men's room at the American Academy, where he taught classical literature in translation, but he didn't think anyone used it. Maybe the women used the one in the faculty women's bathroom. He'd never asked.

The bidet, for Woody, was a symbol of Italy. He spoke the language fluently; he had Italian friends in Rome, Bologna, and Florence; he'd served as vice president of an important political organization, the Association of the Families of the Victims of the Bombing of 15 August 1980; and yet he couldn't seem to get things—things like the bidet—quite right. Every time he turned around he was doing something wrong: drinking a cappuccino in the afternoon, putting Parmesan cheese on *spaghetti alla puttanesca,* or putting too many ingredients on pizza. "The problem with you, Woody," Gabriella used to say—Gabriella was the woman he'd lived with in Bologna—"is that you like too many hybrids. Italian taste is simple, not a weird combination of exotic flavors."

"In Sicily," he'd say, "they put *everything* you can think of on pizza. Not just one or two sparse ingredients." And she'd shake her head in disgust. *"Sicilia . . ."*

Saturday morning. Woody was going to pick up the dog, which had been in the hospital for over a week. He'd been to see her every day, after school—the *ambulatorio veterinario* was on Via Masaccio, only five minutes from the American Academy in Piazza Savonarola—and he'd bought a leash and a dog dish and a supply of dog food and a Frisbee and a heavy rubber ball with a handle. Dottoressa Soldi, the vet who was looking after her, was very nice, really, once it had become clear that Woody was going to assume financial responsibility for the dog. She'd shown him the evidence of previous injuries: burn marks, knife wounds, X-rays that showed that the dog had undergone several expensive operations to reset broken bones, operations that could only have been performed at a very sophisticated animal hospital. The fur on her left shoulder had been scraped away when she was dragged behind the car, and the skin was raw and red, and her throat was still swollen where the collar had choked her, but no more bones had been broken. Dottoressa Soldi had reported the incident to the Ente Nazionale Protezione Animali and to the police, and Woody had received an invitation to appear at the police station—the Questura—on the following Monday, in the morning. He'd have to take time off from school. He considered declining the invitation, but he didn't think it was that sort of invitation, though it had been written in flowery, almost poetic language.

Woody expected the dog to be glad to see him, but when Dottoressa Soldi led her out, all bandaged up, she seemed a strange combination of fear and self-possession. At least she was trying to act self-possessed, Woody thought, looking him over as if she were deciding whether or not to accept him as her new *padrone*. She didn't seem particularly interested. She kept her distance, walking stiffly, deliberately not looking at Woody.

When Woody approached her head on, she squatted down and peed on the floor. "She's afraid of men," the *dottoressa* explained.

"She probably has good reason to be."

The *dottoressa* got some paper towels from behind the counter to mop up the pee.

Woody squatted down on his heels and held out a hand, fingers curved down.

The dog bowed her head and kept it down, reminding him of Laska, his old husky, when she was waiting for something.

He was expecting gratitude. After all, he was doing something great and noble, or at least quite decent, and certainly expensive.

(He suddenly became aware of these feelings, but there was nothing he could do about them.) He put his hand on her head and she started to tremble, and then she gave herself to him completely. She didn't even sniff him. She put her head on his knees. Woody wasn't sure she liked him, but she was helpless and she needed him, and he started to tremble too and had to hide his hands from Dottoressa Soldi.

"Who could harm a dog like this?" he asked, anger surfacing. "It takes your breath away."

"You haven't found out who it was?"

"No, just that he had a fancy car. A Mercedes or a BMW. I haven't tried, really. I have to go to the Questura on Monday. They may know something."

"Take the dog with you," she said. "Let them see what the owner did to her."

"Good idea."

"I think you'll be good friends," she said. "But don't try to rush things."

"Do you think she can make it to Piazza Tasso, or should I take her in a cab?"

"She could use a little exercise. Just take it slow and easy."

On the way home they stopped for a cappuccino and a dolce at a bar in Piazza Santa Croce. Woody looked around, wondering where the American woman's apartment was located. It occurred to him that the dog saved him from getting involved with the American woman. He'd known she was going to invite him up to her apartment, and he'd known he was going to accept her invitation. Two lonely ex-pats. Why not? But he was hoping to go home, and he couldn't afford to get involved with a woman. That was why not. Not now. But what about the dog? What would keep him from getting involved with the dog?

The dog was hungry, and Woody gave her one of the biscotti

that he was dipping in his cappuccino. She liked it and he gave her another one.

"What's her name?" the barista asked.

Woody thought for a minute. "Biscotti," he said. "That was my daughter's name. Cookie."

"*Biscotti*'s plural," the barista said. "But I guess that's all right. *Biscotto* would sound funny. And it's masculine. How about *Dolce?*"

Woody shook his head. "Biscotti."

Woody used one of his own bowls for her water and Biscotti's new dog dish for her food—two cups in the morning, two cups in the evening.

As he was going to sleep that night—Biscotti's first night in Piazza Tasso—Woody tried to remember everything he knew about dogs. King Arthur had a dog, but he couldn't remember the dog's name. Freud had a German shepherd named Wolfe and then a whole series of chows. He kept one of them in the room when he psychoanalyzed patients. The patients were calmer and more forthcoming with a dog in the room. Lincoln had a dog. Odysseus had a dog. One of Woody's dogs had been named Argos. And before Odysseus? The Etruscans. There was a beautiful dog in one of the tombs at Cerveteri. And dog bones in excavations in Iraq suggested that dogs and humans had pooled their resources more than fourteen thousand years ago. He tried to imagine the primordial scene: humans offering food and fire; dogs cleaning up the garbage and keeping watch while the humans slept, barking at the slightest hint of danger.

Woody had put down a blanket for Biscotti by the side of his bed, so he could reach over and touch her and let her lick his hand.

On his way to the Questura in Via Zara, Woody was greeted by a man in uniform whom he didn't recognize at first, one of the guards from the Archeological Museum, which had been closed during August. He was pleased that the guard recognized him. The guard clasped Woody's hands. "We haven't seen you for a while, Professore. You haven't forgotten your stone altar?"

"No, not at all," Woody said, "but I've been getting ready for classes."

"I see you have a friend with you. Looks like she had a nasty scrape."

Woody nodded. "Some *stronzo* tied her behind his car," he said.

The guard frowned.

Woody gave him an answering frown.

"She's been having bad dreams," Woody said. "Running in her sleep. Not eating well. I started giving her a little pasta with butter on it with her dog food. I don't like to leave her alone. She's making progress, though."

At the Questura they were shown into an inner room where Woody was surprised to see Margot Harrington, sitting at a desk, chatting with an impossibly handsome man, a southerner, a *commissario* in a smart uniform. It was a Monday morning. Ten o'clock. Woody, who had his "invitation" in his hand, was right on time. He was pleased to see her, in spite of himself, and relieved, because she didn't look at all distressed, but then he was disappointed when she barely acknowledged him.

The *commissario* greeted Woody warmly and invited him to sit down and stooped down suddenly to greet the dog. Woody didn't have time to warn him. Biscotti squatted and peed on the floor. The *commissario* didn't seem to mind. He waited, offered his hand. Biscotti started to tremble. Woody put his hand on her head to steady her. She raised a paw. The *commissario* took it in his big hand and shook it. A good sign.

"She's a little afraid of men," Woody said.

The *commissario* called someone to wipe up the pee. "It's nothing," he said, tossing his handsome head. "You remember Signora 'arrington, of course," the *commissario* said to Woody, "from the night of the incident."

"Yes, of course," Woody said, shaking Margot's hand.

A young man at a second desk was typing something rapidly with two fingers. They waited for him to finish. He pulled the form out of the typewriter—several carbons—and handed it to the *commissario,* who looked it over. "Very good."

He put it on his desk, facing Margot, who signed it with an expensive-looking fountain pen that didn't go through the carbons, so she had to sign each of the three copies separately. She rose to leave, and the *commissario* shook her hand.

"*Mille grazie.* Thank you very much for coming. And you too, Signor 'oodall." He turned to face Woody. "You Americans have such difficult names."

"It's a problem for me too," Woody said.

The *commissario* struggled to say *w*: "Doppio-vu. And we can't pronounce English 'acca' either. But in any case, thank you for coming."

"It's my pleasure," Woody said. "The *commissario* gave him a funny look. "Well, not exactly a pleasure," Woody added.

The *commissario* sat down and invited Woody to sit down. "Signora 'arrington has given me her version of what happened a week ago Saturday night. Now maybe you could give me your version." The young clerk inserted another thick carbon into his typewriter and aimed his two index fingers at the keyboard. Woody started to give his version of what happened. The *commissario* motioned for Woody to pause every once in a while so the clerk could catch up. When Woody finished, the *commissario* leaned forward.

"Aren't you forgetting something?"

"That turd who was torturing the dog? The *stronzo*?"

"Precisely."

"I forgot about him when the ambulance came. I had to get the dog to the hospital."

"But he hasn't forgotten about you."

"He's all right?"

"Yes and no. He spent the night in the hospital. But you humiliated him in front of his girlfriend. He made *brutta figura*."

"Ah, yes. Ugly figure."

"He would like his dog back."

"So he can cut her throat or burn her? Out of the question. I couldn't do it."

"I quite understand."

"Look at this." He showed the *commissario* the scars and burn marks, covered by hair now, that Dottoressa Soldi had pointed out to him. Biscotti held very still while they examined her. Woody stroked the back of her head. "This dog was very frightened of me at first. She still is. She's been badly abused."

The *commissario* held up a finger and the young man stopped typing. "Unfortunately," the *commissario* said, "this young man, this *stronzo*, as you so precisely call him, comes from an old Florentine family." He leaned forward and whispered confidentially, "A family of turds, of *stronzi*."

"I see," Woody said.

The *commissario* petted the dog. "The higher up you are in the police," he said, "the more . . . how shall I put it?"

"Subject to influence?"

"Yes, exactly. Normally I would not trouble myself about a case of this nature, but you see . . ." He trilled his hand.

"And if I don't give the dog back?"

More trilling. "There could be trouble. Or rather, there will be trouble. No end of trouble. For you, for the family, for me."

"What kind of trouble?"

"Criminal charges, for one thing. Assault. Battery. Threatening the ambulance driver with a knife. The driver, you know, is an employee of the state. If he were to make a complaint, then the police would have no option. You would be arrested. And this is no joking matter."

"I didn't threaten the ambulance driver with a knife. He saw what the *stronzo*'d done . . ."

The *commissario* held up a hand. "I'm speaking hypothetically," he said. "I've spoken with the driver. I don't think you need to worry on that score, at least not now. And I don't think you need to worry about assault charges. Signor Romero is not anxious to have his treatment of the dog made public. But you don't know what people like this will do if they don't get their way."

"I won't give the dog back. I simply couldn't do it."

"I quite understand. Believe me. Which is why, if you will permit me, I will suggest another course of action."

"Go ahead."

"I could arrange for the dog to disappear. My sister in Calabria . . . Three children . . . It could all be done discreetly . . . One day the dog is here; the next day the dog is gone . . . No one knows what has happened . . . The dog will have a good home . . . You will be free to come and go as you like . . ."

This was the kind of solution Woody had been hoping for, and yet he wasn't entirely happy with it.

"Have you ever been to Cerveteri, Commissario, the Etruscan cemetery outside of Civitavecchia?"

"No, I'm sorry to say that I have not."

"Everyone says that the Etruscans had this jolly afterlife, that the spirits of the dead actually lived in the tombs, and that that's why they had all their household things there. But this is too simple. Why is there a door painted on an inside wall of the Tomb of the Four Amphori?"

The *commissario* leaned forward, as if this were an examination question to which he should know the answer but couldn't think of it at the moment.

"You can see a picture of the tomb at the Museo Archeologico in Via della Colonna. That door, it has to be leading somewhere, don't you think? Symbolically?"

"Of course."

"So their understanding of the afterlife . . . It's more complex. . . ."

"Yes."

The *commissario* looked at his watch. "But I'm not sure what you're getting at."

Woody shook his head. "I guess I don't either," he said. "I'm sorry, but we walked past the Museo Archeologico on the way here . . . There's a dog, a wonderful dog, in the Tomb of the Reliefs. I just realized that it looks just like Biscotti. A black Labrador. An Etruscan dog. Do you see?"

The *commissario* smiled. "I think I do," he said, standing up to indicate that the interview was over. "You can't leave the dog here now," he said. "Don't worry. I'll arrange everything. If you bring the dog to Porta Romana at, say, eleven tonight . . ." He trilled his hand. "I'll see to it that you're not bothered by this *stronzo.*"

"I can't do it," Woody said. "You are a *mensch, un uomo molto simpatico.* I appreciate your offer, believe me . . ."

The *commissario* rubbed his eyes with his fists. "Why was I afraid of this? While I was talking to Signora 'arrington, something warned me, but there is nothing else I can do. Legally," he explained, "in Italian law, that is, a dog is a *cosa*, a thing. I'm only a policeman, not a philosopher, not a scholar. But even I recognize the difference between the law and what we might call *justice* in the abstract. The courts, however, will not recognize this distinction, Signor 'oodall. And even if they did, these *stronzi* are very powerful. I am not going to tell you not to follow your heart, signore, but I will tell you that I foresee no end of trouble if you keep this dog. Trouble for you, trouble for me. *E' proprio cosi.*" He paused. "On the other hand, you have served as vice president of the Association of the Families of the Victims of the *Strage* of 15 August." This was a statement, not a question.

Woody nodded.

"Yes. Signora 'arrington told me. That's what I was trying to think of before. That's why I'm not surprised at your decision. I'm very sorry for your loss. You have done Italy an important service, and that will count for something, believe me. You will not be alone. You have resources, friends who will come to your aid. And I will do what I can. You must remember that you have a friend at the Questura. But not a powerful friend, I'm afraid. This uniform . . . , these symbols . . . , not an *eminenza grigia,* as the French say. And of course the Ente Nazionale Protezione Animali will take an interest in the matter."

"I understand. And I appreciate it. It's a pleasure to deal with a man like you."

Woody had never mastered the double air kiss between men, but he was glad to embrace the *commissario* before leaving.

Woody was surprised to find Margot waiting for him, on the other side of Via Zara, looking in the window of a store that sold Persian carpets. She must have seen his reflection in the glass, because she turned and crossed the street.

"I want to apologize," she said.

Woody thought she was talking about her behavior in the Questura, where she'd hardly spoken to him.

"No, no," she explained. "That was because I didn't want the *commissario* to know that we're old friends. Well, not exactly old friends, but something." She looked him in the eye and then looked down. "I saw you with the dog in Piazza Santa Croce," she said. "Out my window. You were feeding the dog cookies, but I didn't come down because I was embarrassed. I'm afraid I made *brutta figura* on Saturday night."

There's something about a woman apologizing that's extremely seductive, and Woody knew, just as he'd known from the beginning that he was going to keep the dog, that he had not really wanted to escape from this woman.

"I make *brutta figura* every time I turn around," Woody said. "It doesn't matter if anyone sees me or not. I'm aware."

"Seriously, Woody. I'm ashamed of myself for wanting to run away. It's humiliating." She put her hand on his arm. "I would have left this poor dog," she said, bending to pat Biscotti on the head. "It makes me sick to my stomach when I think about it. I just wanted to run away. I think I'm becoming too Italian."

Woody was becoming uncomfortable. This was a beautiful woman. Like an actress, but not an American actress, not that fake beauty. More like an Italian actress. She looked like a real woman, full of years, full of experience. *Stagionata,* that was the word he was looking for. Not *aged* but *seasoned.*

"But the *commissario,*" he said. "There's a good man."

"Yes," she said.

"He offered to find a home for the dog. With his sister, in Calabria."

"What are you going to do?"

"I don't know."

"How are you going to keep a dog in Italy?"

"Lots of people have dogs in Italy. Why should it be any different for me?"

"What are you going to do with her during the day?"

"One of my students lives in Borgo Pinti," he said. "The girl who sings like Ida Cox. Maybe the dog can stay there during the day. There's a big courtyard, and another dog to play with. I hadn't realized how lonely I was," he said. "Before."

"And now?"

"It's good to have a dog."

There was nothing more to say. "Coffee?" she asked.

"Let's go to San Marco," he said.

At the bar in San Marco they ordered their coffees and took them to a table. Table etiquette, like bidet etiquette, was one of those things Woody could never be quite sure of. If you sit at a table, you pay more than if you stand at the bar. But what if you stand at the bar and get your coffee and then sit at a table, which is what they'd done? He ordered some biscotti for the dog.

"How did your film meeting go?"

She told him about the yeshiva fire in Severiano, and about Esther Klein, and about koshering the freezer.

"You're excited, aren't you?"

"I'm trying not to show it, but I guess I can't help it."

"It is pretty exciting. I can't imagine it."

"Who do you think should play me?" she asked. Woody struggled, but he couldn't come up with the names of any actresses.

"You don't know any more about movies than I do," she said.

"I've seen *Gone with the Wind*," he said. "In Italian."

"Then we've got something in common." She laughed. "*Francamente, Cara, me ne infischio.*"

Woody laughed too. "Frankly, my dear, I don't give a whistle." He handed Biscotti another cookie. "You'll be like Aeneas," he said when he'd stopped laughing, "when he gets to Carthage and sees the bas-relief with the whole Trojan war laid out and recognizes himself among the Greek warriors: '*Se quoque principibus permixtum agnovit Achivis.*'"

"Which means?"

Woody translated. "He recognized himself among the Greek warriors."

"I see," Margot said, "but it probably won't be quite like that."

"Why not?"

"Well, maybe it will. Isn't that the 'tears of things' passage? *Lacrimae rerum?*"

"Yes, it is."

"My mother used to quote that passage. The 'tears of things.' I never understood what it meant."

"You will when you see a movie about yourself," Woody said.

"Sounds like a threat."

"More like a warning."

"I think I'll be all right," she said. "I'm writing the screenplay myself."

"Good for you. Have you ever written a screenplay before?"

"Of course not, but how hard could it be?"

"I have to teach this afternoon," he said, looking at his watch.

"What are you going to do with the dog?"

"She's coming to class with me today," he said.

"They'll let you get away with that?"

"This is Italy," he said. "Sometimes it's not so bad."

Pitch Meeting

Esther didn't spend any time commiserating with other independent producers, or with producers who'd just been fired, or with producers who hadn't had a hit in five years but were still hanging on. Or worse, with producers who'd given up and now pretended to be glad to be out of the business.

She didn't have time to commiserate. She wanted to finish the exterior shooting before Easter, before Florence got too crowded. She had only three months to set up the film if she wanted to start shooting in January, but she knew what she had to do. She had to start making a lot of noise. She had to act as if she were making the film—attach a director, start casting, fake some publicity—and the rest would follow. In mid-October she took a meeting in L.A. with one of the independent-friendly studios, Leviathan, which was planning to sign a couple of producers to help supply them with movies over the next few years.

Esther had a friend at Leviathan, Dawn Carpenter, an old pal from the early days of WOMPI—the Women of the Motion Picture

Industry—who'd been hired to make "pictures of integrity" with good roles for women, not just for bimbos and virgins, but for real women. They were going to hire women directors, women producers. It sounded like the same old bullshit to Esther, and yet she believed in it. She wasn't a cynic. Appearances to the contrary, no one in Hollywood was really a cynic. They were all dreamers, romantics. Including Esther.

Dawn couldn't green-light a project, nor could her boss, whose name was Gordon Talbot, but Gordon's boss could. "Just be careful you don't women's lib him to death, okay?" Dawn said to Esther in the new commissary, just before the meet. The commissary reminded Esther of her high school cafeteria at P.S. 100 in Brooklyn: Neon lights, trays, the smell of macaroni and cheese. Women in hairnets. Was this deliberate? What had happened to the old commissary, which had been more like a restaurant?

Esther recognized the studio head at a table with a couple of minions, flunkies, including Gordon. "You can't help being aware of him," Esther said to Dawn. "He used to be a gofer, and now it's like Stalin's sitting over there, or Hitler. Or Nero or Caligula!"

"They have to eat too," Dawn said, poking at her salad and dry baked potato. Esther was eating Salisbury steak. "Besides, he's turned this place around."

"Made the trains run on time," Esther said.

Dawn didn't say anything.

"Too many lawyers," Esther said. "Too many execs. What do they do anyway?"

"I'm an exec," Dawn said.

"Sorry."

Esther was too excited to relax. She was getting a buzz in spite of herself. She was her own buzz.

"Here's the deal," Dawn was saying: "New Hope will be the executive producers. Frank Johnson will supervise the music, and Leviathan will advance fifty percent of the budget against North America. The other fifty percent will come from foreign rights. I see Molly Neumann directing, or Alice Arnold. I see Meg Ryan or Heather Locklear as the female lead, and Bobby De Niro as the Italian lover."

Esther's heart was pumping faster and faster. This was going to be bigger than she'd anticipated. "What kind of numbers are we talking about?"

"That depends. There're a lot of variables."

Esther tried to keep a tight rein on her fantasies, but she let herself go a little. Just a little. It was good to be out and about, good to be on her own, feeling her own strength, dealing with this person and that person. Good people. People who could make things happen.

Gordon, whom Esther knew slightly, stopped by their table on his way out of the commissary.

"You look like you could use a hit," he said to Esther.

"Who couldn't?"

"I think she's got one," Dawn said.

"You know how I can tell when I got a hit? By how hard it makes my big dick."

Dawn chuckled. "Esther's got something that'll keep you going all night," she said. "*The Sixteen Pleasures.* Sixteen sexual positions. Wait till you hear the pitch, right, Esther?"

"A book of Renaissance erotica," Esther said. "Discovered in a convent. Sixteen erotic poems by a guy named Aretino, and sixteen erotic engravings by Marcantonio Raimondi."

"Dirty poems and dirty pictures," said Gordon. "A good combination. I hope it makes a fucking ton of money. You got a copy I can look at?"

"There's only one copy," Esther said. "It was auctioned off at Sotheby's and nobody's seen it since."

"I hear Harry's film is wrecking," Gordon said. "Makes you wonder. Harry needs somebody to keep him focused. He's got all that dough and it's confused him. He made a big mistake when he dumped you. You must be feeling good."

"I feel bad about it," Esther said. "We were a team, but what are you going to do?" She shrugged her shoulders.

"He couldn't knock you out, could he? Tough old broad like you. You ought to lose some weight. I'm speaking to you as somebody who'll tell you the truth straight out. Get a lift. Lose that coat too. You get it at the Salvation Army?"

"I thought we were talking about a film?"

"We're going to make this film, if it's everything Dawn's been telling me, and I hope it makes a fucking ton of money for all of us, but for Christ's sake lose the attitude along with the coat."

"You know, Gordon," Esther said, "if you kick me in the ass, I'll kick you right back."

"Who you talking to?" Gordon pretended to look over his shoulder.

Dawn intervened. "Can we hold off till the meet?"

"What meet? We got a meet?"

"Yeah, Gordy, we got a meet, in about fifteen." She looked at her watch and kept looking at it till Gordon was out of sight.

"What the fuck is the matter with you?" she said to Esther.

"Did you hear the way he talked to me?"

"Everybody talks like that around here."

"I've been around here for a long time . . . I never heard anybody talk like that. Not to me. Nobody talks like that to me."

"Well, you'd better get used to it if you want to make a studio movie."

"Look, Dawn, I'm sorry, but . . ."

"You made me look bad, Esther. You could cost me *my* job."

"I'm sorry," Esther said again, but she wasn't sorry. She was just being polite. She wasn't sorry at all, because she knew now that she could walk away from this deal if she had to, and that gave her a boost; it reminded her of something that everyone in Hollywood knew but generally forgot. She'd known it from the beginning, when she first started out with Harry: power isn't money; power isn't reputation or a string of hits behind you; power in Hollywood is passion; power is belief; power is love; power is knowing that nobody in the whole world could make this film the way you want to make it. And Esther had all these things: passion, belief, love, confidence. She knew that *The Sixteen Pleasures* would make a great film. That *she* would make a great film. *An Esther Klein Production.*

Cancer

From his new ergonomic chair in the new apartment on West 74th Street, Michael Gardiner could see, through the floor-to-ceiling window, the Hudson River and parts of New Jersey. If he leaned forward far enough, he could see the dog walkers in Riverside Park. It was a special chair that was supposed to be good for his back. It wasn't as comfortable as the Barcalounger he'd sat in at Macy's, but his wife, Beryl, would never have permitted a Barcalounger. Even though he was dying of cancer. Prostate cancer. He'd skipped his PSA test two years running, and the cancer got away from him and from the doctors. He'd had chemo and then an operation, but the cancer had metastasized to the bone, and his doctors at Sloan-Kettering did not hold out the prospect of death with dignity: weakness, loss of appetite, organ dysfunction, enzyme systems breaking down, pneumonia, urinary infections.

Beryl, a cradle Episcopalian, hadn't offered to pray for him, but he knew that she would anyway, and that she wouldn't tell him. And he was glad for this, glad that she wouldn't tell him, so he wouldn't have to protest.

It was Beryl who'd bought the new apartment and who was fixing it up for their last years together—correction: last year. It was Beryl who'd mustered the energy to move back to New York. Los Angeles had never felt like home. There was no center in L.A., no life on the streets the way there was in New York; people in L.A. didn't understand city life. Yesterday his son had taken the train up from Princeton, where he worked as a computer programmer, and they'd bought ham sandwiches at Zabar's and eaten them in the little park by the Natural History Museum. This afternoon he'd bought a plum on his way back from lunch with Esther Klein. The divorce hadn't slowed Esther down. Maybe she'd made some bad choices. But she knew how to line up financing and how to keep department heads under control and how to bring a film in under budget. Basically good-hearted. Big-hearted. She liked to cook for people, liked to bring people together. She was taking the divorce pretty hard. He and Beryl had tried not to take sides, but it hadn't been easy. Calls from both Harry and Esther in the middle of the night. Harry coming over drunk at two o'clock in the morning. *And Harry wasn't a drinker.* Esther trying to hang on. Asking Beryl for help. Begging her to talk sense to Harry. To lay down the law. You didn't just throw a marriage away, not after thirty years. You'd think a thirty-year marriage would be like a big tree in the forest. Safe for a while. For a long time. Thirty-year marriages in Hollywood were like towering redwoods in a scrub forest. You marveled at them, and you grieved when one of them fell. No more Esther and Harry Klein Productions.

He hadn't told Beryl he was meeting Esther for lunch. Not that there was anything between him and Esther, or that Beryl didn't like Esther. But he'd known that Esther was going to make him an offer, and he'd known that he was going to accept it.

Workmen were still doing things in the apartment. Painting, hanging pictures in the wide hallway, which Beryl had turned into a gallery with recessed lights that could be adjusted to show off her collection—Zulu warrior masks, like the ones that inspired Picasso; a Chagall; an early Barnett Newman (a small one, but floor-to-ceiling nonetheless); a Rembrandt etching; two Japanese prints; a pointillist picture of a dog barking at a man who seemed to be conducting an imaginary symphony, done by their daughter; framed posters of half a dozen lectures she'd attended; still photos, some of them signed, from all of Michael's films.

State-of-the-art projection equipment was being installed in a state-of-the-art screening room that seated twenty people in comfortable chairs. A film library contained his life's work: seventeen feature films and a dozen documentaries, good prints—his own cuts, final cuts—and, for convenience, videos too. The reels were stored in a special closet, like a wine cellar. The piano was being tuned. Mr. Hammond, the owner of the gallery on Ninth Avenue, where Beryl had taken a new acquisition to have it cleaned, had come to deliver the painting and to supervise the installation: *Jesus Restoring Sight to Blind Bartimaeus*. Lots of seventeenth-century chiaroscuro. Beryl, who'd studied art history at Smith, was convinced it was a Michael Sweerts, worth much more than she'd paid for it. Sweerts was somebody not quite famous—at least not famous enough for Michael to recognize the name, though Beryl said he had a painting in the Accademia in Venice. Just as Michael had an Honorable Mention from the Venice Film Festival for his first film, an adaptation of Chekhov's *The Lady with the Pet Dog*.

Mr. Hammond had brought a carpenter with him to hang the Sweerts, which had cost as much as the piano, a rebuilt Bechstein, that Beryl had gotten at an estate sale on Long Island, where she'd also bought the Sweerts.

Everything in the new apartment was intended to cheer him up. There was beauty everywhere. A certain kind of beauty. Nothing to suggest vulgar uplift, but Michael got the message: *in the midst of life, we are in death, but it's okay.* He was going to take up the piano again. Learn to play Chopin's "Ocean Wave Étude." He wasn't particularly depressed, didn't really need cheering up. He was glad, in a way, that it was over. Almost. He was ready to go. At age sixty-five most men might look forward to a few more years, but he'd had enough.

He'd been a "middling" director. *Middling.* That's the word that critics used when they got around to mentioning one of his films. *Middling.* He'd always worked, and he'd always handed the money over to Beryl, who'd managed it, which was why they were rich now; but his first film had been his best—Chekhov's *The Lady with the Pet Dog* in New York and Atlantic City and Princeton instead of Yalta and Moscow and S—. It had been a remarkably "mature" film for such a young director. What he understood now, however, at age sixty-five, was that at age twenty-seven he'd been prematurely mature; he'd been middle-aged from the beginning. Point and shoot. Walk and talk. *Nothing artsy-fartsy,* Esther had said at lunch. *Just tell the story.* That was Michael: nothing artsy-fartsy.

He'd been too old to join in the creative revolution staged by the movie brats—Coppola, Friedkin, Carpenter, Lucas, De Palma, Scorsese, Bogdanovich, Spielberg. He'd been forty-three when Dennis Hopper's *Easy Rider* opened. He'd known something was up, but he hadn't been able to get on board. He could tell a good story, and his fortunes revived with the return of the old Hollywood in the late seventies and eighties.

Mr. Hammond didn't trust Beryl's sketch showing where she

wanted the Sweerts. Michael didn't know what to tell him, except to wait for Beryl. The piano tuner had finished up and wanted a check. Michael assured him that Beryl would send him a check in the mail. He'd be back in two weeks, he said. It would take a while for the piano to settle in. The computer person wanted to show him how to get the computer in *his* study to talk to the computer in Beryl's study. Voices were coming out of the screening room, a man and woman quarreling.

What a lot of work, Michael thought. *What an enormous effort.* Telephones in every room. John Widdicomb furniture. Two stoves in the huge kitchen, two refrigerators, two sinks. For entertaining. As if they were starting out their marriage (with a lot of money) instead of finishing it. How different from their first apartment on the Lower East Side. But Beryl was tireless, and she was fixing up this place for him, because she knew he wanted to come back to New York, back home, though he'd grown up in the Bronx, not Manhattan.

Mr. Hammond decided to wait for Beryl, who was at a meeting, Michael didn't know where. They'd been back in New York less than a month, and she was already active in the American Cancer Society antismoking campaign, she'd been elected to the vestry at St. Francis Episcopal Church, and she was volunteering at Sloan-Kettering, where Michael's cancer was being treated. Meetings upon meetings. She was a type that was becoming extinct: a rich woman who took money seriously and didn't feel guilty about it, a woman who invested shrewdly, volunteered tirelessly, gave generously, raised two children, cooked like a professional chef.

The first thing Beryl saw when the elevator door opened—it opened directly into the apartment—was the Sweerts. It was on the floor, leaning up against the wall. The second thing she saw was the scowling face of Mr. Hammond from the Hammond Gallery on Ninth Avenue. Every two or three years she bought something new and expensive and wildly different. She was always interested to see how the new piece would fit in. How it would change the configuration of the whole ensemble. Michael never thought the new piece would fit, and everyone else she knew, including gallery owners, always agreed with Michael. And at first it wouldn't. But then it would, and everything would be changed.

Besides, she'd always had a good eye for bargains. She'd gotten a bargain on the Bechstein. And she was convinced that the painting would turn out to be a bargain too. If it really was a Sweerts, of course.

She'd just come from St. Francis, where she'd tried out the new kneelers. They worked just fine. She didn't see why everyone had gotten so worked up about replacing the old ones. Martin Haddam, the senior warden, had wanted to replace them with fat little cushions, but Beryl liked the traditional kneelers because they reminded her of the stool in her mother's kitchen that had a little foldout stepladder in it.

She'd knelt on a kneeler in the back of the church, by the Bowton Chapel, and prayed for her husband—not for the cancer to go away, not for him to have the strength to deal with it (he didn't need that). Her prayer was more like giving thanks for so many years with such a good man. Beryl never asked for things. She didn't even make suggestions. It was part of the deal she had with God. She didn't ask for things, and God never made her feel guilty for being rich and happy. She was always amazed at how people couldn't handle happiness. Like her father, an Episcopal priest. If the house got too comfortable in hot weather, he'd turn up the thermostat a little. If it got too comfortable in cold weather, he'd turn it down. So you were always just a little bit uncomfortable.

She didn't ask for things, but she couldn't conceal her hopes and fears. Not from God. What she was hoping for was that Michael would have a good death. Nobody wanted a messy death. What she was afraid of was that his illness would come between them, pull them apart instead of bringing them closer together. Michael was having trouble dealing with the aftermath of the operation.

Neither one of them was afraid of death, though for different reasons. Michael wasn't afraid because there was nothing to be afraid of. There was just *nothing*. And Beryl wasn't afraid because her deepest experiences of life were full of meaning and purpose, and she expected death to be full of meaning and purpose too.

Florid-faced Mr. Hammond was scowling because he was unhappy. He held his shoulders up, as if he were worried that his neck was too long, like a Parmigianino virgin. She could hear her husband at the newly tuned piano. Trying it out. Chopin. She'd tried to get him interested in other composers. She'd like to hear some Mozart once in a while, or *The Harmonious Blacksmith*. She'd given him the music. He'd start to learn new pieces, but he always went back to Chopin. It wasn't healthy.

"Now then, Mr. Hammond, what's the problem?"

"You can see for yourself, Mrs. Gardiner. You're going to have to find another space for the painting. You can't hang a seventeenth-century religious painting on the wall between these African masks and the movie posters. You can see that for yourself."

"That's what Mr. Fischer in L.A. said about the Chagall," Beryl said, "when I wanted to hang it next to the Japanese prints. And now look. My theory—no, it's not a theory, it's a fact—is that no great works of art are incompatible. Maybe no works of art are incompatible. Sometimes I think that the Met would be a better place, a more interesting and exciting place, if they rearranged all the paintings in alphabetical order by title. I have a friend on the board. I may suggest it to her. You'd have lots of startling juxtapositions, and isn't that what art's all about? Startling juxtapositions? Doctor Johnson said something about the metaphysical poets yoking heterogeneous ideas together by violence. Something like that. I'll have to look it up."

"Mrs. Gardiner? What am I doing here?"

"You've put this painting in a lovely frame, and now I want you to tell me that it was done by Michael Sweerts and that it's worth fifty times what I paid for it."

"You know I can't tell you that. Not without a thorough investigation of the provenance. How much *did* you pay for it anyway?"

"You know I can't tell you that." Beryl laughed.

Beryl had experienced a small epiphany while she was praying, but she hadn't been able to bring it into focus. She'd come up to the edge of some insight, up to the edge of a cliff, but she hadn't been able to look over. She experienced the same sensation when she looked at the painting again. Jesus restoring sight to blind Bartimaeus. What does Bartimaeus *see* at that moment? Why does he look so surprised? As if he was seeing something he hadn't expected to see. Had he been blind from birth? No. He asks Christ to "restore" his sight. Maybe he'd had cataracts.

Michael was playing the opening arpeggios of the "Ocean Wave Étude." She went into the living room and sat next to him on the piano bench and turned the pages for him while the carpenter hung the painting. The étude was a difficult piece, too difficult for Michael. But so beautiful. They had several recordings: Horowitz, Rubinstein, Vlado Perlmutter.

They were going to watch one of Michael's films that night if they could figure out how to operate the new projector. They would sit in the dark and she would hold his hand.

He came to the end of the étude. "Esther wants me to do another film," he said. "She wants me to direct."

Beryl looked at him, her eyes open, like Bartimaeus's eyes—seeing something she hadn't expected to see.

"In Italy," he said. "Florence. *The Sixteen Pleasures*. She already has a script. She wrote it herself when she and Harry had the option, about fifteen years ago."

"Could we go to Venice too? I'd like to look at the Sweerts in the Accademia."

"Of course," he said.

"We could stay at that little hotel out on the Lido, like we did before."

"We could stay at the Cipriani or the Daniello," he said.

"Oh, Michael. Let's stay on the Lido. Hotel Buon Pesce. I have a picture of it somewhere. It'll be like a second honeymoon."

He took her hand and she started to cry. Silently. *So this is what she wanted,* she thought. And all the time she'd thought it was something else.

Miranda

When Miranda Clark read in *Variety* that Esther Klein was going to make a film of Margot Harrington's *The Sixteen Pleasures,* she knew that this was the sign she'd been waiting for. She knew with all her might that she had to have this role, knew with all her might that she could play Margot better than anyone. She'd read *The Sixteen Pleasures* her sophomore year at Smith, right after her mother's death, and it had saved her life. She'd dropped French and switched to Italian; she'd dropped Biology and enrolled in Mr. Tonarelli's course in modern Italian Cinema: Rossellini, de Sica, Visconti, Fellini, Antonioni.

She'd been sick of her old life then and had wanted a new one. Ten years later she had a new life, but she was sick of that one too and wanted another new one. She was tired of making the same mistakes over and over again—career mistakes, relationship mistakes—and this was a way out. She called her film agent and left a message. And then she sat at the kitchen table and poured herself a cup of coffee.

She'd been in Los Angeles ten years. Twenty years earlier she'd

have been a starlet, groomed and kept in one of the studio sta-
bles waiting for her big race. Today she was a working actress
with a film agent, a commercial agent, a manager, an entertainment attorney, an accountant, an acting coach, and a therapist
who practiced creative visualization. She'd been in nineteen
movies, twelve of which had had theatrical releases, but no one
had noticed her. She was invisible: the girlfriend of a minor
character; the girl on the beach who notices that the heroine is
drowning and starts shouting; the girl—in *Heavenly Days,* an
Esther and Harry Klein Production—who sidles out of the bedroom clutching her clothes in a bundle in front of her and is
never seen again; the nurse who tells the doctor that the next
patient is ready. And she'd done hundreds of commercials because she had a lot of the white-bread perkiness that sells mops
and toothpaste and toilet paper, so she had what her accountant
called an income stream. Things could have been worse: she
wasn't waitressing at a diner; she hadn't done any porn flicks or
teensploitation flicks, though she'd had some tempting offers. So
she didn't want to complain too loudly.

But it wasn't enough. She wanted to be funny and dramatic and
glamorous. She wanted to see her picture up on the billboard
where Jodie Foster, who was Miranda's age, now looked down at
the traffic on the Glendale Freeway. She wanted to make people
feel what she felt, whatever it was. She wanted people to love her.
She wanted to astonish her high school classmates and her college roommates. She wanted to please her mother, who had sent
her to Smith, even though she'd dropped out without getting her
degree and her mother had died without ever seeing her on the
big screen or on TV. And at the same time she didn't think she
could face another audition, another look-see. And the funny
thing was, when she'd been a senior in high school she'd dreamed
about living in a dorm at Smith with roommates—being on her

own, good friends, wild parties—and boys from Amherst and UMass and even Harvard; and then when she was living in Lawrence House she dreamed about living in an apartment in L.A. with a view of the mountains or maybe the ocean; and now that she was living in Altadena with a view of the San Gabriel Mountains, she dreamed about living at home with her mother—the woman she portrayed in television commercials, enthusing over a new detergent or a new kind of mop or wrinkle cream. And with her father, who had died when she was nine. She'd hardly known him, but she could still close her eyes and hear him in the kitchen with her mother, both of them laughing. What were they laughing about? She'd never know now.

It was only nine o'clock in the morning, but she called her therapist at his emergency number. Her therapist, who answered on the second ring, reminded her that everything is energy— everything!—including our thoughts. When you creatively visualize something you want to see manifested, what you're doing is simply connecting the two frequencies to bring that reality into being. If you can visualize something creatively, then that something already exists.

Miranda wasn't so sure, but she thanked him and put on some water to boil to poach an egg, and then she called her film agent again and left another message: "I want this part. I really mean it. You've got to get me a read. I really, really, really mean it. I don't want any excuses. Do whatever you have to do. Remind Esther that I had a girlfriend role in *Heavenly Days*. Remind her that Harry kept the camera on my legs for a good ten seconds in a pan across the bedroom while David O'Neill's passed out on the bed, and that you can see my face for a second when I bend over and kiss him."

At ten o'clock she got in her five-speed Mazda Turbo II and scooted from one freeway to the next, the Glendale to the Santa

Ana to the Hollywood Extension. The Creative Talent Agency was on La Cienega Boulevard, on the border between West Hollywood and Beverly Hills. She didn't expect her agent, David Greenburg, to show up till eleven, but she wanted to be there early just in case. David might have been the model for Sid in *Doonesbury*—or maybe he'd decided to model himself on Sid. Except he didn't smoke cigars. The doorman eyed her suspiciously. Not much foot traffic yet. Sunset Boulevard was empty. It was too early.

She admired her reflection in the big mirror by the bank of elevators, imagining herself as Margot: a black jacket and man's white shirt tucked into stonewashed jeans. And then she's at the Academy Awards, backstage at the Kodak Theater, waiting to accept her Oscar for her interpretation of the role of Margot Harrington in *The Sixteen Pleasures*, Margot Harrington, the spunky feisty scrappy book conservator who takes Florence, Italy, by storm . . . "I want to thank everyone," she said, improvising, not anticipating, not planning ahead. "I want to thank everyone," she said. The hall was silent.

"You talkin' to me, ma'am?" the doorman asked.

"No, sorry, I forgot where I was. Just daydreaming." But she wasn't just daydreaming. She was using her imagination to bring what she wanted into her life. Billy Crystal is calling her name. Miranda. Miranda Clark. She's wearing a simple chiffon dress. Modest. All the other actresses look gaudy by comparison, their dresses in poor taste, their breasts pumped up like balloons. Miranda was just a simple country girl. Fresh and innocent. But perky—perky spunky feisty scrappy as hell.

"Hey, Mir, what the hell are you doing here?"

"Since you don't return my calls, I had to drive down to see you."

"I'm so fucking busy I can't see straight, you know how it is."

"Well, I'm so fucking unbusy *I* can't see straight. You know how *that* is?"

"Hey, you got residuals up the wazoo. Your turn will come."

"I'm tired of playing my mother on TV. They sent me one of those mop contraptions. I can't make it work. I can't get the cloth part hooked into it."

"They'll explain it at the studio. Besides, that's not my department. Why don't you complain to Billy." Billy was her commercial agent.

"David, I left you a message this morning, two messages, but this is too important to wait. Esther Klein's going to make *The Sixteen Pleasures*. It's a good role. It's a great role. It's just right for me."

"Slow down, doll. You're going way too fast for me."

"Don't 'doll' me. You sound like Esther."

"That's her signature. A real gutsy lady. Too bad about Harry." David shook his head. "We'll see if she can make it on her own. Too bad," he said again. "But that's why you've got an agent to advise and counsel you: no mercy fucks. That's the rule. Tell her to submit a firm offer in writing. That's how we do deals, okay? Money's got to change hands. Don't do anything on spec. Remember, that property's been on the market for fifteen years."

"I'm the one who needs a mercy fuck. I keep picking up my phone to make sure it's working. I can't tell her anything. Esther hasn't called me. I've got to call her. *You've* got to call her. You're my agent. I want you to get me a read. I did a good job in *Heavenly Days*. She should know my name. She should know who I am. She should know I work hard."

"Does she have the rights? Does she have financing? Does she have a script? Does she have a director attached?"

"David, how am I supposed to know these things? That's your job. I just saw the notice in *Variety* last night."

Foot traffic was picking up on the other side of a row of large potted plants that divided the lobby.

"Why don't you go get a facial at Ruby's," he said. "Get the whole works: facial, mud bath, cucumbers over your eyes, massage. You'll feel better."

"I want you to get me a read, David."

"Yes, doll." He laughed.

"I really mean it, David. I'm not kidding you. I really, really mean it."

Miranda thought about going to Ruby's. Was she getting wrinkle lines at twenty-nine? David had told her to get a facial. But then, he'd advised her to get her breasts done too. Was it that bad? She'd always told herself that she'd age gracefully, naturally—that she wouldn't fight it tooth and nail like other actresses. But now it was make-or-break time.

Instead of going to Ruby's, she drove out to Laurel Canyon Park and sat on a bench. From there she could see the Wilson Observatory and the mountains beyond. Mount Wilson, San Gabriel Peak, Strawberry Peak, Evergreen. She stood up and drew the beauty into her body. This was one of her creative visualization exercises. She interrogated the beauty. That's what the exercise was about. Not appreciation but interrogation. Not with words, but with her body, her movements. Every movement was a question. It was more like flying than dancing. Like the hawks moving over Devil's Canyon, tiny specks in her field of vision. She drew them into her body. She felt light, weightless. She was overcoming the weight of her body and then returning to it. Every gesture was like the subtle pressure of wing on air. When she closed her eyes she was in Italy. She was walking to that little town that Margot always walked to. Settignano, looking down on the city of Florence. She's coming to the little cemetery. She's drinking a glass of wine with her mother in the Casa del Popolo. Then she and her mother are waiting in the little piazza for the bus that will take them back down to the city.

She looked at her watch. It was only two o'clock. Maybe she *would* get a facial at Ruby's.

Plot Points

Margot rented a TV and a VCR and got one of her apprentices to hook them up for her and show her how to use the remote. Woody was going to help her write the screenplay. They were going to watch some movies together in her apartment. Woody had bought a book at Feltrinelli on how to write a screenplay. Margot admired his modus operandi: he learned how to do things from books. It wouldn't have occurred to her to go to a bookstore and look for a book on how to write a screenplay.

She was standing in the window, overlooking the piazza, waiting. It was eight o'clock. A few shops were still open. Esther had a director attached, someone Margot had never heard of, and a male lead—Giovanni Cipriani, a wonderful old commedia dell'arte actor whom she'd seen once in a marvelous production of *Volpone* at the Teatro Pergola, and in a movie called *L'accalappiacani (The Dogcatcher)*. Giovanni, or "Zanni," would play her lover, Sandro Postiglione, and she remembered sitting on an orange crate in this very window, waiting for Sandro to cross the piazza. Giovanni had been Mosca in the production at Teatro Pergola, and although the play was a comedy and was hysterically funny, he and Volpone, his partner in crime, had been pretty scary. Nothing had been able to stop them: not the fools they deceived, not the innocent Bonario and Celia, not the state itself. It was only when they turned against each other that they ran into trouble. But in *L'accalappiacani*, he'd been a kind of clown, a kind of Charlie Chaplin figure who shared the life of the dogs he captured.

She and Woody had eaten out together two times at Trattoria la Maremmana—once with a couple of teachers from the American Academy and once by themselves—and they'd taken the bus up to Fiesole and walked to Settignano, a walk she'd taken with all the important people in her life: first her mother; and then Sandro; and then her father, who'd stopped on his way to India; and then Francesca—Sandro's wife—and then an assortment of sisters and nieces and nephews and other lovers; and, finally, with Esther. On one of these walks, just beyond Maiano—she'd been with Francesca—she'd seen them filming the carriage scene for *A Room with a View*. There were no horses on the carriage and Helena Bonham Carter and Julian Sands had bounced up and down as if they were moving, and the driver too, Lucca Rossi, and the *pompieri* from the fire department used up all their water making the rain for the first shot and had to go back to Maiano to fill their tank. Later she'd watched from her window as they filmed the scene between Lucy Honeychurch and the guide in Piazza Santa Croce, a scene that was not, in fact, in Forster's novel. She was replaying the scene in her imagination when she saw Biscotti bound across the piazza and scatter a cloud of pigeons. She stepped out onto the balcony and called: "Woody, over here." She waved, and Woody called the dog: *"Vieni, vieni, vieni mi qua."*

The furniture in Margot's long narrow living room was comfortable and modestly elegant. Two small leather sofas faced each other. A couple of armchairs sat side by side behind a coffee table. On the coffee table: a couple of Clairefontaine notepads. She already knew that Woody wrote with a Parker Duofold with a fine italic nib, and that was one of the things that attracted her to him. Her own Montblanc Meisterstück Le Grand, newly filled with Pelikan *azul-negro* ink, was on the table too. She never left the house without at least two fountain pens in her purse. She'd bought the Montblanc in Rome after Sandro had abandoned her. Next to the pen, a kitchen timer and a video of Michelangelo Antonioni's *L'avventura,* which they were going to watch to get some ideas for their own screenplay. She imagined them sitting in the armchairs, notepads on their laps, fountain pens at the ready, taking notes as the movie unfolded. The TV and the VCR were on the floor between two tall windows that opened onto the piazza. Two smaller windows opened onto Via Verrazzano. Margot buzzed Woody in and opened the door to the stairwell. The dog arrived first. Biscotti. Cookie. Woody bounded up the stairs after her.

Not much happened during the first ten minutes of *L'avventura.* Biscotti went to sleep. Margot worried that Woody might go to sleep too. The timer went off. Margot stopped the tape. Woody opened his copy of Syd Field's *Screenplay.*

"Well," he said. "That's the most important part. The first ten minutes. What do you think? What's the hook? Are *you* hooked? Do we know who the main character is? Do we know what it's *about?* Is the dramatic situation clear?"

"I'm not sure," Margot said. "Maybe we should have watched *Casablanca* or *Shane* or *A Room with a View.*" These were the only three movies they had in common, at least that they could remember. And *Gone with the Wind.*

"Are they having an affair or not?"

"Sandro and Anna?"

"I think Anna's the wife."

"What's the other woman's name? Claudia?"

"Maybe we'd better watch a little more."

Margot set the timer for another twenty minutes and started the VCR. When the timer went off, she stopped the film again.

"That should be the end of Act One, the 'setup,'" Woody said.

"Well, *some*thing's happened. Anna's disappeared."

"But why are they so bored? I mean, the look on Claudia's face when they're making love. You'd think she was doing the dishes."

Margot was expecting to go to bed with Woody that night, and she wasn't bored. She was nervous, excited. She'd changed the sheets. She'd hung her clean clothes in the wardrobe and put the dirty ones in the hamper. She didn't understand how people could be so bored or how they could find sex boring. She assumed Woody would make the first move, but she couldn't be sure. He was an American, a midwesterner. He might need a nudge or a shove.

"That's half an hour," she said. "Have we reached Plot Point One?"

"Right," Woody said. "I've got it right here: 'Plot Point One: something swings the action out of the beginning and into the confrontation.' It's the same thing as the 'dramatic hook,' I think."

"Well," Margot said, "they haven't found Anna yet. We're supposed to be moving toward the confrontation. I suppose they'll have to look for Anna and that the main character— Sandro—will meet lots of obstacles."

"That must be it," Woody said. "I'll make a note. The counter on the VCR says thirty minutes, four seconds." He wrote down "30:04" on his notepad. "But what's it *about*? What's the theme? Boredom? They're so bored with each other."

"I liked the scene with the two women together after swimming. Anna and Claudia, I think. Where Anna sees a shark. Or pretends she sees a shark, and they start giggling. It's a little moment of freshness. You think maybe there's going to be something between the two women, but then nothing comes of it. Put that down: Moment of freshness."

Margot could see that Woody was having trouble writing. "Let me see your pen," she said. She touched it lightly to the page several times, making a series of dots. But some of the dots were missing. "It's skipping," she said. "You probably need to realign the nib. I can do it for you if you'd like."

"It's been driving me crazy. I've been meaning to take it to that pen place on Via Cavour."

"The Casa della Stilografica."

"That's the place."

"That place has been there for fifty years. I know Signor Sacchetti. His daughter more or less runs the place now. She was a year behind me at Liceo Morgagni. But I can fix it for you right now if you'd like."

"You can adjust it? Don't you have to take it apart? This isn't the kind of nib you can just unscrew."

"I know," she said. "It's a Duofold. I won't be able to knock out the nib and feed because they're not accessible from the back of the section. I'll have to use pliers to pull them. Let's go into the bedroom. I've got everything we need."

There was a workbench in her bedroom with a small toolbox for some bookbinding tools she liked to have on hand. There was a little sink too and a Bunsen burner. It was like a high school chemistry lab. She picked up a pair of rubber-coated gripping pliers.

"You won't break it?"

She laughed and ran some water into the sink. "I adjust all my pens," she said. "Did you know that Arthur Conan Doyle used a Duofold to write the Sherlock Holmes stories?"

"I didn't know that," Woody said.

Margot emptied out the ink, flushed out the pen with tap water.

"What's the Bunsen burner for?" Woody asked.

"You can heat-set some of the older pens," Margot explained, "but you have to be careful. I had an old Patterson explode once. It was made out of nitrate-based chemicals. Really unstable. It's still there, in my fountain-pen case."

"Jesus, Margot."

"The newer Duofolds," she said, "have plastic feeds that tend to melt before they can be adjusted." She pulled the nib out with her gripping pliers and examined it through a jeweler's loupe.

"You want to look? You can see that the left tine is sprung. That's what's causing your ink-flow problem. Did you drop it?"

"Not that I know of."

When Woody looked through the loupe he could see that the tines were not lined up perfectly. He handed the nib and the loupe back to Margot, who adjusted the tines with her fingers, checked the alignment with her loupe, and wedged the nib back into the section with her bare fingers.

Woody was admiring a glass-topped display box full of pens. "Why do you have so many fountain pens?"

"Different nibs, different color inks, different heft. Besides, they're so beautiful."

"I never thought of a person having more than one fountain pen."

"It happens all the time." She laughed. "Here, try this Aurora.

You like an italic nib. They're hard to find." She opened the case and took out a pen.

"I thought you weren't supposed to let another person use your fountain pen."

"I'm going to make an exception for you, Woody. Actually, it would take a few years of regular use before it made any difference."

Woody looked at the pen. Forest green. Large. Comfortable. On a piece of paper he wrote, "My soul is an enchanted boat."

"Nice."

"Shelley."

Margot refilled the Duofold and wiped off the nib. She made a row of dots on a piece of paper. It worked perfectly. No skips. She handed it to Woody. "Good as new. I have so many of them I figured I ought to learn how to fix them. It's not that hard. Most of them. I wouldn't knock out my old Parker Snake Pen, but that's a special case."

She was pleased that Woody was impressed. Back in the living room, she started the movie again. "What are we looking for now? Plot Point Two?"

"I think it's *Act* Two," Woody said. "To tell you the truth, I'm not very clear about these plot points. The book says there can be as many as fifteen. I think there's got to be an important plot point at the end of each of the first two acts, but there're other plot points too."

"Like when Anna disappears. That's a plot point."

"Right, but the big ones are at the end of Act One and then at the end of Act Two. We must have missed the one at the end of Act Two. It's supposed to come about page eighty-five or ninety. Two pages a minute. That's forty-five minutes. We're way past that."

"Maybe Italian films are different." Margot thought the film would never end. There were more false leads about Anna's disappearance. Then some smugglers showed up. But the smugglers were a false lead too. Margot could tell that Woody was losing patience.

"Are the smugglers a plot point?"

"I suppose, but they don't change anything. They're a red herring."

Margot was more concerned about Woody's response than she was about the movie. Over an hour and a half had passed. Sandro was running for a train. Sandro and Claudia were on the train. There were a couple of peasants from the provinces with strong accents.

"That's us," Woody said, and laughed. "A couple of midwesterners."

What she was thinking was that the movie was totally and absolutely remote from her experience. She wasn't bored with life. She was nervous and excited, and when the woman—some woman—sashayed through a crowd of workers, she thought, *Finally, someone I can connect with.* She was sure she'd wind up in bed with Woody, but she felt innocent too. They were like a couple of kids.

They didn't pay much attention till Claudia started making faces at herself in a mirror. Margot thought it was the best scene in the movie.

"Do you make faces at yourself in the mirror?" Woody asked her.

"Sometimes." She made a face.

"That's nice," he said.

The movie dragged to an end. Nothing was resolved.

"When did Act Three begin?" Woody asked. "Did we miss

more plot points? Actually, I think the plot-point thing would work better for *The Sixteen Pleasures*. Act One: You get to Florence and start working in the convent, where you discover a book of dirty pictures."

"Erotic drawings," she said.

"Why don't you write this down," he said. She unscrewed the cap of her Montblanc. Woody handed her his notebook. She wrote "Act One: Florence. Convent."

"Then Act Two. You have an affair with Sandro. This ends when you discover that he's trying to swindle you and steal the book." She wrote this down too.

"Then in Act Three you take things into your own hands. All these men are trying to get the book away from you—the bishop, your lover, and finally your father—but you outsmart them all. You auction off the book at Sotheby's for a quarter of a million dollars and give the money to the convent. End of story."

Margot knew that he was waiting for her to say something, but she didn't know what to say. "I kept some of the money for myself," she said.

"A commission," Woody said. "You earned it. Let's get some words on paper. Let me have the notebook." He uncapped his pen and took his notebook from Margot's lap. "Take a look at *On Screenwriting*," he said, handing her the book. "Chapter Thirteen is on screenplay form. It says you don't need to put down anything about camera angles or acting directions."

"That's good."

"Do you want to begin at the beginning?" he said. "Actually, I think we should forget about the train trip from Luxembourg. Just start in Florence. Maybe some stock footage of the flood. There's plenty of it around. You arriving in the rain."

Woody sat next to her. She watched him write:

EXT. STAZIONE SANTA MARIA NOVELLA — NIGHT

"Does that look right?" he asked.
"So far," she said

It's raining hard. A young woman (MARGOT) gets into a taxi.

EXT. TAXI — NIGHT

Taxi drives through the rain.

INT. TAXI — NIGHT — FAVORING MARGOT

Taxi driver drives recklessly. Margot in backseat.

MARGOT

Can you take me to an inexpensive pensione? In the center.

TAXI DRIVER

There ain't no such thing. Not now. You can see for your-self. You got to go to Fiesole. And you won't find anything cheap.

MARGOT

I guess I don't have a choice then.

A muffled noise and the taxi starts to shake.

MARGOT

I think you've got a flat tire.

The driver pulls over, leans his head on the steering wheel, and starts to cry.

CUT TO: EXT. — NIGHT

The driver tries to change the tire in the rain. A man holding an enormous umbrella approaches and holds the umbrella over the taxi driver. The window of the taxi goes down revealing Margot's face.

INT. TAXI — NIGHT

A man's face appears at the open window.

Woody took a deep breath and put the pen down. "This is hard work," he said, laughing.

"You've already thought this through, haven't you? It's a good beginning. You've already got me hooked. The man's face at the taxi window in the storm."

"Is that what really happened?" Woody asked.

Margot nodded.

"That's how you met Sandro Postiglione?"

"That's it. But I didn't know who it was at the time. Not till later, in Piazza Signoria."

"And your Montblanc pen. That's the pen you bought in Rome after he went back to his wife."

"That's the gospel according to Margot."

"And Sandro was your boyfriend's name. I hope he wasn't as boring as the guy in *L'avventura*."

She laughed. "He was a bad man, but he was never boring."

"I suppose that's better than the other way around. You've got a good story. This'll make a great movie."

"You've got the form down, but are you sure you're supposed to put in 'cut to'?"

"Can't hurt. They can always take it out."

"How about some popcorn?"

"Right, I need a break. I didn't know you could get popcorn in Italy. What kind of wine do you drink with popcorn?"

She laughed. "I get it at the Old England Store," she said. "Where I get my peanut butter."

"I'll take the dog out," he said. "You make the popcorn."

She made the popcorn in a saucepan and melted some butter. She put the popcorn in a large wooden bowl and poured the butter over it, and salted it, and then got out a handful of napkins, and then she washed an apple and quartered it.

Woody still hadn't come back with the dog, and she thought, *He's not coming back*. But then she saw his Parker Duofold on the notebook. He hadn't put the cap back on. She capped the pen and went to the window.

Biscotti was off leash, running in circles. She lifted a leg and marked the statue of Dante, and then she circled some more, each circle getting smaller, and squatted to poop. And then Margot saw something she'd never seen in twenty-four years in Italy. She saw a man take a plastic bag out of his pocket and bend over and clean up the mess his dog had made on the sidewalk. She watched him spin the bag around and tie it in a knot and walk across the piazza to drop it in a garbage can in front of the *monte di pietà*, where she'd pawned the jewelry that Sandro Postiglione had given her. Twenty-four years ago. And she knew that this was a plot point, knew that she was in love. Once again. But not hopelessly, because there was something beyond love too, something that wasn't hopeless at all. At the moment that she'd realized what he was doing, she had stopped worrying about whether or not he'd spend the night, stopped worrying about being too forward and frightening him or being too reticent and discouraging him. She put aside her hopes and fears about the future. She would let things happen instead of forcing them. It was enough to watch him, to watch his lips move as he talked to the dog, to watch his strong hands ruffle the dog's fur.

Piazza Tasso

Woody's life had taken a surprising turn: he had a girl-friend, a woman from the Midwest who fixed fountain pens, a woman whose life story was going to be made into a movie. But was this good luck or bad luck? He thought it might be bad luck. The last time he'd gotten involved with a woman, in Bologna . . . Well, actually, that had been good luck.

And he had a dog.

Biscotti had been a problem at first. She pulled away when he tried to pet her. She kept her distance from other dogs in Piazza Tasso, and there were plenty of them. She was afraid of noises, so when Woody played his guitar, he had to play and sing very softly. When she growled at him, he refused to react. After she'd eaten, he would lower himself down to her level and approach her slowly, avoiding eye contact. But it was another dog who taught Biscotti to be less fearful, more aggressive.

On school days Woody planned to leave Biscotti at the home of his student, Marisa Lodovici, on Borgo Pinti. Marisa had a medium-size husky named Bianca, and they thought the two dogs could play together in the courtyard. But at their first meeting Bianca jumped at Biscotti's throat and threw her to the ground and held her down. Woody started to intervene, but Marisa held him back. After a minute Bianca released her hold and lay down on her back, exposing her own throat and waving her paws in the air. By the end of the week, they were taking turns lunging at each other and throwing each other to the ground. Biscotti no longer squatted and peed when Woody approached her. She began to play with other dogs in the piazza in the evening, and Woody started to spend more time chatting with his neighbors, with other dog owners that is, and with the young punks who hung around outside the bar next to Il Tranvai, the little restaurant where he ate once or twice a week, and who called him Professore. He was starting to feel that he belonged here.

It took Woody and Biscotti forty minutes to walk from Piazza Tasso to the American School in Piazza Savonarola. At first they crossed the river on the Ponte alle Grazie and took Via Verdi north to Piazza Salvemini. Woody would drop Biscotti off on Borgo Pinti and walk the rest of the way with Marisa. But after a while he and Biscotti started to vary their route to avoid Signor Stronzo and his friends, who'd begun to follow him. Signor Stronzo—Mr. Turd—would call the dog: Cicciolina, Cicciolina. Woody recognized the name of the porn star who'd been elected to the Italian parliament and who recently had offered to make love to Saddam Hussein as a way of promoting peace in the Middle East. Biscotti was frightened. Sometimes they waited for Woody in Piazza Salvemini, sometimes on the Ponte Vecchio, sometimes in Piazza San Firenze or on Via del Proconsolo, and on Saturday nights they sometimes showed up at the Bebop Club and heckled him. What he felt when he saw them, or when he heard Rinaldo's smooth voice, was the kind of tightening of the stomach you feel at an approaching playground confrontation. Hektor and Achilles. Those were Woody's terms. But was he Hektor or Achilles? He'd always thought of himself as a Hektor person—defending family, city, home—but his anger at Signor Romero made him think that he might be an Achilles person, and it raised Aristotle's disturbing notion that some of the most important virtues flourish only in battle, that some things can be settled only by violence.

Woody was tempted to stop in and see the *commissario*—to seek his advice—but he didn't want to raise any questions, didn't want to get the *commissario* in trouble by suggesting that they were in cahoots.

Woody was putting up a shelf in the bathroom when they rang the bell. He had a hammer in his hand when he pushed the button to see who it was.

"We've come for the dog," someone said over the intercom. *Signor Stronzo himself,* Woody thought, *Mr. Turd.* The voice told Woody to let the dog out. "You give the dog back now, maybe we won't break your fingers. Kind of hard to play the guitar with broken fingers. Just open the door and let her out."

Woody opened the window and looked down. He could see the tips of their cigarettes. They were smoking in unison! Three of them. Mr. Turd and two turd friends.

"Get the fuck out of here," he shouted.

"You give the dog back, maybe we'll break just one finger. How's that sound?"

Woody surprised them by coming down. With Biscotti on her leash. He still had his hammer in his hand. They backed away when they saw the hammer. He could see that they hadn't expected him to come down and that now they weren't sure what to do.

Whatever was going to happen was going to happen. He wanted to get it over with. He walked the dog around the piazza and they followed him. A kind of fury was building inside him. He was a big man, not afraid of a fight. Biscotti was plastered against his leg so tightly that he had trouble walking.

"Call her, Rinaldo," one of the turd friends said.

Rinaldo started to call: "Cicciolina, Cicci, Cicci, come here bitch. Hey, Cicci, hey girl. That's my dog, you know," he said to Woody. "My father's lawyer says you'll rot in jail. And big time too. Dog thief. Time for you to go back to the States."

Woody didn't say anything.

"Fucking Americans. Think you can run the world." This was their second time around the piazza. "That's my dog, you know."

Woody finally stopped in front of Il Tranvai. It was chilly, but there were still tables outside. He had an audience.

"Rinaldo," he said. "So that's your name. I thought it was Signor Stronzo. Go ahead, Mr. Turd. Call your dog."

"Hey, Cicciolina. Hey, girl. Come here. Come to Papa."

A crowd was starting to gather. Waiters from the restaurant, some of the punks who hung out at the bar next door.

Woody unhooked Biscotti's leash. She stayed by his side. Rinaldo kept calling. Biscotti pressed her shoulder harder against Woody's leg.

"Any of you speak English? Too bad. I took the bus to Vallombrosa last fall. It was quite a ride. Up and down, around those hairpin curves. Made me a little queasy. Like looking at you fellows. It turned my stomach. But the leaves were really something. 'Leaves that bloom in the flowery spring.' That's Homer. Young 'squirts,' that's what Homer calls guys like you. But 'turds' is more like it. Stronzi."

"That's my dog," Rinaldo said, appealing to the crowd. "This man stole my dog, you hear that?"

Woody patted the dog. "Excuse me?"

"I said that's my dog. He knows it is. He stole her. She's tattooed. That means the police can identify her."

"The dog doesn't seem to know it, does she?" Woody said.

"You've brainwashed her."

"It didn't take much." Now Woody appealed to the crowd. "You want to know the story? He burned her. He cut her. He dragged her behind his car in Piazza Santissima Annunziata. You read about it in the papers." He turned back to Rinaldo. "You're surprised she doesn't want to go back to you?"

"It's just a dog. *My* dog."

Woody sat down on one of the restaurant chairs and put the hammer down on the table in front of him. He was suddenly depressed. *Where do people like this come from?*

"Don't fuck with us, okay? We've come for the dog."

"The dog's busy right now."

"Fuck off."

Woody stood up and walked up to Rinaldo and slapped him as hard as he could, a real bone-jarring slap that snapped his head to one side. "Get lost," he said to Rinaldo's two friends, "or I'll do the same for you." He put his arm around Rinaldo's neck. "You're a slow learner," he said.

"Fuck you."

"Do you want me to slap you again?"

"You're going to regret this."

"I already regret it. I regret discovering that there are people like you living in our midst, looking just like normal human beings."

He jammed the heel of his hand into Rinaldo's face. "Do you know who I am?"

"You're a fucking American."

"I'm the former vice president of the Association of the Families of the Victims of the Bombing of 15 August 1980. Do you know why I was the vice president? No, probably not, but —"

"How the fuck would I know?"

"Don't piss me off, Rinaldo."

"You got no right to keep me here."

"Because my daughter was killed in Bologna, in the bombing, 1980. You must have been four or five years old. She was killed by someone like you. Someone who didn't give a shit about the harm they do. Now this dog's name is Biscotti. That was my daughter's name. 'Cookie' in English. And I'm going to look after her as if she were my own daughter. Do you see what I mean?"

Rinaldo didn't answer.

"I said, do you see what I mean?" Woody smashed the heel of his hand into Rinaldo's face again. He'd probably broken his nose, but he didn't care. "You want to know something? I went to visit Angela Strappafelci in Regina Coeli Prison in Rome. That's the woman who put the bomb in the station. I pretended I was a journalist and got to go right into her cell, and I almost killed her. I was *that* close." He held up finger and thumb for everyone to see. "And that's how close I am to smacking you again. Angela's out on furlough now. She put a bomb in the station and killed eighty-six people. And now she's out walking around. But I'm going to promise you something: If anything happens to this dog, I'll send you to a place where there are no furloughs. Is that clear? Do you understand?" He released his hold. "Now get the fuck out of here."

Woody was shaking. The waiters took him into the restaurant and brought him a glass of wine and some antipasti. They treated him as if he were the one who had been smacked around. And they were right to do so. That's the way he felt. As if he were the one who'd been threatened and slapped and humiliated and needed looking after.

What bothered him most was the realization that this particular kind of evil was everywhere. Not just in the big things, but in the little things too. It was everywhere. You couldn't escape it, not even in Piazza Tasso.

The waiters put two tables together, and Woody was joined by other patrons. He was the center of attention. The waiters brought more wine, three kinds of pasta. A bowl of scraps for Biscotti. And after a glass of wine Woody thought, *Well, I didn't do too badly, did I?*

Audition

The thing Miranda had been hoping for morning, noon, and night came to pass. She'd been called for an audition. She wasn't sure if it was her creative visualization that had brought it about, or the prayers she had said at the Catholic church by the entrance to the Glendale Freeway—where she sometimes stopped on her way home, even though she wasn't Catholic—or her agent (who wanted to take the credit), or the fact that she'd been sending Esther Klein a humorous card every single day.

What she learned from her agent, when he called with the news, was that Esther didn't have the financing in place yet but that Michael Gardiner was going to direct and that Giovanni Cipriani had been attached as the male lead, and that Esther was looking for a fresh new face to play Margot.

Miranda continued stopping to pray at the Catholic church. She spent two hundred dollars on a Montblanc fountain pen like Margot's. She rented Esther's latest film—*How Happy I Am*—and Michael's—*Last Rites*—and Alessandro Martone's *Love in Venice*, starring Giovanni Cipriani, or Zanni. She practiced her creative visualization exercises every afternoon. She reread her dog-eared copy of Michael Shurtleff's *Audition: Everything an Actor Needs to Know to Get the Part*. She bought a translation of Natalia Ginzburg's *The Little Virtues*—Margot's favorite book. She went to the public library and checked out Luigi Barzini's *The Italians* and a book on bookbinding—*Hand Bookbinding: A Manual of Instruction*. She read through chapter 2 of *Hand Bookbinding* and, using her new fountain pen, made a list of the tools and supplies she'd need. She didn't want to *play* Margot; she wanted to *be* Margot.

She had to do the audition cold, but she didn't mind. She thought it would be to her advantage, in fact. She'd read the book so many times that in a sense she already *was* Margot. She knew Margot's "arc." She could jump into her story at any point.

The audition was held in an office in downtown L.A., near the Grand Central Market, a not-very-impressive office, an old-fashioned office surrounded by dentists and lawyers, with opaque glass windows in every door. The office itself made her a little uneasy. Everything said temporary, low-budget. There were no magazines in the office, just a few chairs and a desk with a secretary behind it. The secretary took her information and handed her a side to look at. Another actress was waiting. She was good-looking, but she wasn't Margot. Her breasts were too big, for one thing, and she was wearing one of the cheap flowered Lycra dresses that were in all the shop windows. Miranda was wearing jeans and a man's white shirt with the sleeves rolled up, which is what Margot had worn when she was working at the Certosa and when she was doing the final restoration work on the Aretino volume. She could hear voices in the next room. Then the voices stopped and the door opened. Miranda got a glimpse of Esther Klein. Esther registered her presence. An actress came out of the office. Esther said good-bye, said she'd let her know. The secretary nodded at the actress in Capri pants and called her name. Miranda didn't think she'd ever heard it before, which was a good sign.

The chairs were uncomfortable, but Miranda didn't mind that either. But when she started to read her side, she didn't recognize the characters, didn't recognize the scene. She thought, *There's been a mistake,* but there was Margot's name in capital letters: MARGOT. Her head was swimming when Esther came out of the office and told Ms. Capri Pants that they'd let her know. The secretary nodded at her and called her name: Miranda Clark.

There were just two people in the little office. Esther Klein, at a desk, and Michael Gardiner. The room was too small. The venetian blinds were sagging. The rubber tree plant was about to expire. She had two seconds to make a good impression. Her instinct took over; she gave good handshakes and introduced herself without stumbling. She told herself that they were more afraid of her than she was of them. She didn't really believe this, but in fact, instead of the usual agony that most actors (including herself) experience at this moment, Miranda was experiencing feelings of anger and contempt. These feelings were stronger than agony, stronger than fear. She opened herself to her feelings instead of fighting them.

"Miranda," Esther said. "Interesting name. Your parents must have been Shakespeareans."

"Actually I picked the name myself."

"Then *you* must be a Shakespearean."

"Not exactly. I picked the name after I got arrested for shoplifting at a department store in Fort Madison. I got off because the officer forgot to Mirandize me. I didn't read *The Tempest* till I was in college."

"I see. You've been sending me a card every day. They're very funny—but effective."

"I've been praying every day too," Miranda said, consciously opening herself up, letting them get to know her.

"That's even funnier." Esther was looking at her résumé. "Always the bridesmaid," she said. "Never the bride."

"My agent thinks it's about time," Miranda said. "I do too. But you remember I was Alice in *Heavenly Days.*"

Esther nodded. "You've done a lot of commercials," she said.

"Well, then," Michael Gardiner said, looking at his watch. "Let's get started."

"Any time."

"We're not looking for a finished performance," Gardiner added. "We just want to see what you can bring to this role. Are you ready?"

Miranda nodded.

"The stage is yours," Michael Gardiner said. "I'll be reading with you."

The scene was set in the little piazza outside the convent where Margot had discovered the Aretino. Miranda had located it on her map and had no trouble conjuring up a *latteria,* a *pizzicheria,* a bar, an arch, the big doors of the convent. She's sitting at a table in the piazza when a man (SANDRO) emerges from the sewer. This made no sense at all to Miranda, but, she reminded herself, *Every scene is a love scene.*

But who was there to love? Oaf meets wimpy girl? And of course there's humor in every scene too. Maybe that was the way to go: Bozo the Clown meets Margot the Prude. Acting is discovery, but what Margot was discovering in this scene was that she didn't want to be there, and that's what Miranda was discovering too. She tried to play the opposite to her lines to bring out subtext, but she couldn't find a subtext, so she did the only thing she could do: she made a strong choice and ran with it. She drew on her own anger in the present moment. She let it fill the wimpy character on the page. She was a powder keg, a ticking time bomb. There was power there. Strength. The poor girl—the wimpy Margot on the page—just hadn't figured out how to tap into it yet.

Michael, looking reasonably pleased, suggested an adjustment, and Miranda knew he wanted to see if she could take direction.

"Let me hear you play the situation, not the emotion," he said. "Try it with a different objective. Your conscious objective is to get this man to go away, but your unconscious objective is to get him to take your clothes off. This will give you a point of contradiction to work with; it will give you more to do."

But Miranda balked. She was too mad. "I don't need another objective to interpret Margot," she said. "I *am* Margot. I read *The Sixteen Pleasures* at Smith, and I've read it a dozen times since. Excuse me. I know this is crazy. I wasn't going to say anything. But I can't help it. How could you do this? How could you do this to Margot? You've turned her into a wimp. She doesn't speak Italian. So what is she doing there? She doesn't drink wine; she doesn't like Italian food. It doesn't compute. And her lover? Why is he such a jerk? He's supposed to be suave and sophisticated. I mean, Giovanni Cipriani, that's great. He's perfect for Sandro. But why is he such an oaf in this scene? Has Giovanni actually looked at this script? And why is Sandro coming up out of the sewer? It doesn't make any sense."

Miranda was pretty shaken up after the reading. Stuck in traffic on the Glendale Freeway, she asked herself, *What would Margot do?* But she couldn't answer the question. She wished she were back in Mount Pleasant, Iowa, living in her parents' house; she wished she were back at Smith, living in Lawrence House, or in Norwalk, Connecticut, where she'd spent a summer at the White Barn Theatre. She wished she were anywhere but where she was. Hollywood was a sham, completely out of touch. People in Hollywood wouldn't recognize a good story if it bit them in the ass.

She was so depressed she couldn't think. It was after six o'clock when she turned off the freeway. She thought of stopping at Corpus Christi to pray and maybe light a candle but decided against it. When she got home she poured herself a glass of white wine and sat in the kitchen with the lights off. She finished the wine and poured herself another glass and unpacked the boxes of bookbinding tools and supplies she'd bought at McManus and Morgan on Seventh Avenue: paper, tape, thread, binding boards, mull (strips of cloth), paste, a carpenter's square, a steel ruler, two bone folders, a folding needle, a right-angle card, a squared card, a sewing frame, a press and a tub, paste brushes, an awl, beeswax, fine sandpaper, a paring knife. She spread everything out on the dining room table and read through the instructions for her first project, which was to make a blank book with a single signature:

- Cut and fold signature paper.
- Cut cover paper.
- Collate.
- Mark up and sew.
- Fold up cover.
- Make and attach label.
- Press.

But before she got started, she had to set up her new sewing frame. The instructions on page 38 of the manual were very clear.

She cut three tapes and attached them to the keys and then fed them through the slot in the sewing frame and attached the other ends to the crossbar. She tightened the crossbar to take up the slack in the tapes. And she thought, *This is what Margot would do.*

But then in the morning her agent called. She had the part. "You took them by surprise," he said. "You brought a lot of spunk to the part. And that's exactly what they were looking for. Spunk. You really spunked the hell out of it."

Second Reconnaissance

Esther didn't believe in hiring talented people and giving them free rein. A lot of talented people didn't know what things cost. Esther knew what things cost because she was the one who wrote the checks—for the film, for the camera package, for the sound and lighting equipment, for the dolly, for the insurance, for the automated dialogue replacement, for the Foley, for the permits, for music and effects, for craft services. A producer wrote thirty-eight checks and she was in business.

She had only three months to set up the film, but everything was falling into place. The principal actors had been attached; she had an acceptable domestic distribution deal with Three Oaks films that guaranteed her three hundred theaters and a prints-and-advertising commitment of 150 percent of the final budget, and a foreign deal with Leviathan with a livable distribution fee and capped expenses. Her line producer, Barbara Cohen, who'd worked on the last two films she and Harry had done together, had already organized the insurance and the completion bond and had prepared a preliminary budget. She'd hired an American cinematographer, Stu Knowles, and an Italian assistant director, Franco Bevilacqua, who was bringing his own department heads on board. Both Knowles and Bevilacqua had worked with Michael before. Knowles was fast and dependable and knew how to work with available light and still get a consistent look. Bevilacqua was an optimistic realist, or a realistic optimist, who knew how to merge characters, reduce extras, cut down scenes, merge locations. He also knew everyone in Florence, including the mayor.

In mid-November she and Michael flew first-class to Rome for her second recce, Michael's first. Michael, who was asleep in the window seat beside her, his long legs covered with a light airline blanket, was tired all the time, and he had to get up to pee every hour. She hadn't known about the cancer when she'd attached him, and now it was too late, and she was starting to worry that he wouldn't make it through production. But he was tractable, so different from Harry. He didn't have the drive that Harry had, but he knew how to put together a coherent story out of bits and pieces, knew where to put the camera and how to move it around, knew how to take command of a set, knew how to bring the best out of an inexperienced actress like Miranda, and how to keep a strong actor like Zanni in front of the camera for more than two takes. The weak link was not Michael but Miranda Clark. She was beautiful, however, and she had spunk, and it was easy to imagine audiences falling in love with her. Besides, when it came right down to it, they really hadn't had much choice, and she *was* a step above the other young actresses they'd auditioned.

Paola Bottazzi, the locations manager, and Franco met them in the lobby of the hotel, and they took a taxi straight to the convent in Piazza San Pier Maggiore, which they were planning to use for a production office, for storing equipment, for wardrobe and makeup, and for most of the interior shots. Margot had made the initial contact, and Paola Bottazzi had done the follow-up. The convent, which had been closed for ten years, had been taken over by the city government, which was planning to turn it into a school, but which hadn't managed to do so yet, though some playground equipment had been installed in the cloister. The convent would represent an enormous savings—bathrooms, a kitchen, changing rooms, green rooms, sets, production office, wardrobe—and Esther wanted to reassure herself that it was going to work. If it did, they wouldn't have to go to Eastern Europe.

Margot was waiting for them in the piazza, and they were soon joined by a government official who had the keys. He opened a small door that was cut out of one of the big doors. Esther was reluctant to enter. It gave her the creeps. One of her girlhood friends had become a nun and had disappeared. But she followed the others into the dark interior, staying close to Margot.

"You were tempted, weren't you?" she asked Margot.

"Tempted?"

"To join."

"For about an hour," Margot said.

"Do you think you could have stuck it out? It gives me the willies."

"Probably not. A religious vocation wasn't what I thought it was. There was always something I couldn't understand. It was a good place for a woman, but . . . a mystery. A place I couldn't get to."

"These three rooms," the government official said, "were the hospice for pilgrims. They're the only rooms that have been converted to classrooms."

"Production office," Esther said. "Right by the front door." In her imagination the room was already full: desks, telephones, computers, fax machine, coffee machine, production assistants and interns. Herself in the middle of it all. Everything was perfect. They could even house the PAs and some of the Italian crew members in the dormitory rooms on the second floor and save another bundle. Esther was relieved to see Michael shake off his tiredness, as if every room were presenting the solution to a problem that had been weighing him down. It was like having one of the big studio soundstages at their disposal. They had seventy pages scripted for interior shots, most of which could be done in the main chapel, which was big enough for two or three sets and which would be easy to light because the ceiling was high enough for the overheads.

In the piazza everyone shook hands with everyone else. Franco and Paola and the government official would take care of the paperwork. Esther could hardly contain herself. She was starting to think this could be big, bigger than she'd thought, and she wanted to take everyone out to dinner, to Enoteca Pinchiorri, which she'd read about in one of her guidebooks.

"Too expensive," Margot said. "Besides, you need a reservation six weeks in advance."

"You know people," Esther said. "Get on the horn, tell them it would be a damn shame if the producer and the director of a great film can't get a table at Enoteca Pinchiorri. Tell them who you are. Tell them you wrote the book."

"It's pronounced *Pinkiori*," Margot said. "The *ch* is pronounced like a *k*."

"What about you, Mike?" Esther said when they were in a cab on the way back to the hotel. "You think Beryl will join a convent after you've popped off? I wouldn't be surprised. Do Episcopalians have convents?"

"You'll have to ask Beryl," Michael said.

The doors of Enoteca Pinchiorri were almost as big as the convent doors and were flanked by potted plants the size of trees. There was no menu posted out in front.

Franco had come for them at the hotel in a taxi. Margot was waiting at the restaurant, along with her friend, Woody. Esther wished that Woody hadn't come because four would have been nicer. Besides, she pegged him right away as a sourpuss, couldn't see him opening up. He sat up straight in the Queen Anne chair, as if he were bracing himself for an attack. And he wasn't dressed appropriately. White shirt, nice jacket, and an okay tie, but jeans. Everyone wore jeans in Italy, but not at the Enoteca Pinchiorri. She knew that he'd worked on a screenplay with Margot and was afraid that this might spell trouble. Unfortunately, at some point she'd have to sit down with Margot and explain the facts of life, explain that she was going to use her own screenplay, not Margot's. Dealing with writers was like dealing with parents of small children. Esther's sister was a schoolteacher in Phoenix. Parents were always complaining, her sister said, because they thought you weren't treating their little darlings properly. Writers were like that with their books. They couldn't grasp certain fundamental concepts: Film is essentially different from narrative. It's a visual medium. It works through images, not through words. Not that dialogue isn't important. Writers thought that story was the heart and soul of everything, including movies, but it isn't. Images are the heart and soul of movies. Moving images. Story is incidental. That's what writers couldn't understand.

Esther was wearing the leather coat she'd bought on her first recce. She kept it on for a while and then took it off and asked one of the waiters to hang it up for her. "The waiters like to push you around in a place like this," she said. "If you want to have a good time, you've got to show them who's boss. You can't let the waiters intimidate you. It's like the old Ma Maison in Los Angeles.

Or the Tour d'Argent in Paris. They tried to intimidate Harry at the Tour d'Argent, and he sent everything back at least once, sometimes twice. The wine, the soup, the steaks. Everything." But Harry was living with another woman in L.A., and without him Esther was just a little intimidated—by the Murano glass chandeliers, the pale pink table linens, the silver water pitchers, the liveried waiters. She was too tired; she was talking too much. There were no prices on the menu, and she was starting to worry about the bill.

They had put five people at a table for four, and Esther complained. Margot tried to shush her, but she wouldn't shush. The waiters knew English, she could see that, but they were pretending not to, and this irritated her. They were going to have to struggle to have a good time here. But she was determined to have a good time, a great time. She ordered a bottle of Prosecco to show them that she knew her way around an Italian meal, and when the Prosecco arrived, she proposed a toast to what was going to be a great film.

They ordered the chef's tasting menu, which was wonderful. Goose liver terrine with figs and star anise; sea scallops with celery and caviar in a basil vinaigrette; lobster with asparagus tips; baked baby lamb with deep-fried brains. Her guests were enjoying themselves. Esther sat between Woody and Franco Bevilacqua, who were talking Italian politics. Margot and Paola were tracking down mutual acquaintances. Esther was relieved that Margot wasn't asking about how they were going to do the flood, and she was relieved that the lambs' brains were edible. Pretty good, actually.

"You're not a film person, are you?" she said to Woody during a lull in the conversation.

"I don't suppose I am," he said.

"Too bad," she said. "Film is the great art form of the twentieth century. Film has pushed everything else into the background. Nothing can compare with it." Woody speared an asparagus tip and put it in his mouth. "It's got everything," Esther went on. "Narrative, scene, intimate detail, visual, sculpture that moves, images that move."

"I liked it better when it was the movies," Woody said. "Painting, sculpture, symphonies, literature . . . They were for the rich. They were highbrow. But movies were for everybody. Like Homer. And everybody could afford it. When I was a kid, it cost fourteen cents for a movie and ten cents for popcorn. If you took a quarter, you had a penny left for candy. I went every Friday night. I don't think I missed a Friday night for two or three years running. I can't remember any of the movies, mostly Westerns, but I can remember what it felt like."

Esther was taken by surprise, ambushed. "You know something," she said, "that's what *we're* going to make — a movie."

After the special desserts and the Vin Santo and the cognac, Esther discovered that her credit card wouldn't cover the bill, which was almost a thousand dollars, and she had to ask Margot to put it on *her* credit card. This was the sort of thing that Harry would have shrugged off, but Esther felt humiliated, even though Margot said it was all right. She remembered Harry sending everything back at the Tour d'Argent, and how the waiters had fallen all over him, apologizing, asking for his advice. And the funny thing was, Harry didn't know squat about French food, but he gave them advice anyway. She thought that if Harry were here they'd take a cab up to the big piazza overlooking the city, Piazza Michelangelo, or they'd go back to the hotel and make love. She thought that if Harry were here she wouldn't feel so alone, but she kept her thoughts to herself and didn't allow herself any tears till she was in the big double bed in her five-hundred-dollar-a-night room at the Excelsior.

Midwestern Christmas

A sign at the base of the tower warned visitors, in Italian and in English, not to make the climb if they had weak hearts. Margot's father had died of a heart attack, but she wasn't worried. She looked at Woody, who was talking to the woman at the counter where they sold maps of the city and official guides to various museums. He didn't look worried either. Florence was a tourist town, no getting around it, but it was her tourist town, and in winter, when the weather was bad, the streets weren't too crowded. Not that they had a real winter. But they'd had rain mixed with a little snow—the first snow she'd seen in four or five years—and they had the tower more or less to themselves.

Margot and Woody had settled into a comfortable friendship. The moment for a little *avventura* had come and gone on the night they'd met, the night the *stronzo* had dragged Biscotti behind him around Piazza Santissima Annunziata. They'd written a screenplay together; they'd watched a lot of movies and they'd eaten a lot of buttered popcorn and a lot of apples. On Saturday nights they'd eat at Trattoria la Maremmana, or at the Osteria de'

Pazzi in Via Verdi, or at the little restaurant in Piazza Tasso—Il Tranvai—or Woody and Biscotti would come over and Woody would fix dinner and they'd watch another movie and eat popcorn and apples, and then Woody would put his shoes back on and head for home.

Margot didn't want him to leave, to go back to St. Clair. She wanted him to stay in Italy, and now every moment they spent together felt charged with meaning, fraught with danger. Something would have to be settled. But how? How did you seduce a man like Woody? With an Italian man, all you had to do was catch his eye and smile and then let him do all the work. But Woody?

On the other hand, Woody was no Puritan: she knew that he'd lived for two years with a woman in Bologna, and he'd admitted, on the way to the tower, that he'd almost lost his job at St. Clair for shacking up with a student whose mother was an important trustee and whose father was a major donor.

Margot pried the details, some of the details, out of him as they climbed the narrow winding stairs to the first level. The mother, Allison, had been Woody's girlfriend at the University of Michigan. She'd taught at St. Clair and when she left she'd recommended that they hire Woody to replace her. The father, Alireza Mirsadiqi, a wealthy Iranian rug merchant, had intervened on Woody's behalf, saving his job, but by the time the scandal had played itself out, Woody had decided to sell his farm and come to Italy for the trial of the terrorists in Bologna. Alireza had insisted that a position be kept open for him at St. Clair. This is what worried Margot.

"Well, Alan Woodhull, aren't you the naughty boy," Margot said. "I had no idea. No idea. Not just the mother, but the daughter too. And then her father takes a shine to you . . ."

Woody laughed. "They've invited me to Rome for Christmas."

"They live in Rome? These same people? Woody, you're full of surprises. Will the daughter be there? What was her name?"

"Turi. Yes. She's teaching at Harvard now. She was a terrific student."

"I'll bet she was."

They had the first landing to themselves. "Two years in Florence," Margot said, "and you haven't climbed Giotto's tower, haven't been up to the cupola of the Duomo, haven't been to the Uffizi, haven't seen Michelangelo's *David* in the Accademia, or Donatello's in the Bargello. I'm going to have to take it upon myself to teach you about the Renaissance."

"As far as I'm concerned," Woody said, adopting a professorial tone, "the Renaissance was the creation of later historians—Michelet and Burckhardt—and accomplished nothing of substance, nothing comparable to the works of Plato and Aristotle, nothing comparable to the institution of chivalry or the gothic cathedrals and universities of the Middle Ages, or to the scientific advances of the seventeenth century. Besides, who reads the Renaissance humanists? Even Pico della Mirandola was a lightweight. There was nothing to compare with Homer or Virgil. Not till Shakespeare."

"What about Dante?"

"Dante, of course. For Dante, Florence was the center of the universe, and by the Quattrocento it really was the center of the universe. But Florence ignored the developing trade routes, ignored the economic opportunities presented by the discovery of the new world. Florence turned inward, and what happened? The kings that the Medici financed went bankrupt, and so did the Medici. Florence never recovered.

"Look at Illinois in the nineteenth century. The old trade routes were north–south. The new ones were east–west. They were made possible by the railroad. Illinois didn't turn inward.

It financed the bridges across the Mississippi that made the rail-road lines possible. Illinois invested in the railroads."

"But Woody," Margot said, "I want you to see what *I* see." They were looking out at the massive red dome of Santa Maria dei Fiori, and she told him the old story: The medieval cathedral builders had learned by trial and error. Some cathedrals in France had collapsed because the builders hadn't known how to calculate stresses. Woody hadn't known that. "The folks who built the Duomo in Florence wanted something to really domi-nate the region, so they built a cathedral so big they didn't know how to put a top on it. Just a big hole."

They looked out through the heavy wire screen in the tower window. Woody put his hand on the screen and tried to shake it. "Like hog panels," he said.

"Florence was a laughingstock," Margot went on. "They had nice cathedrals in Pisa and Siena. But all Florence had was a big hole."

"Till Brunelleschi came along. The egg, and all that."

"It was Columbus who pulled the egg trick. Brunelleschi went to Rome and studied the Pantheon. The Romans knew how to do it, and he figured out how to do it too. Not by trial and error, but by thinking, by figuring it out. That's the difference."

On the second level she explained the double dome construc-tion, which she didn't fully understand. But she understood enough.

"There used to be brick works near St. Clair," Woody said. "I used to go out there with Hannah and the girls. There were arches everywhere formed by the old burned-out kilns."

The problem with Woody, in Margot's opinion, wasn't the Renaissance — the discovery of the world and of man. The prob-lem with Woody was that he lived in a different Italy. Her Italy lay spread out before them, and if you went to the Uffizi, where the paintings were arranged in chronological order, you could see that *something* had happened, something astonishing. Even Woody would have to admit that, if she could get him there. Her Italy was the bus stop on Via del Proconsolo, where you could stand between the Badia, the center of the old medieval city, and the Bargello, the symbol of the new civic authority; her Italy was her old high school and her studio on the Lungarno Guicciardini; it was bars and trattorias where the waiters knew her by name; it was the piazzas where she always ran into a friend or two. But Woody's Italy was the train station in Bologna, where his daughter had been killed by a terrorist bomb; his Italy was the young people who had put the bomb in the second-class waiting room of the station, and the *esecutori,* who had arranged the bombing; and the *mandanti,* the shadowy figures in the background who had commissioned it; his Italy was the corrupt judiciary that had failed to protect Judge DiBernardi from being assassinated; his Italy was the courtroom in Bologna where the terrorists had been tried; his Italy was the old-boy Fascist network that even now had obtained the release of Angela Strappafelci, the young woman who'd put the bomb in the station, dressed like a German tourist; his Italy was Rinaldo, the *stronzo* who'd dragged Biscotti behind his car, who'd threatened him in Piazza Tasso, and who had denounced him and was threatening to sue him to get his dog back. Woody had had to get his own lawyer, someone he'd gotten to know at the trial in Bologna. Rinaldo's father had offered Woody a million lire, almost a thousand dollars, to return the dog, but Woody had refused.

At the top of the tower they were going to create a memory chain. Woody had bought a book on memory that promised to cure absentmindedness and to keep the reader from losing things and to give the reader total recall of names, places, dates, and even shopping lists.

Margot had read the book too and had been helping him with absentmindedness, and she'd noticed a definite improvement. The reason you lose your glasses or your shoes or your shopping list is that you don't register anything when you put them down, so there's nothing in your memory to recall. You need to register the fact that you've put your glasses down on top of the refrigerator by creating a fanciful association at the time you put them there. That way you'll have something to remember. You imagine, for example, that your refrigerator is a big rectangular head that's wearing a pair of glasses. Then when you start to look for your glasses, you'll associate them with this refrigerator head.

The same principle could be used to create a memory chain, a technique that appealed to Woody because it had been developed by the Greek orators. First you create the chain—a list of places. Then, with your chain in place, when you create a list, you put the first item in the first location on your chain and create a fanciful association; then you put the second item on your list in the second location, and so on.

The list that Margot had created for Woody began in Fiesole, the earliest Etruscan settlement in the Arno Valley. From where they were standing now they could see the bell tower of San Romola up in Fiesole. The second location was the Ponte Vecchio, the narrowest spot on the Arno, where the Romans had built the first bridge, part of the Via Cassia that linked Rome to northern Italy. The third location was the Piazza Repubblica, the center of the old Roman *campo,* which had been laid out at right angles. From the top of Giotto's tower they could see it all, the city spread out before them. Margot's memory chain went on in chronological order: San Miniato, the Baptistery, the Badia Fiorentina, Santa Maria Novella, Santa Croce, the Signoria, the Duomo, the Bargello, and so on. It was the story her mother had drilled into her when she was fifteen, and her mother, she learned later, was having an affair with Bruno Bruni, a man who'd befriended them when they first came to Florence, and who was now buried up in Settignano.

"Now Woody, I want you to fix this picture in your mind, okay? You've got twenty locations in your memory chain. That will do for starters. Maybe we'll add a few more later. Now I'm going to give you a shopping list for tonight. I'm going to give you things in random order, and I want you to put each item in one of the locations, okay? Do you want to run through the chain again first?"

"I'm all set."

"Let's start with some *salame toscano*."

"Okay. Fiesole. I'm going to picture the bell tower as a big salami. Next."

"Some olives. Different kinds. Kalamata, and some of those little Ligurian ones."

"I'm at the Ponte Vecchio, but instead of gold in the shop windows they've got all kinds of olives."

"Good."

"I'm going to need some stamps."

"Okay. I'm in Piazza Repubblica, and it's paved with stamps instead of stones."

Margot went through her list till they got to the last two items: *parmigiano reggiano* and *clementini*.

"I'm standing in Piazza Santa Croce. I've just imagined that the statue of Dante is made out of Parmesan cheese, and now I'm looking up at your balcony. You're standing on the balcony, looking down, but instead of your regular breasts you've got about twenty *clementini*, like the breasts on the statue of Artemis in Ephesus."

"Perfect, Woody. Everything's in place. You're ready to go

shopping. You don't need to worry about losing the list because it's up here, right?" She tapped his head. "You'd better run through it, okay, just to make sure."

Woody ran through the list without a mistake. "Pretty amazing," he said. "This is how Demosthenes—"

But Margot put her arm through his. "Woody," she said, "don't go to Rome for Christmas. Stay here. We'll get a tree and we'll put up some lights. We'll make ornaments out of baker's clay, and we'll go shopping and you can roast a turkey. We'll watch *A Christmas Carol* in Italian." Her heart was pounding the way it always did when a man propositioned her, though this time it was the other way around. "We can go to the Christmas Eve service at the American Church and sit way in the back so they don't put us on a committee. I haven't been in years. Last year I went home to see my sisters, and . . ." But she stopped herself because she realized that she was talking too much.

"Sure," he said. "Why not? I've got a meeting in Rome in January anyway. I'll stay with the Mirsadiqis then."

On Christmas Eve, after the service at the American Church, after the traditional Florentine Christmas Eve dinner—*spaghetti alle vongole* followed by barnyard-smelling *cottechino* sausage— Margot asked Woody to undress her in front of the cheval glass. Everything you do after a certain age is a variation on something you've done before. Woody was hardly the first to undress her in front of this cheval glass, which had belonged to Francesca, who'd become her best friend. And yet this didn't feel like anything she'd ever done before. It felt like something new. Like starting over. As if her adventure were just beginning. After they'd made love and had drunk a glass of Vin Santo, Woody started to leave, as he always did, but Margot asked him to stay. "I don't want to wake up alone," she said, "not on Christmas morning," and of course he stayed, but he had to go home to get some food for Biscotti. Margot stood in the window and watched him and the dog cross the piazza. And then she waited right there till she saw him coming back out of Via Verdi into the piazza.

PART II

Production

Miranda Arrives

Miranda was twenty years old when she read *The Sixteen Pleasures* for the first time, shortly after her mother's unexpected death. She'd flown home from Smith for the funeral and then flown back to Bradley International Airport, near Hartford. She hadn't wanted to come back to school, but her aunt and uncle—who hadn't understood why she'd gone so far away from home in the first place—had put her on the plane in Des Moines, and that was that. Someone had left a copy of *The Sixteen Pleasures* in the back of the shuttle that she took from Bradley to Northampton, and she started to read it on the way and kept reading till it got too dark to see.

Back at Smith, she was okay until someone asked her how she was, and then she'd start to cry. She even got to spend a day in the infirmary—almost unheard of unless you were running a fever of over 102 degrees. She missed her mother. Nothing was coming up in her life. She'd been unhappy at Smith from the beginning. She didn't belong. She couldn't afford the clothes she'd admired in the college issue of *Mademoiselle*. She'd never been to the Hamptons, never been to Boston or New York. As a junior in high school she'd played Emily in a production of *Our Town,* and then in her senior year she'd played Juliet in *Romeo and Juliet,* but at Smith she'd been passed over for the role of Nina in Chekhov's *The Seagull,* which she'd studied in her drama class.

She finished *The Sixteen Pleasures* in the infirmary and then she read it again instead of studying for her Art II slide test. She was in despair, but she couldn't get herself to study. The exam was in Sage Hall. The room was dark and you got three minutes for each slide, during which time you had to write down everything you could think of about the ugly statues at the cathedral at Rheims or about Piero della Francesco's *Madonna del Parto.*

The first slide came on and two hundred pens began to write in two hundred blue books. Well, 199 pens if you subtracted Miranda's. She couldn't stick it. She walked out, walked down Green Street back to Lawrence House. She lay down on her bed and started to read *The Sixteen Pleasures* again. *The Sixteen Pleasures* gave her a better sense than Art II of what all the fuss was about. The fuss about art, that is. The fuss about the Renaissance. But what she really liked was the way the plucky heroine — Margot Harrington — pulled herself up by her own bootstraps. The book articulated her needs, her mood, her longing for her mother. She knew that on every page Margot was trying to say what was true. She thought that if Margot hadn't existed, she would have had to invent someone just like her.

Smith had been her mother's idea. Kids from Mount Pleasant went to Iowa Wesleyan, right in town, or Iowa State in Ames, or the University of Iowa in Iowa City, or Grinnell.

A few went east and were never heard of again, but Miranda's mother had read an article about women's colleges in *Reader's*

Digest: it was better for girls to "compete" with other girls in math and science classes than with boys. And at Smith the editor of the newspaper—*The Sophian*—would be a girl. Ditto for Bryn Mawr and Mount Holyoke, which were also described in the article, but Bryn Mawr seemed too intellectual, too mannish, and Mount Holyoke too reticent.

What her mother had really wanted, Miranda realized, but not till after it was too late, was for her to become a certain kind of person—not exactly a "lady," but a Smithie; not Julia Child or Sylvia Plath or Nancy Reagan, but Julie Nixon Eisenhower, who was assistant managing editor of the *Saturday Evening Post* and who'd been voted one of the Ten Most Admired Women in America by readers of *Good Housekeeping,* and who was married to David Eisenhower.

And that's why her mother would have been heartbroken when she dropped out, at the end of her junior year, and moved to L.A. to take a screen test advertised in the back of a magazine. The screen test didn't materialize, but Miranda stayed in L.A.— substitute teaching, working on the switchboard at a talent agency, doing audience work for a sitcom, laughing hysterically and clapping her hands all day long. And then she landed a handful of supporting roles and, ironically, commercials in which she played a younger, perkier version of her mother, immersed in a world of new products: mops, detergents, vacuum cleaners, shampoos.

Miranda sublet her apartment in Altadena and left Los Angeles just before Christmas. She was going to spend the holidays with her aunt and uncle in Mount Pleasant and then fly to Luxembourg on Icelandic and then go by train to Florence. She wanted to spend some time in Florence on her own, before the start of principal photography, to get a feel for the place.

She boarded the Southwest Chief in Union Station on North Alameda with three large suitcases, and three days and two nights later she was in Iowa. She'd passed the time on the train by imagining her new life. By the time the train got to Denver, her Oscar fantasy had lost its power to arouse, and she spent the rest of the trip concentrating on her *Michelin Guide to Italy,* which didn't have any pictures. But it had maps, and she studied the principal piazzas, and she memorized Fiesole and Settignano, and the little Piazza San Pier Maggiore, where the convent was located. And once or twice, as she put the book down and looked out the window of the observation car, a force as powerful as the big diesel locomotives pulling the train thrust her back into adolescence. She was on her way home from Smith, instead of L.A., with her Harvard book bag packed with sandwiches and apples from Lawrence House, more than enough, full of joy at the prospect of seeing her mother again.

But of course it was Uncle Jack, not her mother, who picked her up at the station in Fort Madison, loaded her trunk and the three suitcases into the back of the pickup, and drove her to Mount Pleasant, past corncribs and hog enclosures and Dutch barns. The yard lights in the black distance were like lights on an archipelago or on passing ships. They drove past the Brenner farm where she and Todd Brenner and Jeremy Baker had shot at the hogs with Todd's BB gun and they'd put Jeremy's Saint Bernard, Rufus, in with the hogs and the hogs had chased him till he collapsed and would have eaten him if Todd's dad hadn't driven them off, kicking them away with his wooden leg.

"If you'd married Todd Brenner instead of going out East," Uncle Jack said, "you'd be home."

At home, everything was the same, except older, like her aunt and uncle. And like Miranda herself. *Reader's Digest Condensed Books* sat on the shelf next to copies of some of the books Miranda had used at Smith, her Art II book among them. A paperback copy of *The Sixteen Pleasures* was sitting on the kitchen table. Aunt Lena had read it and had a lot of questions, especially about how they were going to do the flood, and how they were going to do the book restoration scenes and the sex scenes.

Mount Pleasant was the sort of place everyone had made fun of at Smith. And when Miranda had finally gotten settled in L.A., she'd decided she'd never be from Mount Pleasant again. But she'd been wrong. Mount Pleasant contained her life, and she'd been homesick for it in L.A., just as she'd been home-sick for it at Smith—for the public library, where her mother had worked at the reference desk and where she'd done her homework; for Lincoln Elementary and Mount Pleasant Middle School; for the Van Allen House Heritage Center and Midwest Old Threshers Heritage Museum and St. Michael's Episcopal and the Second Baptist and Saunders Park; for best friends and slumber parties and first love and football games and the occa-sional victory parades and Williford Cemetery, where her mother was buried, and her father too, and aunts and uncles, Clarks and Veneclausens.

But the reason she never got over it was that it also contained the life she might have lived, the life that her old friends were living, some of them, anyway. Married. Children. Her first love, Todd, who'd managed to pull her panties down in the backseat of his dad's Packard. But she'd asked him to stop and he had, and after that there was no going forward. And if they had gone all the way, would it matter now?

Everyone was excited about the movie, for about two minutes. Miranda couldn't keep the conversation focused on herself for very long, and gradually she forgot about herself.

On the morning of Christmas Eve, she drove out to the cemetery, to visit her parents' graves. When her mother was twelve years old, she'd gone out to the barn one morning and found her father, Miranda's Grandfather Neumiller, hanging from one of the rafters. He'd climbed up a ladder, tied a rope around the rafter and around his neck, and kicked the ladder away. Miranda's mother, whose name was Ellen, went back to the house and waited for someone else to find him—her older brother, Miranda's Uncle Jack, as it turned out, who was married and lived about half a mile west of them on Highway 34. When Jack came into the house, about fifteen minutes later, he said there'd been an accident and called Doc Grainger. Doc Grainger came, and an ambulance from the Connelly Funeral Home, and the story that came out was that Miranda's grandfather had fallen off a ladder in the barn and broken his neck. No one knew that Ellen had already seen him, swinging from a length of the three-strand rope they used to make halters for the heifers. What upset Miranda more than her Grandpa Neumiller's suicide was the fact that her mother had carried this secret around with her for so many years. Had she brooded on it? Had she allowed it to poison her life? Had she shared it with Miranda's father, who'd been killed in a tractor accident when Miranda was nine? It was as if she'd never known her mother any more than she'd known her father, never known the most important thing about her mother. It was as if a loose thread had been pulled out of a tapestry, unraveling all her memories, her picture of her childhood, her understanding of her own life, her own story.

But Ellen had told her brother Jack, in the hospital, just before she died, and Jack had told everyone, so her secret had become part of family lore, along with stolid Uncle Frank, who'd run a hardware store in Fort Madison and who'd left behind hundreds of passionate letters from a woman in Des Moines. Miranda had a distant cousin who'd been a bank robber and another cousin who'd embezzled a lot of money and fled to Argentina, and still another cousin—Cousin Johnny—who'd killed a man with a spade at the old Clarinda Asylum, back in the time of Polk Wells, the bank robber and Indian fighter. Miranda liked these stories because they spoke of passion and feeling lying just below the surface. But she didn't like to hear her mother's story trotted out. It was too painful, and that's why she went to bed early on Christmas Eve instead of sitting up with her family and sipping hot cider laced with Applejack.

On the train from Luxembourg to Florence, Miranda *became* Margot Harrington, someone who was more real to her than the self she could see, when she didn't have her eyes closed, reflected in the long mirror above the seats opposite her in her compartment, a mirror that was tilted slightly so that it cut off the top of her head. She was larger than this reflected self, wiser, more confident; she had the right touch on life. In this creative visualization, she was on the train from Luxembourg to Florence, but of course, she really *was* on the train from Luxembourg to Florence. She'd cashed in the open ticket from New York to Rome that Esther Klein had given her and flown to Luxembourg three weeks early, so she could try out her new self in Italy. She was following Margot's itinerary: TWA from Chicago to New York; Icelandic from New York to Luxembourg; express train from Luxembourg to Florence.

Lying on her couchette that night, under a paper blanket, she counted down slowly from ten to one, breathing slowly and deeply, till she was standing on the threshold of Margot's apartment in Santa Croce and Margot, the real Margot, was inviting her in and saying how exciting it was to meet a movie star.

She didn't sleep well in the couchette, but she wasn't tired when the train backed into the station in Florence, Stazione Santa Maria Novella. She struggled to get her huge suitcase down from the luggage rack. The conductor had helped her get it up there, but he had disappeared, and it was difficult to maneuver with six people in the compartment. Her other luggage had already been shipped, air freight, to the production office in the convent. Ex-convent.

Waiting in the crush of passengers in the corridor of the train, she was part Margot, part Miranda. But once she stepped off the train onto the platform, she was 100 percent herself again. She was totally unprepared for this experience. Not for being herself, but for being unable to communicate. Her semester and a half of Italian at Smith wasn't going to do her much good. The platform was crowded. There were no porters. Other passengers had found luggage carts, but she couldn't see any. And she had to pee. She should have peed on the train, but she'd been too busy visualizing herself at Margot's doorstep in Piazza Santa Croce. *What would Margot do?* she asked herself. But Margot wouldn't be in this predicament: Margot spoke Italian.

She tried to sashay like Dorothy de Poliolo in her favorite film, *L'avventura,* but it's hard to sashay when you have to pee and when you're pulling a heavy suitcase, and she failed to stir up the collective id.

Gabinetto was the word that she'd tucked away for emergencies, but now the language problem really came home to her for the first time. Everyone at the hotel in Luxembourg where she'd spent the night had spoken English, and so had the people in the train station, and the conductor on the train, and one of the passengers, a doctor from Germany who was coming to visit his son, who'd married an Italian. She looked around for him, but he'd disappeared.

"*Gabinetto*," she said to herself. "*Gabinetto*." What was she saying? *Cabinet?*

Her plan had been to take a cab to Piazza Santa Croce. She'd ask Margot to recommend a hotel, and Margot would either invite her to stay in her apartment, or she'd recommend a hotel.

"Taxi, taxi. You want taxi?"

A rough-looking man wearing a New York Yankees cap was talking to her.

She nodded.

"You come."

He grabbed the handle of the suitcase and pulled it toward the exit. Miranda followed. Out of the station. Down a long flight of stairs. The suitcase banging on each narrow step. Down an underground ramp under a busy street.

The underground passageway, which branched off into other underground passageways, was bright and full of stores of all kinds. Miranda, in high heels, having trouble keeping up with the taxi driver, saw what she'd been looking for, a sign: WC. She shouted at the taxi driver and touched his shoulder: "*Gabinetto*." But the taxi driver kept going, as if he hadn't heard her. And then there were the gypsies, women in shawls, sitting on the pavement and leaning up against the wall of the underpass, holding pathetic-looking babies in their laps, making piercing sounds, and a whole flock of gypsy children, swarming around her like hornets, waving newspapers at her, pawing at her dress with their little hands, exploring her pockets, tugging on the strap of her purse. The cab driver gave one of them, a little girl, a savage kick and she fell to the ground. He shouted something in Italian. The gypsies backed away. Miranda was starting to panic.

They came to another fork in the tunnels. Miranda had had enough. She wanted to go back to the WC. *"Gabinetto,"* she shouted in the driver's ear. "Stop." She gave the suitcase a push so that it fell over. The driver stopped and looked at her.

"No taxi," she said. "No taxi." But the driver righted the suitcase.

"Fuck you," Miranda shouted. "Fuck you, fuck you, you bastard."

A crowd started to gather. The driver let go of the suitcase, shrugged his shoulders, walked away.

"Gabinetto," Miranda said to a middle-aged woman in a black dress as people started to move on, but the woman shrugged her shoulders too, like the taxi driver.

Miranda backtracked. She wanted to find the WC without confronting the gypsies again, but she was soon lost. She came to a flight of stairs and managed to lug the suitcase up to the street. The sidewalks were crowded, and the streets were incredibly busy, but there were no taxis. She sat on the suitcase and tried to take her map out of her purse, but her purse was gone. The strap was there, but it had been cut at both ends.

It took her an hour on foot to reach Piazza Santa Croce, which she did by repeating *"Dove Santa Croce?"* over and over, as if it were a mantra. The suitcase had wheels that had rolled okay in the underpass and that rolled okay on the sidewalks, but on the cobbled streets it kept tipping over. She would have followed her guidebook advice and stopped in a bar for a coffee and *then* asked for the *gabinetto,* but now she had no money to pay for the coffee. She'd lost everything: her money, her passport, her traveler's checks, her return ticket.

When she finally spotted a row of taxi cabs, she was already at Piazza Santa Croce. She recognized the church at the far end of the piazza, but the statue of Dante was not in the middle of the piazza where it belonged. She was trembling, still on the edge of panic. But maybe it was just because she was so cold. She knew it was January, but this was Italy. It shouldn't have been so cold. Her jeans kept her legs warm, but her feet were freezing. *What will Margot make of me?* she asked herself. *Will she be glad to see me or will she be annoyed? What will I say? What will the real Margot be like? Will she be the same as the Margot in* The Sixteen Pleasures? She should go to a hotel, she thought. Call American Express. Call the American Consulate. But there weren't any hotels in the piazza. No *pensiones*. Nothing but leather shops and shops with postcard stands in their open doorways. And gold shops and a pawn shop. Only one bar that she could see.

She remembered the address, which she'd had to pry out of Esther, but there were two sets of numbers, blue numbers and red numbers, that didn't seem to be related to each other. She started with the red numbers and worked her way around the piazza. No Margot Harrington. There was a *Postiglione,* however—the name of Margot's lover. It had been his apartment. His wife's, actually.

She pushed the button and then pushed it again. She waited and waited some more. There was a bit of static. And then a man's voice.

"*Chi é?*"

And again: "*Chi é?*"

Miranda could tell it was a question. "Margot Harrington," she said.

A pause. "Margot Harrington? Are you sure?"

"Of course I'm sure."

"Who?"

"Margot Harrington," she said again.

More static was followed by a heavy click.

Miranda didn't know what to do.

The voice said, "You have to push on the door when you hear the click."

She heard the heavy click again, more of a thunk than a click, and pushed the door. It opened.

The corridor was gray, dark, not what she'd imagined. She was in the right place. But who was the man? There were two sets of stairs. She was halfway up one when she heard a door open. A dog started to growl, and she closed her eyes.

"Wrong stairs," the man's voice said. She opened her eyes, but she couldn't see him. He was up too high. She banged the heavy suitcase down one set of stairs and up the other. The man was standing in an open doorway buttoning his shirt. He looked like someone from her hometown.

"We were just taking a nap."

"You live here?"

"Yes."

The dog, a black Lab, kept looking up at the man's face, as if waiting for the signal to attack.

A woman came out of another room and looked at her. Miranda didn't recognize her. She had a just-fucked look, a look that was hard to imitate: face glowing, hair tousled, feet bare, eyes unfocused. The woman shook her head back and forth and held a robe closed around her. She was about Miranda's mother's age—the age her mother would have been if she hadn't died—but Miranda's mother would never have come to the door in just a robe.

"Who are you?" the woman said, "and why did you say you were me?"

"I'm sorry. I didn't mean to interrupt." Miranda was embarrassed.

"Oh, it's all right. We were just taking a little Sunday afternoon nap."

Miranda shifted her weight from one foot to the other. "You're Margot Harrington, aren't you? I can't believe this. I mean, that I'm here, that you're here. Just like the book. I figured out where your apartment had to be, but the statue of Dante. Did they move it? In the book it's in the center of the piazza . . ."

"I suppose it was in the center of my imagination," Margot said. "It was always scolding me for something. But you still haven't told me who you are."

"I'm Miranda Clark. I'm going to play you in the movie."

"Ah. I see. Do you need to use the bathroom?"

"Is it that obvious?"

"Yes. You might as well come in. Let me get dressed. Don't mind the dog."

The dog had settled down on its haunches. The man patted its head. "Come on, Biscotti, out of the way."

The bathroom, which opened off the entrance hall, was long and narrow. It had two sinks and a tub and shower at the far end. And some kind of foot bath. Sitting on the toilet, Miranda was flooded with emotion, but it was unfocused.

She looked at herself in the mirror over one of the sinks. She'd slept in her clothes because there hadn't been room to open her suitcase in the railway compartment, not that she would have undressed in front of everyone anyway. She tried to smooth out her mascara with her fingers. She poked at her hair as if she were getting ready to go on camera. *Lights, camera, action. Ready for Take One. Roll 'em.* But she wasn't ready to go on. She'd forgotten her lines and had no idea what her objective was. She wasn't even sure who she was, but she thought she was about to find out.

Standing inside the bathroom door, her hand on the knob, she slowed down her breathing, she took her time, she reminded herself that everything she needed was already within her. But she couldn't set her objective, couldn't bring her energies into focus, couldn't muster enough positive energy to make a dent in the universe.

"Miranda Clark. What a lovely name," Margot said. "I was so pleased when I first heard it. 'Clark' gives it a nice strong finish."

"O brave new world, that hath such people in it," the man said. "I'm Woody."

Miranda thought that Woody might spell trouble. She couldn't place the quotation. *There ought to be a law against quoting like this.*

"End of *The Tempest*," he said.

"No, sorry," Miranda said. "Not Shakespeare. I was arrested for shoplifting when I was twelve and my uncle got a lawyer. The judge dismissed the case because the officer forgot to read me the Miranda warning. It was pretty new then—the Miranda warning—and they weren't used to it. I started calling myself Miranda when I went out to L.A., but when I go home I'm still Mary. Mary Clark." She tried to judge the impression she was making. *Did they believe her? They should. It was true.*

"Have I seen you in anything?" Margot asked.

"Not yet. But you will." She was trying to hit a confident note.

"That's all right. I've hardly seen any films anyway. Is this your first?"

"No, but it's the first time I'll be the lead."

"The star. I can't tell you how excited I am about this film. I try to tell myself it's nothing, but it's come as such a surprise after all these years. It's been optioned so many times . . . But how did you get here?"

Miranda tried to give her adventures a light touch—the station, the cabbie, the gypsies. When she described the gypsies she twisted and turned her body as if she were brushing away the little hands. "And my suitcase. Well, you can see. It was like dragging a big dog around. Bigger than you." She reached down to pat the dog on the head. "What did you say his name was?"

"*Her* name. Biscotti."

"Anyway, the suitcase kept flopping down, the way a dog flops itself down. It was like a scene from a bad movie. Or maybe a good movie." She laughed.

"You don't speak Italian?"

"I started Italian at Smith, right after I read *The Sixteen Pleasures,* but then I dropped out and went to L.A. I took Latin in high school. Everyone said it would help you understand English better, but it's a dead language."

"*Vera incessu patuit dea,*" Woody said.

Miranda thought she was going to cry.

"Don't tease her, Woody."

"I wasn't teasing her," Woody said. "I was telling her that she walks like a goddess."

"Let me get dressed," Margot said, giving Woody a pointed look, "and we'll have some coffee."

Miranda stood at the window while Margot got dressed. She could hear Woody in the kitchen, making coffee. There was a dining table in the middle of the living room, covered with books and papers. There was a funny-looking fireplace with a grill and little vents at the bottom. Passages opened off the room in different directions. It was disorienting. She closed her eyes and imagined herself looking out at the piazza: she was Margot again, waiting for her Italian lover.

Her objective was starting to clarify itself: she wanted to stay *in here;* she didn't want to go back *out there.* An image was coming into focus: a kitchen table, a glass of wine, a pot of water on the stove. She could feel the positive energy building up inside her, like the water coming to a boil. She let it go, sent it out into the universe. When she opened her eyes, she *was* looking out at the piazza, and Margot was standing beside her, pointing out how high the water had come in the flood. All the way up to the second-story windows. It was hard to believe.

"How will they do the flood in the movie?" Margot asked.

Miranda believed that acting was a way of telling the truth, but the moment of the lie came and went so quickly that she hardly noticed it. It was like a split-second driving decision: Take the Washington Boulevard exit or stay on the expressway. You aren't ready. You're talking about something else or listening to the radio. And all of a sudden it's too late.

Or maybe she simply lied instinctively.

"Oh, I don't know how they'll handle that." She didn't want to tell Margot that there was no flood in the movie. And that that wasn't the worst of it. She'd find out soon enough. Let Esther explain.

"But you must have some idea."

"Stock footage," she said. "Sometimes they make a model. To tell you the truth, I'm more worried about the gold-tooling scene. I've done a little bookbinding myself. Let me show you something."

Miranda opened her huge suitcase, which was still in the entryway, and got out the copy of *The Sixteen Pleasures* that she'd bound at her kitchen table. She could see now that the fake leather bands weren't quite parallel and that the gold lettering on the label was uneven. It was embarrassing. But it was better than talking about the flood.

Woody came in with coffee. Little cups, little spoons. Like a doll's tea party.

Miranda blurted out the speech she'd been rehearsing off and on over the past few days. "I want to know everything about you," she said to Margot. "For the movie. Is that all right? I want to follow you around for a couple of weeks."

"I'm afraid I already told the whole world everything about me. There wasn't anything left to tell. At the time, anyway."

"I can't tell you how much I love your book. I read it after my mother died. I've always thought if I could talk to you, you could set me on the right path."

"I used to feel that way about Tolstoy," Woody said. "Till I read his wife's journal. He was a bad man. When you read the novels, you think Dostoyevsky was crazy and Tolstoy was the sane one, the wise one. But if you read their wives' journals, you'll see it was the other way around."

"I loved *Anna Karenina*," Miranda said. "Did you know that Basil Rathbone asked Greta Garbo for an autograph on the set, and she refused! Can you believe it!"

"They left out the main story in that movie," Woody complained. "Have you read the novel?"

"No, but I've always wanted to."

"You could get a copy at the Paperback Exchange," Margot said. "Or you could borrow Woody's. He's always talking about Tolstoy and Homer."

"Oh, no thanks. I don't think I'll have time now. I'll be too busy being you."

"If you were Margot," Woody said, "you'd have read *Anna Karenina* already, or you'd find time to read it. But never mind."

"All right, I'll read it."

"You won't be sorry. How about *The Iliad*?"

But Margot intervened. "Woody, leave her alone. You can see she was badly frightened. She's got a lot on her plate." Turning to Miranda: "Why don't you stay and have supper with us. Woody's a good cook." She put her arm around Woody. "You might as well spend the night too," she said to Miranda. "We can call the credit card companies right now, and then tomorrow we'll go to the Questura and report the theft; you may get the purse back, but not the money. And to the American Express office to sort out your traveler's checks and to the American Consulate—I know the Consul General—and apply for a new passport."

Miranda was so relieved she burst into tears, and she was so tired from the flight and the long train trip she went to bed right after supper, but before she went to sleep she started *Anna Karenina*. While she was reading about Oblonsky's affair with the governess, she could hear Woody playing a guitar, and later she could hear Woody and Margot talking, could hear suppressed laughter. She sank down into the warm mattress under the warm covers. She was in a safe place, a safe place where she could just be herself. Little Mary Clark. At least for tonight.

Anna Karenina

The thing about Miranda, who was staying with Margot and Woody for three weeks, until rehearsals began, was that she was always right there with you, asking questions: your favorite color (forest green), your favorite food (*spaghetti alle vongole*), your favorite sexual position (none of your business). But Miranda made everything her business. She wanted to know more about Margot than Margot knew about herself. Margot felt like a witness to a serious accident or a crime who has to go over what she saw again and again, or like a patient in Freudian analysis who's unwilling to disclose her secrets even to herself, or like a hostile witness being cross-examined by a hard-nosed prosecutor: "How did you *really* feel when you learned about your mother's affair with Bruno Bruni? Did your father ever find out? What were you *really* feeling when Sandro undressed you in front of the cheval glass? Did you *really* try all the positions in the Aretino book?"

"What are you looking for, Miranda?"

"I want to be in harmony with the natural principles that govern the universe."

"And you think I can help?"

Miranda nodded. "It's like Woody's feelings about Tolstoy."

What Margot *thought* was that what Miranda's quest to be in harmony with the principles that govern the universe boiled down to was this: should she sleep with her co-star, Giovanni Cipriani—Zanni—or not? She was afraid of the man, but excited too, and couldn't stop talking about him. And Margot couldn't blame her. Margot didn't remember any sex scenes in *L'accalappiacani,* which she'd seen years ago, with Francesca— just Zanni and a dozen or so dogs—but the way he'd put his hands on the stray dogs made you think that this was the way a man ought to touch a woman. Miranda was full of questions: How old was Zanni, really? Had he been married? Had he really had an affair with Ingrid Bergman, and that Scottish actress, Morag something-or-other? Why had he been denied a visa to return to the United States? Why had he been denounced by the Vatican? and banned from Italian television?

What Margot *said* was, "Well, if you're looking for the principles that govern the universe, I suppose this is as good a place as any."

They were eating breakfast in Bar Badia on Via del Proconsolo, just down the street from the Badia Fiorentina. On the other side of the street tourists were queuing up, even in January, to get into the Bargello.

"This was my mother's favorite place in the whole city," Margot said. "Every time we had hot chocolate here she'd say you could feel the tension between the old medieval view of the universe as a meaningfully ordered cosmic hierarchy—that's the Badia—and the new Renaissance worldview, the discovery of the world, *this* world, and of man—that's the Bargello, the new

civic authority. But maybe it was just that she liked the hot chocolate at this bar. They thicken it with potato starch."

"I can feel it," Miranda said. "It's like when I was thinking of
joining a convent. Did I tell you that? When I read those chapters
at Smith after my mom's death. I mean, the convent in the book,
it was such a wonderful place. I'm not even Catholic, but I could
feel *some*thing pulling me, and it was either that or go to L.A. *You*
almost joined, didn't you? I mean, you thought about it . . ."

"I was pretty upset at the time," Margot said.

"That was right after Sandro dumped you, right? But you
thought about it?"

"I suppose I did."

"Have you ever been sorry you didn't join?"

"Not sorry enough to keep me awake at night."

"Do you think Zanni will dump me the way Sandro dumped
you?"

"You haven't even met the man yet."

"No, but he's the kind of man I want to attract into my life."

"I don't get it. Zanni's a notorious womanizer, and he's old
enough to be your father."

Miranda nodded. "It's in the nude scenes that things get serious. I think Michael's planning to get quite a few of the sixteen
pleasures into the film, you know. The different positions."

"How on earth are you going to do that? What about the
script? That's not what Woody and I wrote. Some of those positions are not even possible. *La Gondola*. It can't be done." Margot
was starting to worry seriously about the final version of the
script. She'd tried to get a copy from Esther, but Esther had put
her off with vague promises, and she'd been trying to get straight
answers from Miranda, but Miranda was evasive.

"Everyone says nude scenes are just boring hard work," she
said. "You've got your body propped up with two-by-fours, and

there are twenty guys running around trying to keep out of the sight lines, and the camera's in your face, and the director's telling you to lift up your knee or run your fingers through your hair, and you can't look your partner in the eyes because if you do, you'll look cross-eyed on the screen. But that's just what they say because they don't want to admit how exciting it is. But it is exciting."

"You've done it before?"

"Not exactly, but it's got to be exciting. You want the audience to feel that you're telling them a secret about yourself, and you can't fake that. You really have to tell them a secret. I'll wear a crotch patch, of course, but even so . . ."

Margot made a lemon face.

"It's no big deal," Miranda said. "You use wig glue to hold it in place."

"I guess there are some things I don't really want to know about," Margot said.

"I'm a little worried about the cunnilingus scene, though."

Margot looked around the bar to see if anyone had picked up on the word, which is the same in Italian as it is in English. She thought the barista was smiling. "Oral sex," she said, "is known as *l'arte bolognese*. But what is it that worries you? It seems to me that cunnilingus is the last thing you've got to worry about. Once you get past the initial absurdity of it . . . It's—what do they say about works of mercy?—supererogatory. It's a supererogatory pleasure. It's not necessary, but it's so delicious."

It was Miranda's turn to make a lemon face. "There's a big cunnilingus scene with Zanni in the movie. I can't imagine how Michael's going to film it. I'm supposed to hold a piece of chocolate between my teeth and Zanni sticks his head under the covers and, you know, till I come, and then I bite down on the chocolate."

"Good Lord. Tell them you won't do it."

"It's in my contract."

"In your contract?"

"All this stuff. How much breast. Nipple. Pubic hair. One cheek, two. How much of your crack. Everything. They can't *show* everything because they'll lose their R rating, but they *shoot* everything, and then they cut and paste — jump cuts, head-and-shoulders, close-ups, soft focus."

"Just one of those things you have to accept because it can't be changed?"

Miranda nodded.

"The old serenity prayer," Margot said. "They've got it in Italian too. But cunnilingus isn't in the book anyway. Where did that come from?"

"Yes, it is. You wrote about it. Don't you remember? You called it an unexpected gift. You said it reverberated like the throat-singing those Tibetan monks do."

Margot laughed. "I'd forgotten about that." She was flattered by Miranda's attention — the kind of crush a young girl might have on an older married woman. And she was happy to give advice, but in doing so she surprised herself. Why was she so cautious, so eager to warn Miranda?

"If you're going to fall in love," Margot said, "wouldn't it be better to do it wholeheartedly, not holding anything back, instead of trying to accumulate a checklist of interesting and exciting experiences?"

"What about you and Sandro?" Miranda asked.

"That was different."

"What about your mother and Bruno Bruni?"

"That was different too."

"Well, this will be different too." Miranda laughed.

"I suppose it's always different," Margot said.

Galileo Codex 72 was on the director's desk at the Biblioteca Nazionale. The codex contained, among other things, about two hundred loose sheets with Galileo's manuscript notes on his discoveries in mechanics, notes that would shed light on the shift from Aristotelian to classical physics. Normally, independent conservators like Margot had to bid on jobs sight unseen—*here are ten books, here's what needs to be done, submit your bid*—but the Galileo codex was something special, and there was grant money available from American institutions, the Smithsonian and the National Science Foundation. Margot and the director and Miranda, who'd stayed with Margot instead of going to the Bargello, were looking at the manuscript, which was full of diagrams and freehand drawings. "It's like the physics book I had at Smith," Miranda said.

It was hard to concentrate with the director and Miranda looking over her shoulder, but Margot was excited and enjoyed showing off her knowledge as she examined the codex. "You can see the traces of a previous conservator," she said. "Probably someone in the eighteenth century. Look at these tears that have been mended and these holes and losses that have been filled using too much adhesive on paper that was already too thick. All these unsympathetic mends will have to be removed using controlled applications of distilled water." She pointed out several "unsympathetic" mends in the first gathering. "It looks like a kid did it," she said, running her finger over one of the mends. "It's not impossible," she went on. "This might have been a child's job in an eighteenth-century binding shop."

The director, a handsome man in his fifties, took Miranda out for a coffee while Margot prepared her condition assessment— identifying the format, materials, and construction of the codex;

determining the extent of physical damage and deterioration; examining the structural components; deciding on treatment options. When they came back, she thought five minutes had passed, but it had been over two hours.

In the evening they went to the Bebop Club. Woody played a set with Marisa Lodovici and her band and then persuaded Miranda to get up on the small stage and sing the chorus of "Sweet Home, Chicago" with him, and then a couple of old hymns—"Amazing Grace" and "Nearer My God to Thee."

The next night, Tuesday night, Miranda wanted to watch a movie.

"All the English-language films are dubbed into Italian," Margot said. "No subtitles."

But Miranda wanted to watch *L'avventura*. She knew it so well she wouldn't need subtitles, she said.

Woody laughed.

"What's so funny?"

"Antonioennui."

"That's *not* funny," Miranda said. "But seriously, I didn't like it either, the first time I saw it. You've really got to see it over and over again."

"Why would you want to? It's torture. Nothing happens."

"You *think* nothing's going on, but it's all so subtle."

"We weren't even sure they were sleeping together!" Woody said.

"Who?"

"Sandro and Claudia."

Miranda laughed. "What did you think they were doing?"

"Well, in the hotel . . . She won't make love. I thought he was chasing her . . . You know . . . the hunt."

"You're thinking of the scene where Claudia says she feels guilty," Miranda said. "That's earlier. She still has some principles, some real feelings. The whole film is a critique of eros in art."

"The best scene is where she makes faces in the mirror. Everyone's done that. But it's still torture."

"You need to see it again."

"Torture."

"Antonioni's a genius . . . You probably grew up on American films, like I did. You've got to realize that Antonioni was breaking new ground. It's not entertainment. He invented a new language for film: tone, mood, light and shade, composition. It's an exhausting film. So much is going on. No one understood it when it was first screened at Cannes, and two years later *Sight and Sound* called it the second-best film of all time after *Citizen Kane*. It was one of Susan Sontag's favorite films. She called it the equivalent of the new novel."

"The characters don't have any lives," Woody said. "They don't have jobs."

"That's the point. They reach out to each other, but all they find is boredom, emptiness."

"That's the fallacy of imitative form. Maybe life is boring, but art shouldn't be. Jane Austen's Miss Bates bores the people in the novel, but she doesn't bore the reader."

Margot intervened at this point. She couldn't help herself. She wanted to clear something up.

"Miranda, is this what your life is like right now? Is this the way you see the world? I'm astonished. I'm really astonished. Look at you. You're going to be the female lead in a feature film, you're going to star with Giovanni Cipriani, and all you see is boredom and emptiness? Is that the way you feel here, with Woody and me? When you said you thought I could set you on the right track, I was flattered, but I didn't take it seriously. But now I think I can help you out." She laughed. "*L'avventura* my foot. Miranda, your life is full of love and excitement—this is your great adventure. Don't miss out on it. Forget *L'avventura;* let's watch Zanni in *The Dogcatcher, L'accalappiacani.* Zanni's like Charlie Chaplin. You don't have to know a word of Italian, you'll see. Woody, you make the popcorn. Miranda and I will go and rent the film."

What Miranda wanted to do the next day was hang out in Margot's *studio,* a long, L-shaped work space with four benches perpendicular to the windows (so that everyone got a view of the Arno). The large equipment was spread out along the back wall, where a special rack built over the back counter held the long-handled rolls and hand tools used for tooling leather. There was a small staff kitchen at the base of the *L.*

Margot didn't blame Miranda. She couldn't divide her own life from this space. Her craft was not separate from her life; it was an intensification of her life. That's what she'd learned from Signor Cecchi, the conservator in Prato who'd helped her restore Aretino's *I modi.*

Miranda wanted to do the restoration scenes in the movie herself and had persuaded Margot to help her. Instead of doing her own work, Margot walked Miranda through the whole process. They opened up one of the last of Rabbi Kors's books, a children's book, with a lifting knife and put it in a nipping press and spread paste made of wheat starch and thinned out with deionized water over the spine to soften the lining.

While they waited for the paste to soak in, Miranda explained creative visualization. "First you have to know what you really want," Miranda said, "and you have to be specific; you have to visualize something specific."

"You mean Zanni?"

"Exactly. Now you have to remember that you can't control the actions of another person. All you can control are your own attitudes and actions."

"If you can't control Zanni, how are you going to get him to do what you want?"

"That's the beauty of it. You don't need to control anything. You let it happen. You train your mind to visualize whatever it is you want, and when your mind wanders, you call it back, like calling a dog. You let it happen by itself."

"All I can say is that it's a good thing that most people's fantasies *don't* come true. Can you imagine —"

"Fantasies are important. They show us what we really want. They give us hope. They help us initiate positive life changes. Fantasizing about a goal is the first step toward making it come true."

"Do you know what I'm fantasizing about right now?"

"You're fantasizing about the Galileo book."

"Codex." Miranda was right, but Margot didn't want to admit it. "I'm fantasizing about an espresso," she said. "I'll make a pot right now. Just a small one. Let's go in the kitchen."

As they were waiting for the water to boil in the little Alessi *caffettiera,* Miranda suggested that Margot try some creative visualization. "You should fantasize about the Galileo. Send good intentions about it out into the universe and it will come to you."

"I've submitted a bid to do the restoration work, along with half a dozen other conservators."

Miranda reached across the small table in the little staff kitchen and touched Margot's hand. "I know I'm not as wise as you," she said, "but I do know *some* things. You mustn't let any negativity into your thoughts. I want you to form a picture in your mind of the manuscript or codex, or whatever it is, right here on your own workbench, waiting for you to start working on it. Will you promise to do that?"

Margot laughed. "I can't *stop* picturing it there," she said. "But we'll see." The *caffettiera* began to sputter. Margot turned off the gas. "The coffee's ready."

After they'd drunk their coffee, Margot showed Miranda how to scrape off the paste with her bone folder and peel back the starched spine lining from the sections. "Be careful not to scrape away any of the paper," she said. "Now you've got to pull the text before the sections dry out." Margot opened the text block at the center of the first section, lifted up the threads with a pair of hemostats, and clipped them with scissors. She closed the section and pulled it away from the text block. "If you did this dry," she said, "you'd tear off the backs of the sections. You think you can do it?"

Miranda nodded.

Margot watched while Miranda pulled the next section.

"That will keep you busy for a while. If it sets too dry, you'll have to apply more paste."

After the flood, after being dumped by her Italian lover, after the sale of the Aretino at Sotheby's, Margot had worked at the Certosa Monastery for two years, overseeing a triage operation that had rescued thousands of valuable books from the city's library and abandoned thousands of others that were beyond repair. After that she'd apprenticed herself to Signor Cecchi in Prato, even though she'd already worked for several years with Paul Banks at the Newberry Library in Chicago and was an experienced conservator. For three years she took the train to Prato every day, five days a week, never quite realizing that Signor Cecchi was famous throughout Europe for his conservation skills and for his own one-of-a-kind leather bindings. When Signor Cecchi died, his wife gave his hand tools to Margot, and the abbess at the convent arranged to buy the large equipment: the large board shears and the guillotine for cutting paper and boards; the big standing presses and the finishing presses and the job backers. And Margot had set up a studio in the convent itself where she supervised the work on the books in the convent library. When the convent was closed after the death of the abbess, Francesca Postiglione — her ex-lover's wife — had helped her move her *studio* to a palazzo on Lungarno Guicciardini.

Margot had always tried to emulate Signor Cecchi in everything, tried to convey the same deep love of his work to the nuns who had worked for her in the convent, and then, later, to the young people, mostly young women who'd begun to enter the profession since the flood, whom she took on as apprentices. And this is what she tried to convey to Miranda as they washed the pages of the rabbi's book in deionized water that Margot warmed up on the stove in the little kitchen. The deionized water would remove the soluble acids in the paper. She expected Miranda to become impatient with the repetitive task of laying out the open quartos on sheets of wet-strength paper, placing them in the deionized water in the photographic trays, changing the water at half-hour intervals. But in fact it was Margot herself who soon became antsy. "'It takes too long to wait,'" she said. "That's what Woody's daughter used to say."

"Cookie? The one who was killed?"

Margot nodded.

At the end of the day they prepared a buffer — carbon dioxide that had been bubbled through a large glass container of magnesium carbonate powder and mixed with deionized water — to neutralize any remaining acids, and placed the quartos on drying racks to air-dry. Margot slapped her hands back and forth to indicate that they'd done a good day's work. It was after seven o'clock.

On the way home they looked in the lighted shop windows on the Lungarno. Leather goods, stationery, haute couture, beautiful mosaic tables that cost thousands of dollars. Above them they could see the lights of Piazzale Michelangelo. In Piazza Santa Croce they could see the lights in Margot's apartment, and when Margot opened the big door to the palazzo, they could smell the garlic. Woody was making tomato sauce for pizza. The smell of garlic filled the hallway, as if Woody were some *meridionale,* a southerner.

"Italian pizza's good," Margot said to Miranda as they took off their coats in the front hall, "but not as good as Woody's."

There was a chunk of *parmigiano reggiano* on a cutting board on the kitchen table, and a bowl of fruit next to an open bottle of Chianti and three glasses. Margot thought it looked like a still life by Chardin, one of those paintings that make you see the beauty in the everyday things all around you.

Woody was pitting olives. "So how's *Anna Karenina* coming?"

"I really love it," Miranda said. "I just got to the scene where Levin and Oblonsky have dinner together in the restaurant, and the waiter keeps translating everything Oblonsky says into French. Oblonsky worries about the menu and then changes his plans when he learns of a fresh shipment of some kind of oysters. Levin's not interested in the food."

"From Ostend," Woody said. "The oysters. I love that passage." He was spreading tomato sauce over the pizza dough in three small pans. "I admire Levin," he said, "but I'm afraid I'm more like Oblonsky. *What shall we eat? What shall we drink?* That sort of thing."

"Oh no," Miranda said, "I don't think so. I think you're more like Levin."

Margot could see that Woody was pleased to be compared to Levin, but not when Miranda added, "No sense of humor."

"What are you talking about?" Woody said. "I've got a highly developed sense of humor."

"Tell us a joke then, something funnier than *Antonioennui.*"

"I can't ever remember jokes. I've heard a million jokes, but I can't remember them."

"You must remember one. If you've got a sense of humor."

"That's enough, Miranda."

"But Levin's so sweet," Miranda said. "He can't imagine fooling around with a woman. He can't even understand what Oblonsky's talking about."

Woody was filleting large anchovies that had been preserved in salt.

Margot said, "I can't imagine either one of them making pizza, can you?"

And Miranda said, "No."

In the morning the bells from Santa Croce summoned the faithful to Mass. Margot could see a few old women entering the church. Miranda announced her intention of going to Mass.

"But you said you're not Catholic," Margot protested.

"It doesn't matter," Miranda said. "Why don't we all go." And for some strange reason they did. Miranda received Communion, though Margot tried to stop her. Margot and Woody sat in the back by the empty Dante tomb.

Then they ate lunch at the Osteria de' Pazzi on Via Verde.

"I remembered a joke," Woody said.

"Let's hear it," Miranda said.

"I don't know."

"You have to tell us, now that you mentioned it."

"It's from when I was in junior high. It's the first dirty joke I ever heard."

They waited.

"This city slicker," Woody said, "moved out to the country and wanted to start a farm, so he went up to a farmer and said, 'I want to buy a rooster,' and the farmer said, 'We don't call 'em roosters; we call 'em cocks.' The city slicker says, 'Okay, then, and I want to buy a chicken.' The farmer says, 'We don't call 'em chickens; we call 'em pullets.' The city slicker says, 'Okay, and I want to buy a donkey.' 'We don't call 'em donkeys,' the farmer says, 'we call 'em asses.' So the city slicker pays for the animals, and he's walking back down the road, and a woman's coming toward him, and all of a sudden the donkey runs away. 'Excuse me, ma'am,' the city slicker says to the woman. 'Would you hold my cock and pullet while I run after my ass.'"

"Woody," Margot said, "that's not funny."

But Miranda was laughing.

"Miranda thinks it's funny," Woody said.

"No, I don't," Miranda said, wiping her eyes with a napkin. "It's not funny at all, that's what's so funny."

They called a cab from the apartment. Woody banged Miranda's big suitcase down the stairs. *It was like sending a daughter off to college,* Margot thought. Who knew what adventures lay in store for her? Woody'd been through it before. Three daughters. She thought of her father waving to her at O'Hare when she left for Italy. She'd never lived at home again. Her father had sold the house in Chicago and moved to Texas to raise avocados. Her sisters had moved to California and Florida. And then her father had sold the avocado grove and gone to India. He'd stopped to see her on the way. On his last day in Florence he went to see Bruno Bruni, his wife's lover, and then in the afternoon he and Margot walked from Fiesole to Settignano, but he never told

Margot what he and Bruni had said to each other. He'd been cremated before she and her sisters arrived in Assam. In a Hindu ceremony. His ashes had been scattered in the Brahmaputra, a river so wide Margot hadn't been able to see the other shore. But she remembered his eyes searching for her in the airport, finally focusing on her just as she went through the last door.

Protestant Cemetery

Beryl Gardiner walked from the comfortable apartment she and Michael had rented on Via Pietrapiana to the American Church on Via Bernardo Rucellai. She walked along the river because, although it was a longer route, it was simpler than trying to find her way through the city center. She could have taken a taxi, but she needed the exercise, wanted to get out. She wore her sensible walking shoes till she got to a little roundabout at the end of Via Rucellai and then changed into the navy blue pumps she'd bought because they were an exact match for her new pin-striped coat dress and because she needed cheering up. As an art history major she'd taken three years of Italian at Smith, and this was her third extended stay in Italy, but she found life in Italian very stressful. It was one thing to buy shoes and dresses on Via Tornabuoni, where everyone spoke English; it was quite another to schedule a doctor's appointment for Michael at the Policlinico and to shop in the *pizzicheria* in Piazza San Pier Maggiore and at the Mercato Sant'Ambrogio and at the little *ortomercato* in Via degli Albizi. They could have lived in a hotel, but the idea of spending three months in a hotel had been too depressing.

She was lonely too. There were chatty letters from their daughter in Philadelphia, with pictures of the two grandchildren, and telephone calls from their son in Princeton. There were dinners with Esther and with the Italian assistant director, but she had no friends here, no gossips. The shooting script had been locked down for a week, but Michael still spent most of his time at the production office, and he'd skipped the doctor's appointment that Beryl had managed to schedule and then reschedule for him, so she knew that he wouldn't get his leuprolide injection unless she escorted him personally to the Policlinico.

So the sight of the church was refreshing, reassuring: nineteenth century, Victorian, like the Episcopal churches you find in English villages or in wealthy suburbs in the United States, like the church Beryl had grown up with in Upstate New York, her father's church — an oasis, a comfortable respite, smelling of old incense. The kneelers were like the new kneelers in St. Francis, but older, and softer.

It was the third Sunday after Epiphany, a down time in the Christian year — Christmas a distant memory, Easter not yet on the horizon. Beryl didn't pay much attention to the lessons, which were read by members of the congregation, but the gospel was one of her favorites — the wedding at Cana. The old words washed over her. Water into wine. A lot of wine. Six water pots, each one holding two or three firkins. Filled to the brim. Beryl looked around. How many of her fellow worshippers knew what a firkin was? It's half a kilderkin. Eleven gallons. Beryl knew these things because her father had been an Episcopal priest — he would have been made bishop if he hadn't had a heart attack — and this was the sort of thing they'd talked about at the dinner table when she was a child. She'd done the calculations in her head then, and she redid them now: A firkin was 11 gallons. So somewhere between 12 water pots × 11 = 132 and 18 water pots × 11 = 198 gallons of wine. It must have been quite a wedding reception. They'd already finished off the wine provided for the party. Now they had another four or five hundred bottles!

Beryl smiled inwardly. She loved miracles. Her faith came easily to her, in part because she was not too particular about what she believed. What she aimed at was not a creed but a general affirmation that ultimate reality—whatever is *out there*—is consistent with her inner reality: full of purpose and intention and love. She stuck with the Episcopal Church because she wanted to tie this general affirmation to something specific, give it an institutional home, locate it in the cycle of the church year that had always given shape to her life, and to life in general—Advent, Christmas, Epiphany, Lent, Easter, Pentecost, and then back to Advent. You always knew what to do. You weren't simply at the mercy of your emotions. It was like getting dressed up for a party, or a funeral. Maybe you didn't feel like going. But you put on the appropriate clothes and you went, and if it was a party you had a good time, and if it was a funeral you grieved.

What was the alternative? Existentialism? She'd seen through the existentialists from the beginning, in her French class at Smith. What to tell Sartre's poor young man who didn't know whether to join the resistance or look after his mother? As far as Beryl was concerned, the young man's dilemma just demonstrated that there were values *out there.* If you just made them up as you went along, there wouldn't be any dilemmas. Everybody knew that, whatever they claimed. Almost everybody. There were very few exceptions—a few madmen, Svidrigailov in *Crime and Punishment,* or Meursault in *L'Étranger.* Those were the only ones she could think of.

The congregation was sparse, but not embarrassingly sparse. Beryl could see the pillars of the church scattered among the nave, like the pillars that held up the roof. A handful of men and women whose expensive tailored clothes distinguished them from the tourists. She recognized them, and she knew, without a word being spoken, that they had already recognized her.

In his sermon the priest—who turned out to be an interim priest—said the usual things about Cana: it was Christ's first public miracle; it confirmed marriage as a sacrament; and so on. Beryl didn't expect much from sermons. She'd heard too many of them. But marriage was very much on her mind. Her own marriage. What Michael wanted, it seemed to Beryl, was to make one last film and then die, get it over with. He was embarrassed by his condition. She could understand that. He wasn't incontinent, but his body was leaking. He wasn't impotent; he could still get it up, but he couldn't keep it up. And once he started the leuprolide, he wouldn't be able to get it up at all. What she couldn't understand was that after all these years he was too embarrassed to trust her. *In sickness and in health*—that's what she cared about. But for the first time Beryl was starting to think that *things might not work out*. This was a new feeling for her. In her experience things had always worked out, one way or another, always arrived at a happy ending. Her mother had gone away for a while, like Margot Harrington's mother, but then she'd come back.

The sermon came to an end, and the priest plunged into the Mass. Beryl was not inclined to bewail her manifold sins and wickedness, nor did she feel unworthy to gather up the crumbs under the table, but she joined in the holy mysteries wholeheartedly, the way she did everything else: "We do not presume to come to this thy table, O merciful Lord, trusting in our own righteousness, but in thy manifold and great mercies."

At the coffee hour, in the rectory behind the church, Beryl was greeted warmly and got a good look at herself as others saw her: a handsome woman who had money and good taste, and who was also a good person, just the sort of person you'd like to have on your committee, and by the time the coffee hour was over she'd been invited to serve on the search committee for a new priest. "Well," she said to the senior warden, who'd been sounding her out, "I suppose it makes a kind of sense: my father was active in the national church, and I have a lot of contacts in Los Angeles and New York." And then she said, "This is where Margot Harrington's mother met her Italian lover, isn't it?"

The senior warden, who was also the headmaster of the American Academy of Florence, laughed.

"It just occurred to me," Beryl said. "My husband's directing the film." She looked around. "I don't see anyone here today who fits the bill."

The senior warden laughed again. "Miss Harrington's a lovely woman," he said, "but ever since she wrote that book, we've had no end of American women looking for that man!"

"Bruno Bruni, that was his name. 'A man who preyed on American women.'"

"Yes. He was quite a character."

"He's dead now?"

"Oh, yes. Many years ago. He was seventy-five years old and still causing trouble."

On her way home Beryl thought she could see things more clearly. She'd buy the three-volume Moncrieff-Kilmartin translation of Proust she'd seen in the window of the Paperback Exchange. Museums in the morning, search committee three afternoons a week, *Remembrance of Things Past* in the evenings. That would get her through twelve weeks and then she'd get Michael back to Sloan-Kettering in New York where he belonged.

Michael was alone in the production office at the convent when he heard the bell—Beryl bringing him some lunch; Beryl, who'd never lost faith in him, who loved him more for being "middling" than if he'd been Scorsese or Coppola or Steven Spielberg; Beryl, who washed out his stained underpants because she knew he didn't want her to take them to the *lavanderia*.

Middling. His first film had been his best. That was the hard fact he had to live with. After seventeen feature films he was still introduced—when he *was* introduced—as the director of *The Lady with the Pet Dog*. He'd shot it with a few friends from his acting class at NYU and a dozen extras. They hadn't had a shooting script, not really, but he'd had every scene clearly in his mind, and what had started as a demo of what the film was going to be about turned into a full-length feature.

Maybe it had worked because he'd internalized the Chekhov story, had come to see it as an extension of his own life. His father and his father's secretary had been killed in a car crash in the Poconos when he and his mother had thought his father was at a convention in Chicago. His mother never got over it, and Michael didn't think he'd ever get over it either, till he read "The Lady with the Pet Dog" in a Russian Lit class, and suddenly everything had become clear and he had to rethink everything he'd always believed about his parents' marriage. He'd been a nervous wreck on the first day of the shoot, but the woman who was his assistant on this picture, fresh out of Smith College—somebody else's girlfriend at the time—put her arm around him and said, "You can do it. You can do it. Just get up and put one foot in front of the other and drag your ass around." That was Beryl. And now he and Beryl were the age of the protagonists in the story, Gurov and Anna.

He opened the small door cut out of a big door that opened into the piazza. Beryl was wearing the glow she always had after church. The neck of a wine bottle, the cork pulled halfway out, poked out of the plastic Standa bag she was carrying. "I thought we'd have a picnic," she said, smiling. "You need to keep up your strength."

"How much prosciutto can a man eat?" he asked. He seemed to have more energy than ever, but he was never hungry.

She touched the back of his hand. "A lot," she said.

Beryl spread the picnic out on one of the folding tables in the big refectory: prosciutto, salami, day-old *pane toscano* that she'd kept wrapped in damp paper towels so it wouldn't get too hard. Olives, olive oil, salt, cheese, a tomato. Paper napkins. Mineral water, *frizzante.*

Michael saw his wife close her eyes as she said a silent grace. She poured a little olive oil on a piece of the hard bread and sprinkled it with a little salt, then prosciutto, cheese, tomato.

"So," she said, "how's the storyboarding going?"

Michael was redrawing some of the storyboards he'd done back in New York. He worked quickly, and the sketches were beautiful, with a life of their own. He didn't do every scene, but he always acted out every scene, so he wouldn't have to ask the actors to do something he couldn't do himself.

"Where are you going to shoot the bedroom scenes?"

"In the chapel."

Beryl laughed.

"Don't worry," he said. "It's been deconsecrated."

"It's just the idea of it. I guess it tickles me." She started to fix a piece of bread for him, pouring a little olive oil on it. "Too bad you couldn't afford a flood. It would have been nice to link the movie to a real historical event."

"I don't want to get into it," he said. "I read the script, not the book. The book doesn't exist for me."

"It's just that . . ."

"Beryl," he said.

"Okay, okay. But you know what I worry about, Michael?"

"What?"

"I worry that you're not having fun. Why are you doing this if you don't enjoy it?"

Michael had to stop and think. "Because," he said, "because I don't know what else to do."

"Why don't you come with me this afternoon to the Protestant Cemetery. I want to see Elizabeth Barrett Browning's grave."

"A cemetery is the last place I want to visit."

"Sorry."

"What's she doing here?"

"She lived here. In Casa Guidi, by the Pitti Palace. She and Robert. We could go there instead. I'll see if it's open on Sundays."

"*The Barretts of Wimpole Street*. With Jennifer Jones and Sir John Gielgud."

"What a story. So romantic. I used to think that was our story."

"I'm sorry I'm such a disappointment in the romance department."

"Michael, you've never been a disappointment. Not ever. You know that. We've had a great life. Together. It's all been good."

"And now it's almost over."

"Death isn't the worst thing."

"It is if you're the one dying."

"The worst thing, Michael, the absolute worst, is not making the most of the time we have together. That's what's worse than dying. At least eat your prosciutto."

"I'm not hungry," he said. "We'll go to Venice. We'll go at Easter. We've got to shut down anyway. Everyone's got to be out of the hotels during Easter week. All the rooms were booked months in advance. The production crew's going back to Rome."

"Okay," she said. "Venice it is. It's a date."

She leaned over and kissed the top of Michael's head, and then she finished his bread and prosciutto and cheese and tomato.

Beryl was so unused to being unhappy, or out of sorts, that she hardly knew what to do. When she got back to the apartment, which was only two minutes away from the production office in the convent, she turned on the television and sat in the big *poltronaletto,* an armchair that could be opened up to make a bed, a very comfortable bed. She couldn't understand a word, but she could understand that Italian television is even stupider than American. She watched for a while anyway, and then, with the television still on, she looked through her guidebook till she found a page and a half on the Protestant Cemetery, which was listed as the "English Cemetery" in the index, though according to the book the cemetery had been built by the Swiss in 1827 and was still the property of the Swiss Evangelical Reformed Church and administered through its "consistory." When it was built it had met with a lot of opposition from local Catholics, who destroyed the first graves. The nearest Protestant Cemetery at the time had been in Leghorn, near Pisa.

The most famous people buried there, after Elizabeth Barrett Browning, were Walter Savage Landor; Arthur Hugh Clough; Frances Trollope, mother of the novelist; and the famous American preacher Theodore Parker, whom she'd never heard of. She put the book on a coffee table and opened one of the big windows and looked down at the people walking up and down Via Pietrapiana. It wasn't raining, but it was threatening. Good cemetery weather.

She looked at her watch. Four o'clock. She must have dozed off. Michael was still at his office in the convent and she knew he wouldn't be home till late. She had two chicken breasts in the refrigerator for supper. *I don't know what else to do,* he'd said. And she'd thought he wasn't afraid of death . . . *Death isn't such a bad thing,* she thought, *but neither is a little fear of death.*

She stopped by the Paperback Exchange on the way to the cemetery, but it was closed. She could see the translation of Proust in the window, all three volumes. She'd read "Combray" twice in English and once in French, but she'd never managed to make it through "Swann in Love," maybe because she found Swann so exasperating. Swann needed professional help. He should have written to Ann Landers.

She was thinking about the Brownings. At Smith she'd done a paper on *Sonnets from the Portuguese,* in the days before feminism. In those days EBB had been the heroine of a love story rather than a poet in her own right, and nowadays Beryl supposed you could find bad things to say about her marriage, but no one could maintain that she hadn't *thought* she was happy with Robert. But how on earth had they managed to stay in love like that for so many years? *Instead of reading Proust,* she thought, *maybe she'd get a biography of EBB and see for herself.* Maybe she'd find a crack in their marriage, and maybe she wouldn't. It didn't matter. She had a project, a quest. She felt better already. And just at that moment the sun came out. When she looked down the street and up, she could see Fiesole.

The Protestant Cemetery was at the end of Borgo Pinti, one street over. According to the guidebook, the schedule was irregular, but you could usually get the custodian to let you in. Beryl didn't really want to deal with a custodian, but she'd cross that bridge when she came to it.

The cemetery was on a little island, protected by a *viale,* or boulevard, the way a castle might be protected by a moat. It seemed to be built on an unstable mound of dirt, enclosed by a wrought-iron fence, and held together by a crumbling stone wall. She could see tombstones and cypress trees and a few mausoleums and a gatehouse. She could see that the front gate was open and was relieved that she wouldn't have to deal with a custodian. One less thing to worry about. But she couldn't figure out how to cross the busy *viale*. There were no zebra crosswalks in evidence, and by the time she was able to dash through an opening in the unrelenting traffic, the sky had clouded over again and it was starting to drizzle.

A sign on the gatepost at the front of the cemetery repeated some of the information in the guidebook about EBB, Clough, Landor, etc. Beryl went through the gate and followed the main path under an arch in the gatehouse that led to the cemetery itself. A bicycle leaned against one wall. Beryl looked in the windows but couldn't see much. She picked up a booklet from a table outside the door and left a five-thousand-lire note as a donation. The cemetery had seemed small from the outside, but inside, it seemed huge. It was not well cared for. Trees and bushes needed trimming. There were no signs to guide you, like the signs in Père-Lachaise, where she and Michael had visited Proust's grave—that was when she was reading "Combray" in French—or in the Protestant Cemetery in Rome, where she'd sat at a bench near Keats's grave: "Here lies one whose name was writ in water."

She had no trouble locating EBB's neoclassical tomb, however, which was pictured in the booklet. The sarcophagus itself, supported by six Corinthian columns, bore her initials (E-B-B), the date of her death (1861), and a laurel-crowned woman in bas-relief flanked by two Florentine lilies. *How do I love thee? Let me count the ways.* Beryl could remember struggling with her paper in her room in Baldwin House. She'd been in love herself at the time, not with Michael but with a boy from Amherst who drove a hearse with a mattress in the back and who rolled his own cigarettes.

When she heard a noise she stepped behind the sarcophagus. She peeked around the corner and saw the figure of an old woman standing in the archway. The custodian. Beryl stayed put and watched while the old woman walked her bicycle down to the front gate. And then she heard the sound of the gate closing. She ran to the gatehouse in time to see the old woman ride off on her bicycle, merging smoothly into the flow of traffic. She could see that the gate was now closed. And she soon discovered that it was locked as well.

She stood at the locked gate, holding onto the bars, like a prisoner. She was puzzled at first but not really alarmed. Just a little uneasy. It was getting dark, but traffic continued to zoom around the cemetery. She could see people walking on the sidewalks on the other side of the *viale,* but not on the sidewalk that circled the cemetery.

"Oh, bother," she said, as if she were Winnie the Pooh. She was a little annoyed, but she maintained her sense of humor. *This will make a good story,* she thought, and she imagined telling it at a cocktail party. And then she got a little angry. No, not angry, indignant. What kind of a place was this anyway? No posted hours. The custodian just going off and locking you in?

It was getting darker. There were fewer people on the other side of the *viale.* She shouted but she couldn't make herself heard over the traffic. She had a good command of the present, imperfect, and past perfect tenses, but she didn't have a very good handle on the imperative, so she tried several different forms: *Aiutame, aiutami, mi aiutare.* She made the circuit of the cemetery, which took about twenty minutes. By the time she got back to the front gate the streetlights had come on. She shook the gate. She started to panic and then pulled herself together by breathing deeply and by doing one of the spiritual exercises recommended by Father Sam at St. Francis back in New York, only instead of imagining Christ on the Cross, she imagined the scene at Cana, all those firkins of wine. Christ didn't even need to stick his finger in the water to turn it to wine. He just told them to fill the water jars with water. Did the water turn to wine gradually, as it was being poured into the water jar? Or all at once, the moment the jar was full to the brim? And then it was her own wedding she was imagining, her father presiding over the ceremony at St. Andrew's in Troy, New York. She and Michael had been sleeping together for over a year. How handsome Michael had been. Still was, just a little gaunt. And when *The Lady with the Pet Dog* had been screened at the Venice Film Festival, how they walked up and down the Lido every night, eating octopus and other things in a little *ciccheti* bar on the other side of the island.

It's just another one of your adventures, Michael will say, *like the time you got off the Orient Express in Belgrade thinking you were in Athens, or the time you got stuck in the laundry chute in the house on Blackstone.* She walked back up to the gatehouse and sat on the bench, out of the drizzle. It was too dark to read the booklet. She held the booklet in her hand and pictured the cemeteries in her life. There was only one, really. Only one that really mattered. Elmwood Hill Cemetery on Belle Avenue, where her parents were buried, and her brother, who'd been killed in Vietnam. And her aunts and uncles.

Like many of her high school classmates, Beryl had ridden her bike in the cemetery, had learned to drive a stick shift in the cemetery, had parked at the back of the cemetery, had lost her virginity there, with a boy named David Logan, with whom she still exchanged Christmas cards.

When the drizzle let up again she walked around, looking for a good spot for her and Michael, the way they used to drive around Beverly Hills, when they first moved to L.A., to pick out their ideal house. She didn't see signs of any new graves, but it was too dark to see very well. Maybe a few of the urns were new. And then she found the ideal spot. In the center, where the sounds of the traffic were muted. It wasn't too far from EBB. A little farther down the main path, where she'd seen the Shakespeare grave — two sisters, Shakespeare's last relatives. Michael would like that.

It wasn't till she heard the old woman at the gate that the tears welled up inside her and she realized she'd been holding them in. She didn't want to startle the old woman, but she simply couldn't hold back her tears. She wasn't used to crying. What she really wanted to do was rush past the old woman and out the gate, but the woman was holding up her bicycle with one hand, already locking the gate behind her.

"*Mi trovo in difficoltà,*" Beryl said in a loud voice.

The old woman looked around, startled.

"*Chi è? Che cosa fa?*"

"*Mi trovo in difficoltà,*" Beryl said again. "I find myself in difficulty."

The old woman walked her bicycle up to the gatehouse. When she saw Beryl's tears, she said, in Italian, "You poor dear, you got locked in, didn't you? I didn't think anyone was inside the gates when I left. I usually go to the movies on Sunday nights. *Dimmi, dimmi,* speak to me. Are you all right?"

"I am locked in," Beryl said in Italian. "I wanted to see the grave of Elizabeth Barrett Browning, and then the gate was closed and locked."

"Ahh, ahh, ahh. Elizabeta. Signora Browning. Ahh. Our most famous resident. *Si si si. Si si si. È molto famosa.* What a beautiful story. So romantic. Ahh."

The old woman unlocked the door on the left side of the gatehouse and asked Beryl if she'd like a cup of tea. Beryl said yes and watched while the woman boiled water in the small kitchen. The nice little house seemed to hold her in an embrace. It was a combination of her father's study and her mother's sewing room. The walls were covered with pictures; the windows were shuttered; the rugs were thick. A spiral staircase led to the upstairs.

"You live here?"

"My husband was the caretaker, for twenty years." She handed a tray of tea things to Beryl. "Put them on the little table." Beryl did, and they sat next to each other on a sofa.

"My husband," Beryl said, "is here to make a film."

"In Piazza San Pier Maggiore? *Nel convento vecchio?*"

"You know about that?"

"I get my vegetables at the little shop in Via degli Albizi. Usually I go at noon, just before they close. A film. Very exciting."

"I shop there too, but it's very difficult for me. I can shop all right, by pointing at things, but for a week I was buying *bietola* thinking it was lettuce, and wondering why the lettuce in Italy is so tough; I washed my husband's things in fabric softener, thinking it was detergent — it had a picture of a woman putting clothes in a washing machine on the bottle — and the meat is impossible. I've always been good at math, but there are too many conversions to consider at the same time: kilograms to pounds, *etti* to ounces, lire to dollars.

"We *could* live in a hotel, but I couldn't stand it. And anyway my husband is dying," Beryl said. "That's all right. I mean, it's not all right, but . . . I thought it would bring us closer together." She started to cry again. "I am doing everything to make him comfortable. But he's going farther and farther away from me. Every day, farther and farther. I thought we were all through with films. And now . . . But we're going to go to Venice during Easter week. We were in Venice after his first film. He won a prize. We stayed at a hotel out on the Lido."

Robert Hellenga

The old woman touched Beryl's arm. "Men," she said, as if she were offering an explanation. "And now?"

"He doesn't want to be with me. I don't know if it's the sickness. *Cancro.* I don't know what to do."

"My husband has been dead for twenty years, signora."

"Do you miss him?"

"Every day," the old woman said, and she started to cry too, and Beryl put an arm around her to comfort her. These were companionable tears, shared by two women. Beryl was starting to enjoy herself. And then suddenly she realized that she'd been having this conversation in Italian, and she caught a glimpse of herself in Italian, as this kind old woman saw her. The way you might catch a glimpse of yourself in a shop window when you're not expecting it, not prepared for it. She hardly recognized herself. Where was the sophisticated woman of the world who'd sent back a two-hundred-franc bottle of wine at Le Piramide, who wore shoes from Ferragamo and Prada and dresses from Chanel? Where was the hardheaded woman who'd made money in the stock market in the seventies and eighties, who'd kept her husband's taxable income under fifty thousand dollars a year for the last fifteen years? Where was the practical woman who'd taken over as chair of the stewardship committee at St. Hildegard's Episcopal in Los Angeles just when it looked like the church was going down the tubes? And who was this timid, shy woman who was afraid of shopkeepers? who was afraid to confront her butcher when he overcharged her? who couldn't find the cornstarch in the Standa and didn't know how to ask? who was afraid to answer the telephone because it might be someone calling in Italian?

She didn't know who this other woman was, but she thought she'd like to find out, thought that maybe this was what God had in mind for her in Italy.

Rehearsal

Michael's prognosis was not good. His chances of dying with dignity were almost nil. The cancer had metastasized to the bone. He'd lost his appetite; he couldn't sleep; he couldn't fuck. He had plenty of energy, but the energy was generated by the very tumor that was killing him. A massive heart attack would have been better, or even a long lingering illness, with Beryl taking care of him. He could imagine himself lying in bed, like a sick child—but not too sick to read. He could imagine eating soft-boiled eggs with strips of buttered-toast soldiers, and, in the evenings, watching his films with Beryl in their new screening room, which they hadn't used yet because of a problem with the electronic focusing mechanism.

But Beryl was right. Death wasn't the worst thing. The worst thing was that his last film had been too ponderous, too heavy handed—not a critical disaster, not a financial disaster, just not much of anything. He'd clung to scenes that should have been cut; he'd tried too hard for profundity. It had been too walkie-talkie, as if he'd forgotten how to use images to create drama, to deepen the characters, to further the story. He wanted to go out on a lighter note, plenty of movement, lots of jump cuts, lots of crosscutting, lots of color, lots of romance, lots of sex, lots of life itself.

He was a very organized director. He liked to arrive on the set with everyone already knowing how the scene was blocked and how he wanted to shoot it. So during the two weeks before he started rehearsing, he tried to anticipate every question that anyone might ask him. He went over the script a hundred times; he knew what he was looking for in the characters so he could coach the actors; he created backstories for every actor, which no one had to follow, but which gave everyone an idea of what he was looking for. He thought that by being organized, he could be more flexible, so that when the unexpected happened, he could put it to use. He watched the production assistants, who were crowded around a large American coffeemaker at the end of the big refectory. Most of them had been through film school, but they couldn't figure out how to work the coffeepot. It was a big electric pot, like a giant samovar, a church-basement pot. It was plugged into an adapter, but it just sat there. A little red light blinked off and on. There was coffee in the pot. And water. But it wouldn't start perking. There had to be a secret switch somewhere, but no one knew where it was. He experienced the familiar feeling of inadequacy. *Middling.* It was always like this at the beginning of a film; everyone standing around like the kids at the coffeemaker. Not knowing how to get it started.

What about Craft Services? What did they call it in Italian? Michael didn't know. Esther had hired a company called Piccolo Mondo, a catering company that supplied food to airlines, but Piccolo Mondo probably didn't know how to make American coffee. There were no pastries either. Esther would know what to do when she showed up with Zanni. Michael, too nervous to intervene with the coffee urn, made himself invisible by studying a plan of the convent on the wall of the refectory. Almost all the interior scenes would be shot in the convent, and the set construction was on schedule, but Miranda Clark, the female lead, didn't like the script and kept pushing for changes, and she suddenly didn't want to do the cunnilingus scene. Her Italian lover, Giovanni Cipriani—Zanni—was a commedia dell'arte actor famous for not taking direction, famous for refusing to acknowledge any authority outside himself. He'd been denied a visa to reenter the United States after ridiculing President Bush and Vice President Quayle at Harvard in one of his pantomime routines; he'd been banned from Italian television for ridiculing the government of Giulio Andreotti; he'd been denounced by the Vatican for ridiculing the Pope. Michael wasn't anxious to become another target of his satire.

He asked the PAs to rearrange the long school tables, to put them back the way they'd been originally, in a square, and set out ballpoint pens, notebooks, and fresh scripts at each place, as if this were a business meeting in an airport conference room.

People from the production office began to bustle in. The production designer, costume designer, second assistant director, the script girl, the editor, and the director of photography. The second assistant director was full of questions. "We still don't have permission for the bar in Piazza Signoria. The guy wants too much money. Do you want the shelves in the library to run lengthwise or sideways?"

"Isn't there another bar in the piazza?" Michael asked.

"There's one bar, that's it. The one on the northeast corner, by Via Calzaiuoli."

"Find another piazza; build another bar; talk to Esther; build the shelves the way they were in the convent; you only need one wall; do what you have to do."

By eight o'clock all the actors except Zanni had arrived and were schmoozing with the PAs to show that they were just regular people, which they were. Everyone wanted coffee, but no one had figured out what to do except complain about Piccolo Mondo, till Zanni arrived with Esther. Zanni took one look at the coffee machine and sent Esther and a team of PAs out into the piazza to get real coffee and plenty of pastries.

Michael got everyone settled and ran through the story while they were waiting for their coffee.

"Act One. Here's the setup. Margot Harrington, twenty-nine years old, dysfunctional family, father a broken-down blues musician, alcoholic; mother dead for years, a cold, unfeeling woman. Margot is a book conservator at the Newberry Library in New York. Some of the books in a convent in Florence—this convent, actually—have been damaged by water from a broken drainage pipe. The nuns run an ad in a book conservation journal for an American book conservator. A woman. They want an American woman because they're afraid an Italian man will give in to the bishop, who wants to move the books to San Marco. Margot answers the ad. She comes to Florence. But she's lost. She doesn't speak Italian. She doesn't drink wine because her father's an alcoholic. She doesn't drink the water because she's afraid of getting sick. She doesn't eat the food because she's afraid of getting fat. She's afraid of life.

"She's sitting in the piazza outside the convent when a man, Sandro, comes up out of the sewer and offers to buy her a glass of wine."

"Michael," Miranda interrupted. "For one thing, the Newberry Library's in Chicago, not New York, and for another I still can't figure out what Sandro's doing in the sewer."

"Let's worry about the library later," Michael said. "And Sandro, Sandro's been trying to sneak into the convent through the sewer to look at a famous fresco in the cloister."

"Ah."

Michael went on: "Sandro notices Margot and offers—in English—to buy her a glass of wine, but she tells him to get lost.

"Later, he follows her to a restaurant and sits down at her table and renews his offer. She gets up and runs out of the restaurant."

The coffee arrived at Plot Point One. Trays with little cups of espresso, each cup expertly covered by a napkin. Packets of sugar. The PAs served the coffee.

"In the convent Margot discovers a book of Renaissance erotic drawings, pornography. Sixteen different sexual positions. This is the plot point that hooks us into Act Two.

"Act Two," Michael went on. "The abbess takes Margot under her wing and asks her to sell the book on behalf of the convent. This is the through-story that shapes the confrontation. The bishop wants the book, and Margot needs help. She turns to the man who has been pursuing her: Sandro. Sandro is middle-aged, a widower, an art restorer. The book has been damaged by the water from the drainage pipe. Margot restores it in Sandro's apartment; they look at the pictures together; he undresses her in front of a cheval glass; they go to bed. She's too uptight to respond, so Sandro finds a piece of chocolate in a dresser drawer. He unwraps it and tells Margot to hold it between her teeth but not to bite down. He performs cunnilingus till she orgasms and bites down on the chocolate.

"In the subplot Sandro offers to save the fresco in the convent."

Miranda interrupted again: "Has this fresco been damaged by water from the drainpipe?"

"No," Michael said. "It just needs to be restored. Okay?" He waited. He knew that Miranda didn't like the screenplay, but there was nothing he could do about it. There was nothing she could do about it either.

"Sandro restores the fresco in the convent," he went on, "and then helps Margot trick the bishop, who wants to get his hands on the book. But then Sandro steals the book himself, because he needs some money if he's going to marry Margot. When Margot figures out what's happened, she demands the book back and then dumps Sandro.

"All Margot has to do now is sell the book at Sotheby's to save the convent, but the bishop figures out that he's been tricked and calls in the Vatican Police, who try to get the book away from Margot. Technically the book belongs to the church, not the convent. This is the plot point that hooks us into Act Three.

"Act Three. Margot takes the book to Sotheby's to auction it off. The Vatican Police are waiting for her, but Sandro shows up just in time to rescue her. At the auction he bids on the book himself, even though he doesn't have any money. He risks everything for Margot. Margot forgives him. He proposes. She says yes. He stops bidding just in time. Margot will get the money for the convent, and Sandro will show her how to live.

Miranda again: "Michael, why does Sandro bid on the Aretino in the first place? If he wins the bidding and can't pay, then he's in big trouble and nobody gets any money. It doesn't make sense. They'd have to have another auction. In the book . . ."

"I'm reading the script," Michael said, "not the book." He looked around. "At the end," he said, "they get married in the Palazzo Vecchio. Margot's father comes to the wedding and plays his guitar. It's very life affirming."

Michael thought that the first read-through, although not inspired, went smoothly enough. Some of the love scenes—especially the cunnilingus scene—were a little hard to negotiate, but that was always the case with love scenes, and he expected that Zanni would soon seduce Miranda and then they could work things out between them. He could see that she was a little afraid of him, but that was okay. She'd need to use her fear, hang onto it. It would give her an edge. He still hadn't figured out how to frame the cunnilingus scene. It would be easier to listen to Miranda's objections and make it a regular love scene, but he didn't want to take the easy way out. Besides, how many great cunnilingus scenes are there in movies? Not many. He wanted to give audiences something to remember.

The lunch that Piccolo Mondo delivered to the convent was unacceptable to the Italians, who'd never seen sandwiches wrapped in plastic before. Esther was upset and sent the sandwiches and the Piccolo Mondo truck away.

Zanni offered to make polenta while Esther left to order a meal at one of the restaurants in the piazza. The Italian department heads and crew recognized a cue and started clapping as Zanni pantomimed a starving man, rubbing his stomach and opening his mouth wide to mimic hunger pangs. Suddenly at his feet an enormous pot appeared, which he filled with cornmeal and water and then began to stir with a large wooden paddle. He was getting hungrier and hungrier, rolling his eyes, inhaling the smell of the polenta, brushing off a fly that buzzed round his head. He continued to do battle with the fly and to stir the polenta. In the end the polenta turned out to be nothing more than a starving man's fantasy. Only the fly was real. Zanni's hand shot out; he caught the fly and ate it.

By the time he had eaten the fly, Esther had returned with several bottles of wine and the promise of pizza from Maistro Ciliego, just around the corner. What had struck Michael the most, he realized as Esther was opening the wine, was Zanni's delight in himself, his pleasure in being Zanni. Michael had seen this in actors before—in Jack Nicholson in *Five Easy Pieces* and in Toshiro Mifune in *Seven Samurai*. But not like this. And he knew what he had to do—not when the film opened, not when the final cut had been printed, not when they wrapped, not when principal photography had begun, not tomorrow, not after the second read-through, but now, this very moment. He had to take pleasure in being himself, in being Michael. He had to remember that he was doing what he wanted to do; he had to remember that this was his vocation.

Tribunale

The examining magistrate's desk at the Tribunale on Via Magazzini was piled high with papers in official folders. Rinaldo Romero and his father and their lawyer were already seated when Woody and his lawyer entered the room on the second floor, which overlooked a courtyard that now served as a parking lot for the police station at the back of the Badia. According to Woody's lawyer, the examination of witnesses would probably not be carried out according to the provisions of article 244 of the Code of Civil Procedure but rather in a free-form discussion similar to the procedure used in criminal trials. The civil judge, in other words, would enjoy exceptional discretionary powers that could affect the balance of power between the parties to the proceedings. Everything depended on what evidence the judge was willing to admit.

Rinaldo's family wanted to reduce the case to a single issue: the tattoo on the dog. If the tattoo indicated that the dog was registered to Rinaldo, then there was nothing more to discuss.

Open and shut. They had wanted Woody to bring the dog to the Tribunale.

Rinaldo's lawyer, Woody had learned from the *commissario,* had bribed the ambulance driver to change his story. This was Rinaldo's trump card. The driver was now willing to testify that Woody had threatened him with a knife and prevented him from taking the injured Rinaldo in his ambulance. But if Rinaldo played his trump card, then the matter would be immediately transferred to the criminal courts, and various embarrassing consequences would follow. For Rinaldo as well as for Woody.

Moreover, Rinaldo hadn't counted on Woody's aggressiveness. Woody had instructed his lawyer to depose the veterinarian, the *commissario,* witnesses from the restaurant in Piazza Tasso, Rinaldo's girlfriend, who was now his ex-girlfriend. Woody had also solicited briefs from the Ente Nazionale Protezione Animali, and from the *pubblico ministero* in Bologna, and from Signor Secci, the president of the Association of the Families of the Victims of the Bombing of 15 August, and from the luthier on Via Verdi who had located a new resonator and a new cover plate for Woody's guitar, which had been damaged by Rinaldo's knife.

These briefs, or *carte,* were what took up so much space on the examining magistrate's desk.

Rinaldo's lawyer spoke first: Rinaldo's family, he said, had made a good-faith effort to settle the matter out of court by offering Signor Woodhull a substantial sum as compensation. Signor Woodhull had refused all reasonable offers, however, and now, after all, it was really a simple matter of fact, not a matter of interpretation or of philosophical disagreement: either the registration tattooed on the dog's ear indicated that the dog belonged to Rinaldo or it didn't. Signor Woodhull had been ordered to bring the dog, but he had not brought the dog. *Res ipse loquitur.*

Woody's lawyer objected at this point. Signor Woodhull had not been ordered by the court to bring the dog. He had been ordered by Signor Romero's attorney, which was a very different matter. The dog's presence was not necessary, in any case, because Signor Woodhull was willing to concede that the registration number tattooed on the dog was the same as the number registered in the name of Signor Romero. Moreover, if it was a simple matter of fact, then the principal fact was that Signor Romero had abused the dog. He had dragged her behind his car and, according to the brief from the veterinarian, he had abused her in various other ways as well. There were burn marks, evidence of knife wounds and of broken bones . . .

Rinaldo's lawyer objected: "This is not a criminal proceeding against my client. It's a proceeding to determine who owns the dog. If Signor Woodhull stipulates that the number tattooed on the dog corresponds to the number registered at the regional canine registry, then there's nothing to discuss. The dog should be returned to its rightful owner. As you know"—he turned to Woody's lawyer—"under Italian law, a dog is a *cosa,* a thing. My client may have punished the dog for misbehaving, but that is his right. It's true that article 727 of the penal code contemplates the crime of mistreating an animal, but in point of fact an animal is considered by law to be a *cosa,* not a living being. Public morality and common sentiment do not apply in the case of animals."

Woody's lawyer rose to his feet: "Not only is there a strong movement afoot to repeal article 727, but the law itself is open to interpretation. Ownership gives the right to enjoy and dispose of things within certain limits established by law." The lawyer put a great deal of emphasis on the phrase *entro i limiti,* a point that led to a long debate about the definition of property.

The judge had still not indicated what she was going to admit as evidence. She asked Rinaldo's lawyer once again why this wasn't a criminal trial. If Woody had in fact threatened the ambulance driver with a knife . . .

But Rinaldo's lawyer interrupted her: "Thank you, your honor, for bringing us back to the point. This is not a criminal trial. All these depositions, all these *carte,* are irrelevant. The only thing that's relevant is whether the number tattooed on the dog corresponds to the number in the registration. The accused has already stipulated that it does correspond. *Res ipse loquitur.*"

The judge, however, declared that this was only a preliminary hearing. She needed to look at the depositions.

Woody's lawyer assured him that it would be at least nine months before they could take the dog away from him.

Instead of going back to the American Academy and eating lunch in the cafeteria, Woody went to his favorite spot in Florence, the Etruscan wing of the Archeological Museum, which involved only a slight detour. He'd been struggling with the Etruscans for years. After the trial of the terrorists in Bologna, after the guilty verdicts, after an ugly episode in Regina Coeli Prison in Rome, where he'd almost strangled the bomber, Angela Strappafelci, Woody had visited the Etruscan cemetery at Cerveteri, had entered the Tomb of the Reliefs—the dog, the goose, the mysterious eggs, the naked slaves stooping to the wine jars, the happy couples embracing under their sheets of stone, the couple about to engage in anal intercourse. And he'd experienced a sense of profound relief. He'd bought all the books and had read them, but of course what he wanted to know was not to be found in Haptonstahl's *Etrusker Grammatik* nor in the *Notizie degli scavi di antichità,* which he read in the Biblioteca Nazionale. Nor in D. H.

Lawrence's *Etruscan Places,* though Lawrence pointed the way, pointed toward a time when the whole universe was vitally alive and our business was not to figure out what we believed but to open ourselves to this vitality, to draw it into ourselves.

The guard at the ticket window—the one he'd met on his way to the Questura—asked about the dog, but Woody had to be back at the Academy at one o'clock for his mythology class and didn't have time to chat. He ran up the stairs to the Etruscan exhibits on the second floor. Past the stone sculptures and cinerary urns in Rooms IX and X; past the famous bronze Chimera, which the Medici, who had invented Etruscan ancestors to balance the claims of the Pope, had adopted to establish their power; past the special exhibit on the third floor, curated by Professor Roncalli from the University of Naples, whom Woody had met after a public lecture. (Roncalli was overseeing the excavations at Severiano.)

What he wanted to see was simply a flat stone and a table from the Etruscan site at Severiano. The stone itself was raised a little bit above the floor, but not much. This was not a popular exhibit because there wasn't much to it—just a flat stone and a stone table that reminded Woody of the trainmaster's desk that his wife had bought for him when the old Burlington depot was torn down.

This stone altar and table were the domain of the haruspex, said to be descended from Tages, the grandson of Jupiter. He was represented as a shepherd—a figure from an even earlier culture, from outside the community—who came with the seasons, or who brought the seasons by his coming, like the musicians Woody and Margot had heard the other night in the piazza, who come down from the mountains in the Abruzzi at Christmastime. The altar didn't *represent* a threshold between this world and the invisible world, it *was* the threshold, though no one, not even Roncalli, was sure just how it worked. Except that the haruspex stood on it, probably while examining sheep's entrails for signs at the stone table.

It was Friday noon. Woody had Room X to himself. He stepped over the velvet cord that cordoned off the altar. Then he stepped back. He was an academic. A man who obeyed the rules. But then he stepped over the cord a second time. He raised his left foot to place it on the altar, and then he put his foot down carefully, as if he were stepping onto a bathroom scale. Then his right foot.

And he tried to peer into the future. He had compelling reasons to go home. Financial reasons. The job at the American Academy did not pay well and he had to supplement his income by playing at the Bebop Club and the Osteria dei Poeti on Via de' Macci. He wanted to teach Ovid and Virgil and Homer in Latin and Greek at the college level, not in translation. He felt that his work in Italy was over, and he believed that Cookie herself, whose charred remains had been buried in St. Clair, no longer made her presence felt in Italy—not in the Protestant Cemetery in Rome, nor at the University in Bologna, nor at the morgue on Via Irnerio where he'd cradled her broken, burned body in his arms for the last time. His daughters wanted him to come home, and his ex-wife, Hannah—now in her fifth year in the Ursuline convent west of Davenport—was seriously ill and wanted to see him before she died. He was afraid of this visit. The nuns were cloistered, and he'd spoken to her only once since she'd completed her novitiate, at the burial service for Cookie. He was afraid that Hannah had changed her mind about her vocation, that she wanted to escape. He couldn't bear this, the thought of all those wasted years.

There was the dog, Biscotti, and there was Margot. But he could take Biscotti with him. Dogs flew on airplanes. And maybe he could take Margot with him too. He was thinking of proposing. Maybe she could get a job in Iowa City. The University of Iowa had an important book conservation program. An hour and a half away. Even if she stayed in Iowa City during the week . . . Or the Newberry Library, in Chicago, where she'd started her career as a conservator. Farther away, but she could take the train and come home on weekends.

Standing on the stone altar Woody felt, to his surprise, that he had entered a familiar place, felt that he'd been stepping onto this stone all his life. He stood at the altar as he had often stood at his trainmaster's desk, writing his notes for his classes, or reading his Homer, or puzzling over a difficult passage in Aeschylus or Thucydides. But now he was standing on a threshold: his dad's funeral, his first date, first cigarette, his first taste of alcohol, his first ride on the Twilight Limited, his first Greek class at the University of Michigan, first sexual intercourse, the exchange scholarship to Iran, proposing to Hannah, the birth of Cookie, his first job at St. Clair, signing the papers for the house in the lawyer's office on Cherry Street, the birth of Sara, the birth of Ludi, and then the *strage* in Bologna, Cookie's death, Hannah's breakdown and the divorce, Hannah leaving for the convent, the affair with one of his students that had turned the dean against him, selling the house and going to Bologna for the trial of the terrorists, playing his guitar for the first time in Gabriella's trattoria, Gabriella herself, the job at the American Academy, Margot. He'd been standing on this threshold all his life. There was no end of new lives, renaissances, rebirths. But how many times can a man be reborn? He thought this might be the last time. The trainmaster's desk was gone. The house was there, but other people were living in it now, raising their children. His own children had left home. Sara, who had three children, was an exhibit developer at the Museum of Science and Industry in Chicago. Ludi was a vet in Florida. His wife had left him and was living in a convent. And yet they weren't gone. Nothing was gone. Nothing had been lost. Not even Cookie and the trainmaster's desk. And he had decided to go home. He was overwhelmed with happiness. He felt it along his pulse and in his heart. He would have been content to die at this moment, standing on the threshold of yet another new life, whatever it was going to be.

He thought he heard a sound in the corridor. One of the guards. He stepped back over the velvet rail and glanced at his watch. Just enough time to get back for his afternoon mythology class: maybe he'd tell them about the vitality of the Etruscans instead of soldiering on with *Oedipus*.

La Maremmana

Beryl was sitting in the Osteria dei Pazzi with Michael and Zanni. Michael was finding reasons why he couldn't do any of the things that Zanni was suggesting.

"A crane. But we'd need a crane."

"You're the director, Michael. Tell Signora Klein you need a crane. We have cranes in Italy."

"But five minutes with no sound?"

They had ordered the *antipastone* and the waiter was arranging crostini on their plates.

"You should always imagine you're making a silent film," Zanni was saying. "Then you have to use the camera to think visually. Think about it. The first meeting. Instead of Sandro emerging from the sewer, which is ridiculous, we see a young woman who's been excluded by her American colleagues from a Thanksgiving dinner at I Tatti. She wanders out into the piazza, on the edge of tears. She sees a girl chasing her dog. She shouts at the dog to stop. There you might allow the audience to hear her voice. She calls the dog; the dog stops. And who is watching her beside the audience? *You*. You're looking down from on high. You *see* her. You see the man who is going to become her lover approaching from behind. He's been watching her too. They speak. *We don't hear what they have to say because we don't need to.* It's classic. She's angry. She pulls her whole body away from him. She jerks away. They speak some more. And then they walk across the piazza to a bar. Not a word; do you see what I mean? One long shot that takes in the piazza, the fake *David*, the Uffizi in the background. Simplicity itself. What do you think?"

Michael, who'd been looking at his dog-eared copy of the script, shook his head. "We'd have to get a crane, a big crane."

"We have big cranes too."

"But it's not in the budget."

"Tell Signora Klein to put it in the budget."

"I'm afraid of heights."

Beryl's heart sank. She knew why her husband had never won an Oscar.

"If I didn't have to be on the ground, I'd shoot the scene for you," Zanni said, "but you can watch it from below on a video tap. That's what most directors would do. Send the director of photography up in the basket."

Beryl didn't think that Zanni was speaking sarcastically, but if he was, he'd taken the edge off it. "Seriously, though," he went on, "you ought to try it. It gives you a new perspective on things."

The waiter brought more antipasti: squid, fish, little octopuses. Beryl knew that Zanni was stealing the movie, which they'd decided to call *The Italian Lover*. Everyone knew it, and everyone was happy, except Miranda.

Beryl stopped listening to Michael and Zanni when she suddenly realized that she could understand what the couple at the next table was saying. Her intensive Italian class at Linguaviva was paying off. She wasn't even stopping to translate. They were arguing about a sofa (*divano*) that the woman had ordered without consulting her husband. She didn't realize that she needed to consult him about every little thing (*ogne cosa piccola*). A sofa, he said, was not a little thing. It was huge (*enorme*).

The waiter brought more food. "Get the crane," she said to Michael. "I'll talk to Esther if you don't want to. It's a great idea." *Antipastone*. Beryl finally realized what it meant: big antipasto. They weren't going to eat a regular meal. They were going to eat one antipasto after another. Including *lardo Colonnata*. Paper-thin slices of lard that had been cured in special marble tubs in Colonnata. She didn't think she could do it. Eat straight lard. But she did, and it was delicious.

When they'd finished their *lardo* and the waiter had brought fresh plates, Michael, who hadn't touched his lard, asked Beryl for a piece of paper, which she produced from her purse, and began jotting down some notes. The waiter brought a platter of deep-fried anchovy pastries, but Michael, who'd hardly eaten anything, wasn't interested. He wanted to get home to call Esther about the crane and then rethink the shooting schedule. "We could shoot the library scene tomorrow," he explained, as if he were justifying himself to Esther. He stood up to leave. "Then we can shoot the new piazza scene when we've got the crane."

"But we haven't finished eating," Zanni said.

"You stay," Michael said. "I'm going to call Esther."

"I don't think I can eat anymore," Beryl said in Italian, as one waiter cleared their plates and another brought a tray of prosciutto and *salame toscano* with big chunks of white fat in each slice. "I can't believe that I ate straight lard."

Zanni answered her in Italian: "They'll keep bringing more dishes till we tell them to stop."

Beryl tried to explain to Zanni, in Italian, that she was a different person in Italian—not her usual confident self, but timid, attentive. She had to stay alert all the time in Italian. She told him about the woman at the Protestant Cemetery, where she sometimes stopped for tea after her Italian lessons. About her teachers at Linguaviva. It was like starting her life over or starting another life. She wasn't sure who she was or who she would turn out to be if she kept it up.

They finished their wine. Zanni told the waiter not to bring any more food, just a little fruit and some Vin Santo and maybe a plate of biscotti. Beryl knew she was in danger. She wasn't going to make anything happen, but she wasn't going to stop it from happening either. They continued to talk in Italian. They dipped their *biscotti di Prato* in little glasses of Vin Santo; they ate their fruit and drank two coffees, corrected with grappa. Beryl paid the bill with her Visa card.

Walking with Zanni down the Via de' Macci, Beryl said, "Let's get this over with." At least that's what she meant to say, though she wasn't sure about the subjunctive in Italian, and so they turned south instead of north, south toward Santa Croce instead of north toward San Pier Maggiore, down winding streets on the other side of the piazza—Via Torta, Via della Burella—into Piazza San Firenze, past the Bargello and the Badia, where Michael was planning to film some exterior shots. They crossed the right-angled streets of the old Roman forum, under the arch to Via Tornabuoni. This route was imprinted on Beryl's mind at this time, and she didn't think she'd ever forget it. This city was no longer Renaissance Florence. It had become something more personal. But she was afraid that one word of English would send her back to her old self, a self that could never do what she was doing. She couldn't always understand what Zanni was saying, but she understood that they were going to his hotel. She could sense another self—her English-speaking self—walking beside them. When she checked their reflections in the window at Versace, pretending she was just looking at a pair of shoes, she saw just two people, but when they were walking along, not looking in the windows, she seemed to glimpse this other self out of the corner of her eye. She had to struggle to keep the conversation going in Italian. She was afraid that Zanni would become impatient and start speaking in English, and she knew that if he did, she would turn around and go straight home. To Via Pietrapiana. But Zanni must have understood this too, because he did not become impatient.

Zanni whispered his room number in her ear. *Trenta-sei.* He would go in first, he said, and she should wait five minutes and then take the elevator. No point in bumping into Esther in the lobby. Maybe, she thought, he was giving her a chance to back out—a second chance—time to think things over. But there was nothing more to think over.

She walked down the street to Via Tornabuoni and then back to the hotel, which had very fancy glass doors—large glass windows set in beautiful dark wood. A sign indicated that the hotel accepted various credit cards. The lobby was empty. Arches sprang from Corinthian columns. There were two desks. A man at one, a woman at the other. Both looked up. *Let them look,* Beryl thought. What were they going to do?

In the mirrors in the elevator Beryl thought she looked especially handsome in a velvet halter that showed off her shoulders without being overtly sexy. She was a little shaky, but she knocked firmly on the door. Numero 36. *Trenta-sei.* She thought she had it right, but for a minute she imagined a perfect stranger opening the door. Or Esther or Miranda.

"*Avanti.*" Zanni opened the door. The first thing she noticed was that there were two single beds in the room.

Beryl knew how Sandro proceeds in *The Sixteen Pleasures*. He undresses Margot in front of a cheval glass. Michael had talked about this scene. She knew that Miranda was nervous about it. But what did a beautiful young body like that have to worry about? What Beryl wondered was, how would Zanni proceed? They never really show this part in films—a man trying to get out of his pants, a woman trying to unhook her bra. Nude scenes in movies all had the same shape, acted out the same cultural fantasy.

"*Vieni.*"

"*Sicuro?*"

"*Si, si.*" Zanni patted the bed and she sat down beside him. You'd think she'd know what to do by now, but Michael was the only man she'd been to bed with since Smith. She wasn't thinking that way now, though. In Italian she'd done this lots of times. In her imagination—Darren, the point guard at Troy High; Mr. Alexander, the friend of the family; Paul, the server for her father and her date for the senior prom; Barry, her coworker at Bergdorf Goodman's before she met Michael. And after that: Duncan, an editor at *Advertising Age;* the priest at St. Hildegard's back in L.A.; her husband's colleagues; men she'd passed on the street or seen in a restaurant or on an airplane. She'd had a dozen lovers since she'd come to Florence. She'd slept with the barista at the bar where she stopped for a cappuccino every morning, with the man at the *pizzicheria* and the *ortolano* on Via degli Albizzi, with Franco Bevilacqua and the good-looking dolly grip. She couldn't begin to count them, the lovers she'd held in her arms at night, in Italy. And now they all came crowding together in this hotel room, sitting next to her on a single bed in the person of Giovanni Cipriani.

"*Vuoi mettere i letti insieme?*" she asked. Do you want to put the beds together?

"C'e sempre un diviso sconfortabile nel mezzo," he said. *"Domani chiedero una camera con un matrimoniale."*

"Va bene. E stasera?"

He laughed. *"Faremo il meglio possiamo."* We'll do the best we can. He touched her. *"Permettimi."* He started to remove her dress, but there were too many buttons.

"They're fake," she said. "It unhooks. Like this. My wedding dress," she said, "had hundreds of buttons, and my mother kept getting them misaligned. I was half an hour late for the ceremony."

He entered her with all the force of her imaginary lovers—priest and plowman, young and old, short and tall, stout and thin. They whispered to her in Italian. She didn't know what to say in Italian, so she didn't say anything. She'd exhausted her supply of Italian and just wanted to be quiet, to experience all these lovers at once, after so many years of behaving herself.

Zanni insisted on walking her home or calling a cab. Not because Firenze is dangerous at eleven o'clock at night, but because it was the thing to do, but Beryl refused, because she wanted to be alone, to savor this moment as she retraced her steps back to the restaurant, Osteria de' Pazzi, and then got a little lost and wound up in Piazza Sant'Ambrogio, where Saint Ambrose had spent a year, living with a local family, in 403. Ambrose, the church's chief opponent of Arianism in the West. When someone asked her the time—*Che ore sono?*—she couldn't understand a word. The man had to point at his watch.

Back at the apartment, Michael was hard at work on the new crane scene and hardly noticed that she was late. "Hello," he said, and when she put her hands on his shoulders, she was her old self again. He'd already talked to Esther about the crane, he said. She waited for the sadness to kick in, the melancholy, the postcoitum triste, the guilt, the shame. She tried to pretend, but she couldn't. She was too full of life and joy and love, and her earlier feelings about her husband—her knowledge that he was middling—turned into tenderness. He was so excited, and she thought that just maybe this film would turn out to be something great for him. He seemed to think so. He wanted to talk about the new plan for the crane. At first Esther had objected, he said, but he'd insisted, and she seemed happy enough. She was going to talk to the production manager in the morning, start adding time to the schedule. If Michael wanted a crane, he'd get a crane.

So they both went to bed happy, their arms around each other, at first, and then just touching. Beryl thought about last Sunday's lesson—Paul warning the Ephesians against fornication and uncleanness, against filthiness and foolish talking, against whoremongers and idolaters and vain words; she kept waiting for something bad to happen, but it didn't.

Hump Day

Sunday afternoon. Esther was in the production office with Guido Graziano, the dolly grip. Guido was talking on the phone in Italian, talking to his father, who owned the movie-supply house in Rome that had provided the camera, the lighting package, the dollies and that was going to supply the crane they would use for Michael's piazza shot. There was to be some kind of demonstration in the piazza on Wednesday, and Esther wanted to reschedule the crane for Thursday. She had the impression that Guido and his father were talking about something else, but whenever she coughed or tapped the desk, Guido would smile and move his hand up and down as if he were patting a dog on the head. *He was a beautiful man,* Esther thought, *and a good worker.*

They were four weeks into the shoot. Almost halfway. Wednesday would be hump day. The weather had been cooperating, not good for tourists, but a string of gray days that could pass for midwinter, which is just what they needed. The sun had come out on Friday for a while and she'd thought they'd have to scramble to find an interior shot they could do, but then it clouded over again.

Esther liked the Italian crew, and the Italian crew liked her, especially after she'd hired an old Italian couple, Gina and Rosario, who cooked special dinners at the American Church, to fix a proper Italian lunch every day in the big convent kitchen. Everything they needed—pots, pans, glasses, tableware—was in the kitchen. All Esther had to do was hire a plumber, an *idraulico,* to hook up the eight-burner restaurant stove.

They'd been making their days, getting through the exterior shots on schedule—a difficult car shot in Fiesole, the walk to Settignano. The dailies looked good, and if Zanni was stealing the show, that was all right. The man was too full of life experience to need the attention of the camera, and for that reason the camera was drawn to him.

Her own life experience in Florence, she thought, *was totally different from shooting with Harry.* Maybe all the craziness, all the shouting and yelling, wasn't really necessary. Maybe it was better to plan ahead, the way Michael did; keep the whole movie in your head, instead of just plunking down the camera and trying to figure out coverage on the set.

Even so, when she thought of the days ahead, she experienced a nameless dread. Margot—the real Margot—was demanding a copy of the script, and Esther wasn't going to be able to put her off much longer. Leviathan was objecting to the crane, even though the last cost report showed that the crane would not put them over budget. Esther had ignored the faxes from Los Angeles and ordered the crane anyway. It was going to be a difficult shot, a huge scene to mount, and she still didn't have written permission to use the piazza, though the mayor, whom she'd taken to lunch at Cibreo, with Franco Bevilacqua and Michael, had promised her that there would be no difficulties.

And they still had the sex scenes to do, and they'd have to be careful because they couldn't release the film with an NC-17 rating.

But Esther's biggest worry was the affair between Zanni and Beryl, which everyone seemed to know about except Michael and Miranda. An affair between Zanni and Miranda would have been fine. A man like Zanni. A young woman like Miranda. It would have been good publicity. Stars are the gods and goddesses who embody the romantic dreams of people not in the business. When they come together on the screen, sparks are supposed to fly. It has to be real, and the audience has to know it's real.

But an affair between the male lead and the director's wife was another matter. It could disrupt everything. Esther'd seen it happen. And Beryl of all people. Beryl was the last person Esther would have expected to have an affair. Beryl was a nice person, a good woman, an Episcopalian, a good friend to her, and to Harry too, during the divorce. Sitting up late all those nights, holding her hand, taking her shopping on Rodeo Drive, taking her for sauerbraten at Mussos. How could she do this to a man like Michael? The man was dying. He was bound to find out. And then what would happen? How would he keep going? What if he lost heart? How could she, Esther, protect him? She could almost imagine him turning to her, leaning on her the way she'd leaned on him and Beryl when Harry had dumped her. What would she say to him as a friend, an old friend? What advice would she give him? Beryl was a bit older than Esther, more sophisticated, and she was still beautiful. Beryl knew how to dress. She had class. But who would have thought that a man like Zanni would prefer her to a young woman like Miranda?

And Miranda. She'd been in love with Zanni from the start. What if she went to pieces? lost it? balked? clutched? panicked? How would they get through the love scenes, the sixteen pleasures?

Esther was depressed. She was sorry for everybody, and most

of all she was sorry for herself, because she knew that no one would ever again feel about her the way Zanni felt about Beryl.

Guido was still sitting in Esther's office chair, behind her desk. She didn't know how long he'd been off the phone. "Sorry," she said. "I was daydreaming."

"They'll bring the crane on Wednesday," he said. "We'll get it set up in the piazza that night, but you have to have the permission papers for the right day."

Esther nodded. "The mayor promised," she said. "He said he'd see to it that things arranged themselves."

"That's good," Guido said, "but I have to have the papers in my hand by Wednesday night."

"Wednesday's hump day," Esther said.

"Hump day." Guido repeated the words after her.

"It means halfway. You're over the hump."

He laughed. "It sounds like something else."

"Guido," she said, "I think we should have a party. Harry and I always had a hump-day party on our shoots. We'd cook for everybody. What do you think?"

"Un botte di vino," he said, *"fa più miracoli che una chiesa piena di santi."*

"Which means?"

"A cask of wine works more miracles than a church full of saints," he said.

"Do you think we need a miracle?"

He shook his head. "Not at all," he said. "I just think it would be a kind of miracle to have a producer cook for us."

"We always made sauerbraten," she said, "wherever we were. And potato dumplings. Do you think Italians would like sauerbraten? It's pot roast, beef marinated in vinegar for three days . . ."

"Maybe like a *straccotto?*" Guido said. "And dumplings?"

"Potato dumplings. You boil the potatoes and put them through a ricer"—she demonstrated with her hands—"and then you roll them into little balls with some eggs . . ."

Guido nodded: "*Gnocchi*. Listen, Signora Klein, did you ever hear the story about *il Papa* and the producer who went up to heaven together?"

Esther shook her head.

"Well, the producer and the Pope go up to heaven. When they get there everyone makes a big fuss over the producer—would the producer like a glass of wine? would the producer like some pasta?—that sort of thing. San Pietro himself shows the producer around: would you like this villa or this beautiful apartment? The producer can't figure it out. So finally he asks San Pietro: 'Why is everyone so nice to me, and nobody's paying any attention to the Pope?'

"Now San Pietro's surprised. 'We've got a lot of popes up here,' he says, 'but you're the first producer.'"

Esther *had* heard the joke before, more than once, but this was the first time it made her really laugh.

Esther enjoyed shopping and cooking so much that she forgot to worry about Margot and the love scenes and the crane and Beryl's affair with Zanni.

On Monday she bought ten kilos of beef at the *macelleria* in the piazza. She didn't recognize the Italian cuts of meat, but whatever she bought was expensive and looked like it might be bottom round or sirloin. She bought two liters of red wine vinegar at the Grana Market and poured them over the meat, and then she added two bottles of red wine, six large yellow onions, a handful of bay leaves, caraway seeds, and peppercorns. She sent one of the Italian PAs out to find juniper berries.

On Tuesday she took two PAs with her to the Mercato Sant'Ambrogio, at the end of Via Pietrapiana, and bought fifteen kilos of potatoes, and then she bought two cases of Sangiovese di Romagna, because the Roman crew didn't like Chianti.

On Wednesday she bought lettuce for the salad and fruit for dessert, and she bought seven loaves of *pane toscano* at the bakery in Piazza San Pier Maggiore. They were shooting a scene in the piazza, and Esther stopped to watch as Sandro delivered Japanese rice paper to Margot in the convent and the romance got under way. In the afternoon members of the crew kept popping into the kitchen to see what she was doing, and after the wrap several of the men helped her form the potato dumplings, which, as everyone kept observing, were just oversize gnocchi.

The dinner was a great success. No one wanted to leave, and Esther didn't want anyone to leave, but the crane was arriving that night and Guido and the *macchinisti*—the grips—wanted to be sure everything was in working order before the six o'clock call in the morning. Double overtime, but Esther didn't care. Michael, in jeans and a sweatshirt, looked beat, but Beryl was her usual elegant self in a simple black dress and a pearl choker and bright pink shoes. Michael and Beryl stayed on a bit. Three old friends. Someone had brought a bottle of grappa, and Esther poured the last of it into their little espresso cups while the PAs attacked the dishes.

They chatted a bit about the old days, and then it was time to go to bed.

"You know," Michael said as he stood up to leave, "a movie set is absolute chaos, the work is grueling, the difficulties are overwhelming. But everyone cooperates, everyone works together, everyone cares about everyone else. Wouldn't it be great if the world worked this way, like a film set, everyone pulling together toward a common goal?"

"You're absolutely right," Esther said, and she meant it.

The Crane

It took a week to get the big Titan crane from Rome to Florence and to get all the permissions taken care of. In the meantime, they'd completed a lot of the exterior shots, and the sets in the convent itself were almost finished, so they were on schedule. The director of photography thought Michael should stay on the ground, but Michael now wanted to be up in the air, as Zanni had suggested—up in the wild blue.

Michael had never known how to be anything other than what he was, how to do anything other than what he'd always done. He arrived on the set every morning at seven o'clock, went over the shot list with the assistant director and the DP, talked with the DP about how they were going to cover the first scene, went over the scene with the actors, walked through a camera rehearsal, started shooting, broke for lunch, looked at the rushes from the previous day, started shooting again, wrapped at seven, replanned the next day with the AD, sat in the cutting room with Eddie Franklin to view the day's editing. Then supper with Beryl.

But up on the crane, which was mounted on the back of a truck, he felt something new happening. At first he thought it was just his fear of heights, but suddenly he wasn't afraid anymore, and he began to understand how God must have felt on the morning of creation, just before he shouted "Action." Everything had been perfectly scripted, yet the actors were free to fuck up. All they had to do was follow the script—he could see them below him, in their places (Miranda, Zanni, Mr. Woodhull, holding a cloth Frisbee, and the dog, and the girl, who was one of Woodhull's students, the extras), and yet they were free to fuck up. Bevilacqua had done the paperwork for the girl actor, but not for the dog. They were supposed to have a licensed animal trainer on the set, but Woodhull, Woody, would have to do.

Esther had grumbled more about the changes in the script than at the expense of the crane. They'd scrapped the original first-meeting scene, where Sandro comes out of the sewer. She had fought Michael till he started to scream, the way Harry used to scream. But he'd brought every day in on time, and they were saving a fortune by using the convent for offices, sets, dormitories, meals.

Michael didn't like to discuss a shot with Esther because Esther always brought the conversation around to the way Harry would have done it. Esther was a hands-on producer. Michael liked that. He was not afraid of suggestions, constructive criticism. But he didn't want to hear about Harry. Harry'd had a different approach. Harry was a screamer. Always over budget. It bothered him that he was actually trying to become more like Harry—to take more risks, to go for the jugular, for the primal scream; to plant the camera and let something happen instead of storyboarding everything to death. Harry'd made a lot of bad films, but some great ones too.

And now, up on the crane, not the single long take Zanni had originally imagined, with the camera locked down, but the most complex and ambitious shot Michael had ever tackled. He was nervous, but excited. Looking down like God. He could see all his creatures, right where he'd placed them: Woody and the dog and the girl in front of the Banco Ambrosiana; the others by the Palazzo Signoria. When he closed his eyes, he could see Miranda coming out of the side entrance of the palazzo—another expensive permission. The camera takes in some of the fountain and all of *David*. It follows Miranda to the Loggia dei Lanzi, panning across the Piazza degli Uffizi, past Benvenuto Cellini's *Perseus,* past the *Rape of the Sabine Women,* past Hercules and Nessus. Margot will stand on the steps. They've blocked off part of the piazza— paid for by the square meter—a sort of "path" for Miranda to follow. The camera will have to stay focused on this path and avoid the railings used to keep people back.

The camera will see Zanni walking behind Miranda, following her from the Palazzo Signoria. Then Woodhull will throw the Frisbee, and the dog will run around. Miranda will watch the girl—Woodhull's student—chase the dog, and Zanni will watch Miranda watching the girl. Then Zanni will come up behind Miranda and speak to her. She will rebuff him. He'll press her. She'll put up more resistance. The dog will keep running. Zanni will shout at her, and then she'll stop. At least Michael hopes she'll stop. If the dog doesn't stop, it won't matter. That's the beauty of it. In either case Miranda-Margot's resistance will start to melt. She and Zanni-Sandro will cross the piazza to a bar. The shot will end with them going into the bar.

Cut to the bar.

This was what he could see in his mind's eye. This was what he was praying for. Miranda would have to hit nine different marks, Zanni six. The camera would have to find fifteen different points of focus as it glided from a wide shot to a close-up and then boomed up, tilted down, and panned 180 degrees to follow Miranda and Zanni across the piazza to a bar. And there were the wild cards—*the dog* and the people in the piazza. It was almost impossible to stop them from staring up at the camera on the crane. They couldn't afford to block off the whole piazza. That would just make it worse. Because there would be no way to keep the crowds at the edges out of the frame, even with the long lens. He'd done the best he could. The AD had hired enough extras to surround Margot. Lots of things could go wrong, but that was okay. He was doing what he wanted to do, and something new was happening.

He watched the PAs herding the extras into position— seventy-five of them, whose main task was to fill the frame. Miranda and Zanni were standing outside the doorway at the side of the Palazzo Vecchio. Esther was there too. And Beryl. He could see Woody and the dog in front of the Banco Ambrosiano. The extras were milling around. And then he saw Beryl, who'd skipped her language class to come to watch, reach up and adjust Zanni's tie. She squeezed the knot of the tie and ran her hand underneath the fabric. And Michael's heart sank. She might as well have kissed him. Where was Miranda? Miranda was talking to Esther.

The knot in Michael's stomach tightened when he looked at his wife again. He thought he understood what was happening better than she did herself. He knew he could stop it right now. He could tell one of the PAs to ask Zanni to . . . to do something, or to ask Beryl . . . But what to ask? He was God looking down on Eve and the serpent. And he hadn't even shouted "Action" yet.

Is this the way God felt? Dizzy? It wouldn't take much for him to throw up over the edge of the basket. There was no safety railing. He could fall over the edge. He could let Beryl know that he was watching, but that would be like God calling to Eve. He decided to let it go. He'd deal with it later. There was too much going on right now in this unscripted moment just before creation, just before the big bang.

"Two minutes," the AD, Franco Bevilacqua, said into his walkie-talkie.

Miranda and Zanni disappeared into the Palazzo Vecchio. Woodhull knelt beside the dog on the steps of the Loggia dei Lanzi. The dog looked calm. The girl too. Woodhull had the Frisbee in his left hand. It had gone fine when they'd rehearsed yesterday.

It was time. "Quiet, please," Bevilacqua yelled through his megaphone, in English and then in Italian: "*Silenzio, per favore. We're going for a take!*" It took about thirty seconds for the piazza to quiet down. Most of the tourists were staring up at the crane. "Please don't look at the crane," Bevilacqua yelled. "Just go about your business," and then he yelled, "Roll sound" to the production recordist, who yelled, "Sound rolling, and then, "Sound speed."

The camera assistant, up on the crane, held the slate in front of the camera.

The camera operator, sitting next to Michael, yelled, "Framed."

Bevilacqua yelled, "Roll camera." The camera operator started the camera and yelled, "Rolling," and then, after a moment, "Speed."

Bevilacqua took a deep breath and yelled, "Slate it!" The camera assistant said, "*The Italian Lover,* scene 109, take 1—Mark!" and clapped the slate. Michael put his hand over his heart. He'd been expecting the worst, but everything started smoothly. As planned. The camera followed Miranda from the north side of the Palazzo Vecchio to the side of the fountain, where she stopped to adjust her shoe—unscripted, but a nice bit of business—and then to the Loggia dei Lanzi. Zanni followed and soon appeared behind her, in front of the statue of Perseus. She climbed the stairs and turned toward the piazza. Woodhull tossed the Frisbee and released the dog, Biscotti. The dog started to run across the piazza after the Frisbee, and the girl chased after the dog. The dog kept running, and the girl kept chasing her. Michael willed the girl to keep chasing, otherwise the dog would stop and run to her.

The camera followed the dog till it was time for Zanni to yell, "Down, down." Zanni yelled, or rather, Woodhull yelled: "*Stai, stai, stai Biscotti.*" They'd dub in Zanni's voice later. The dog stopped. Perfect. But then a second dog appeared, a big German shepherd, and Michael's heart sank. "Stay on the principals," he said to the camera operator, but it was too late. The camera was already tracking the dogs. Michael started to say "Cut" but couldn't get the word out. The dogs stopped, circled each other, sniffed each other's butts. Michael watched them on the videotape and then over the edge of the crane. The camera stayed on the dogs. The extras were watching the dogs. Everyone in the piazza was watching the dogs. The camera operator was on his own now. The dogs continued to circle and sniff butt.

Where was Woodhull? What was the girl doing? The camera panned back to Miranda and Zanni. They were laughing. They walked across the piazza together. Toward the bar. Zanni opened the door for Miranda. They disappeared into the bar.

Michael yelled, "Cut."

They had time for four more takes before their permit expired—takes without the mysterious German shepherd, whose owner had appeared, dragging the dog's leash.

"Boom down," Michael said into his walkie-talkie. Below him he could see Esther passing out release forms to some of the extras who'd arrived late. Beryl had disappeared. So had Woodhull and the dog. Zanni and Miranda were standing in front of the bar. Everyone was looking up at the crane.

The boom didn't move. Michael looked over the edge. The crane operator was looking up. "Boom down," Michael said again into his walkie-talkie. The crane operator turned to one of the grips. Esther was there now.

"What's going on?" the camera operator asked Michael. The camera operator and the focus puller were both looking down too. The grips were scurrying around.

"This doesn't look good," the camera operator said.

"What's going on?" Michael asked into the walkie-talkie.

This time Esther answered. "Something's wrong with the crane."

"Well, get it fixed."

"Just sit tight." *How could he sit tight?*

Esther said. "I'll let you talk to Guido. The dolly grip."

"Hello?"

"Hello? Guido? What's going on?"

"Could be a lot of things. Maybe something caught in the gears."

"What are you going to do?"

"Can you see me?"

Michael looked over the edge. "Yes." He could feel his godlike powers ebbing. He was getting dizzy from looking down. He closed his eyes, but that only made it worse. "What the hell is going on?" he shouted over the edge, not bothering with his walkie-talkie.

Everyone in the piazza—cast, crew, tourists, extras—was watching, staring up at him. "Go about your business," he wanted to shout, but there was nothing he could do. Beryl reappeared. She was looking up at him too. He avoided her gaze. Soon he heard a shout.

"The pivot point's jammed," Guido shouted.

Michael nodded.

"You see this box at the end of the beam? That's what holds the counterweights. That's why we had to weigh everyone, so it balances just right — the turret at one end, the counterweight at the other."

"But what are you going to do?"

"I'm going to walk up the beam till I add enough weight to bring it down."

Michael watched as Guido removed his tool kit and his jacket and climbed up on the weight box and then onto the beam itself. Holding onto the outer edges of the beam he started to climb, like a monkey climbing a coconut tree. Michael closed his eyes and waited till he felt the floor start to sink beneath him, like a slow elevator. When he opened his eyes, Guido had almost reached the turret.

When the boom finally came down, Michael tried not to show how happy he was to be back on terra firma, with his big scene in the can. But it was only when he saw the rushes in the morning that he realized what a gift he had been given. The dogs had said all that was necessary. Dialogue would be superfluous. *No, not a gift,* he thought, *a reward.* He hadn't spoken to Beryl, hadn't warned her what a dangerous course she was about to embark on. It wasn't that he didn't care; it wasn't that he wasn't jealous. He didn't know what it was. Two roads were diverging in a yellow wood. He was taking one; she was taking the other.

Cheval Glass

When Michael arrived on set at seven o'clock to go over the sequence with the director of photography and the production manager, the grips were hanging lights and mounting the camera on a crab dolly. He was excited; he was thinking on his feet, taking risks; he was cutting in camera with only a few additional angles for coverage. It was like working a high wire without a safety net. He'd been awake most of the night, rehearsing the scene in his imagination. It would be so much simpler if he didn't want the over-the-shoulder mirror shot requiring body doubles. But he did want it, wanted to bring the viewer into the scene, wanted the viewer to be standing right behind Zanni, looking at Miranda in the mirror as her clothes come off.

They were filming at one end of the long chapel, which had been divided into three sets: Sandro's bedroom, his living room, and the Lodovici Chapel at the Badia, where Sandro restores the fresco. Sandro's bedroom consisted of two semipermanent walls and a backing for the reflections in the mirror. The set was almost bare—just the cheval glass and the double bed, a *matrimoniale*. And a big Italian wardrobe, the door partly open, which the production designer had filled with Sandro's clothes. And he could see the camera already mounted on the dolly, which had an extra seat for the camera assistant, and the dolly tracks and the cables coiling like snakes, and the Chinese lights in the corners, rigged on C-stands.

When Miranda and Zanni arrived from Makeup, he went over the shot with them. The choreography for the two-shot sequence was simple enough for the actors, and he didn't want to put them through another rehearsal. He did remind them, though, that they've been looking at the Aretino pictures together and have been carried away, like Paolo and Francesca in *The Divine Comedy*. Now they're in Sandro's bedroom. He didn't want them to carry around too much information or to think more than two or three shots ahead. Zanni was never a problem, but Michael didn't need Esther to tell him that Miranda seemed a little shaky. Twitchy. But she told him anyway.

By nine thirty the scene was falling into place, and Michael was anxious to expose some film. The lighting stand-ins came on. The DP, still worrying about the sight lines, kept repositioning the cheval glass and the stand-ins and telling the grips to rebalance the flags and the lights. The continuity girl was trying to make herself invisible. The set was closed, but Gordon Talbot, a suit from Leviathan, had bullied his way in. Michael didn't need Gordon on the set, telling the grips what to do, giving advice to the DP on how to tweak the cheval glass, but there he was.

Michael ran through a camera rehearsal with stand-ins. The sequence was simple enough for the actors, but the camera moves were tricky. The dolly grip and the camera operator would have to tie several complex moves together. What Michael had in mind looked like this:

144. INT. SANDRO'S BEDROOM—AFTERNOON

CU. SANDRO is looking over MARGOT's shoulder

CAMERA PULLS BACK to reveal beveled edge of cheval glass, then the back of SANDRO's head (BODY DOUBLE's head) as he looks over MARGOT's (BODY DOUBLE's) shoulder. Behind the cheval glass is a double bed and a wardrobe with the door partway open, revealing clothes inside. CAMERA looks over the shoulders of the BODY DOUBLES at the reflection of MARGOT and SANDRO in the cheval glass. Margot is wearing jeans and a man's white shirt. Sandro is elegant in a camel hair sport coat, a white shirt, and a yellow tie.

SANDRO
The mousy librarian. (laughs)

MARGOT
It's book conservator, not librarian.

Sandro takes off his coat, rolls up his sleeves, reaches around Margot and unbuttons her blouse. He tosses her blouse on the floor and unhooks her bra. He drops the bra on the floor and begins to remove his tie. Margot leans forward and points at the three goddesses on the frame of the cheval glass.

> **MARGOT**
> Which one would you choose?

> **SANDRO**
> I would choose you.

Sandro pulls down her underpants slowly.

CUT TO:

145. INT. SANDRO'S BEDROOM—MOMENTS LATER

PROFILE TWO-SHOT. SANDRO and MARGOT face each other in front of the cheval glass, which is to their left. (No reflection.) The body doubles are gone. Margot steps out of her underpants and walks out of the frame. THE DOLLY CRABS LEFT 5 FEET, AND THE CAMERA PANS RIGHT TO THE BED. Margot walks back into the frame, crosses the room, and sits down on the edge of the bed and then lies down. THE CAMERA WATCHES MARGOT, as if Sandro were watching her, THEN DOLLIES FORWARD, TILTS, AND BOOMS DOWN FOR AN ECU OF MARGOT'S FACE. Margot looks up at the camera and smiles.

For the U.S. release, Michael will cut away, when Sandro pulls down Margot's underpants, to the three goddesses on the cheval glass. And he'll cut away again, this time to the bed, when she walks out of the frame. European audiences will get seven seconds of Margot as naked as Eve before the Fall. U.S. audiences will get about one second.

Michael won't need much coverage—medium profile two-shots of Margot and Sandro standing in front of the mirror, a cutaway to the three goddesses on the frame of the cheval glass, a cutaway of the bed. *Basta.*

When an actress is in love with her costar, her most honest, truest, deepest self emerges, especially after they start shooting. Miranda could feel this happening, could feel her Margot-self emerging. Zanni brought out the best in her. He always seemed to be improvising, acting without a script, and at the same time he always hit his marks, he was always in his light, he always knew his lines, and he always looked her in the eye. And she responded in kind, staying in the moment, leaving herself open, turning herself inside out.

But it wasn't till the café scene that she felt she'd been properly seduced, seduced at least a dozen times in a single scene, acknowledged by her costar not simply as a character but as her real self. Michael got his master shot in four takes and Zanni's close-ups in four, but he made Miranda do take after take. On each take Zanni—off camera—would look deep into her eyes and smile and surprise her as they talked nonsense about the Anglo-Saxon love of Italy, and every time he looked at her and smiled her insides turned to jelly.

She didn't sleep the night before the cheval glass scene, but she wasn't tired. She was very excited and trying not to show it.

"What is it about librarians?" Zanni asked, coming up behind her.

"Book conservators," Miranda said.

"They're so easily transformed into radiant beauties."

She wished that he would touch her. Put his hand on her shoulder.

"All they have to do," Zanni went on, "is take off their glasses and let down their hair."

"I'm not wearing glasses," she said, but she could feel what he meant. Her hairdo—up in a bun—couldn't hide her beauty. Makeup, continuing to fuss with her face as the DP waved his light meter around, couldn't tone it down, couldn't stop her eyes from shining, her lips from swelling, as if for a kiss. But at the same time, she wasn't thinking about her beauty, wasn't worrying about which was her good side, or about keeping her chin up, or moving two inches to the right or to the left.

"You look very handsome yourself," she said. "I hope Michael knows what he's doing." Michael and the DP were fussing with the cheval glass.

Zanni laughed, elegant in his camel hair jacket and a bright yellow tie with tiny ivory dots in it that shimmered. "I see we have company," he said.

The set was closed. They were down to essential crew, but there were still a dozen people milling around—the camera operator and the focus puller, and the assistant director, and one of the Italian grips, who'd had his head shaved for the mirror shot, so that from the back his new bald spot matched Zanni's. And there was a studio exec on the set, making a lot of noise.

"Let him look," Miranda said. "You can tell he's a pain by the way he keeps getting in everyone's way."

The DP was positioning the stand-ins and the body doubles,

and the studio exec kept looking over their shoulders and making suggestions.

When the DP was finally satisfied, Michael called the actors to their marks and Miranda, still clutching her robe, took her position facing the cheval glass, but off to one side. Zanni stood behind her, looking over her shoulder. The body doubles—an American PA and the Italian *macchinista*—stood to their left, the *macchinista* behind the PA. Behind the *macchinista*, Miranda could see the eye of the camera, which would catch the body doubles from behind as it looked into the cheval glass, where it would see the reflections of Miranda and Zanni.

When Makeup was finally satisfied with her face, Miranda took off her robe and handed it to Wardrobe. She was down to bra and sensible white underpants. A lot of thought had gone into those underpants: bikini versus "sensible." Michael thought that in this case "sensible" was actually sexier than bikini. More down-to-earth.

The last thing she heard before the AD called for quiet on the set was the voice of Gordon Talbot, the studio exec: "Nice heinie."

"Motor. Roll 'em."

The camera assistant held up the slate.

Behind her Miranda could hear the camera running. In the mirror she saw not her own reflection but the reflection of the American PA and, looking over her shoulder, the face of the *macchinista* who was doubling for Zanni, and over the shoulder of the *macchinista*, the camera itself.

Zanni, standing behind Miranda, removed his jacket and dropped it on the floor. The *macchinista* mirrored him, removing an identical jacket and dropping it on the floor. Zanni rolled up his sleeves. The *macchinista* did the same. In rehearsal he'd had trouble figuring out which arm to start with.

Miranda felt rigid, but that was okay.

Zanni and the *macchinista* rolled up their sleeves. Zanni bent to kiss her neck. The *macchinista* bent to kiss the PA's neck. As Zanni unhooked her bra, the *macchinista* pretended to unhook the PA's bra. Miranda's bra fell to the floor.

Miranda was supposed to point at the three naked goddesses on the cheval glass and say, which one would you choose?, but she couldn't move her arm. She was buried up to her neck in wet sand. She couldn't speak. Finally she managed to croak: "I can't move my arm."

Before Michael yelled "Cut" she'd broken free, started to run, out into the corridor, down the long hallway, past boxes and cables and lighting equipment, past a row of Chinese lamps, past the soundman, past Wardrobe, past the production office, out into the cloister, and then back into the convent through a different door and down another corridor till she came to the bathroom opposite the door to the refectory. WC it said on the door. She took her pants down and sat on the bidet and waited three or four minutes for a knock on the door and the sound of the door opening.

"Are you all right?" It was Michael.

She didn't answer him.

"We're waiting."

"I know."

"Do you remember our discussion about being temperamental?"

"I'm not being temperamental."

"You're holding everything up. We've got to get this shot this morning before we break for lunch."

"I can't help it."

"May I come in?"

"I don't care."

Michael's face appeared around the corner. "That's a bidet," he said when he saw her, "not a toilet."

"I know what a bidet is."

"Then—never mind. This is a romantic comedy. We're supposed to be having fun."

"What's that supposed to mean?"

"You've got to figure out a better objective, so you'll have something to work with."

"My objective is that I don't want to be there."

"Not wanting to be there is never a good choice for an actor. It's not very interesting. Just think a minute. Relax. Why are you there? In this man's bedroom?"

"Because it's in the script."

"Miranda, you know that's an even worse choice. You're there because you're attracted to this man. You're there because you don't want to be afraid of sex all your life."

"I'm not afraid of sex."

"I'm talking about Margot, not you personally, okay? I'm talking about the choices you need to make to play this scene. Okay? Which choices give you more to work with? You're disgusted and just want to be somewhere else, or you're afraid because you've never been to this place before, but you're also attracted because you've never been to this place before."

"I'm not disgusted. That's not it. I have been to this place before. You don't understand. I just freaked out, that's all."

"I do understand," Michael said. "It's an ordeal, taking your clothes off in front of the cast and the crew. And knowing you'll have to do it again and again. You don't have the exhibitionist tendency that some actresses have that gets them through it. You need a strong director to look out for you. I'm sorry if I haven't been that director. But at least I got Gordon off the set. I told him I wouldn't expose another inch of film till he was gone. He had no business talking like that."

"Michael, it's not your fault."

"What I want you to do," Michael said, "is dig down and discover something about yourself and reveal that something to the audience, something strong and sexy and life affirming that you've never revealed to anyone before because you didn't know about it yourself."

The door opened. It was Esther. "Get your butt out there. Goddamn it, Miranda, you're not fucking Sigourney Weaver or Melanie Griffith. You can't get away with this. I want you to deliver the scene. Do you want me to get your contract out and read it to you? If you're not out there and on your mark in two minutes, this will be your last film. Here, I've brought your robe."

Miranda knew that she meant it. "Okay," she said. "I'm all right now."

They did a dozen takes, and the first three or four times Zanni pulled down her underpants she started to panic again, but after another couple of takes she started to feel comfortable. Her head started to spin, as if she'd drunk just a little too much wine. She could feel the male energy in the room focused on her, like sunlight brought into a smoldering focus by a magnifying glass. She started digging deeper on each take, deeper and deeper, till finally she discovered what she'd been looking for all along, something strong and sexy and life affirming that she hadn't even known was there. She could feel it coming up from deep within her, like an orgasm, rising to her face like a blush as the camera dollied in, tilted, and boomed down for an ECU.

Cut. Print.

Before leaving the set, she picked up Zanni's tie, which was still lying on the floor in front of the cheval glass. Always alert for instances of synchronicity, she saw the tie as a sign. She was too churned up for lunch, but she drank a glass of wine. Back in her room, she threaded the tie through her underpants and pulled it back and forth between her legs.

Zanni always took a little nap after lunch when he didn't have to be on the set. She gave him a few minutes to get settled, but not enough time to go to sleep, and then she took the tie to his room on the fourth floor—the third floor, the way the Italians counted. They were both free that afternoon.

She had done everything she was supposed to do. She had visualized Zanni opening the door and smiling at her; she'd banished all negativity and opened herself to the unexpected. Even so, she was a little nervous.

He didn't answer the door at first. She knocked again. It hadn't occurred to her that he might not be there. She kept knocking and knocking, not knowing what else to do, till he opened the door, and she smelled a woman's perfume, and she wondered why Zanni would be wearing perfume and suddenly everything became clear.

"Sorry," she said, handing him his tie. "You left this on the set."

"*Mille grazie*," he said. "You were terrific this morning." He closed the door.

She went down to the lobby and sat in an armchair and waited. She couldn't find a clock and had to keep asking the desk clerk for the time. What did it all mean? What about her smile at the end, looking straight into the lens of the camera? And she still had the cunnilingus scene to go through, and fourteen other "pleasures." She didn't know how she could do it. She did *not* know.

She'd done the right thing when she'd run away. She was proud of herself for running because it showed she was sensitive and vulnerable, not one of those actresses with an exhibitionist streak. *Nice heinie.* It was so disgusting.

How could she have been so wrong about Zanni? How could she have misread all the signs? Probably everyone else knew he was involved with another woman, so she'd made a fool of herself. That's what hurt.

She went back to her room, got Woody's copy of *Anna Karenina,* took it down to the lobby and settled into a wingback chair to read. Who was she now? All along she'd been thinking of herself as Anna, but in fact she was poor little Kitty, jilted by Vronsky.

What was she trying to accomplish right now by waiting in the lobby? Did she really want to know who would come down? Who could it be? Alessandra Martelli, the woman who played the abbess? But then Alessandra entered the lobby from Via Porta Rossa and stopped to chat for a minute. What was she going to do or say when the woman emerged? Would she be alone or with Zanni? Miranda couldn't imagine what she'd say, but she knew she'd say something.

About an hour and a half later, Beryl Gardiner emerged from the door to the stairs, a black winter coat over her arm, her hair pulled back tight on her head, like a French woman's. She was wearing a simple black sheath, with pearls and classy pumps that gave her a well-balanced, put-together look. They didn't have women like Beryl in Mount Pleasant, but Miranda recognized the type. Beryl was a Smithie, the kind of woman her mother had wanted her to become.

Miranda didn't put two and two together—Beryl had to be in

her fifties, maybe even sixty—till she caught a whiff of the perfume.

"Why, hello, Miranda," Beryl said, slipping on her winter coat as if nothing had happened. "Do you want a *caffè?*"

Miranda nodded. Didn't Beryl realize that it had been Miranda knocking on the door?

"There's a nice bar behind the post office," Beryl said. "It's just around the corner. You won't need a coat."

Miranda nodded again and followed Beryl out of the hotel onto Via Porta Rossa.

In the bar, Beryl motioned Miranda to a table and stood chatting a bit in Italian with the barista while he pulled two espressos. Miranda would have preferred a glass of wine, but it was too late. Or a whiskey. There were whiskey bottles in all the bars, but she never saw anyone drinking whiskey.

Beryl brought the coffees to the table. "Do they still do those nude posture pictures at Smith?" she asked.

"How did you know I went to Smith?"

"It's in your bio."

"Oh," Miranda said.

"I'm class of fifty-eight," Beryl said. "The posture photos were the high point of orientation when I was there. *All right, Banks, drop the sheet.* Banks was my maiden name. I don't think anyone had ever seen me naked before, not since I was a baby. Things were different then. I wound up with a C− for posture and had to take Basic Motor Skills—how to walk gracefully, how to sit down properly, how to lift a suitcase up to an overhead rack on a train without losing your balance, how to put on your coat without twisting around too much. And how to gallop. And I don't mean on a horse. That was the worst. I don't suppose they teach that anymore."

"Those posture pictures," Miranda said. "They turned out to

be a hoax. Somebody at Harvard claimed to be doing anthropological research."

"What did they do with the photos? When I was there everyone was afraid that the boys from Amherst would break into the gym and get their hands on them."

"No idea."

Beryl had finished her coffee. Miranda looked into her cup. She still had a sip left.

"I'm going to give a talk next week," Beryl said, "to the Smith students on the Junior Year Abroad Program. The office is right around the corner, in Piazza Repubblica. Maybe you'd like to come along. I'm surprised they didn't ask *you*, in fact. I'm just somebody's wife, but you're an actress."

Miranda couldn't tell if Beryl was serious or if she was making fun of her. "To Virtue, Knowledge," Miranda said, the Smith motto. "What the hell does that *mean*? I hated Smith," she went on. "Every minute of it. I hated Lawrence House; I hated House Meetings and House Inspections and Quiet Hours and the Honor System, and all the talk about *gracious living,* and the Harvard book bags, and the Ivy League scarves, and Mountain Day. I didn't graduate, but you must know that if you read my bio."

"Well," Beryl said, smiling, "I take it that's a no."

Miranda didn't say anything.

"Miranda," Beryl said, "how old are you?"

"Twenty-nine. I mean, I just turned thirty."

"There are still some things you don't understand about life."

Miranda started to disagree, started to say that she understood, all right; but before she opened her mouth, she decided that Beryl was right.

That night Miranda wanted to eat by herself. She sat at a table in a back corner in Trattoria la Maremmana, behind the table of antipasti, and the waiter, who recognized her but who treated her as if she were a civilian, rather than a movie star—which she appreciated—brought a basket of the kind of Florentine bread that needed salt and a large bottle of red wine and told her, in English, to enjoy. She wasn't in a mood to enjoy, but she poured a large glass of wine. They would charge her by how much she drank. She wasn't hungry either, just restless, wanting to blot out the day, the humiliation, everyone except her and Michael knowing about Zanni's affair with Beryl, her humiliating encounter with Beryl. This wasn't the script she'd been visualizing.

And the smile. She couldn't forgive herself for the stupid smile she'd let loose at the camera at the end of the shot. She was like Oblonsky, smiling a stupid smile at his wife after he's been caught having an affair with the French governess. Well, maybe she wasn't like Oblonsky, but she'd caught the eye of the dolly grip as he was cranking the camera in tight for a close-up of her face, and he'd smiled, and then she couldn't stop herself.

She poured herself some more wine and ate a piece of the Florentine salt-free bread. She drank more wine and ate more bread and tried to order a *tris*—three different kinds of pasta— but the waiter said you had to have three people to order a *tris*, so she ordered the *lasagna al forno* and drank more wine and at some point she was joined by Esther and the studio exec from Leviathan, the one who'd said "nice heinie," the one who'd been kicked off the set. Gordon.

Esther and Gordon were both really excited about the dailies, and Miranda started to feel better. They all had dessert, and afterward Esther tried to talk her into going back to the hotel, but she wasn't ready to go back because Gordon, who kept pouring more grappa from the bottle the waiter had brought to the table, kept talking about how her career was about to take off and how he was definitely going to make some things happen for her.

By the time they left the restaurant, she was too drunk to walk. Gordon asked the waiter to call a taxi. She fell asleep in the back of the taxi, and when she woke up she was in the lobby of the Excelsior. There was a party. People were all dressed up. Someone was playing a piano, and Gordon was saying, "You're the star. I can't understand why Esther didn't put you up here." And then he was steering her toward the elevator, but she was pulling away from him. She broke loose and plopped herself down in an oversize chair. The lobby started to spin as she curled up in the chair. She couldn't get it to stop, and she couldn't figure out how she'd almost let Gordon Talbot into her life.

Settignano

A dreary Saturday morning. Margot, whose bid on the Galileo codex had not been accepted, sat on a wooden stool at her workbench in her *studio* paging through a copy of the shooting script of *The Sixteen Pleasures* that Miranda had brought her.

"What I have to do now," Miranda was saying, "is detach myself from the outcome." Margot nodded. "But I shouldn't *have* to detach myself from the outcome because the outcome should have been different. What's the point of visualizing an outcome in the first place if you're going to have to detach yourself from it at the end?"

"How about a cup of tea?" Margot asked.

"I don't know what I was thinking."

"It's called puppy love," Margot said. "That's what my mother used to say when I fell in love with one of my teachers."

"I'm too old for puppy love," Miranda said. "Besides, the man's a total jerk. I don't know what I saw in him anyway."

"He's a lovely man, Miranda."

"How could he be having an affair with Beryl Gardiner? She must be in her fifties!"

"*I'm* in my fifties," Margot said.

"Sorry."

"It's all right."

"And she's the director's wife."

"That makes it awkward."

"It's unprofessional."

"I'm sure it is," Margot said.

"And I still have to do the cunnilingus scene."

"Just lie back and think of England," Margot said.

"What's that supposed to mean?"

Margot didn't explain. Miranda was preparing for the conservation scenes in the movie, which were going to be shot in Margot's *studio.* Margot was helping her assemble the dummy book that was going to serve as the Aretino volume.

"How much of the Aretino restoration will they actually film?" Margot asked.

"They'll probably do mostly medium shots," Miranda said, "with a few cutaways to show the results. I'll do some of the sewing, but I'll just pretend to do the gold tooling, like Helena Bonham Carter pretending to play the piano in *A Room with a View.* But it isn't *just* pretending. It's important for me to really understand what I'm doing."

Margot didn't comment. The kettle on the stove in the staff kitchen had started to whistle, and she poured boiling water into two cups. She was anxious to finish reading the script, but she wanted to conceal her anxiety from Miranda.

The plan was to sew the dummy book on two half-inch linen tapes that Miranda had already attached to a sewing frame. When they were finished, they'd glue the tapes to the covering boards to attach the text block securely. They'd already marked up and pierced the signatures, and Margot was demonstrating to Miranda how to weave the needle up and back through two sections at a time.

"I know how to do the kettle stitch," Miranda said. "That's the stitch you taught the nuns in *The Sixteen Pleasures*. There's a whole chapter on sewing up in my book on hand bookbinding."

"Just don't pull the thread too tight," Margot said.

"My mother taught me to sew," Miranda said.

Margot had been trying to get a copy of the script from Esther for several weeks, but Esther kept making excuses, and now Margot knew why. The shooting script didn't look anything like the screenplay she and Woody had written. She'd known that Esther had tweaked it, and she'd braced herself for changes and thought she would be ready, but she wasn't prepared for the extent of the damage, just as she hadn't been prepared for the extent of the damage caused by the flood when she'd come to Florence in November 1966.

Two pages into the script and it was clear that there was no flood, and it soon became clear that someone had moved the Newberry Library from Chicago to New York, and that her father was an alcoholic blues musician and her mother a coldhearted bitch who cheated on her husband and drove him to drink.

It took Margot two hours to read the script. Miranda had sewn about two-thirds of the signatures of the dummy book. Margot sat at her workbench with her head in her hands. Instead of making her own way in the world and finding herself, at the end, in the place where she wanted to be, in Piazza Santa Croce, Movie Margot was going to marry Sandro, who'd rescued her from the Vatican Police.

Margot was thinking about love, about how she'd waited for the real Sandro Postiglione to propose, and about how he hadn't, and about how difficult it is to see clearly when you're in love.

Especially with an Italian man. Like Sandro, or Zanni, or Bruno Bruni. What had her mother seen, she wondered, when she'd fallen in love with Bruni? Her father had gone to see Bruni, alone, when he'd stopped to visit Margot on his way to India, but he'd never told Margot what they'd talked about. Whatever it was, he'd been happy to have Helen back home again, and Margot didn't think that he ever held the affair with Bruni against her, didn't think they'd ever been so solid as they were at the end, when her mother was dying. He hadn't fallen apart. He'd been strong. He'd held the family together.

Margot thought that this was the kind of love she wanted and that this was the kind of love Woody offered. Woody had asked if she'd marry him, and she'd said, "In two shakes." But he wanted her to go back to the States with him. The dog too. Not to Chicago, but to St. Clair, a small town in the middle of nowhere, and she didn't think she could do it, didn't think she could leave this city where she still met her mother on every street corner, at every *angolo,* in every museum, every theater, every piazza, even though she'd resisted her mother's lectures and the enforced trips to the museums; even though she'd refused to speak Italian at home, in the beautiful apartment that Signor Bruni had found for them. Now every memory seemed precious: how her mother had ordered *bollito misto* at a fancy restaurant in Siena and was served a plain chunk of boiled turkey breast with no sauce; how one night they were going to take the bus up to Piazzale Michelangelo, but when a number-23 bus pulled up to the stop on Via Verdi just as they were walking by they took it. It was dark and the bus went a long way. They were going to ride to the end of the line and then ride back, but when they got to the end of the line, the driver told them to get off. The bus wasn't going back into the city. This was it. They had to get off the bus. It was an industrial area. There were no people around. Mama finally flagged down a car and asked Margot to talk to the driver. She explained what had happened. The driver laughed, and his girlfriend laughed too, and they gave Margot and her mother a ride back into town. And afterward her mother was very proud of her. They never figured out where they'd been because the *capolinea* of the number-23 bus is off the edge of all the maps.

In the afternoon it was still raining—the skies were gray; the river was gray. But Margot had one of the big green umbrellas from San Gimignagno, and she and Miranda walked to the bus stop on Via Panzani and took the number-10 bus up to Settignano, so that Miranda could see the Casa del Popolo and the little cemetery. Margot was still upset about the screenplay. "My father played the blues," she said, "but he was an avocado broker, not a broken-down alcoholic bluesman. And my mother had an affair with Bruno Bruni, but she wasn't trash. It doesn't make any sense. And in the end, I turn my life over to Sandro. We're going to get married and be poor but happy! It's unforgivable. If Esther liked the book so much, why didn't she stick to the story? I mean . . ."

"I know what you mean. That's the way I felt."

"Then why did you take the part?"

"I blew up at them. Believe me. At Michael and Esther. At the audition. I really gave them hell. I thought I'd blown everything, but they liked it. They called my agent the next morning. They thought I had spunk."

Margot could have pointed out that Miranda hadn't answered her question, but she didn't.

"They always change things," Miranda said. "It's part of the culture. You should talk to Esther. They can only imagine one kind of ending."

"I don't think I'll be able to speak to that woman again."

It had stopped raining by the time they got to Settignano. "You can't see the city from here," Miranda complained as they drank a glass of wine in the Casa del Popolo.

"So I fudged a little," Margot said.

"Like you did with the statue of Dante, putting it in the middle of the piazza?"

"That was just a simple mistake."

"But looking down on the city from this place?"

"Well, I liked the idea of looking down on the city."

"That's what moviemakers do. They go with what they like. What else did you fudge?"

"Oh, heavens, I have no idea."

"Sandro undressing you in front of the cheval glass?"

"No, that was the real thing."

At the little cemetery on the edge of the town, they located Bruno Bruni's grave, and Miranda studied the photo on the tombstone. Margot remembered him from when she was fifteen, when he'd been her mother's lover, though she hadn't known it at the time. He'd helped her with her schoolwork, and later in life she'd known him socially—if he saw her in a restaurant he'd stop at her table to have a word. But she'd never talked to her mother about him or to him about her mother. And then one morning she'd read in *La Repubblica* that he was dead, and she'd gone to the funeral, at the little church in Settignano. The priest, she learned, was Bruno's brother, and she wondered what he could possibly say about this man.

What he said was this: "My brother was a man who loved life. He was always happy. Everyone loved him. When you were with him, you were happy too. It was a gift from God, this happiness, a sign that God wants us to be happy. When he came into a room, everyone was glad. The party was a success. All awkwardness, all reserve, would disappear. People would begin to open their hearts to each other in his presence. When we were boys . . . ," and he went on to reminisce about their childhood in Settignano, how they had climbed the cave walls in Maiano and found an underground passage.

This was as close as Margot ever came to the mystery of Bruno Bruni.

He'd died on August fifth, four days after her birthday. Nineteen eighty-one or eighty-two. She couldn't remember. It had been hot, and the church had been full of flowers and full of people, but of course Bruni had known everyone. But who were all the women, she'd wondered, some of them clearly American? And who was the woman glowering at her from the pew on the opposite side of the church?

After the funeral, the glowering woman came up to her and said, "You're very beautiful—I can see why Sandro was so fond of you. Now how about getting out of my apartment so I can sell it?"

Beautiful. It was the first time a woman had ever called her beautiful, and she was pleased. But she was conscious of being in the wrong too. Sandro had said she could stay in the apartment after he went back to Rome, to his wife, but it was not really his apartment to dispose of. It was hers. She came from a rich banking family and could have afforded to let Margot stay in the apartment, but instead she sent lots of letters and even telegrams. She had the phone cut off. But Italian laws make it very difficult to evict a squatter, even a foreign squatter.

"You're Sandro's wife?" Margot said.

"Yes."

"Are you going to the cemetery?" Margot asked.

"Did you sleep with Bruni *too?*" she asked back.

"No," Margot said, "but my mother did. Years ago. We spent a year in Florence when I was fifteen."

"He was an unusual man. Did you notice all the women at the funeral? It was almost all women."

"And you?"

"Bruno and I were old friends."

"I thought you'd given up on the apartment," Margot said.

"To tell you the truth, I'd sort of forgotten about it, but when I saw you sitting there, I had to say something."

"How did you know who I was?"

"Sandro kept a picture."

"Really? I mean, I can see how it would rub you the wrong way."

"Do you want to walk to the cemetery?"

"Treviso?"

"No, no. He's being buried right here, in Settignano."

"*That* cemetery? I thought it was full."

"A man like Bruni," she said, "there's always a table for him at a restaurant that's booked solid, always a room at a hotel, an extra seat on the plane. Why not an extra plot in the cemetery?"

"I'm sorry about Sandro," Margot said. "I never sent a card. I didn't know what to do."

"It's all right," she said. "He was a good lover but a bad man."

"No, no," Margot protested.

They walked to the cemetery, at the end of the procession that followed the coffin, which was trundled along on a kind of gurney. Margot was thinking about her mother. How they'd always been surprised when the little cemetery came into view at the end of their walk. They'd stand at the wall and look down. The cemetery was always full of flowers. Signora Postiglione, Margot thought, was very beautiful. Younger than Sandro but older than Margot. Her name was Francesca.

Margot and Francesca stood at the wall and looked down as Bruni was lowered into the ground. They stood where Margot and her mother used to stand, where Margot and Miranda were standing now.

The weather had improved. "We could walk to Fiesole," Miranda suggested. "We could see the field full of flowers."

"It's wet," Margot said.

"I don't mind. Besides, we're both wearing sensible shoes."

Margot looked down at her feet, as if to make sure.

"I've never walked it backward," Margot said. "I've always started in Fiesole."

"It will be a new experience. Do you think you can find the way?"

"I'm not sure I can find the field full of flowers, but we can't get too lost."

Margot didn't tell Miranda about Francesca. There were some things she wanted to keep to herself. Francesca was dead too, now, but she'd left Margot a life interest in the apartment in Santa Croce. Her brothers had tried unsuccessfully to break the will.

They found the field full of flowers, where Julian Sands kisses Helena Bonham Carter in *A Room with a View*. The scene was hardly recognizable in winter, except for the little shed in the back of the field. And then they went on to the lane where the carriage scene had been filmed.

"The carriage driver, Lucca Rossi, still drives a cab—a horse cab—in the city, you know," Margot said. "I met him at a wedding reception in Palazzo Vecchio."

"He was so handsome. And so dangerous looking."

"Maybe I'll introduce you, but he doesn't speak English. You'd have to work on your Italian, but that might be a good thing."

Walking the familiar path backward, as if they were walking into the past, Margot felt that she was growing younger with each step, walking backward into childhood innocence, backward into a time before this time, before Francesca, before her father's death in India, before Sandro, before the flood, before her mother's death in Chicago, till by the time they got to the outskirts of Fiesole she was a young girl again and her adventure was just beginning. But they met an old couple setting out on their own walk, and Margot realized she had the wrong metaphor.

"Did you see the way they smiled at us?" she said to Miranda. "They thought we were mother and daughter."

Our Town

Wednesday evening. Woody and Biscotti waited in the lobby of Albergo Porta Rossa for Miranda to come down. The drama club at the American Academy was putting on a performance of *Our Town,* and the students had persuaded Woody to ask Miranda to come to one of the rehearsals. Woody was afraid she might not show. Margot had told him the whole story—how Miranda had been expecting Zanni to seduce her and then had discovered Beryl Gardiner in Zanni's hotel room—but had sworn him to secrecy.

He looked up when he heard the elevator door open and took in the tragic expression on Miranda's face just as it gave way to a wan smile. She was Cookie's age, the age Cookie would be if she hadn't been killed, and his heart went out to her. He thought that an affair with a man like Zanni would have been a good experience for her, but he couldn't help thinking that being passed over by a man like Zanni might be an even better experience. "I appreciate your doing this," he said. "The students are very excited."

They left the hotel and walked down Via Porta Rossa toward Piazza Repubblica. "I have no idea what I'm supposed to do tonight," Miranda said as they passed under the fake triumphal arch and entered the piazza, "and no desire to do it."

The piazza was brightly lit and they had to pass through a crowd of children waiting to ride a merry-go-round that had been up since Christmas.

"For heaven's sake, Miranda," Woody said, "you played Emily when you were in high school. What can go wrong? It's just a bunch of students. Good students too. That makes it easy— Emily's from San Francisco; the Stage Manager's an Italian. George is an Iranian. Mr. Webb's from Hamburg, and Mrs. Webb is an Italian."

Miranda thought for a minute. "It's hard to imagine Grover's Corners peopled by Italians, Germans, and Middle Easterners. How can they possibly understand *Our Town?*"

"The same way anybody understands anything," Woody said. "Isn't that the purpose of art? To see through others' eyes?"

"I can never win an argument with you," she said.

Biscotti tugged on the leash and squatted. They waited for her to pee.

"I wasn't arguing," Woody said, stooping to pat the dog's head; "I was explaining."

The Drama Club met in a small theater—Teatro le Laudi— on the side of Piazza Savonarola opposite the American Academy. The set had been dressed like a piazza for a different production. On one side there was a bar with a few tables in front. On the other, one of those little shops that sold fruit and vegetables. One of the tables had a Cinzano umbrella that seemed, to Woody, to be too large for the small stage.

They were greeted by about thirty students, cast and crew, who fussed over the dog, and over Miranda, and by Polly Winston, the English teacher who was directing the play. Woody was fond of Polly, who had a clear hierarchy of needs that included adjourning faculty meetings after one hour and opening a bottle of Prosecco in the staff lounge on Fridays at four. She'd surprised everyone at Epiphany by coming to school dressed as the *befana* and handing out candy to everyone. She was wearing jeans and a white shirt and was smoking a cigarette. She was about Miranda's age and seemed perfectly confident as she and Miranda exchanged air kisses. Woody was a little nervous. He wanted the visit to go well.

What Miranda did, after a brief introduction, was ask the students, who were standing on the piazza stage, to form groups of three and brainstorm about what daily life would have been like in a small New Hampshire town, and to compare it with daily life in their own hometowns. But the students had already done that. What they wanted to know, one of the girls said, was how to kiss.

Woody, who was sitting in the front row next to Polly Winston, looked around. "I'll bet some of you could give lessons in kissing," Miranda said. Everyone laughed. "There's only one kiss, isn't there? In the wedding?"

"End of Act Two," Polly said. She leaned toward Woody and whispered: "I'd kiss Nasser myself—he's playing George—but I don't want him to fall in love with me."

"Well, then," Miranda said, "let's do it. George? Emily? Maybe everyone else could sit in the front rows."

Nasser, an Iranian, was swarthy. That was the only word for him. Emily, from California, was small and fragile.

"What you want to know," Miranda said, "is the difference between real kissing and stage kissing, right?"

"And movie kissing," someone said.

"It can be scary," Miranda went on. "But it doesn't have to be. You've got to get to know each other when you start blocking the scene, but I assume you've already done that." Some laughter. "Now in stage kissing, your lips don't actually have to touch, okay? The guy—usually it's the guy—will have his back to the audience, so the audience won't see that your lips aren't touching. A kiss is stage business, like crossing stage left and sitting down on a chair. It's part of the blocking."

The students were skeptical. "What about movie kissing?" Nasser asked. "When Agnese Nano kisses Jacques Perrin in *Cinema Paradiso,* you can see that their lips are touching."

"And not just their lips," someone said. More laughter.

"One thing at a time," Miranda said.

Emily spoke up: "Polly—Ms. Winston—says that she wants the audience to *see* the kiss. If George has got his back to the audience, he might just be licking my cheek. What's the point?"

"All right," Miranda said. "I just said your lips don't *have* to touch, but there's no law against kissing on stage. It's just . . ."

"Are you going to kiss Zanni in the movie? Will your lips touch?"

"Let me tell you something," Miranda said. "Screen acting is just posing for the camera. It's all cut and paste. You don't have to *act* at all. There's no give and take, no buildup, no rhythm. There's no consistent arc. You do the same shot over and over and over," she said, "and then it's cut together later; all the reality is edited out. It's mind-numbing. There's no rapport with the audience, with real people. When you're on the stage, the audience is there with you, in the same moment, sharing the same space.

"All right," she said. "Let's start over. Again. If you want a real kiss, and you want everyone to see the kiss, then just take it easy, open your mouths a little and join your lips together and press, but not too hard. The main thing is you need to communicate. The kissers have to trust each other. If you're afraid that the other kisser's going to stick his tongue in your mouth, then it's impossible to act natural."

The students wanted a demonstration.

"George," Miranda said, "come over here." She crooked a finger and beckoned.

"What about Emily?" George asked.

"I'll be Emily," she said. "Has somebody got a script I can borrow?"

Polly stood up and handed her a script.

"Come on, Nasser. George. You don't mind if I call you George?"

Nasser said he didn't mind.

Miranda looked at the script. "Well," she said, "we might as well do the whole thing. Let's see, I'm Emily, so I'll need to be stage left. We're going to need the Stage Manager and we're going to need Mrs. Soames. I think that's it." She looked again. "No, we need Mr. Webb too. All right, everybody, hit your marks. Or I guess I should say, 'Take your places.'"

The students positioned themselves on the stage, Miranda and Mr. Webb stage left, George and the Stage Manager stage right. Mrs. Soames found an extra folding chair and sat downstage right, in front of the Italian fruit and vegetable stand.

"Can someone give us the 'Wedding March'?"

Polly ta-tummed the opening of Lohengrin. George stood next to the Stage Manager. Miranda started down the aisle with Mr. Webb. They stopped in front of the Stage Manager, and George stood next to them while the Stage Manager performed the ceremony. Mrs. Soames started jabbering.

George produced the ring and put it on Miranda's finger. The moment had arrived. They turned to face each other. Miranda, who was slightly taller than George, looked him in the eye. "Put your arms around me," Miranda said. Woody saw George stiffen.

Miranda stopped and put her hands on George's shoulders: "I'm remembering my first kiss," she said. "And I want you to do the same—your first kiss on the lips, and then all the other kisses." Everyone's eyes were on them. Woody could see George soften, could almost feel his lips meeting Miranda's as Miranda pulled him toward her. Woody was remembering his first kiss, Carolyn Draper, on the steps of the high school gym after a dance, their lips colliding rather than meeting, and then the Stage Manager was launching into his cynical remarks about marriage.

"That's all there is to it," Miranda said, taking George's hand and turning to the audience.

Polly Winston thanked Miranda for what she'd said about stage acting. Miranda sat down in the front row, and they watched as the students ran through the last act—Emily's return to Grover's Corners to relive her twelfth birthday.

At first Woody was distracted by the Italian stage set. The vegetable stand and the white tables in front of the bar and the big Cinzano umbrella pointed his imagination in one direction, and it was hard to point it back at Grover's Corners. Biscotti had gone to sleep at his feet. He was tired too. But then he was imagining that the dead were speaking to Cookie, not Emily, in the little cemetery in St. Clair, trying to dissuade her from going back—that it was Cookie, not Emily, who was reluctant to let go of her earthly life, Cookie who had to learn that the living don't understand. It was true. Woody didn't understand.

The students wanted a critique. Miranda said she couldn't find anything wrong. "It's better than I remembered," she said. "I saw it at the Goodman Theater in Chicago when I was in high school, with Tony Mockus as the Stage Manager and Harriet Hall as Emily, and then I saw it again at the Lyceum in New York with Spalding Gray and Eric Stoltz and Penelope Ann Miller, so I know what I'm talking about. You guys are doing a great job, wholehearted, that's the main thing, and not sentimental. I'd forgotten how hard-edged the ending is." And then she went on to offer some suggestions to Emily on how to find the rhythm inherent in her lines by saying them over and over with the emphasis in different places, and to George, who was having trouble flinging himself down on Emily's grave. "You've got to figure out your objective in this scene," she said. "Do you want to join her? to protect her? to bring her back?" George tried flinging himself down several times with different objectives in mind.

"I think I want to protect her," he said.

"There you go," Miranda said.

Woody chatted with Polly while Miranda signed some autographs.

On the way back to the hotel, Miranda asked Woody Emily's question: "Do any human beings ever realize life while they live it?—every, every minute?" And Woody gave the Stage Manager's answer: "No."

"What about Margot?"

Woody laughed. "What about Margot? She's no different from anyone else."

"I wish I could go back to the opening night when we did *Our Town* in high school," Miranda said. "Emily wants her mother to see her. 'Mama, just look at me one minute as though you really saw me.' But my mother did see me. I could feel her eyes on me. 'Just look at me one minute as though you really saw me, Mama.' She did see me. She always really saw me. She saw me when I was playing on the swings in East Lake Park, or just reading in the public library—she worked at the reference desk. She saw me when I was Helen Keller in *The Miracle Worker,* and when I was Juliet in the junior play and when I played Emily in my senior year. She saw me on the platform at the station when I left for Smith and when I got off the train the first time, at Christmas.

"What about you?" she said.

"Me?"

"You. If you could live over just one day, what would it be?"

"I don't want to go back. I'm like the dead. I already know what will happen. Cookie will be killed in the bombing . . ."

"But if you didn't know . . ."

"I couldn't stand it. I couldn't stand not knowing. It would be too painful."

"But you wouldn't know, so it wouldn't be painful."

Woody just shook his head. "And that my wife was going to divorce me and join a convent. Who would have imagined such a thing?"

"But you'd know that you were going to meet Margot, wouldn't you? You'd have that to look forward to. And me!" She laughed. "You'd know you were going to meet *me*."

Woody laughed too. "How would I know?"

"But if you picked just the right day. That's all I'm asking. One day. The most important day in your life."

Woody stopped and thought for a minute. They were in Piazza San Pier Maggiore, outside the convent. The dog started pulling toward Via Verdi.

"Say something, Woody."

"*I* see you," he said, thinking of what she'd said about her mother. She laughed and took his arm. "I see right through you!" he said, and she laughed again.

They turned down Via Albizzi, but Biscotti kept straining toward Via Verdi. "This reminds me of one of the hunting scenes in *Anna Karenina,*" Woody said. "Levin wants to go in one direction, but the dog, Laska, knows where the game is. Levin keeps going one way, and the dog keeps trying to get him to go in a different direction."

Woody jerked on the leash, and Miranda said, "Maybe Biscotti knows where the game is!"

"You want to go to Margot's? I thought you had a six a.m. call."

She looked at her watch. "It's only ten."

"All right," Woody said. "I'll walk you home later."

"You don't need to do that," she said.

"But I'll do it anyway."

They turned around and started down Via Verdi. Biscotti jumped up and down and pulled harder and harder. When they came to the piazza, Woody let her off the leash and she immediately ran to the statue of Dante and raised a leg, though she usually squatted to pee.

"Did you teach her to do that?" Miranda asked.

Woody laughed. "She always waters old Dante." Biscotti headed for the apartment. The shutters were closed but Woody could see that the lights were on in the living room. Margot greeted them in her bathrobe. "How did it go?"

"Beautifully," Woody said. "And now we need a drink."

Margot got out a bottle of Vin Santo and some cookies. Biscotti watched hopefully.

"Maybe I'll go up to Fiesole this weekend and walk to Settignano all by myself," Miranda said, once they were seated at the kitchen table. She dipped a cookie in the Vin Santo.

"You must be desperate," Woody said.

"Or maybe I'll go to the Bargello. Margot's been trying to get me to go there ever since I got here."

"Good idea," Margot said. "The Bargello."

"Maybe I won't do anything."

"Take the weekend off," Margot said. "You've been working hard."

"Maybe I'll go to the Paperback Exchange and get a detective novel."

"I've got a stack of them," Margot said. "You could borrow one. Nero Wolfe. Travis McGee."

"Maybe I'll keep on reading *Anna Karenina*."

"Where are you now?" Woody asked.

"Levin's brother's just died, and Kitty's pregnant."

"If you start now," Woody said, "and read right straight through, you should get to the hunting scene by this weekend."

"You still haven't picked the day you'd like to go back to." Miranda rehearsed their earlier conversation for Margot, who'd never seen *Our Town*.

"I think I'll stay right where I am," Woody said, reaching down to scratch Biscotti behind the ears. "At least for tonight."

Auction

There's a day in every shoot when everything that can go wrong does go wrong, and this was it. It was Esther's fifty-fifth birthday, March 22. They'd had a long day yesterday, and everyone was tired. A roll of film had been left in the developer overnight in the lab in Rome, and now they'd have to reshoot the exterior shots for the scene in which the novice who discovers the Aretino volume flees the convent and meets Margot in the piazza; Miranda, who'd been demanding some script changes in the auction scene at Sotheby's, had given her copy of the shooting script to Margot, and Margot had been hostile when Esther called her in the morning to see if she could get someone to unlock the gate to the Giardino dei Semplici on the opposite side of Via Capponi, where they were going to park the camera truck, which was now blocking the street; the Italian second assistant director had called in sick; one of the PAs was complaining that her stomach hurt and that she wanted to go back to the convent; the stills photographer was an hour late. Esther called his manager from the porter's lodge at Sotheby's, and the manager said that the photographer had had to be somewhere else, so Esther fired him.

Esther's job was to exude confidence. She was standing in front of Sotheby's Florence branch. They were still waiting for a city official to open the Giardino dei Semplici. A traffic policeman had arrived and was using various elaborate gestures to order the driver of the camera truck to move on. The driver was Guido, the dolly grip, the one who'd saved the day when the boom of the crane got stuck up in the air. Guido wasn't arguing, but he was moving his hands and touching the policeman, first with one hand, then with the other. Esther approached. There was a strike, Guido explained in English, a *sciopero*—not a strike like in the U.S., but a slowdown. That's why the official hadn't arrived to open the gate.

The art department had dressed the exterior of Sotheby's on Via Capponi to look like the London headquarters, flanked by Tavernier on the left and Richard Green on the right, and when Esther turned around to go back to the porter's lodge she was transported for a moment to New Bond Street in London. Harry had bought her a pair of diamond earrings at Tavernier for their twenty-fifth anniversary, and afterward they'd bought a Rembrandt engraving at Richard Green. She still had the earrings, but Harry had taken the engraving. Her transport lasted only a moment. She had something stuck between her two front teeth, and when she tried to dislodge it with her thumbnail, she got a sliver of thumbnail stuck too. It was tiny, but it made her head feel like it was swelling up on one side. She turned her back to the porter in the porter's lodge in order to floss. She always kept a spool of floss in her purse. But the last bit of floss frayed, and a piece of it got stuck along with the sliver of thumbnail.

Things had been going well. Too well. They'd been shooting four pages a day; thanks to the convent, they were significantly under budget in spite of the crane; Gordon Talbot from Leviathan had been really excited about the dailies and about the scenes Eddie Franklin was cutting together. He told Esther not to cut corners, told her he was looking ahead to other projects. But today was going to be difficult, and whatever they had to do had to be done before the sun went down, because it was the last day before Easter week, and everyone had to be out of the hotels the next morning since all the rooms had been booked a year in advance. Miranda was going to stay with Margot and Woody. Esther thought she might stay in the convent.

The set dresser was afraid of giving a lighting estimate that was too short and wanted an extra hour. Esther tried to calm her down by going over, once again, the shots they'd need. They would have to light the auction room—the *sala monumentale*—only once, so there shouldn't be a problem. Some of the extras, distinguished older Americans and Brits who'd been rounded up at the American and British churches and outfitted at the convent, had arrived early and were crowding the entrance on Via Capponi, where they were going to shoot the Vatican Police scene. It was ten o'clock in the morning, and they were already an hour behind schedule.

Guido was still talking to the traffic policeman. Esther gave him a fifty-thousand lire note and asked him to see if the policeman might find someone to open the gate. She asked Zanni, the only one who seemed to be enjoying himself, to use his contacts to locate another stills photographer. She deployed Michael to handle Miranda, when she arrived from Makeup. She herded the extras into the Sotheby's courtyard where the PAs could get them to sign their releases and warn them about flashing the camera.

When the policeman returned with an official and they got the gate open and the camera truck off the street, Esther sent one of the PAs to get more dental floss, dental tape too, if she could find it.

Michael shot the Vatican Police scene with two cameras so that any shots he wanted to cut together would work smoothly, but they were still behind schedule when they finished the scene, and the extras were getting anxious.

The auction scene was long and complicated, the most expensive scene in the film. They had to do only three setups, but there were lots of actors—the bidders, the auctioneer, the Sotheby's men, who reminded Esther of the soberly dressed men in suits who stood around at funeral homes. And lots of extras to fill the seats. They really needed two days, but Sotheby's schedule had made it impossible. They could have filmed on the weekend if they hadn't had to get everyone out of the hotel rooms.

Michael had accepted Miranda's script change, so that *she* was going to bid on the Aretino instead of leaving it to Sandro, but she seemed unsure of herself on the first two takes, and then Margot showed up in the middle of the third. Margot was blazing. She entered the *sala monumentale,* not through the big doors at the back but through one of the big windows overlooking the garden. Michael saw her and yelled "Cut."

Esther knew that she had to face Margot alone, had to protect Michael. She could see that he was feeling the pressure. He'd been fussing about small things that didn't usually bother him, and she figured he was upset about Beryl's affair. It would have been so much simpler if Zanni had taken up with Miranda instead. It would have settled Miranda down. But that hadn't happened, and now Esther needed to protect the shot. It was two o'clock.

Margot was heading straight for her, for Esther. "When I finished reading the screenplay," she said in a loud voice, "I thought

I wasn't going to say anything. I didn't think I'd be able to speak to you"—she was almost hissing—"but when you called this morning and asked me to find someone to unlock the gates to the Giardino dei Semplici . . . You push and push and push. You want more and more and more."

"Can we talk outside?" Esther asked.

"How could you do this to me? I thought we were friends. You said you thought of me as your daughter, and now —"

"Shhh. We've got to finish this shot today. It's now or never."

"This isn't what Woody and I wrote. This is a piece of shit. It's worse than the original screenplay for MGM."

"Please, Margot, let's go outside. I'll explain everything."

"You've trashed the story. There's nothing left of it. There's not even a flood. A broken drainage pipe floods Piazza San Pier Maggiore *and* the Badia? The Badia is two kilometers away. It's the most ridiculous thing I've ever heard of. How can there not be a flood?"

"Do you have any idea what it would cost to do a flood? A flood would double our budget."

"There's all kinds of stock footage you could use, and all you'd have to do is pile a little mud up in San Pier Maggiore to get the effect. But that's your job, not mine. And you've totally misrepresented the convent. The convent was a wonderful place, a feminist enclave, not a prison. And my parents? a drunk and a slut? And Margot marries Sandro in the end? What are you thinking of? You've got to get Sandro out of the way so Margot can do her thing. On her own. Without a man to rescue her or take over her life. I don't mind all the extra sex. Why not? Miranda Clark has a beautiful butt. Why not put it out there for the whole world to admire? But why does she have to be such a nitwit? She can't even speak Italian in the movie. There's no reason for her to be in Italy. It's the stupidest thing I've ever seen in my life. And

Sandro. He's supposed to be sophisticated, not a dope. Who's going to want to see a dope and a ninny fall in love. You betrayed me. You stabbed me in the back, Esther."

"Margot, listen to me. You can't have the male lead disappear halfway through the movie."

"Why the fuck not? If that's the fucking point of it all? Why the fuck is he hanging around? Get him the fuck out of there. Why did you want to make this film if you're going to give all the important stuff to Sandro? It's *my* story, not *his* story. It's *my* story that you're fucking up. *My* life. As far as I'm concerned, you can go to hell. You belong right down there with the betrayers in Dante—the *traditori*. Judas and Brutus and Cassius. And now Esther."

"You got paid, didn't you?" Esther shouted. "You cashed your checks. Ninety thousand dollars for a screenplay that I had to rewrite and . . ."

But Margot was already climbing out the window, the same way she'd come in. No one was in a mood to linger. They did the master shot in one more take, and Michael said "Cut, Print," and then they set up for the medium shots and the close-ups. Esther checked the window. There was a balcony and an outside stairway, so she knew that Margot hadn't jumped.

Esther was upset—who wouldn't be?—but by the time they wrapped, her take on it was that maybe things weren't so bad after all. Margot had no control over the script, and she'd seen worse. Authors were always a problem. She could tell some stories that would curl your hair. One thing was sure: they couldn't have afforded a flood. And you really couldn't have the male lead disappear halfway through the film. You just couldn't. She didn't know how she could have done things differently.

Easter Week

Beryl was not completely surprised by the person she turned out to be in Italian. She'd had a glimpse of this person when she was drinking tea with the concierge in the Protestant Cemetery, and again when she was eating supper with Zanni and Michael in Trattoria la Maremmana. Instead of being witty, sophisticated, in control, she was tongue-tied, awkward, and vulnerable. What did surprise her was that in Italian she was a nicer person. She couldn't afford to be angry because she had no weapons. Sarcasm and irony were beyond her linguistic competence. In English she didn't suffer fools gladly, but in Italian she couldn't tell a fool from a font of wisdom, and so she talked to everyone who was willing to talk to her and was on a first-name basis with the butcher and the baker and the woman from whom she bought her vegetables at Mercato Sant'Ambrogio, and the checkout clerks at the Standa. She liked this new person, and she tried to be this person with Michael: open, vulnerable, interested in everything. But as soon as she started speaking English, this new self disappeared. In English she was fully formed, congealed. In Italian she was still malleable. In English she thought of marriage as a fruitful collaboration, adultery as an irrational heat. She and Michael had been joined together in English *for better or worse, for richer or poorer, in sickness and in health.* In English she did not see marriage as a prison and adultery as an act of rebellion. But in Italian . . . In Italian she could still be hopelessly in love, and so with Zanni she spoke only Italian, because she was afraid that one word of English would destroy everything, like the prohibitions in fairy tales: *Don't look back; don't peek in the box; open any door but that one; eat from any tree but that one.*

But now that the thing that all secret lovers long for, a romantic holiday all to themselves, was in Beryl's grasp, why was she risking everything—ecstasy, heaven on earth—by asking Michael to come with her to Venice, as they had originally planned? Was she sure he wouldn't change his mind and go with her, as he'd promised back in New York, back at the beginning? If he said yes, the affair would be over. She'd tell Zanni that she was going with Michael instead, and that would be that.

Did Michael know what was going on? He had to know. Everyone else knew. Then why didn't he say something? Why didn't he show more spunk?

"You remember the hotel," she said. "Hotel Buon Pesce, out on the Lido. I've already reserved a room. You remember how tiny our room was? But nice. We could look out and see the canal, and the top of the campanile, and at night we could see the lights along the other shore. We could eat in that little fish place if it's still there. What did they call those things? Not a regular meal, not antipasti. *Cicchetti*, that was what they were. *Polpo* and calamari and all those little fish we didn't recognize, so we just pointed at them. They probably take credit cards now. We thought the wine prices were for a bottle, but they were for a glass, remember? And we barely had enough money to pay the bill.

"We could go to the Peggy Guggenheim Museum and sit in front of the Jackson Pollock. That's when I realized that modern art is, well, art. And you could see the reflection of the canal in the glass over the painting—the palazzi on the other side of the canal—and then the museum guard came and closed the blinds."

Michael was at the kitchen table that served as his desk doing some storyboard revisions for the *strappo* scene in the Badia. It was the biggest challenge that remained. "It's going to be spectacular," he said.

Poor Michael, she thought. He worked so hard because it was all he knew how to do at this point. All he could do. All he could talk about. How to shape this scene or set up that shot. He was always willing to start over with every film. He was dependable and always had work. He never gave up. He was always confident that the film he was working on would be his masterpiece. He was dedicated to his craft. But she knew—and it broke her heart—that he was never going to have a huge success, never going to fulfill the promise of his first film. Such a lovely story it had been too. *A story about older people falling in love.*

"You've got a doctor's appointment on Friday. At the clinic at Santa Maria Nuova. It's only half a block away. Turn right at the end of Borgo Pinti; don't go under the arch. Just stay to your right."

He nodded.

"You won't forget? You've got to get another leuprolide shot."

It was hard to get him to keep his appointments, to take his medicine. Was it an affectation? No. It was the only way he knew how to be.

"You're sure you won't go? To Venice, I mean."

"I'm sure," he said, sketching. "You have a good time."

She looked at his drawing. He'd gotten carried away and was sketching not the shot but the fresco itself, the one that Sandro restores — Saint Francis dancing before the Pope. He'd made a lovely drawing.

She knew that he knew, and that this trip was his gift to her. He was being magnanimous. She hated magnanimity, but what could she do?

Michael needed a vacation. From Beryl. Beryl was the only woman he'd ever loved, but he needed some quiet time, needed to be out of the spotlight of her attention. She wanted to keep his spirits up by entertaining interesting people. Last week she'd invited all the students in her Italian class to dinner — Germans, Argentines, Japanese, a couple of Americans — and the instructors too. Twenty-five people. The week before it had been the search committee from the American Church. That was on Tuesday, and then after the wrap on Wednesday, she'd prepared an osso buco for the principal actors, Esther, the Italian assistant director, and an American nun she'd met at the Badia Fiorentina. She'd furnished their little kitchen with a complete *batterie de cuisine.* She wanted to nourish him. She cooked something special every night. Every night she served him something better than the baked baby lamb he'd eaten at Enoteca Pinchiorri. She wanted him to have a certain kind of space. She'd bought a book on feng shui and rearranged the furniture so that the apartment — large but nondescript — seemed more *Italian,* and she had a way of adjusting the lights to highlight the strips of fifteenth-century fresco that had been left on the walls when the apartment was remodeled, which gave the room a warm glow.

She threw herself into her language class so she could look after him out on the street, could make restaurant reservations, make special arrangements at the Uffizi and the Pitti Palace, so he wouldn't have to wait in line, not that he had time to go to these places. She'd taken charge of his health from the beginning, had researched everything: different treatments—radiation, chemotherapy, radical prostatectomy—and finally, when his PSA went off the charts, the leuprolide, the only alternative to castration. Except death. The drug suppressed testosterone and would eventually do permanent damage to his testicles. He couldn't maintain an erection, but Beryl was happy just to cuddle. At least that's what he'd thought.

He'd known about the affair ever since the crane shot in Piazza Signoria, and he knew that she was going to Venice with Zanni. He'd stepped outside himself a second time, just as he'd stepped outside himself up on the turret of the crane. Just as if he were now looking down with the same Godlike perspective, as if he were watching a genre film that had taken on a life of its own and become unpredictable, like *The Godfather* or *Singin' in the Rain*. He told himself that this was Italy, where things like this happened. He told himself that he'd had affairs and that Beryl had taken them in stride. His plan had been to be a heroic martyr, a saint, magnanimous. He'd thought he'd be able to gut it out, but alone in the empty apartment, it wasn't so easy. What if she left him? What if he had to face his death all alone?

The dominant sound in the apartment was the sound of the accordion player on the street below, Via Pietrapiana. Michael looked out the window. It was cold, but the street was busy. It was always busy. All night long you could hear people talking. The accordion player wasn't very good. He knew only three or four songs, which he played over and over, but the music was comforting. On his way to buy bread and salami for lunch, Michael ignored the accordion player, but on his way back from the Grana Market, he gave him a ten-thousand lire note. In the apartment, he made coffee in Beryl's special *caffettiera*. He waited for the little explosion that aerated the coffee so that it would have the same *crema* that you got in a bar.

Michael had figured out early on that the way to become a director was to write something first, so he wrote a screenplay for Chekhov's *The Lady with the Pet Dog*. He had liked the expression "tutored by bitter experience," which he repeated endlessly, and he liked the way the second ending snuck up behind the first and took you by surprise, like the second mountain appearing behind the first in Wordsworth when he steals the boat: just when you thought you'd come to the end and understood what was going on, real love cut through Gurov's cynicism and Anna's conventional romantic illusions.

He'd been working at NBC and had shopped the script around in New York, but there hadn't really been a movie colony in New York at the time, and he hadn't wanted to go to L.A. *Tutored by bitter experience,* he finally decided to make the film on his own. He and a group of friends pooled their resources and rented a 16mm Arriflex M camera from a movie-supply house on Tenth Avenue and drove down to Atlantic City to do the exterior shots.

The gambling interests had begun to take over, and many of the old hotels had been torn down to make room for casinos, but the Dennis was still operating and Mr. Busbee, the manager, remembered Michael as a little boy and gave him permission to shoot the café scenes in the outdoor restaurant along the boardwalk.

When Michael and his parents and his sister, Jordan, had vacationed in Atlantic City, before the war, they'd been picked up at the station by a carriage and taken to the Dennis. Michael couldn't afford to shoot a period film, but he could remember the carriages and the special wheelchair track along the board-walk and the auctions at Wing Fat. One night his father had bid three hundred dollars on a huge Chinese rug that was eventually knocked down for three hundred fifty, and right after the auctioneer banged his gavel, the manager of the hotel, Mr. Busbee, came running out and burst into tears. "That rug was worth a million dollars," he said. "You sold it for three hundred fifty dollars." And Michael thought the manager was going to fire the auctioneer.

Walking back to the Dennis that night, Michael was on the edge of tears, but he kept his thoughts to himself. It wasn't till he tried to borrow money from his father for *The Lady with the Pet Dog* that he brought the subject up. "A million dollars, Papa. If you'd bought that rug at Wing Fat . . ." And his father explained that it had been an act. The rug was worth about three hundred dollars. *Tutored by bitter experience.*

Back in New York, everything went wrong. There was a fire on the set, a warehouse in the south Bronx that they'd fitted up for the interior shots. The actress who played Gurov's wife got a role in a feature film and left for L.A.; there was a break-in and the thieves stole a work print, which they tried to ransom.

His assistant, Beryl—who'd become his girlfriend by this time—got her father, an Episcopal priest, to come all the way from Troy, New York, to bless the set. Everything was okay after that—no more fires, no more actors leaving, no more break-ins or ransom demands.

The film got into some festivals, was a strong contender at Venice, got distribution, did quite a bit of business. Critics called it remarkably "mature." In retrospect Michael could see that he'd skipped over the "Young Turk" stage of his career and gone straight to middle age. *Lady* was his best film. He got plenty of offers after *Lady,* and he made a lot of films. But Pauline Kael, in an offhand remark in a review of someone else's film, had lumped him together with a group of "middling" directors. And the word stuck to him as if it had been a clever nickname, like Meatball or Shorty or Red. He made films that got great reviews but didn't do much business; and he made films that got panned by the critics but did a lot of business. But he couldn't get shut of "middling."

Even so, he always expected the film he was working on to be his best. So maybe he hadn't been tutored by bitter experience. Because in the editing room at the convent, looking at some of the scenes that Eddie had already cut together, he felt the old flutter of excitement that you get when you see a really great film for the first time.

His plan for the week was to go over all the scenes that Eddie had cut together. Eddie himself had gone to Palermo, but Michael had lined up an Italian projectionist, and he thought he could find his way around the editing room, which was in one of the dormitories on the second floor. His confidence in the film was becoming stronger every day, as one great shot followed another: the dogs in the piazza, Zanni's face in the window of the taxi during a rainstorm, Zanni walking across Piazza Santa Croce, Zanni's face in the cheval glass as he removes Miranda's underthings. Zanni brought out the best in everyone, kept the tone consistent, even when he wasn't on camera, so that all the actors seemed to be making the same movie. And when he *was* on camera, he confronted you, even in the rushes, as if the screen were not there, as if there were no artifice, as if he were about to confide some delicious secret.

At lunch Michael drank some of the red wine left over from Beryl's last dinner party while he fixed himself a salami sandwich, though he wasn't hungry. He mixed wine from different bottles—something that Beryl would never have allowed.

Revenge of the Pink Panther was showing at Cinema Astro at nine. It was one of his favorites, the best of the series. He sat down in the *poltronaletto* and paged through Beryl's paperback biography of Elizabeth Barrett Browning, but he was tired and couldn't concentrate. As he was sinking into sleep, he could almost *see* Beryl and Zanni in the hotel, unpacking their bags like two characters in a film. He could picture Beryl's enormous suitcase wide open on the bed, Zanni looking out the window at the lagoon. A pair of middle-aged lovers, like Gurov and Anna in *The Lady with the Pet Dog*.

When he woke up from his nap he was depressed. He'd been dreaming of Sganarelle in Molière's *The Imaginary Cuckold,* whose jealous rage is tempered only by his cowardice. Michael had directed a film version of the play, back in the seventies, but they'd never managed to get the language right. Outside, the accordion player was still playing his gypsy medley. Michael ignored his hopeful look as he walked past him. He walked without paying any attention to where he was going. He walked past the synagogue, where carabinieri with submachine guns were posted; he walked past the Protestant Cemetery. He thought he might go in and have a look at the grave of Shakespeare's last descendants, but the gate was closed. He wound up at the Paperback Exchange.

Miranda was the last person he wanted to encounter, but there she was, glaring at him, at the end of the mystery aisle, just as he'd turned up a John D. MacDonald novel he thought he might not have read. He hadn't spoken to her since the big blowup about the script at Sotheby's.

"Do you know where your wife is?" she said.

Michael kept reading, trying to remember if he'd read this one before. Miranda's voice seemed to be coming from a long way away. He couldn't hear her words, but he could make out what she was thinking: *You're not a man. How can you let your wife go off for a week with that monster? You should have challenged him to a duel. They're fucking up a storm right now. You know, don't you? I don't have to tell you. And you've let Zanni steal all the scenes. It was supposed to be a film about a woman, and now you're going to call it* The Italian Lover. *You identified with the male lead. You let Esther walk all over you. Margot was right. And I knew it beforehand. I should have told her everything at the very beginning. You took everything away from me except the T and A scenes. Esther told me Margot wrote the screenplay, but that was a lie. She lied to everyone. As far as I'm concerned, you can all go to hell.*

Michael looked up from *The Lonely Silver Rain.* "How old are you, Miranda?"

"Twenty-nine," she said. "Well, thirty."

"There are still some things you don't understand about life."

"That's what your wife told me," Miranda said. She started to cry, and he put an arm around her and invited her to go to see *Revenge of the Pink Panther* that night.

There were a lot of things about life that he didn't understand either.

Beryl and Zanni arrived at Santa Lucia Station in Venice on Saturday afternoon and took the vaporetto down the Grand Canal and out to the Lido. Zanni had nothing but bad things to say about his native city: it was sinking into the sea; the Public Works Ministry had halted the controversial gates project that was supposed to protect the interior of the city from flooding; the young people were leaving; there were no jobs; Mestre — the industrial city on the mainland — was dominating the economy; Venice was a tourist town that had lost its soul, its raison d'être, like Christianity. On and on he went as they passed the Fondaco dei Turchi and the Ca' d'Oro and the Rialto and the Accademia and then stopped at San Marco before heading out into open water.

The Lido was at the end of the vaporetto line, and the Hotel Buon Pesce was at the end of the bus line on the Lido. There were two bus lines. One went clockwise and one counterclockwise. Beryl remembered taking the wrong bus with Michael and getting worried, but then it hadn't mattered because both buses went to the hotel and turned around in a circular drive in front. She'd forgotten about the military installation farther out, but the road was gated and there were NO ENTRY signs posted everywhere. It was not as fancy as Beryl remembered, but it had a view of the lagoon, and in the distance they could see the campanile and San Giorgio Maggiore and the lights along the shore.

The garden was bare, but Beryl remembered the bright blue and yellow fuchsia that had been in bloom during the film festival, and how the lobby had been full of flowers. She didn't remember, though, that their room had been this small, almost cramped, and she had to wonder, *what are we going to do all week? In this little room!* Maybe that was the problem with being middle-aged.

Michael met Miranda at the bottom of Via Tornabuoni, and they pushed their way through the crowds in the center to the little theater across from Vivoli, the ice cream place. Miranda started to apologize but he stopped her.

"It will be a good film," he said. "You've got a career ahead of you. Don't worry, all right?"

"All right," she said, "but I really am sorry. It's just —"

"It doesn't matter," he said. He didn't ask her "just" what? He was hanging onto his Godlike perspective vis-à-vis his wife and her lover, didn't want to let it go. God with a sense of humor. It would be easy to lose that too.

"*Every*one's in love with Zanni," she said. "I don't understand it."

"Because he enjoys being who he is. I could see that from the beginning, when he did his polenta routine at the first rehearsal. He takes whatever's at hand. Like Falstaff. It's his commedia dell'arte background. Improvisation. Everything's fresh. He's got the secret of life."

"He's good at catching flies," she said. She put her arm through Michael's. In the little piazza outside the Cinema Astro they ran into the dolly grip, his collar turned up against the cold. Michael was conscious of the fact that, like everyone else, the dolly grip—Guido—knew about Beryl and Zanni, and probably pitied him and found him ridiculous, but he was also conscious of the fact that his appearance with Miranda, who still had her arm through his, might look as if he and Miranda were having an affair, which would counter the Beryl-Zanni affair. If it were true.

"I'm here to practice my English," Guido said.

They sat together on uncomfortable folding chairs, Miranda in the middle. The theater was shabby—more like a church basement than a proper movie theater—but Michael experienced the familiar thrill when the lights went out and previews started. *Excalibur.* Another old story tortured on the rack. He wished they still showed cartoons, but then, *Revenge of the Pink Panther* was a cartoon, and he was buoyed up by the movie, even though they showed the reels out of order. It didn't really matter. His favorite part was when Clouseau disguises himself as the old Swedish sailor with an inflatable parrot on his shoulder. But there were so many great moments: the bomb sequence, Clouseau disguised as Toulouse-Lautrec, the kung-fu fight between Cato and Clouseau with the slow-motion ending.

Outside, in the cold, Michael, wanting to prolong the special companionable feeling you get after watching a movie with someone, offered to buy ice cream at Vivoli. He could see that Miranda was already forgetting Zanni. He could already see what was going to happen as surely as if it were the beginning of a romantic comedy.

There was a large crowd on the street in front of Vivoli and they had to wait.

"I couldn't understand anything," Guido said. "Nothing. Nothing at all. Were they speaking French?"

"It's hard to hear in there," Michael said.

"But this Pink Panther. I don't understand . . ."

"He's supposed to have a French *accent*." Michael imitated: "It's a *bimb,* it's the *lieuw.*"

"Is it some kind of satire?" Guido asked.

"Movies are never about what they seem to be about," Miranda said. "They're always about *how* they're about it."

Guido looked puzzled.

"What Miranda means," Michael said, not wanting to pursue this line of thought, "is that they showed the reels in the wrong order. They showed the third reel second and then the second reel last. Not that it makes much difference!"

"Oh." Miranda covered her mouth with her hand.

"That's why the credits showed up in the middle instead of at the end."

"I couldn't understand that," Guido said.

Michael laughed. "I still know a thing or two."

"The ice cream here is fantastic," Miranda said.

"Almost as good as at San Crispiano, in Trastevere."

"I'm sure everything's better in Rome," Miranda said.

They got their little cups of ice cream and their little wooden spoons and found a seat. Miranda had *nocciola,* Guido had the *stracciatella,* and Michael had pistachio. When they'd finished, Miranda asked Guido if he were working on anything.

"Working on anything? I'm pushing the dolly every day."

"I meant a screenplay."

"Why would you think that?"

"Because," Michael said, "everyone in this business is writing a screenplay."

"Not in Italy," Guido said. "But if I *were* going to write a screenplay, it would be a romantic comedy, and I'd avoid all the clichés."

"What kind of clichés?" Miranda asked.

"You know, the lovers meet in some funny way —"

"If you eliminate all the clichés," Michael interrupted, "there's nothing left. Isn't that your experience?"

"Well," Guido said, "you meet a woman at a party . . ." He stopped, pushed his lips out, and tipped his head to one side.

"What about Shakespeare?" Michael asked. "Benedict and Beatrice, Rosalind and Orlando?"

"Maybe everything's a cliché," Guido said. "If a man and a woman fall in love at first sight, that's a cliché. If they can't stand each other at the beginning, that's a cliché, because you know right away that they're going to fall in love later. If a man tries to kiss a woman and she slaps him, that's a cliché; you know they're going to fall in love. If she slaps him and then he kisses her, that's a cliché. Look at *Strega della luna.* It's all a cliché. They can't stand each other. She slaps him. They jump into bed. If they go to bed and it's fantastic, that's a cliché. If they go to bed and nothing works right the first time, that's a cliché too, and you know it will get better and pretty soon it will be fantastic."

Miranda didn't recognize the title — *Strega della luna.*

"With Cher and Nicolas Cage," Guido explained.

"*Moonstruck,*" she said. "But that was a terrific movie."

"And avoiding clichés is a cliché too," Michael said. "Sometimes it's even worse than the clichés themselves."

Guido laughed.

"If it's going to be a romantic comedy," Michael said, "somebody's got to fall in love."

"I suppose."

"Clichés aren't the enemy," Michael said. "Intentionality is the enemy. Don't plan too much. Don't think too much. Let things happen. Don't try to illustrate a theory. Write your screenplay without stopping. Don't try to squeeze it out, like toothpaste out of a tube. Don't worry about originality. Don't be afraid of clichés. Just let something happen."

"Is that the way you work?"

"No, I've always planned too far ahead. I've always been afraid."

"Afraid?"

"Afraid to steal what I wanted! Don't be afraid to do that. If you like the way de Sica gets behind his characters in *The Bicycle Thief,* framing them in windows and doorways, looking at them around corners, do it. If you like the way Claudia makes faces at herself in the mirror in *L'avventura,* go for a mirror scene. If you like the way Jewison sets up the bedroom scene in *Moonstruck,* learn from it."

"That's not a great scene."

"No," Michael said, "but you can learn from it. You can learn to shape a scene, to pace it. Use what you love. Don't be afraid of clichés. But don't just plunk them down—put them to work, make them sweat. The main thing is, don't be afraid of what you don't understand. Go for the deep truth." Michael leaned forward and paused dramatically. "No, *truth* is the wrong word.

Forget *truth*. *Mystery*'s what you want. At the center of every good story there's a mystery that can't be explained. If you could explain it, you wouldn't need a story. Stories are for the things you can't explain. If you stick to that, everything else will take care of itself. Don't be afraid to break all the rules, and don't be afraid to follow them either.

"And don't be afraid to surprise yourself. You've got to put yourself in a discovery mode, do you know what I mean? When you sit down to write, or when you sit down to set up a shot, you want to leave room for surprises. Intentionality is the enemy. Let things happen."

"This is very good advice. Maybe I *will* write a screenplay." Guido laughed. "But what's the *mystery* in the *Pink Panther*? What is it that you can't explain so you have to have a story, a movie like that?"

Michael was stumped: it was a mystery film, but it didn't really matter who'd committed the crime. There was something more. He thought about it and then it came to him. "It's the inflatable parrot, isn't it? What's at the heart of things—silliness or rationality? *The Iliad* is a great story because life is war. *The Odyssey*'s a great story because life's a journey. *The Canterbury Tales* are great because life is a pilgrimage. And *The Pink Panther*'s pretty good because life is a joke—the parrot. You can't explain it. It's just there. And you can't get it into words either. That's the key. You have to *see* it."

Sunday morning. Beryl thought she might be experiencing a paradigm shift, a Copernican revolution, and she was going to church to find out, to find out if there was anything out there strong enough to balance the kind of bodily ecstasy she'd experienced the previous night in the *matrimoniale* of the little room in the hotel. She stood on the open deck of the vaporetto and let the wind muss her hair.

Sunday morning. Palm Sunday. It would be a long service, the longest of the year. Her father's service, at St. Andrew's in Troy, always lasted almost two hours, but that was because her father had included all the old rituals he'd come across over the course of years. The tension would start building at Ash Wednesday and keep on growing till it reached a climax on Easter Sunday.

Zanni had offered to take her to the English Church in Campo San Vio, but she had it marked on her map and wanted to find her own way. She took the bus from the hotel to the vaporetto landing, and the vaporetto to the Accademia. The streets on her map were not all named, but she'd crossed the bridge and found the church without much trouble—St. George's Church. Diocese of Gibraltar.

She couldn't tell anything about the church from the façade, but inside it was pleasantly simple. The priest was already reading the collect from the old prayer book to a congregation of about thirty-five people, most of whom, she guessed from their clothes, were British tourists. She thought of her father, how his faith had increased as his congregation dwindled.

The gospel of the palms was sung so beautifully by a young man in a red cassock and white surplice that Beryl's whole body responded, reverberating like an echo of her orgasm the previous night. But it was only an echo, not the real thing. It didn't convulse her entire being.

She knew what her father would have said: "You cannot belong to Christ Jesus unless you crucify all your self-indulgent passions and desires." It was just what Saint Paul had said to the Galatians, except Saint Paul hadn't called the passions "self-indulgent."

But bodily ecstasy. What could it mean? No sermon could match bodily ecstasy, *orgasmo*. The priest spoke of acknowledging our sins, our shortcomings. However embarrassing, however painful, however shameful. But Beryl wasn't embarrassed; she wasn't in pain; she wasn't ashamed. And this was what scared her. She should have felt guilty. She would have welcomed guilt, because then she would have known where she was. But she'd crossed the border into another country, and what frightened her was the thought that the border police might not let her go back again to her native land, might glance at the stamp on her passport and shake their heads.

At the end of the service the congregation marched around the piazza—Campo San Vio—waving their palm fronds and singing "All Glory, Laud, and Honor." A small crowd of Italians gathered at the newspaper kiosk to watch. Beryl did not go back into the church for the benediction. She had not found what she was looking for. She was already looking forward to fucking Zanni. She was imagining him waiting for her in the bed, or in the lobby, or the breakfast room, or the garden. Zanni, who could have been spending the week with Miranda Clark, a real beauty, but had chosen to spend it with her.

"You got a philosophy of life?" Guido asked.

"You mean like Zorba?" Miranda laughed. "Swallow life whole and take your clothes off and dance?"

It was Monday night. Miranda and Guido were sitting at one of the small tables in the back at Vivoli, eating ice cream. They'd just watched *Zorba the Greek*, which had succeeded *Revenge of the Pink Panther* at Cinema Astro.

"You're not convinced?"

"He's only got one note," Miranda said. "His son dies, and

what does he do? Dance dance dance. Basil's too uptight to say anything to the widow. What does Zorba advise? Dance dance dance."

"Do you like to dance?" Guido asked.

"Yes, as a matter of fact I do," she said. "I just don't think it's the solution to everything."

"When I asked my pop if he had a philosophy of life," Guido said, "he thought I was in some kind of trouble!"

"Did he have one?"

"Sort of: Always be ready to go to work at call time; always have your tools in order; never walk in the ozone without a fall-protection strap; never repeat anything you hear on the set; don't get too familiar with the people above the line."

"Is your dad in the film business too?"

"My dad, my uncle, my cousins, my sister —"

"Don't get involved with people above the line," she said. "You mean like me?"

"Like you."

"Why not?"

"Could be trouble."

"Like what?"

"Like when you saw me smile at you when I was dollying in for a close-up and then you started to choke on the piece of chocolate, and then Zanni made everybody laugh by pretending there was a fly buzzing round his head. If you had complained that I was looking at you the wrong way —"

"It wasn't your fault," she said. "It's just that I was upset; it was so stupid."

"You can afford to get upset; I can't. You could have me fired. You wouldn't even have to give a reason. Maybe you don't like my face." He snapped his fingers.

"Guido, I wouldn't do that."

"I'm not saying you would."

"Sounds like you've adopted your dad's philosophy of life. Maybe Zanni could fire you, but I don't think Esther'd let me do it." She laughed.

"Take my mama, now," Guido said. "She's a deeply religious person. I respect that. Priests, the Virgin Mary, the saints, rosaries, crucifixes, all that stuff. When you've got religion, you don't need a philosophy of life."

Miranda nodded. "Did you come up with anything?"

"I thought that my philosophy of life would have to include getting laid a lot." She looked at him, expecting a significant glance, but he was just talking, talking to her as a friend. "But I was already getting laid a lot. I was looking for something more. I started thinking maybe it was time for me to get married, that's one thing, and then I went to Sicily to work on *Cinema Paradiso*. My uncle was the key grip. We shot the whole thing near Palermo, different places.

"Maybe we should rent that movie tomorrow night and then I can show you something. You remember when they're out in the country, chasing each other through the field of wheat? Just before the chase. They're waiting for the light to change, a cloud passing in front of the sun, and the dolly grip has to take a leak. They're waiting, and I can see that it would be great to catch the transition, you know what I mean? It's light, and then the cloud . . . I'm just a *macchinista,* but I tell the cameraman, whose name was Roberto, to sit on the camera while I push it along the tracks. He doesn't want to do it. Cameramen tend to be *altezzosi,* snooty. But the director—Signor Tornatore—tells him to go ahead. So I start pushing the dolly and he starts filming. Great opening tracking shot, but he took all the credit for it."

"So, you could see the light, and nobody else could?"

"No, everybody could see the light. You couldn't miss it. But I'm the one who knew how to push the dolly."

"So that's your philosophy of life? You want to be a dolly grip? You don't want to direct?" She realized that this was not a good thing to say, but Guido didn't seem to notice.

"A director? No, maybe a gaffer or a key grip. I could go either way."

"Those are jobs, not a philosophy of life."

"Maybe so."

"So you don't want to direct. Do you want to act? Maybe write a screenplay?"

"A screenplay maybe. I could see writing a romantic comedy—with no clichés." He scooped the last little bit of his ice cream out of the cup with a little wooden spoon and licked the spoon. "But I'll probably stay below the line. There's nothing wrong with being a dolly grip. Some producers think they're hiring you from the neck down—*don't think, just do.* But it's not like that. You've got to be on top of all the camera moves, right? The camera's got to get from A to B to C, right? It's not so simple, especially with a director like Signor Michael, who likes to keep the camera on the dolly all the time. It's a Zen thing. You've got to answer to your own boss, the key grip, and to the director of photography. You've got to be in sync with the camera operator and with the actors, or they'll blow a lot of shots. You've got to anticipate every move. You've got to know the dialogue so you know when to start moving or when to arm the center post for a high-angle shot. You've got to be calm when the talent's freaking out waiting for someone to bring more film or a different lens. You've got to move fast or slow, A to B to C. It's the only thing the DP can't control directly. If he's shooting with a 300mm lens he's going to be *scontroso,* crabby, guaranteed. You've got to tune everything out—the producer's mad because you're in over-time; the PAs are trying to flirt with you; you've got to keep the talent in the frame; and everything, starting and stopping, has got to be smooth. That's called *feathering*. That's the toughest thing. Let me show you."

Vivoli was still crowded, but Guido stood up and began to demonstrate with his chair. "You just sit there and I'll move around you." He looked down at his feet. "This floor would never work, too many bumps. You'd have to build a dance floor or you could lay down a track, but the track's got to be level and the pieces have to come together in a straight line. That doesn't always happen. Maybe the track's been run over or it's fallen off a truck or it's been overtorqued. Signora Klein understands that. She's paying for C-rails with skateboard wheels."

Miranda—and everyone else eating ice cream in the back at Vivoli—watched as Guido pushed the chair around the adjacent tables. "Some guys hate the square track," he said, "but I like it because you can lay down a wider arc. Just hold still now, we're moving in for a close-up. Turn toward me a little." Miranda turned. Guido pushed the chair till he was almost on top of her. "With this crab dolly, you see, I can come right in on top of you, like when you were lying in bed in the cheval glass scene, just looking up at the camera and smiling."

Guido moved like a dancer, and Miranda was thinking that things had worked out for the best, that she'd rather be here at Vivoli with Guido than in Venice with Zanni.

"I don't blame you," she said. "I mean, for staying below the line. I've just about had it with *the industry*. They're the worst people in the world—lying, ass licking, backstabbing phonies. And the talent are the worst. They think that because they embody everyone's dreams they should get special treatment. Look what they've done to *The Sixteen Pleasures*. Talk about clichés.

Instead of a woman's empowerment film, Margot's going to marry Sandro. And that's not even the worst. And I've gone along with it. I'm just as bad as the rest of them. Maybe I'll go back to New York and do some real acting."

Guido just laughed.

"I'm serious," she said.

"I know you are," he said.

Esther had been looking forward to the break, though it was costly and inconvenient. There was plenty of room in the convent, and Esther had been planning to throw a party for everyone, but the convent was empty except for Guido. The Italian crew members had gone back to Rome, and the American PAs had gone off with Italian boyfriends. Esther didn't want to stay there when it was so empty. It was too spooky. If Miranda had been staying there it would have been different, but Miranda was staying with Margot and Woody. Esther managed to find a room at the Excelsior, which was charging six hundred dollars a night during Easter week.

Esther didn't mind Christmas. When she was a little girl in Fairfax (L.A., not Virginia), they'd had a Christmas tree. But Easter was oppressive, especially in Florence. The streets were so crowded you couldn't walk. The lines at the museums were endless. You couldn't find a place in a restaurant, not even at the kosher place next to the synagogue.

Passover began on Saturday. Esther had nowhere to go for the Seder, and she couldn't stop herself from thinking about Harry. How if Harry were here with her the crowded piazzas would seem festive rather than oppressive, that the break in the filming would be a special time for them to walk up to Piazzale Michelangelo or to get on a city bus and ride to the end of the line. To do nothing, or to do something, it wouldn't have mattered. How, if Harry were here, he would take her hand and make a joke. One of his Lieberman jokes. She couldn't tell them herself, but she could hear them inside her head: Lieberman clinging to a stick of a tree on the side of a cliff, the ground thousands of feet below him, shouting at the Red Cross helicopter that's come to rescue him: *"I gave at the office."* Lieberman clinging to the same tree, looking up and shouting: *"Is anybody up there?"* And the voice of God saying, *"Lieberman, let go of the tree; I'll look after you."* And Lieberman looking up and shouting: *"Is anybody else up there?"* That's how Esther felt at the moment, standing outside Ruth's Kosher Vegetarian Restaurant, looking at the menu in the window—Italian first courses and Middle-Eastern second courses. The menu was in English and Italian. She wouldn't have minded some "cuscus" or some "pearch fish" in foil, and maybe a blintz, but she'd have to wait over an hour and she was hungry. She ate two slices of pizza, at two different places, on the way back to the Excelsior. The pizza looked good, but the bright-red topping turned out to be paper thin, like a layer of fingernail polish.

On Tuesday she went to the Jewish Museum and tried to interest herself in the cases of books and documents and the ceremonial accessories and an eighteenth-century Sefer Torah from Venice, but it was the Seder table that got her attention. The table was covered with so many objects—like the table at her aunt Pearl's—that she didn't see how a person could eat. But they'd eaten, and her younger brother had read the Haggadah, and after the adults had drunk their fourth glass of wine they'd sung a song that involved a lot of animal sounds, and she always got to be the goat.

She stood in line at Ruth's again, and by the time she got a table, which she had to share with a family from Hamburg, they were out of the "pearch fish" in foil. There was going to be a Passover Seder at Ruth's, but it was too late to sign up. She was desperate enough to call Margot to see if Margot could put her in touch with the rabbi, Rabbi Kors. Rabbi Kors owed her for koshering the freezer for his precious books. She wasn't sure Margot would speak to her, but she called anyway when she got back to the Excelsior. "It would be a real mitzvah—a good deed—if you would put me in touch with the rabbi."

"Rabbi Kors?"

"The one with the books."

"Esther, you've got a lot of nerve."

"Margot, I'm desperate. Believe me, I wouldn't call you if I weren't. The rabbi was a nice man, and he owes me."

"In Severiano?"

"Didn't you say there was an Etruscan site there? Maybe Woody would like to go?"

"Esther, I'll take you. I can't stand to hear a grown woman cry."

"Baruch atah," Esther said. "Bless you."

It was their third date in three days. They'd just rented *Cinema Paradiso* and were going to watch it in the common room at the convent, which Esther had had fitted up with a TV and a VCR and a couple of old couches.

They'd bought some popcorn at the Old England Store on Via Tornabuoni and were popping it on the restaurant stove in the convent kitchen. There was no regular cooking oil, so Miranda used olive oil.

"This is the way we do it in the United States." There was no coffee table, but Guido, who'd taken off his shoes, propped his long legs up on an apple box. Miranda set a big bowl of popcorn on another and went back to the kitchen for napkins and apples. She sat down next to Guido so that their upper arms touched. She wondered if she *could* have him fired if she wanted to. It was a strange feeling. She held the remote and started the video.

They had finished the popcorn by the time the opening credits were over. They washed their hands at the sink in the kitchen.

There were no subtitles, but Miranda had seen the film when it came out and then again a year later. Salvatore loses his virginity on the floor between the seats of a theater. The prostitute (Teresa) laughs at his nervousness. Salvatore is very awkward, sweating profusely. The scene made Miranda nervous. She felt awkward and clumsy herself. She sat close to Guido and didn't move.

"I always wondered what happened to Elena," she said.

"Her story was cut in the American version," Guido said. "There was too much explicit sex for you Americans. The story didn't make sense after the cuts, but nobody cared. But it's all here," Guido said.

Miranda couldn't hold still. She held Guido's arm. She snuggled. She put her hand on his leg.

"Wait. It's coming."

"What's coming?"

"My shot."

They watched the field. The camera started to move.

It seemed perfectly ordinary to Miranda, but Guido stopped the film and rewound it so they could watch it again. "Look. You see how the camera moves? You see the light there? This isn't a very good print, but you can see it. Isn't that fantastic?"

There was plenty of sex in the fifty-one minutes that had been cut from the American release—Salvatore's sexual coming of age. "No matter what we do now," Miranda said, "it will be a cliché."

Guido laughed. "Here? There's nobody around, so it doesn't matter."

"There might be."

"But there isn't now."

So they made love on the couch with the film still running. It seemed to Miranda that they were making a lot of noise, and she thought of Father Arnold, back in Mount Pleasant. She imagined that God was looking down on them, looking down at her over Guido's shoulder, or listening, and she wondered what He was thinking. She thought of Margot and Sandro and of Woody and Margot, fucking in the morning, and trying not to make noise and then laughing. And then the montage of kisses came on at the end of the film, and the voices inside her grew quieter. It was dark and warm. She closed her eyes, and when she opened them, the TV screen was dark. The only sound was the whirring of the video rewinding automatically. Then, for a while, nothing at all.

And then, after a truly satisfying orgasm, it was time for a cigarette, but neither of them smoked. Miranda had fallen in love lots of times. She thought that this time would be different. But that's what she always thought. She knew the drill.

"Was what we just did a cliché?" she asked.

"It didn't feel like a cliché," he said. "It was like the director got up the courage to get right up close to the big emotions without going over the edge, you know what I mean? Without getting sappy or sentimental."

"I know what you mean," she said.

Beryl and Zanni climbed the campanile (which had fallen down in 1902 and been rebuilt), admired the Basilica of San Marco, went for an expensive gondola ride all the way out to San Michele, passing a black and gold funeral gondola on the way. They drank tea in the Chinese room at Café Florian, where Zanni was recognized by the owner. They walked along the Lungomare Marconi, but the Cinema Palace and the casino were closed, and their view of the Adriatic was blocked by the fences that kept the private beaches private. At the Accademia, Beryl was disappointed to discover that the Michael Sweerts self-portrait she wanted to see was *in restauro,* and then delighted to find, in the lobby at the end of their route, an entire exhibit devoted to Giorgione, including many works from other museums. She had seen so many reproductions that she'd forgotten how brilliant the original was—*The Tempest.* And yet it didn't compare with the bodily ecstasy she experienced, like Psyche, in the dark of night at the Hotel Buon Pesce.

It wasn't till they went to the Guggenheim Museum that she found what she was looking for, something to challenge the supremacy of bodily ecstasy as the ultimate good, the way fresh sweet corn challenges the supremacy of the finest French dishes. She was taken by surprise as they sat in front of Jackson Pollock's *Alchemy,* where she and Michael had sat thirty-five years earlier, after *The Lady with the Pet Dog* had been screened at the film festival. She could sense Zanni's impatience, but she wasn't going to be hurried.

After all of the old museums, full of annunciations and Madonnas-and-child and crucifixions and depositions, the Guggenheim was like a breath of fresh air. When she had visited with Michael, she'd been shaken. She had always disapproved of modern art in general and Jackson Pollock in particular. It was too easy. Anybody could splash paint. But in the Guggenheim you could see, you could feel, why modern art was necessary. What she remembered most clearly was sitting on this bench with Michael. Anyone could splash paint, but not everyone could splash paint like this. And Michael had held her hand. They'd been married only six months; their future stretched out before them. The shoots in Hollywood and other exotic places—Rome and Algeria and West Africa; the ups and downs, good reviews and bad reviews; after the kids were gone. Reading in bed together. Traveling with the dogs. This was their story, the story they'd written together. Zanni was only a footnote.

In the glass that covered the painting, she could see the reflection of the palazzi on the opposite side of the canal. Superimposed. And then a guard came and pulled the blinds. And then it was time to go back to the hotel. It seemed so far away.

"I need to go back to Florence tomorrow," she said to Zanni. He took her arm. "Of course," he said.

In the morning at the train station they learned that there was a strike on one of the train lines, and they had to change their tickets and take an interregional train instead of the express. The train was very crowded and they had to stand in the aisle, and they didn't arrive in Florence till almost eight o'clock. Beryl kissed Zanni good-bye and took a taxi from the station to Via Pietrapiana. She'd been thinking about this moment all day, but she didn't know what to expect, and she didn't know what she'd do or say if any of the things that might happen happened. What did she *want* to happen? She wasn't sure, but she rather thought she'd like to be scolded. If God wasn't going to scold her, then at least Michael could scold her. She didn't think she'd be able to bear it if he were magnanimous, or if he pretended that nothing had happened. She wouldn't know what she'd do till she did it. She'd just have to surprise herself.

And she was surprised, because when she entered the apartment, Michael wasn't there. She checked the wardrobe in the bedroom. His clothes were still there, so he hadn't walked out on her. The suitcases were still stored in the little passage that went from the bedroom to the front hallway. She opened the window and looked up and down the street.

She kept looking out the window, though it was cold. She turned the television on and then turned it off again. She put on water for tea, but turned the kettle off before it boiled. She tried to read Margaret Forster's biography of Elizabeth Barrett Browning. Had Elizabeth even gone to Venice? Robert had died there, but that was later. In Ca' Rezzonico, on the Grand Canal. Zanni had pointed it out to her from the vaporetto. As she was drifting off to sleep it occurred to her that this is what it would be like when Michael was gone, dead. Their story was almost over. They didn't have much time left to work out a good ending.

On the way to Severiano, conversation was awkward. Woody had come along to have a look at the Etruscan site. He sat in the back of Margot's little Fiat, which must have been fifteen years old. Margot had called the rabbi and convinced him to invite Esther to the Seder. Esther didn't want to know what she'd said to him. She was having second thoughts.

"We couldn't afford a flood," she said, out of the blue.

"I don't give a damn about the flood," Margot said. "But how could you keep Sandro around?"

"I've already told you. Think of all the romantic comedies you've seen, Margot. The male lead has to be there at the end."

"Romantic comedy? My life was a romantic comedy? No wonder you got it all screwed up. What were you thinking?"

Esther was starting to cry. "Of course it was a romantic comedy. What else could it be? I was thinking that you were my daughter. The daughter I never had. I wanted you to be happy. That's why I did what I did. I'm sorry. I just wanted you to be happy."

Woody, who was sitting in the backseat with the dog, reached forward and massaged Esther's shoulders.

Margot said, "I had a boyfriend at the end. Tony. From Sotheby's. I *was* happy. Why didn't you just let me be happy with Tony? I could have married Tony, but I didn't want to move to London."

"You couldn't have a second lover," Esther said, back on familiar territory. "Not in a romantic comedy. It would violate Hollywood morality."

Margot exploded: "Hollywood morality? Isn't that like *Army Intelligence?*" But then she laughed, and Esther started feeling better. She was worried, though, about the rabbi. He didn't speak English, and he was ultraconservative. She wasn't sure what she'd gotten herself into, and she was thinking she'd like to go back to Florence. She didn't want to ask, it would be too embarrassing, but she asked anyway. "I could take you out to dinner," she said.

"Enoteca Pinchiorri again?" Margot said. "You still owe me a thousand dollars. Why don't you pay up?"

"I don't know, Margot. I think that maybe if I still owe you the money, we're still connected. There's still a bond between us."

"I already talked to the rabbi," Margot said, "and I talked to his wife. She's a nice woman. You'll like her. She speaks English. She's Lithuanian, but she learned English in Israel. That's where they met. It's just family and a few friends. Some of them speak English too."

Margot and Woody stayed in the car and waited while Esther went up to the door and rang the bell. Esther felt the way she'd always felt when her parents had dropped her off at Camp Alonim. Someone buzzed the door open and Esther went in. She was greeted by the rabbi's wife, whose name was Lital. She was a solid woman, like Esther herself. Margot and Woody drove off. She and Lital stood under a cloisonné mezuzah, like the one in her grandfather's house. Esther looked around. Lumber was stacked on the floor. Sheets of drywall leaned up against the wall.

"We're doing some remodeling," the rabbi's wife explained. "My husband got into an argument with the contractor and he stopped coming for a while. We can't use the kitchen. We can't sit in the dining room. But don't worry, Esther. We've got everything we need in the *cantina*. A kitchen with everything, all the Passover dishes and pots and pans—everything, you'll see—and my grandmother's Kiddush cups. It's all ready. There'll be twenty of us. We're glad to have you."

"I'm glad to be here. It's very nice of you to have me."

"My husband says you koshered the freeze-drying unit at the produce market for his books."

"I was glad to help."

"You don't forget something like that. He was at his wit's end. And Signora Harrington, she's the only one he'll let touch those books."

"She's very good."

"She says you're making a movie about her book. I haven't read it, but it must be very exciting for her."

"I'm not sure she's happy with the way it's turning out, but it's always that way with authors."

Lital showed her to her room. Esther wished she'd brought something to read. She went over the shooting schedule in her head, and then over the next week's shot lists. The loneliness returned to her in her room. There was nothing to read. She sat on the edge of the bed, on the edge of tears. Again.

What had happened to her life? Why was she sitting in an empty room in a stranger's house? In a little godforsaken town in a foreign country? She remembered the Seders at her aunt and uncle's. Singing the animal song, the "Chad Gadya" it was called. But the room wasn't empty. It had been a child's bedroom, and a *tzedaka,* or charity box, sat on the dresser. Colorful folk paintings hung on the wall: grandmothers in babushkas, peasants, lions of Judah, doves of peace, stars of David, a picture of the King David Hotel in Jerusalem. And pictures of a dog—a golden retriever. The room was full of books, children's books in Hebrew and Italian, prayer books, dictionaries, travel books, some stacked on their sides.

Lital came back in a few minutes with a plate of challah rolls. "The problem," she said, as if she were picking up on their previous conversation, "is that when Pesach falls on Shabbat, you can't eat matzo on Shabbat because you have to eat the matzo at the Seder with a big appetite. But it's difficult to keep *challot* for *hamotzi* in the home on Shabbat when all the *hametz* has been removed. We've been eating all day. It's a good thing we have time to rest before the Seder."

Esther didn't understand what she was talking about. She couldn't remember any problems caused by Passover falling on Shabbat. "These challah rolls are delicious," she said. And she started to tell Lital about Harry. How they had no children. Just their films. And now she was a lonely old woman. At odds with everyone. She told Lital how she was sent to fire him, Harry, and then he invited her to go to dinner. In the back lot at Paramount. And now? There'd never been another man in her life to regret. Harry was it. They'd been married in Temple Beth Am in L.A., and now he was sleeping next to another woman. It would have been easier if he'd died, she said. Easier for her, maybe not for

Harry. She could have grieved. Everyone would have comforted her. But Harry was alive and kicking. And the woman he was kicking with was her own age, Esther's age.

Lital put her arm around Esther. "You want to come and look at my table?"

Because it was Shabbat, Lital explained, the Seder wouldn't begin till nine o'clock. The Seder table in the *cantina* was as elaborate as the one in the Jewish Museum and as familiar as the one at Uncle Harry and Aunt Pearl's. The Seder plate at the center of the table. The horseradish and parsley. The salt water. The fruit relish. The roasted shank bone and a roasted egg. There were fifteen adults and five children under twelve. The children spoke English and took turns talking to her, as if she were an unfamiliar aunt, explaining what was going on: Everything was familiar now, but she listened to the explanations. The lighting of the candles, the first cup of wine, the washing of the hands, hiding the bit of matzo as a symbol of the redemption to come.

Esther couldn't follow the reading of the Haggadah, but she recognized the essential question: Why is this night of Passover different from all other nights of the year? This was the question that Harry always asked when they'd set out to make a new film. Why is this night different from all other nights of the year? Why are we beginning here? Why are we telling this story?

They ate crostini with chopped chicken livers, with matzo for the bread, and then rice and chicken soup with chicken balls instead of matzo balls, and then a boned leg of lamb with potatoes and tomatoes that had been roasted in the oven. The salad was spinach and fennel; the dessert a walnut tort and hazelnut pie. Esther hadn't eaten so well since she'd come to Italy, not even at Enoteca Pinchiorri. It was one o'clock in the morning by the time they drank the fourth cup of wine. The children were drowsing off. Only one thing disappointed her: they hadn't sung "Chad Gadya." Esther asked Lital about it. She spoke to her husband, who was wearing a bow tie. Everyone was merry. Rabbi Kors said that they would sing "Chad Gadya" if Esther would be the goat. The other animals were assigned to the children. They sang the song in Yiddish and then in Italian. Esther didn't know the words in either language, but she'd had a lot of practice bleating like a goat:

> *Then came the Holy One, blessed be He, and slew the angel of death that killed the Shochet who slaughtered the ox that drank the water that quenched the fire that burned the stick that beat the dog that bit the cat that ate the goat, that Father bought for two zuzim.*
> *One little goat, one little goat.*

When Michael came home on Saturday night, he was surprised to find Beryl asleep on the couch. He'd been to see *Zorba the Greek* at Cinema Astro—the film that launched a thousand package tours. Was he playing Alan Bates's Basil to Zanni's larger-than-life Zorba?

He watched Beryl sleep because he didn't know what else to do. How quickly it had melted away, his life, their life together. Thirty-some years. Seventeen films. One miscarriage, two children. Marriages went under all the time. He'd left her alone too much. He understood that now. She'd had the church, the PTA, the committees, the charities. But he'd always been preoccupied with the film, whatever it was. There she was, though, asleep on the couch, breathing evenly. Still a beautiful woman. Directors went under too, but he'd always worked, and on Monday morning he'd be on the set in the convent chapel, which had been dressed to look like the Lodovici Chapel in the Badia, and Zanni would strip a fake fresco from the wall.

What he felt was gratitude. That she'd come back. *Intentionality is the enemy,* he thought. He shouldn't try to plan ahead too much. He shouldn't force the story; he should let it unfold by itself.

Esther got a ride back to Florence on Sunday with Rabbi Kors and Lital. By the time she got back to the Excelsior, she knew what she had to do. "You've got to get your *nashoma* back," Lital explained. "You've got to get a Jewish divorce. You were married to the same man for thirty years. Your *nashoma* is still wrapped around him. You have to call him right away and ask him to send you a *get.*"

Esther sat on the edge of her king-size bed in the Excelsior and calculated the time in L.A. Five o'clock in the morning. Harry would be at home in bed.

She thought how much he would have enjoyed the Seder. Harry knew a little Yiddish. He could have sung along on "Chad Gadya." She prepared herself to hear his voice again. She could hear it in her head. Another Lieberman joke.

She dialed the number. Their old number. He'd kept the phone number, even though he'd moved out and Esther had kept the house in Santa Monica. She held her breath while the phone rang. What she was really hoping was that he'd tell her that he was all alone and that his film was wrecking and that he needed her to sort things out, but that isn't what happened. A woman answered the phone. Finally she got to talk to Harry.

"Hefty," he said, his old nickname for her, "is that really you? What's going on?"

"Harry," she said, "I just wanted to hear your voice," and she started to tell him about the Seder, and the animal sounds, just like at her aunt and uncle's.

"What's really going on that you call me at five o'clock in the morning?"

"I wanted to be sure you were home."

"I'm here; I'm here."

"Harry, I need you to do for me a mitzvah."

"Is everything okay?"

"Harry, I need a *get*. Will you do that for me?"

"A *get*? You mean from a rabbi?"

"That's what I mean, Harry." It was so good to hear his voice. She could picture him propped up on one elbow, scrunching his thick neck to hold the phone in place.

"You find somebody else?"

"No, Harry. There's nobody else. You were one of a kind."

"Hefty, I'm sorry. I keep hoping I'll hear that you're getting hitched again, a dynamite woman like you."

"Thanks, Harry. It's good to hear your voice. I can hear it in my head all the time, but it's not the same."

"Hefty, you don't want to wait till you get back to L.A.?"

"No, Harry, there's a rabbi here I know. I want him to do it."

"I'll find a rabbi tomorrow, okay, who'll make up the papers. Maybe we should have done it earlier."

"Thanks, Harry. Let me give you the fax number at the production office. You can send it there."

She gave him the number and then she said good-bye. *If she could just make it through the rest of the day,* she thought, *she'd be okay,* and she started going over in her mind the shot list for the coming week.

Frisbee

The *sentenza* was handed down not by the examining magistrate who had originally heard the case but by the Sostituto Procuratore del Tribunale di Firenze. It was handed down in record time. No one had expected a decision for at least nine months. But the judge had determined that there was no reason not to regard Biscotti as a *cosa*, a thing, a piece of property, and had ordered Woody to return her to Rinaldo Romero. Woody was at the American Academy when he got the call from his lawyer. He had one week to surrender the dog.

Woody was furious, full of *lyssa*, the wolf rage that Homer invokes when he wants to describe the anger of Achilles. Margot had trouble keeping him from going up to Settignano and attacking Rinaldo and his father in their villa, which was located just below the town, on a narrow road that slopes down to the railroad tracks and the river. Woody's anger was shared by the country at large. There was a public outcry. Articles appeared in *La Repubblica* and *Corriere della Sera*, in all the national papers.

RESTITUITO IL CANE
MALTRATTATO AL TORTURATORE
CONDANNATO

How had the Italian legal system moved so nimbly? Everyone agreed that money had changed hands, but no one knew what to do about it except to file an appeal, which Woody did, once he'd calmed down. The president of the Ente Nazionale Protezione Animali was interviewed on Rai Due. New impetus was given to the movement to change article 727.

Every night that week Woody and Margot sat up late drinking wine and trying to make a plan. They could rent a car and drive to Calabria or Switzerland, but then they'd be in Calabria or Switzerland. Woody could fly back to the States with the dog. But not without the necessary papers—not without a certificate of ownership, not without a certificate from a veterinarian confirming that she'd been vaccinated for rabies and parvo.

Woody proposed to Margot for the fourth or fifth time, and she accepted for the fourth or fifth time. But she didn't want to live in a small town in the Midwest, and he didn't want to live in Italy. They addressed the problem rationally, rehearsing once more all the pros and cons, and a rational solution always seemed just around the corner. But Woody was too angry to be rational. How could anyone choose to stay in such a country, he wanted to know. Margot pointed out that Woody was a member of an important political organization, that he had more friends in Italy—in Rome, in Bologna, in Florence—than he had in the States, that he had a good job, that he had regular gigs as a bluesman. And Woody pointed out that she'd admitted that she was homesick, that she kept circling around and around her desire to go home, wondering if her real life was waiting for her back in the States.

You'd think that when two people love each other—and there was no question about that—they'd be able to work through their differences. But by the end of the week, it became clear that there was no solution. An irresistible force had encountered an immovable object. Woody was shaken, depressed. And he thought that Margot was shaken too. He didn't need to go to the Archeological Museum and stand on the stone altar to see into the future. Suddenly everything had become clear.

He was supposed to surrender the dog on Friday, but he did nothing. The *commissario* he'd met at the Questura called to warn him that if he didn't surrender the dog voluntarily, the police would come for her, but still he did nothing.

On Saturday morning he did what he did every morning. He got up early and took Biscotti out to play Frisbee while the piazza was more or less deserted. Two street cleaners stopped to watch and share a cigarette, as they did every morning, and a pair of Franciscan nuns also watched as they crossed the piazza on their way to prepare for the early Mass at Santa Croce, and that was it.

It seemed to Woody that Biscotti was running faster than ever and leaping higher than ever, and that he was sailing the Frisbee higher and farther and faster than ever. He had a large rubber ball too, which for the most part he held in his hand. When Biscotti returned with the Frisbee, she would bang the ball with her snout and drop the Frisbee. If Woody wasn't holding the ball, she wouldn't drop the Frisbee, and Woody would have to grab her collar and shout at her. Sometimes Woody threw the ball too, and she'd race after it, batting it with her paws till it banged up against the statue of Dante or the steps of the church. If she already had the Frisbee in her mouth, she could pick up the ball with no trouble; but if she had the ball in her mouth first, it took her a while to pick up the Frisbee because she couldn't get her lower jaw under it.

Every time she brought the Frisbee back to him, she'd toss it into the air for Woody to catch, and Woody would bend over to kiss her head and to caress her well-muscled shoulders.

He didn't know what he was going to do when the police came, which they did, at six thirty, so he knew that someone had been observing his routine. They parked at the taxi stand on Via Verdi at the far end of the piazza. He'd been expecting *poliziotti,* not *carabinieri* in their smart uniforms.

Biscotti seemed especially full of joy this morning. She had no idea what was about to happen, and Woody hadn't been able to explain, though he'd tried. *Lyssa.* Wolf rage. That's what he felt. But then he saw that they were boys, two boys, like the boys that Agamemnon sends to Achilles' tent to take away the girl Briseis, and he could see that they were more afraid of him than he was of them.

He looked up and saw Margot watching from the window.

He threw the Frisbee into a crowd of pigeons. The pigeons scattered, but not quickly enough. Biscotti caught one in her strong jaws and brought it to Woody, wagging her strong black tail happily. "Drop it," he said, holding up the blue ball. He took the pigeon from her mouth and tossed it into the air.

The two *carabinieri* were embarrassed, apologetic. One of them held a leash.

"You're just following orders," Woody said. "Take good care of her."

The one with the leash snapped it onto Biscotti's collar. The other one said, "We will; don't worry."

Biscotti looked at Woody and then at the *carabiniero,* and then, as she was being led across the piazza to the waiting Alfa 75, back over her shoulder at Woody, who was picking up the Frisbee.

PART III

Postproduction

What Would Margot Do?

Principal photography was completed late Wednesday. The wrap party, on Thursday, was held outside in the piazza. Miranda and Guido were drinking Prosecco in front of the convent. Esther hadn't cooked, but she'd outdone herself, ordering food and wine from all the different shops and restaurants in the piazza, and inviting all the people who worked in these little shops and restaurants—Natalino, Maistro Ciliego, the Grana Market, the *pizzicheria,* the *ortolano,* the *latteria.* At eight o'clock the shops were just closing, the restaurants just opening. Shopkeepers and waiters mingled with the cast and crew and helped themselves to the food, which was set out on tables that had been brought from the convent. Each person there had come to the end of a chapter in his or her life, to the end of a journey, to the end of a story. At least a dozen love affairs were coming to an end. But everyone was happy and shouting and hugging and kissing. Miranda had tried to persuade Margot to come, but Margot was still angry at Esther.

Miranda had gotten everything she'd wanted. She'd starred in a feature film; she'd played the heroine of her favorite book; and there were more roles on the horizon: Gordon Talbot wanted to cast her in a sex comedy/thriller called *The Babysitter,* based on a short story by Robert Coover. She wouldn't have to send out new head shots every three months. But as is often the case, getting what you want doesn't necessarily make you happy. At least not perfectly happy. She'd betrayed the real Margot. And she didn't really ever want to see Gordon Talbot again, not if she lived to be a hundred, and she didn't want to sit in a bathtub and inspire outrageous sexual fantasies in the boy she was babysitting and his father.

She'd had a more or less successful affair with an Italian too—not the star but the dolly grip. Someone below the line, though "below the line" wasn't what rankled. What rankled was not that Guido was below the line but that he'd dumped her. Well, not dumped, but refused to sleep with her during the rest of the shoot. It was against his philosophy of life, he explained. It was okay for the Italian crew members to be in and out of the dorm rooms of the American PAs all night long, up on the second floor of the convent, but it was not okay for the female lead to fuck the dolly grip. Guido didn't say "fuck," but Miranda thought *fuck.* It was too disruptive, Guido said. It was unprofessional. It created jealousy and suspicion of favoritism. What Guido wanted her to do was wait till after the shoot and go to Rome with him.

What would Margot do? That was the question she kept asking herself. She'd asked Margot too, at lunch with Woody and Margot in a little restaurant in Piazza Santa Croce, and Margot had repeated her earlier advice about doing whatever she did wholeheartedly. And Woody had said she could keep his copy of *Anna Karenina,* as if it had all the answers. And after lunch Margot had taken her to the Uffizi and walked her through the Renaissance, from Cimabue and Giotto to Raphael and Titian. But the Renaissance was more than these paintings, more than a period of art history. It was the discovery of reason and truth. It was the discovery of the world and of man, the discovery of *this* world, the wind in your hair, the rough pavement beneath your feet, a man's hand on your breast. And then they went for a gelato at a little place on the Lungarno, near the hotel, and then, in the lobby of the hotel, Margot told her that Woody was leaving, going back to the States, and they both started to cry.

Miranda nibbled at a small piece of toasted bread that had been rubbed with garlic and a fresh tomato. Three more days in Florence, then the train to Rome and the fifteen-hour flight to L.A. She was going to take a bus up to Piazzale Michelangelo; she was going to walk from Fiesole to Settignano all by herself; she was going to climb Giotto's tower, and on Sunday, Margot, who'd refused to come to the wrap party, was going to take her to the Bargello. And then she was going to pull herself together and take charge of her life, go back to New York, get back into the theater.

When Guido, standing beside her, touched her arm tentatively, she raised her head up and then lowered it. He was going to drive the grip truck back to Rome in the morning and asked her again if she wanted to go with him.

"What about your philosophy of life? Not mixing with people above the line?"

"That's during the shoot. I already explained. Now the shoot is over . . ." He shrugged, putting his whole body into it, throwing his hands into the air, opening his eyes wide. Incredulous.

What *would* Margot do? She had no idea, but maybe what she needed was a down-and-dirty weekend in Rome with somebody below the line, somebody who wasn't working on a screenplay or who didn't want to act or direct, so she said yes. They'd have to leave early, he said. He wanted to stop in Montepulciano on the way to buy several cases of Vino Nobile.

The tables were loaded with traditional Florentine specialties— *pane toscano,* white beans, crostini with chicken liver pâté, raw vegetables, *ribollita, pappa al pomodoro,* tripe, sliced pork roasts, and, of course, *bistecca alla fiorentina*—big rare steaks cooked on a grill in the piazza. They stuffed themselves and drank San Giovese di Romagna, and later on Esther cleared a space in the middle of the piazza so they could dance, which wasn't easy on the rough paving stones. Miranda kicked off her shoes and later had trouble finding them.

In the morning she called Margot to say she was leaving early. She had trouble explaining and started to cry, but Margot said she understood perfectly, and Guido was waiting for her in the lobby when she went down, so she felt better. They took a cab to a little street just north of Piazza Santa Croce, not far from Vivoli, and loaded Miranda's luggage onto the back of the movie truck. Miranda didn't see how Guido could possibly get the big truck out of the maze of little streets, but she supposed if he'd gotten the truck in there, he could get it out.

"Getting it in is always harder," he said. "Especially when you don't know the territory."

Maybe it was just that things looked different from below the line, or maybe it was that Miranda had been so intent on having other people look at her that she'd forgotten to look at other people. How could she have missed so much? What she'd learned from Guido, by the time they turned off the *autostrada* onto the narrow road that led up to Montepulciano, was that Michael was dying of cancer and probably wouldn't live long enough to make the director's cut; that Beryl had become fluent in Italian in only two months and spoke with a beautiful Tuscan accent; that Woody had been the vice president of an important antiterrorist organization in Bologna; that Margot ran an internationally famous institute every summer in which some of the leading book conservators from England and the continent offered their services to pass on their skills; that Zanni had been married to a German-speaking woman who'd been killed in a climbing accident in the Dolomites, northwest of Venice; and that as far as the crew was concerned Esther was the best hands-on producer they'd ever worked for: she'd made sure the second AD had the call slips out on time; she'd learned everyone's name, even though she didn't speak Italian; she'd known how to stroke the department heads as well as the talent; she'd been willing to haul lights after a wrap; and she'd made sure that everybody got paid on time and that everyone ate well — real Italian food, Florentine food — with a glass or two of red wine.

"How do you know all these things?" Miranda asked.

"Below the line," Guido said, "you hear everything. You pay attention."

"How about me?" Miranda asked. "Is there anything about me that I missed?"

"Maybe so. Maybe it's this: You don't respect yourself enough. You don't give yourself enough credit. You know how to take direction, for example. You listen. You give the director something new every take. Even after eight or ten takes, you don't just go through the motions. I admire that. And you don't act like a star. Not usually. No temper tantrums. You got a little worked up in the first nude scene, standing in front of the mirror, but if you ask me that was a good sign. Who wouldn't get worked up? I couldn't do it myself."

Montepulciano was on such a steep hill that Miranda was afraid the movie truck wouldn't make it to the top. They were passed by several racing Alfa Romeos. Then they met the Alfa Romeos coming back down again. They pulled over at a turnoff where a German film crew was shooting the Alfa Romeos. Guido stopped and talked to the film crew in German. It was for a TV commercial. It was hard to get the truck moving again.

The Vino Nobile was for Guido's father and for his uncle. They left the truck in a *parcheggio* outside the city walls. Sunday. Restaurants were not open yet, so they stopped for a sandwich at a bar: the barista had some salami, but the only cheese he could offer was Kraft Singles. Miranda thought this was very funny and kept talking about it, even though she could see that it embarrassed Guido.

The woman from whom Guido bought wine was named Lavinia. She lived in a large apartment behind the main piazza and apologized profusely when Guido told her about the Kraft Singles. She wrapped up some local cheese for them and some nasty-looking, homemade blood sausages. And then she followed them in her car to the wine *fattoria*.

The small *fattoria* didn't look very picturesque to Miranda, but Guido said the wine was exceptional. When they were leaving, Guido asked about the turns. He wanted to take the secondary road to the highway without going back to Montepulciano. Lavinia said there wouldn't be a problem, that he should follow her because the route was a little tricky. Guido explained this to Miranda later, when it turned out there was a problem. There wasn't room for the big movie truck to turn from the secondary road onto the two-lane highway that would take them back to the *autostrada*.

The secondary road stopped at the highway, forming a T. The opposite side of the T was lined with a row of houses. Guido pulled forward as far as he could so that the front of the truck was blocking the door of one of the houses. A woman opened the door. Miranda looked down at her startled face. The woman closed the door again.

Traffic started to pile up.

A German Pullman driver soon took over the situation, barking orders at Guido, who inched the truck back and forth. People got out of their cars to watch. Traffic was soon blocked in both directions as far as Miranda could see.

The German bellowed orders—*vorwärts, halt, züruch, halt*—and Guido inched the truck back and forth, back and forth. It took fifteen minutes to maneuver the truck around the corner. Traffic began to move again.

"When we get to Rome tonight," Miranda said, "I'm going to fuck your brains out."

He didn't say anything.

"I'm sorry I said that," she said. "I didn't mean it the way it sounded. I mean, I meant it, but the tone was all wrong. For a romantic comedy. That's what this is, isn't it? A romantic comedy?"

"It could be," he said. "Or it could be a farce."

They were quiet for a while, till they came to Orvieto, another hill town.

"I really *am* sorry," she said again. "There are a lot of things about life I don't understand. At least that's what everyone keeps telling me."

"What's there to understand?"

"Love and marriage, for one thing. Or two things. Beryl and Zanni, for example. And Michael. You'd think Michael would have been more upset. They've been married forever and ever. I mean, directing Zanni and knowing . . . all the time. Beryl going off to Venice with him. They were together in Venice the night

the three of us went to Vivoli after *Revenge of the Pink Panther.*"
Miranda waited for him to say something. When he didn't she
went on: "Before that, after the cheval glass scene, I saw Beryl
coming down from Zanni's room at the hotel. We had a coffee
and talked about Smith and that's when she said there were a lot
of things about life I didn't understand. And you know what?"

"Speak."

"Michael told me the same thing in the Paperback Exchange.
Those were his exact words: *There are a lot of things about life that
you don't understand.* He's probably right. I mean, look at Margot
and Woody. They love each other. The happiest time I had in
Florence was when I first came and stayed with Margot and
Woody for almost three weeks. It was like being a family. And
now Woody's leaving. He's going back to the States. I don't
understand. Margot told me on Wednesday, after we went to
the Uffizi. I don't understand. Then there's Michael and Beryl.
They're still together. And look at Anna Karenina. You can see
why she'd leave Karenin, but what goes wrong with Vronsky?
Why does she become so spiteful? And Kitty and Levin. That's
so beautiful, but look at Tolstoy and his wife. The things Woody
told me about that marriage . . ."—she pushed out her lips and
made a burring sound—". . . forcing her to keep a diary and
then insisting that they read each other's diaries and then getting mad about everything, and not letting her have any of the
money from his books, and then running away at the end, and
he wouldn't let her see him when he was dying in a railway station in the middle of nowhere."

She looked at Guido: "You've got a philosophy of life," she
said. "You explain it."

"I've never read *Anna Karenina,*" he said.

"You can borrow my copy. But seriously, Guido."

"I don't think anyone can understand a long-term marriage," Guido said. "A long-term marriage is the most mysterious thing in the world. Take my mom and dad. Now you expect an Italian man to fool around a little, right? And my mom puts up with it. In an Italian marriage there's a little wiggle room —"

"For the man," Miranda interrupted.

"True. But when you think about it, for every man that fools around, there's got to be a woman that fools around too, right?"

"Unless all the men are fooling around with the same woman."

"I hadn't thought of that," he said. "She'd have to be pretty busy, or maybe you've got a hundred different guys fooling around with fifty different women. That's probably more like it. But the principle is the same."

"What's the principle?"

"The principle is . . ." Guido said, but then he hesitated, and then he laughed.

They passed Orvieto, towering above them on their right, and were coming to Montefiascone, but Guido still hadn't figured out the principle.

They discussed the rules of marriage, of Italian marriages and of American marriages. They asked each other, are the rules the same for men and for women, and are they the same for couples who've been married twenty or thirty years as they are for young married couples? Is it okay for young married people to fool around because they are, well, young and hot-blooded, or is it bad for them to fool around because they're newly married and should still be in love? Is it okay to fool around after a certain age — say fifty — because you've stuck it out for a long time with the same partner and deserve a little holiday now and then? Or is it bad to fool around when you're past fifty because you should know better, you should have figured out by now how to control your passions? And are there men like Zanni, strong men full of the life force, who are exempt from the rules of ordinary morality? Men like Picasso? Goethe? Guido's dad? And are there women like this?

Guido couldn't think of any examples.

"How about Peggy Guggenheim?" Miranda asked. "Or Maria Callas? Or Catherine the Great?"

Guido didn't know.

"And who makes up the rules anyway?" Miranda wanted to know. "Are these rules based on anything really *out there,* or are they just customs based on resentment, the resentment of those who are too afraid to take what they want from life, so they don't want others to have it either?"

They reached the outskirts of Rome at about seven o'clock without having resolved a single one of these important questions.

There was someone else Miranda hadn't "seen." Guido himself. Guido was the son and nephew of the two men—I FRATELLI GRA- ZIANO—who owned the movie-supply company, who owned the dollies and the big crane and the Panavision camera and the Chinese lanterns and the klieg lights and the miles of cable and the generator and the rain machine. She realized this when they pulled into the lot on the outskirts of Rome, near Cinecittà, and were greeted by the night watchman.

"The boss's son," she said. "And I thought you were just a dolly grip."

"*Just* a dolly grip?" he said, and she knew that she still didn't have it right.

"Sorry," she said. And then she said, "Why am I always apologizing to you?"

"I told you," he said. "You've got to treat yourself with more respect."

It was already dark. Guido didn't have a car, so they had to ride his Vespa down Via Tuscolana all the way into the city, about five kilometers. She held on tight and kept her eyes closed most of the time, wondering what she'd do for a nightgown that night and for clean clothes in the morning, and remembering bits and pieces of *Roman Holiday,* one of her mother's favorite films, with Audrey Hepburn and Cary Grant. Or was it Gregory Peck? Princess Anne takes a holiday from being a princess and rides around Rome on the back of a Vespa, and then when Cary Grant, or Gregory Peck, parks the Vespa outside the Colosseum, she takes off and knocks over fruit stalls and café tables and artists' easels. Miranda thought maybe that was what she needed too: a Roman holiday, a holiday from being herself.

But when Guido finally dismounted, outside the Graziano family palazzo in Trastevere, where he had his own apartment, she was too tired to do anything but take off her clothes and climb into bed while Guido went to get his dog, Peppino, who'd been staying with his parents. Lying in bed, she tried to remember Roman history. She'd taken a special topics course when she thought she was going to be a history major: "Women in the Ancient World: Sappho, Artemisia, Cleopatra, Cornelia, Julia (Augustus's daughter, or granddaughter?), Octavia, Agrippina, and the vestal virgins who would have been buried alive for doing what she'd come to Rome to do. She was thinking about the vestal virgins, about being buried alive, and the next thing she knew it was morning and Guido's dog, some kind of hunting dog, was nuzzling her face, interrogating her with his nose, asking her, with his tongue, *who are you and what are you doing here?*

There was a note from Guido taped to the bathroom mirror: he'd gone to get their luggage from the movie truck at the lot.

Guido's father, mother, aunt, uncle, grandmother, and sister and her husband and their three children all lived in the same palazzo, and they all ate Sunday dinner together.

Miranda had expected Guido to keep her a secret. "Do they know who I am? What did you tell them?" she asked.

"I told them you were someone special."

"Does your dad know that I'm above the line?"

He laughed. "Not anymore you're not. The shoot is over."

Miranda wasn't sure she wanted to be someone special, but she didn't have a choice. She sat with Guido at one end of a long table, near Guido's uncle, his sister, and his sister's husband, who all spoke English.

Guido's father sat at the other end of the table and talked directly to Miranda, explaining the different dishes that Guido's mother kept bringing in from the kitchen and the wine, pausing from time to time to let someone translate for him. He asked her about Florence as if it were a foreign country. What did the people eat there? Was Chianti wine as acidic as they said it was? And about the movie: He wanted to hear about the boom of the crane getting stuck, about how his son had saved the day. He wanted to hear it in Miranda's own words. Where was she when it happened? What did the director do? And he explained in some detail how he personally was going to replace the old ball bearings on the pivot point with oil-impregnated sleeve bearings. Guido's sister, Lucia, translated, and Guido's mother kept up a running commentary of her own, which was translated by Lucia's husband, insisting that a star like Miranda wasn't interested in ball bearings and pivot points. What Guido's mother was interested in was the love story, the romance with Zanni. She was almost in love with that man herself, she said. She'd seen every one of his films.

At the end of the dinner, which lasted most of the afternoon, Guido's father went down to the cantina and came back with a bottle of Fragolino from the year of Miranda's birth, 1961 — she was two years older than Guido. He toasted her in Italian, and Lucia translated, though Miranda suspected she wasn't translating everything. He went on to say that Guido was almost thirty years old and that it was time for him to get married, and then Lucia refused to translate anymore, and they dipped their little cookies, *cantucci,* in the Fragolino, which tasted, to Miranda, like strawberries.

That night Guido and Miranda made love like an old married couple, as if they'd skipped over a stage in their relationship. If Miranda was uneasy, it was because she thought that Guido was on the edge of saying he loved her. She recognized the signs: he'd start to say something and then say something else, and he kept asking inappropriate questions: does this feel good? does that feel good? would you like me to . . . ? She thought that Guido was waiting for her to come before saying what he had to say, but she was too tired, and too full, and after a while what they were doing started to feel like work, and she told him to go ahead, and she could see that he didn't know what to do, that he didn't want to go on ahead and leave her behind, but she cocked her body so that he couldn't hold himself back, and then for a few seconds he was gone and she was alone in the dark. He went into the bathroom to dispose of the condom. She heard the toilet flush. When he came back she was curled up on her side. He curled up behind her, and she thought that now he was going to tell her that he loved her as a sort of consolation prize. But he didn't say anything, and pretty soon he was asleep, and she didn't know if she was relieved or disappointed.

In the morning, Guido wanted to show Miranda the city, his city, the real Rome, Trastevere, where the most authentic Romans lived. He wanted to show her the mosaics in Santa Maria in Trastevere, the oldest Christian church in Rome, and then drink a *caffè* in the piazza and look at the fountain. Then lunch at Casa della Fornarina, where Raphael's mistress had lived, and after lunch they could climb up to the dome of San Pietro. "It's really wonderful," he said. "You're in this tight little winding stairway. It's steep. It's hot. It's dark. There aren't any windows. It's like being in the womb. You can't go back down, and it takes forever. Sometimes people panic, but you really can't go back down. There's no room. Not with people coming up behind you, like other souls waiting to be born. And then you step out into the light. It's like being born again. You'll see."

But Miranda didn't want to see, didn't want to be born again. At least not yet. She wanted to have her own Roman *avventura,* wanted to discover something by herself, wanted to follow the real Margot's itinerary on the day that she'd followed the real Sandro to Rome and said good-bye to him in the train station. She could see that Guido was disappointed, but he took her to the station on his Vespa. They bought a map and he helped her locate all the places that had been important to Margot. She didn't know when she'd be back, she said. Probably late afternoon. Then they could do something together. You could still climb the dome at five o'clock, he said, but after that it's closed.

She waited for Guido to leave, and as he left she pretended she was Margot, watching her lover, Sandro, walking arm in arm with his wife, walking out of the station and out of her life, never looking back. From the station she walked to Santa Maria Maggiore to see the confessionals lined up like porta-potties. Margot had tried to make a confession here, but the priest had shouted at her and turned her away. Then Campo dei Fiori, where Margot and Sandro had stayed, and then the French church, San Luigi, where she'd looked at the Caravaggios with Sandro, and then the Pantheon. She circled the Pantheon till she found the fountain-pen store where Margot had spent her last lire on a Montblanc. Miranda already had a Montblanc, but the pens were so beautiful she was tempted to buy another, an Aurora or a Pelikan or an eight-sided Omas.

She stopped for a dolce and a cappuccino on her way to the English-language bookstore near the Spanish Steps. She wanted something to read for the trip home. It was three o'clock. She asked for directions at the American Express office. There were two English-language bookstores nearby, one in Via dei Greci and one in Via della Vite. She cashed five hundred dollars' worth of traveler's checks. She had plenty of money and thought she'd go back to the fountain-pen store. Margot had more than one fountain pen, after all.

In the Anglo American Book Company on Via della Vite she picked out one of Margot's favorite Nero Wolfe novels. She scanned the fiction section for *The Sixteen Pleasures* and found three copies of the American edition. There was a British edition too, and an Italian translation. She looked at it and thought of buying it, and then another browser, a woman who looked like her mother—or what her mother would have looked like if she'd been Italian—spoke to her in Italian. Miranda had to apologize. "*Non parlo italiano,*" she managed to say. The woman spoke to her in English.

"It's really very good," she said. "I've read it in English and Italian." She asked Miranda where she was staying and offered to walk with her as far as Largo Torre Argentina. "It's not a tower," she explained, "in case you're wondering. And it's got nothing to do with Argentina. The earliest temples in Rome are there, and an unofficial cat sanctuary—like the ones at the Protestant

Cemetery and the Colosseum. We're working to get a law passed to make it illegal to *sfrattare* cats from places where they've established a home. To kick them out."

The woman had been a singer in the Coro Romano but had been forced to take early retirement. She'd always loved cats and had become a *gattera*, a cat lady.

The cat sanctuary was in one of the temples that had been excavated in the piazza, forty feet below street level. The cat ladies came every morning at eleven o'clock. There was no running water. They brought water in buckets to clean the cages. They needed volunteers, the woman said, and contributions. Miranda, who had seen the collection box for cats in the Protestant Cemetery, gave her all the money from the traveler's checks she'd just cashed. Thousands of lire, huge banknotes. "Signorina," the *gattera* protested, "it's too much." But she put the banknotes in her purse.

Miranda got out her map, and the *gattera* showed her how to get back to Guido's. It wasn't far. Just across the Ponte Sisto to Trastevere.

Miranda stopped on the bridge and looked down at the sluggish Tiber. She remembered that she'd never told the *gattera* that she was the actress who was going to play Margot in the film. It was four thirty. Guido would be waiting for her, but it was probably too late to be born again. What Miranda knew was that love is a choice, a commitment. Love is moving on past infatuation, past fantasy, to reality. But everybody knew this. She thought of Margot's advice: whatever she was going to enter into, she should do it wholeheartedly. With no reservations. But she barely knew Guido.

What would Margot do?

She still had no idea, but it didn't really matter. She was on her own now.

Director's Cut

Michael had been afraid that after the break it would be hard to find their rhythm again, but everything had gone smoothly. Zanni had ripped the fake fresco off the fake wall of the fake Badia Fiorentina, and Miranda, with minimal coaching from Margot, had stitched together the gatherings of the fake Aretino. Sitting on an apple box, Michael had watched it all happen.

He had not gone to the clinic for another leuprolide injection, and no matter how much Beryl scolded and wheedled, he'd refused to make another appointment. He was through with leuprolide. He'd agreed to check himself into Sloan-Kettering as soon as they got back to New York, and then the children were coming to the city for a reunion, and then he'd see. Beryl had made all the arrangements.

He and Beryl left the morning after the wrap party, but instead of going to Venice, as planned, they changed their minds at the last minute and flew to Naples. Neither of them had ever been south of Rome. They wanted something different. Beryl had gone to the little travel agency in Piazza San Pier Maggiore and booked a room in a small hotel on the Spaccanapoli which, according to her Red Guide to Naples, bisects the city, following the course of the old Roman Decumanus Inferiore. She'd bought several guidebooks, in fact, and had a long list of things to see in addition to Naples itself: Pompeii, Herculaneum, the Amalfi Coast. The hotel—Soggiorno Sansevero—would arrange all the trips.

Michael didn't want to see anything. He wanted to be somewhere where he could just *be*. Somewhere where he didn't know anyone. Somewhere where nothing was familiar. He remembered going with Beryl to Mykonos as a young man after a shoot in the south of France. What a pleasure: there was absolutely nothing one felt obligated to see. No monuments. No museums. One hot afternoon they'd walked across the island to a deserted beach. They'd eaten a picnic lunch and drunk a bottle of Samos Sec in a little cave and were drowsing off and they'd seen a woman walking along the deserted beach. They'd watched as she took off her swimsuit and swam out into the Aegean. She swam out so far they couldn't see her anymore, and then she swam back, put on her suit, and walked back along the beach.

Of course, there was plenty to see in Naples. It wasn't in Beryl's nature not to see as much of it as she could. Michael was weak, and he'd been losing weight, but he thought that his appetite had been improving since he stopped the leuprolide. A private car and a guide—arranged by the hotel—would take them to Pompeii and Herculaneum the next day and then for a drive along the Amalfi Coast on Wednesday. But as they were walking back to the hotel from the Duomo, a young man on a Vespa roared by and grabbed Beryl's large Vuitton handbag. The taxi driver had warned them—one of several warnings—but now it was too late. Beryl was dragged by the arm down Via Tribunali. "Let go," Michael shouted, but it wasn't in Beryl's nature to let go. She rolled to one side and managed to tip the

Vespa over. The young man took off running. Beryl still had her bag. And a sore shoulder and a broken nose.

These robbers are called *scippatori,* the policeman explained, while they were waiting for an ambulance. They usually work in pairs, one to drive the Vespa and one to grab the handbag. If there had been two of them, the policeman went on, Beryl would not have been able to pull the Vespa over. Some men had given chase, but they had returned empty-handed, though the Vespa was still there, lying on its side. A crowd gathered. Another policeman arrived, and an ambulance. The crowd was indignant and sympathetic, full of advice and questions. Beryl spoke to several different people in Italian, though her nose had been broken pretty badly and she was in pain.

Michael rode with Beryl in the modern, boxlike ambulance to a hospital, where she spent several days in a long ward. No private rooms were available. That night Michael sat on a hard chair next to the bed till she sent him back to the hotel. There were over twenty patients in the ward, and Michael watched as relatives came and went, bringing toilet paper, clean sheets, hunks of cheese, bottles of wine, bowls of pasta.

In the morning Michael walked along the Spaccanapoli, which was like an open-air museum, from the *pensione* to the hospital, which was less than a mile away. Beryl was cranky. Other patients in the ward wanted to hear the story. Michael couldn't tell it in Italian, and Beryl had trouble talking because her nose had been packed, but by the end of the day she'd created an exciting story line, and she'd managed to call Sloan-Kettering to reschedule Michael's appointment, and to notify the insurance company and the people who were looking after their apartment. She gave Michael her Red Guide and sent him off to visit the Gesù Nuovo church in Piazza del Gesù Nuovo. Michael didn't go into the church. Instead he walked up and down the Spaccanapoli, poking around the labyrinth of narrow alleys that branched out on either side. He bought some toilet paper for Beryl, and when he got tired, he walked back to the little piazza next to the hospital and read the guidebook so he could describe things to her later.

At lunchtime he thought he might be able to eat something in a little restaurant in Piazza Calenda, next to the hospital. It was still early and the restaurant wasn't crowded. He could see from the street a sign for *toilette.* The waiter didn't speak English, but the owner did. He came out of the kitchen and took Michael's order. A simple plate of spaghetti with tomato sauce and a salad.

The spaghetti tasted like something he'd been looking for all his life, or something he remembered. It was what his childhood food memories would have been if his mother had come from Naples instead of from the Bronx. He wanted to take some of the spaghetti back to Beryl and asked the owner for a doggie bag, which he had to explain. The owner was happy to wrap the plate in foil and provide silverware.

Back at the hospital he described Chiesa Gesù Nuovo, which he'd read up on in the guidebook, while Beryl ate the spaghetti — the diamond-point rustication, the seventeenth-century doorway, the Baroque interior, the statue of the Madonna. When she'd finished he held her hand for a while.

He returned to the same restaurant in the evening, to return the plate and the silverware, and to eat a little supper, and then he returned every day that week. On Tuesday he was supposed to go to Pompeii, so he didn't go to the hospital till that evening. He spent the day in Piazza Calenda, his piazza. He chatted with the proprietor of the restaurant. *Dolce far niente.* The sweetness of doing nothing. Michael went early at lunch and in the evening to chat with the *proprietario.* When the *proprietario* learned that he'd just shot a movie with Giovanni Cipriani—Zanni—he, Michael, became something of a celebrity.

The *proprietario* had once had a small part in one of de Sica's neorealistic films, where they used real people, not actors, and asked Michael what he thought about the future of Italian cinema. Would it ever return to the glory days of Cinecittà? It was a fair question. Michael thought that Roberto Benigni's *Johnny Stecchino* and Daniele Luchetti's *Il portaborse* were powerful films, and Gabriele Salvatores's *Mediterraneo.*

The food was so wonderful it overpowered the bad taste in Michael's mouth; it overwhelmed his lack of appetite. He hadn't been hungry—really hungry—in ages. He thought maybe the cancer had gone into remission. The owner explained all the dishes, all the sauces. He made fun of ragù Bolognese and of "thin" northern dishes. "They don't know how to cook up there," he said, tossing his head in a northerly direction.

After lunch Michael sat at a table outside the restaurant. He wrote postcards to his children, to make up for his long silence. He chatted with friends of the *proprietario* who began to gather in the late afternoon. There was always someone who spoke a little English. No one had heard of him in Italy, but it didn't matter because he'd just directed Zanni in a feature film! They wanted to know about the film, about the book, about the *sceneggiatura,* and about Zanni himself. The only problem with Zanni, they said, was that he was not from Naples, which the *proprietario* and his friends regarded as the real Italy. Michael believed them. What was that song about filling up your senses? Naples filled up his senses. One last time.

He always took some food to Beryl, always something special, something not on the menu. Like zucchini soup with cheese and eggs, a homey dish not found in most restaurants. He carried it to the hospital in a cardboard box. The food was always on real plates with real silverware.

It wasn't till Beryl's last day in the hospital that she figured out that he hadn't gone to Pompeii, hadn't set foot in the Gesù Nuovo or Santa Marta or the Palazzo Filomarino, or Santa Chiara—all the important sites along the Spaccanapoli.

"So, what *have* you been doing?"

He took her hand but she pulled it away.

"Just sitting around at this little restaurant. *Dolce far niente,* isn't that it? It's sweet to do nothing."

"What about the driver? The trips to Pompeii and the Amalfi Coast were expensive. Did you pay him?"

"He picked me up at the hotel and I had him drop me off in Piazza Calenda."

"How much did you pay him?"

"The hotel paid him. They'll put it on the bill."

"You should have canceled."

"Beryl."

She didn't answer.

"Beryl," he said again. "It doesn't matter. None of these things matters. Not any longer. Did you know that you can still see part of the old Greco-Roman wall in the piazza? Blocks of tufa. I did study that."

He took her hand again, and this time she let him hold it. He thought that they'd already said most of what they had to say to each other, but now the talk came freely. He described the piazza and the restaurant, and he told her that the Neapolitans didn't eat the thick outer crust of their pizza.

She had things to tell too. Her Italian was really good. At first, in Naples, she'd worried that she wasn't going to be able to understand anything at all. But the nurses talked to her all day. And the doctors, and the other patients, and so she had lots of stories.

He went out for supper at the restaurant, and he brought her back some more of the zucchini soup. He brought some special wine too. And another roll of good toilet paper.

When Beryl was released from the hospital, they took a taxi to the hotel, and then another taxi back to the restaurant in Piazza Calenda. Everyone praised her Italian and asked her about her impressions of Zanni. They all promised to see the film as soon as it opened in Italy. Michael didn't know when that would be, but he knew that there was a good chance he'd never see the inside of the editing room, never hear the score or see the final cut. But in his imagination he could see a broad smile spread across Miranda's face as the camera dollies in for an extreme close-up; he could hear Zanni's dubbed footsteps as he walks across Piazza Santa Croce, and see him stirring his imaginary polenta, taking his time, making use of whatever was at hand—a long thin rolling pin, a copper pot—just taking pleasure in being who he was.

The Get

The last few days had been excruciating—an impossible call list, fourteen- to fifteen-hour days, four hours to reshoot the *strappo* scene, which had been out of focus, a whole day for the gold tooling, which they had to do without Margot. Michael was on the verge of collapse. Esther wished she could have helped him more.

Ten days after the wrap, the production office was still open, but stripped down to two computers, two desks, two filing cabinets, a telephone, and a fax machine.

The rest of the convent was empty. The rental company had removed the beds and dressers that they'd rented, and the TV and VCR in the common room, and all the tables and chairs. The *idraulico* had disconnected the big stove. Props and costumes had been inventoried, equipment returned, leftover stock sold, location problems ironed out, vendors' contracts vetted, and bills settled.

Michael and Beryl had gone to Naples instead of Venice and

then to Sloan-Kettering for a checkup. The plan was to meet in L.A. at the end of the month, but in fact Esther didn't expect to see Michael again.

Miranda had gone to Rome with the dolly grip.

Zanni had disappeared.

Esther didn't know what they were going to do if they needed any automated dialogue replacement. Maybe fly everybody to L.A. Except Zanni would need a visa.

Esther was going over the books with the production accountant and firing off faxes to the postproduction office in L.A. when the *get* emerged from the fax machine. It was from Temple Beth Am in Fairfax, where she and Harry had gotten married. Now she'd have to ask Margot to take her to Severiano again.

Half a dozen men filled the small office at the synagogue in Severiano, all in wool suits and yarmulkes. The rabbi himself wore the same bow tie he'd worn at the Seder. He sat at his desk. Esther was glad to have Margot with her. She was very nervous, expecting the rabbi to disapprove, and was prepared to endure a sermon, which Margot would have to translate. Divorce was not a good thing. But everyone seemed cheerful, especially the rabbi, and Margot joked with them in Italian.

"What are they saying?" Esther wanted to know.

"That it's a nice day," Margot said.

"They're saying something more than that."

"Esther, just be quiet. I can't hear what they're saying if I'm trying to listen to you."

Rabbi Kors said something directly to Esther, and Margot translated: "He wants to know if you've got the bill of divorce, the *get,* from your husband."

Esther looked bewildered. "It's in your handbag," Margot said.

"Right," Esther said, opening the big leather bag she'd bought at the San Lorenzo market.

The six men stood around the rabbi's desk.

"You have to give Rabbi Kors the *get*," Margot said.

"I can't find it," Esther said. Her hands were shaking. She was remembering her wedding day, the klezmer band, and the accordion player, who wasn't Jewish. And the rabbi, ultraconservative, and her father, who was not religious, dancing in the old way. Skipping. Like Saint Francis dancing before the Pope in the Lodovici fresco in the Badia, the one that Zanni had *strappoed* off the wall. And Harry dancing too. Harry and her father and the rabbi. Like peasants in that Brueghel painting. She remembered firing Harry, and then going to dinner with him at Musso and Frank's. And their first film together, *The Bagman*. And their first apartment, a two-bedroom flat on Brooklyn Avenue in East L.A., over a kosher bakery. Cannes. Venice. One of the first successful films at Sundance. The films were the children they'd wanted. They'd brought them into the light of day, or the light of the movie theaters. Given them life. Some ups and downs. A couple of turkeys. *Oh Harry, Harry,* she cried to herself. Only yesterday.

"Esther, Esther," Margot said. "Pull yourself together." She looked in Esther's bag. "It's right here."

"What do they want?"

"You have to answer some questions."

"Don't be angry." Esther was in tears.

"I'm sorry, Esther."

The rabbi read the *get* in Hebrew, and one of the other men translated it into Italian as he went along. Then Margot translated it into English for Esther.

"I am the agent . . ." (Hebrew)

"I am the agent . . ." (Italian)

"I am the agent . . ." (English)

"to deliver the *get*"

"to deliver the *get*"

"to deliver the *get*"

"to Esther Sarah Klein."

"to Esther Sarah Klein."

"to Esther Sarah Klein."

"Here I have the *get*"

"Here I have the *get*"

"Here I have the *get*"

"and the document"

"and the document"

"and the document"

"proving that I was duly delegated"

"proving that I was duly delegated"

"proving that I was duly delegated"

"by the husband."

"by the husband."

"by the husband."

"You, Esther Klein, consent to receive the bill of divorce sent to you by your husband, Harry Klein." Margot translated.

"Yes."

"Si. Just say 'si,'" Margot said to Esther. "Then I won't have to translate 'yes' every time."

"You agree," the rabbi said, "of your own free will and without compulsion."

Margot translated.

Esther: "*Si.*"

"If there is anyone who has a claim against the validity of this *get,* he will come forth now before it is too late to state his objection."

They looked around them. No one came forth.

"You hold your hands this way," the rabbi said in Italian, holding up his hands to demonstrate.

"And my assistant will hold the *get* over your hands and let it go. You catch it." Margot translated, and Esther held up her hands.

"Don't let it go till I tell you," the rabbi said.

"I know," his assistant, a man in his sixties, said. He held it over Esther's hands.

"This is your *get*, the bill of divorce," the rabbi said, "which your husband sent to you and therewith you shall be divorced from him from this very moment and permissible to anyone. Lift it up high."

Esther held it up high.

"Now put it under your arm."

Esther put the *get* under her arm.

"Now walk away."

Esther walked away.

"Okay, come back to me. Give me the *get*. That's all. When I cut the *get*, you are cut open. You are not allowed to marry for ninety-two days. God bless you and grant you peace and fulfillment."

Margot translated.

"I need to sit down," Esther said.

"You still have to do the whipping," the rabbi said. Margot translated.

"The whipping?"

But it wasn't so bad. The rabbi gave Esther a whip made of willow switches and told her to whip the floor five times. Esther looked at Margot. "It's easier if you get right down on the floor," the rabbi said. Margot translated, and Esther knelt down.

"Go ahead. Whip the floor five times."

Esther whipped the floor five times.

"There shall be five sweetened severities," the rabbi said, "through striking the willow switches on the floor." He asked Esther to read. The book was in Italian, and Margot translated the words of a prayer of thanksgiving, and Esther repeated them after her. "The Lord will open for you His bounteous treasures, the heavens, rain for your land in season, and bless all the work of your hands. Amen."

Dognapping

They sat companionably on the *rapido* from Florence to Bologna, where Woody had some business to take care of at the Association of the Families of the Victims of the Bombing. Their shoulders and upper arms touched; they were absorbed in their reading, or pretending to be. Neither one felt like talking. Everything had been settled. There was nothing more to talk about. Woody had given up trying to persuade Margot to come back to St. Clair with him. And Margot had given up trying to persuade Woody to stay in Italy, and maybe they were both a little relieved, ready to step back into their old lives. Margot had crossed a line and couldn't go back. Not to small-town Illinois. She couldn't leave her *studio*. She had circled round to this place for the last time. She couldn't *go* home because she *was* home.

Margot was reading *La Repubblica*. Andreotti's new coalition government, which was almost identical to his old coalition government, was proposing new initiatives to deal with pressing economic and social problems. The new initiatives were almost identical to the old initiatives. General elections had been set for 1992, and the Socialists and the newly renamed Communists were beginning to test the waters. A Sicilian businessman had been gunned down in front of his home in Palermo. A rear admiral, who'd been forced to give up his command in January for saying that the Persian Gulf War might have been avoided, was going to speak at the University of Florence. Tough new immigration laws were being enacted to stop the flow of Albanian refugees into southern Italy.

Woody was reading the *Odyssey,* in Greek, in his Oxford onion-skin edition. Odysseus, entertaining King Alcinous and his guests on the island of Phaeacia with tales of his adventures, was about to reveal his true identity:

> *But first let my name be known to you,*
> *and if I shrink from pitiless death,*
> *friendship will bind us, though my home lies far away.*

What Woody found in the great Homeric poems was a way to affirm the goodness of life without lying or deceiving himself, which was the problem with Christianity, which always wanted you to affirm things you knew weren't true. That's why he couldn't get through Dante. He just couldn't do it. Dante was too teleological.

Margot looked up from the newspaper as if she'd heard the word *teleological.*

"The fall of Troy," Woody said. "It's all in a day's work. It's not the big stories that matter; it's the small ones: Hektor's love for his wife, Odysseus's wanting to hold his mother in his arms. Homer's so clear-headed," Woody said, "compared to Dante. Look at Odysseus in the underworld. Odysseus's old

comrades—Agamemnon, Achilles, Aias—have learned nothing. Their deaths have canceled out the meaning of their lives.
They're like the sinners in the Inferno. But Odysseus sees
clearly."

"What does he see? What keeps death from canceling out the
meaning of *his* life?"

Woody folded the book around his thumb. "I'm not sure," he
said. "Whatever it is, I can almost see it myself, out of the corner
of my eye, but I can't focus on it directly."

At the office of the association, on Via Polese, Margot chatted
with the secretary while Woody met with the president and vice
president.

"You don't have to tiptoe," the secretary said. "This isn't a funeral home."

Margot laughed.

"You should have seen Woody when he first came here," she
went on. "So shy and timid. But only for a little while. We're going to miss him."

"I'm going to miss him too," Margot said.

Margot had always found Bologna dark and gloomy. She was a
Fiorentina and thought that ragù Bolognese was overrated. But
walking under the porticoes with Woody, and seeing through
Woody's eyes, Bologna appeared to her as a real city, not a tourist destination. A university town. That's the way Woody thought
of it. But the tour Woody gave her was personal rather than edu-
cational: the office of the association; Piazza Maggiore, where
the families of the victims assembled every year on the anniversary of the bombing for their march to the station; Santa Maria

della Vita, where his wife had had a nervous breakdown or had seen an angel, depending on your point of view; and the Osteria del Sole, where they stopped for a glass of wine, and Woody laid out, for the first time, his plan for kidnapping the dog.

Rinaldo's family lived on Via della Capponcina, which started in the little piazza in Settignano and ended at Via di Rocca Tedalda at the bottom of the hill. Woody sketched a rough map on a paper napkin. His plan was to come up to the villa from the back, through an olive grove and then a maze of narrow alleys that serviced the villas that lined the main road, and use a bolt cutter to cut through the bars of the fence. He'd arrange for a driver to wait for them—for him and Biscotti—at the gas station across from the bus stop on Via di Rocca Tedalda.

The whole thing made Margot nervous, and she drank more than her share of the bottle of Prosecco that Woody had ordered. She wanted something to eat, but there was no food in the *osteria,* one of the oldest in Italy. Only wine. When the *osteria* got too busy, Woody told her, the old men who ran the place threw everyone out and played cards.

Margot felt a little dizzy when they got back out into the sunlight. They walked to the morgue on Via Irnerio and went inside. Margot held back, but Woody pushed through a door that said ABSOLUTELY NO ADMITTANCE and was greeted warmly by a man in green scrubs. There was a body of a woman on an autopsy table. This was where Woody had said good-bye to his daughter. Margot braced herself, expecting him to burst into tears, but he accepted a cup of coffee, an espresso brewed on an alcohol burner, and chatted with the doctor. From the morgue they walked to Gabriella's *osteria,* just inside Porta San Mammolo, where they were going to eat lunch.

Margot had always thought of Woody as the opposite of Bruno Bruni, and yet like Bruni, Woody had left a trail of lovely women behind him. Margot expected to dislike these women, but instead had found in them potential friends: Allison Mirsadiqi, whom she'd met in Rome, who had invited her to come back to Rome for a special viewing of the restoration work on the Sistine ceiling, which was nearing completion; and Allison's daughter, Turi, who as a student had gotten Woody kicked out of St. Clair; and now Gabriella. She was a stunning woman. Margot didn't expect her to be friendly, didn't expect such warmth. She sat down next to Margot while Woody was in the men's room and wanted to know how Woody was doing. It was too bad he was going back to the States. But Gabriella told Margot that he was always homesick, even when he was happy. Like Odysseus. And Margot understood that Gabriella could be a real friend, like Francesca, and put her hand on Gabriella's. Gabriella served them a wonderful lunch—her own ragù Bolognese, and filets in a sauce made of garlic and *balsamico*. Afterward Margot asked Woody, "How could you let go of such a splendid woman?"

"Gabriella?"

"Of course, Gabriella."

"I was thinking of you," he said.

On their way back to the station, they went out of their way so that Woody could point out the apartment that Cookie had rented on the day before she was killed, in Via Zamboni, the main artery of the university. But it wasn't until they got back to the station and entered the second-class waiting room and saw Cookie's name on the *lapide* above the crater where the bomb had been placed—Carolyn Clifford Woodhull—that Woody let himself go. He sat in front of the stone with his head in his hands, and Margot sat next to him. She had her own loss to deal with, but there was no time for that now. The loudspeaker was announcing that the Adria Express from Basel was arriving on *binario uno* on its way to Florence and Rome. This was the train Cookie had been waiting for when the bomb went off.

On the day before the dognapping, Woody stayed in Margot's *studio* while she examined the Galileo codex that she'd bid on earlier. He was restless and kept checking his tickets. He had two: one from Leonardo da Vinci Airport to Chicago's O'Hare, to throw off would-be pursuers, and the one he was actually going to use: from Ciampino to New York. He was worried about the bolt cutters he'd bought: would they be strong enough to cut through the wrought-iron fence? What if the dog didn't want to come with him? But Margot was glad he was there to occupy Sterling Pears, a historian from Harvard who had become the world's foremost authority on the Galileo manuscripts.

What had happened was that the inexperienced independent conservator who'd submitted the lowest bid to the Biblioteca Nazionale, and had been awarded the contract for the Galileo codex, had severely damaged some of the badly cockled pages by trying to flatten the codex in a nipping press before disassembling it. It was Pears—the conduit for funds from the Smithsonian and National Science Foundation in the U.S.— who intervened and arranged for the codex to be transferred to Margot's *studio*. He'd brought it himself, actually, in a taxi, accompanied by an armed guard from the Biblioteca Nazionale.

All the paperwork had been done, all the photo documentation, and Pears was understandably impatient for Margot to get started. But he'd arrived at the *studio* at an inconvenient time, and Margot, who had known Pears for years, refused to be hurried. She didn't want Pears handling the damaged manuscript, so she sent him out with Woody to have a *caffè*.

Woody and Pears were both academics, but their specialties didn't overlap, so there was no rivalry between them, and Woody was happy to share Pears's enthusiasm for the codex as they crossed the Ponte Santa Trinità.

"It would have belonged to Giovanni Battista Clemente de' Nelli at that time," Pears explained. "He bought as many holographs as he could for his biography, and it's a good thing he did. That's the core of the present Collezione Galileiana. The collection could have been lost then, or again after his death, when his sons tried to sell the manuscripts, and then again in the flood. Another five inches and it would all have been lost. You can't imagine what a disaster that would have been. Without it we'd never understand the transition from Aristotelian to classical physics. It's never been translated, never even been adequately published.

"I'm talking about the notes that begin in 1589 when Galileo was at the University of Pisa and go right up to the time he was arrested by the Inquisition at Arcetri. He'd given the manuscript to Aggiunti because he was afraid of the Inquisition, and when it disappeared he felt 'un dolore e afflizione intolerabile.' Think of it: 'an unbearable sorrow and affliction.'

"There are some letters, too, bound in at the end of the notes. From his daughter. He put her in a convent, you know. He could see the convent from Arcetri."

Through the window of the bar where they were sitting they could see Margot's window in the palazzo on the other side of the river. Woody could picture her standing at her big workbench, but in the window all he could see was the reflection of a few thin clouds in the pale gray sky.

"You know," Pears said, "her bid for the codex job was over seven million lire, and now she wants another two million to repair the damage done by the idiot on Via Faentina. His bid was only four million, but if I hadn't kept my eye on him he could have ruined the whole thing, all the corners would have been lost."

"But it's worth it, right? The extra money?"

"Oh yes," Pears said. "Absolutely. But tell me something— you're leaving us. Margot says you're interested in buying a place in the country."

Woody nodded. "It's not far from my old home. Not far from the cemetery where my daughter's buried."

"The one who was killed in the *strage?* I'm terribly sorry. What a blow. *Animae dimidium meae.*"

Woody nodded.

"Like one of these Medici villas," Pears said. "Have you been out to Poggio a Caiano?"

"More like Horace's *villa rustica,*" Woody said.

"Of course," Pears said, rattling off the Latin: "on me unde-ceitful fate has bestowed a small country estate, and the slight inspiration of the Grecian muse, and a contempt for the malig-nity of the vulgar."

"I haven't closed yet," Woody said, "but they've accepted my offer."

"*Tristis eris si solus eris,*" Pears said. "You will be sad if you are alone. I couldn't take it, living out in the country."

"*Minus solum, cum quam solus esset.* I am never less alone than when alone."

The two men traded more quotations and drank more espresso. Pears left to go back to the Biblioteca Nazionale, where he was preparing a new edition of his biography of Galileo. Woody went back to Margot's *studio.*

Margot had finished her final assessment and wanted to show off the codex.

"I thought you didn't want us pawing through it," Woody said.

"I don't want Pears pawing through it. He's a great scholar, and he's single-handedly saved a lot of the manuscript from being completely ruined. That's why he had the clout to get the codex away from Balentari. Balentari's a nice man, but he was out of his depth here. He had no business bidding on this job."

"But Pears?"

"He dog-ears everything he touches."

"I want to see the letters from Galileo's daughter," Woody said. "Are they in Latin or Italian?"

"I'm not sure," Margot said. She opened the codex to one of the later gatherings. The pages were smaller. They looked at the first letter, which was in Italian:

> *As I have no cell of my own to sleep in, Sister Diamanta kindly allows me to share hers, depriving herself of the company of her own sister for my sake. But the room is so bitterly cold that with my head so infected, I do not know how I shall remain well, unless you can help me by lending me a set of those white bed-hangings which you will not want now. I would be glad to know if you can do me this service. Moreover, I beg you to be so kind as to send me that book of yours which has just been published, so that I may read it, for I have a great desire to see it.*

Woody was as upset by the letter as if it had come from Cookie, come from beyond the grave.

Woody had shipped most of his stuff airfreight. His papers were in order. The false papers that matched Biscotti's tattoo were in order, and Woody had various certificates from the vet who'd treated her after she'd been dragged behind Rinaldo's car. The arrangements at Fiumicino airport were in order. The driver had picked up Woody's big suitcase at the taxi stand in Santa Croce.

Woody had a sack of food and a bottle of water for the dog. He was too keyed up to understand what Margot was saying. He kept fiddling with the bolt cutter, which was wrapped in a blanket. What she was saying was, "I'm going with you. To Settignano."

"It's too dangerous," he said, when she finally made him understand. "You could get in trouble. What would happen to your career if you got arrested for kidnapping a dog?" Margot agreed. It was impossible to imagine such a thing. But she remembered her moment of cowardice on the night Woody rescued the dog from Rinaldo, and she was determined to expunge that moment.

"What about you?" she asked.

"I'm an American, they'd just throw me out of the country. It'd be worse for you. You've got dual citizenship. You'd have to come home."

Woody engaged a taxi. Margot got in too. They drove to an Agip station on Via di Rocca Tedalda, at the bottom of Via della Capponcina. They were early. The driver wouldn't be there till it was dark. They wanted coffee, and there was a bar just down the street, but they didn't want to be seen.

"They're sure to figure out who did it," Margot said.

Woody put his arm around her. "But I'll be long gone."

At eight o'clock the car arrived, a dark Alfa Romeo sedan. Margot sat in the back of the car while Woody went over things with the driver. At nine o'clock he and Margot crossed the railroad tracks and then left the road. There wasn't much of a moon but it wasn't totally dark.

"Did you bring a flashlight?" Margot asked.

"I don't need one."

Margot had to resist the impulse to run away. "What if the police . . . ? What if . . . ? What are you going to do with a dog when you get home?"

"You don't have to *do* anything with a dog. It's just a dog."

Their footsteps made no sound on the soft ground. The stone walls along the road were topped with broken glass. They walked up the slope through an open field, past a hunter's blind, and then through an olive grove. At the upper end of the grove they came to a narrow alley, just wide enough for a car, that led to the back gate. There was a surveillance camera here, just as there was at the front gate.

They waited. The dog didn't come. Woody unwrapped his bolt cutters.

"My God, Woody, what are you going to do? You said the dog came here every night."

"I'm going to cut through this bar next to the gate." The bar was thick, but the bolt cutter was at least four feet long. The bar rang like a church bell when Woody cut through it.

"Can you bend it out now?"

Woody shook his head. "I have to cut through at the bottom too. It's too heavy to bend. I want to wait a little while. I didn't think it would make so much noise."

"Where's the dog?"

"Margot, I don't know. The dog has been here every night."

Ten minutes later he made another cut. Another ringing sound. But no dog.

"She may be chained up."

"Why would she be chained up? They've got this fence."

"I don't know."

"What are you going to do?" she said again.

"Don't panic, Margot. I'm going to look for her."

"Woody, you can't. It's too dangerous. Please."

But Woody was already squeezing through the gap he'd made in the fence.

It was darker now. A cloud had covered the little bit of moon.

Margot couldn't see the house from here. Just the surveillance camera. A little glass window. She had an impulse to ring the bell and look in the little window, but she stayed hunched down.

What to do? How long could she wait in the dark? She was afraid Woody would break into the house. She listened. A car went by on Via della Capponcina. Then another car. And then she heard someone walking, someone with a stick. Someone coming down the alley from the town. She hid herself behind the laurel hedge. It was an old man. He opened the gate with a key and went inside. He was too old to be Rinaldo's father. He must be the grandfather.

Margot imagined God watching her. What circle of hell would He put her in? There was no circle for kidnappers or dognappers. Maybe stupidity. Was stupidity a sin? No circle for the stupid. But maybe there should be.

And then she heard the dog, heard someone talking to the dog. Not Woody, but the old man: *"Fai pipì, Cicci, fai pipì."*

Woody, crouched down behind some bushes, heard the old man too: *"Cicci, Cicci. Fai pipì."* He heard the dog too. *"Buona ragazza,"* the old man said. Woody thought the dog was going to go back in the house, but she'd caught his scent on her way and came to him. The old man kept calling her. *"Cicci, Cicci."* Woody talked to her while the old man called. He could have grabbed her collar, but he didn't. He just talked to her: "Biscotti," he whispered, "you can stay here, or you can come with me, it's up to you." The dog stayed with him, and he heard a voice from inside telling the old man to leave the dog out. Then the shutting of the door.

Woody came back with Biscotti. "I think they forgot to let the dog out," he said. "The old man let the dog out, but then he wanted her to come back in."

"He sounded nice."

Woody nodded. "He did, didn't he?"

Down the alley they went, through the olive grove, past the hunter's blind in the field, back onto the road. Crossing the tracks to the Alfa Romeo in the Agip station.

Woody opened the door and the dog jumped into the back.

"You could come with me," Woody said.

"To Rome?"

"Home. To America. I've got a credit card for the plane."

"This isn't a romantic comedy, Woody. This is real life. I have a job, responsibilities, an apartment, a grown-up life. Besides, I don't have my passport."

"Right right right. I'm sorry. I wasn't thinking."

He put his arms around her and they kissed. She'd known for a long time that she wouldn't go back with him. Even so, the thought that Woody hadn't pursued her with the same determination that he'd pursued Biscotti made her sad.

Woody rolled down the window and Biscotti put her head out.

"The woman," the driver said—the driver had been hired by Woody's lawyer—"she's a good friend?"

"Very good friend."

The driver nodded. "Always tough to say good-bye. At least you got the dog."

When they got to the *autostrada*, Woody reached into the backseat and patted Biscotti's head. He was thinking back to the stone altar in the Archeological Museum. Maybe he had glimpsed into the future after all. Everything seemed familiar. He stroked the dog's head. Dogs' heads are shaped just right for hands.

They passed a sign for Siena. The driver lit a cigarette and offered one to Woody. Woody was tempted. He hadn't had a cigarette in years. The smell was wonderful. His wife, Hannah, had

had to give up smoking when she joined the convent. She said it was the hardest thing. Giving up cigarettes. The thought of it brought Woody to the edge of tears.

"You okay?" the driver asked.

Woody wanted to explain, but he didn't understand it himself.

Margot took the number-14 bus back into the center, but instead of getting off the bus in Piazza Santa Croce and going home, she went all the way to the train station and then took a cab to her *studio.* She looked at herself in the mirror in the slow, slow elevator. She could see that she'd been crying, without even knowing it — but just a little. She negotiated the locks and the alarm system. The Galileo was on her workbench.

She got out her lifting knife and her Japanese water stones from the library cabinet where she kept her tools. She'd made the lifting knife herself, when she first went to work with Signor Cecchi in Prato, out of a hacksaw blade. She'd clamped the blade in the job backer, snapped it in half, ground down the teeth, taken the angle back on a grinding stone, finished it by hand, and wrapped the handle in leather. Signor Cecchi had held her hand every step of the way, and she could feel something of his spirit in the knife as she held it in her own hand, a spirit that would help her face the uncertainties that lay ahead of her, that would help her overcome them and master the art of living.

She put the Japanese stones in a bucket of water to soak while she fixed a small pot of espresso. Standing at the bench, waiting for her coffee to brew, she could look down on the Arno. She could see the shops on the other side of the Arno, the leather shop where Esther had bought her multicolored coat. The river moved as slowly as the elevator. She'd lived in Florence ten years before she'd been sure which way the Arno was flowing. She knew it flowed from Florence to Pisa and from Pisa to the sea, but for ten years she hadn't known north from south.

By the time she'd drunk her coffee, the stones were saturated. She slipped the coarsest one into a wooden holder she'd built to hold it over the sink and moved the blade of the knife across the top in long even strokes, running a little water over the stone from time to time so the pores wouldn't clog with tiny particles of metal from the blade. Then she moved to the second stone, and then to the third and finest stone. She continued to move the blade back and forth till the edge was so sharp it approached nothing, and then she honed it on a piece of rawhide.

She looked over her survey sheet and paused for a moment. Like a surgeon, she slid the lifting knife under one side of the soft crumbling leather of the codex and lifted the spine off the back of the text block. There was no turning back now.

The Italian Lover

AN ESTHER KLEIN PRODUCTION

The industry was struggling to recover from a string of big-budget disasters. Harry's film had tanked, followed by Clint Eastwood's *The Rookie*, Sean Connery and Michelle Pfeiffer's *The Russia House*, Robert Redford's *Havana*, and—the biggest disaster of all—Brian De Palma's *The Bonfire of the Vanities*. There was a lot of breast-beating in the industry about the need for a reality check, about the need to economize. Hollywood was in the mood for a modest romantic comedy with an Italian twist, and *The Italian Lover* generated a buzz. The marketing execs at Leviathan put some serious money into the trailers and production stills and advance screenings and press packs. And much was made of Michael's death. He'd been making films for thirty years; he knew everyone. Everyone knew him. How could they not come to the opening?

The Italian Lover opened in December on over a thousand

screens across the country. Esther saw it in L.A. She'd already seen it five hundred times—dailies, rough cuts, fine cuts, Eddie's cut, her own cut, the Leviathan cut. She'd worked with Eddie on what passed for a back lot at Leviathan in Burbank on one of the new Avid systems, a first for Esther. No film bins, no editing tapes, no splicers. It was amazing. It was like using a word processor instead of a typewriter. You could save a sequence the way you had it originally, try it two or three different ways, and then watch them all. Without pulling anything apart the way you had to do on a Steenbeck table.

Leviathan had tested two endings. One version ended with Sandro's passionate speech in which he proposes to marry Margot, even though she's going to give the money to the convent. He'll teach her how to live: they'll sail the Mediterranean, tread grapes in their bare feet, go camping in Sardinia, make love on a mountain peak. The other version ended with Margot walking down London's New Bond Street—or Via Capponi dressed to look like New Bond Street—by herself, looking in the shop windows. In her purse she's got the money from the sale of the Aretino volume at Sotheby's. She admires something in the window of an antique shop, an Etruscan statue of a little girl. She enters the shop. THE END. But the second ending had been a waste of time. Viewers preferred the first ending nine to one.

It's always unnerving to see your film in front of a "real" audience, responding to the film, scene by scene, as it unfolds on the screen. It's like watching your daughter at her first piano recital. You can't relax till it's over. But Esther didn't have to wait till it was over. The dogs sniffing butts in the opening sequence said everything that needed to be said at that moment—the audience loved it—and the long take of Zanni walking across the piazza while Margot watches him from the window of his apartment was like watching Chaplin in the long shots in *City Lights* or *The Gold Rush,* everything working on five or six levels. They cut the second Settignano sequence, which slowed down the narrative too much, but that was it.

The Italian Lover opened at the Fox on Hollywood Boulevard. It was a preview for "the community." It was everything a gala is supposed to be: a giant searchlight illuminated the heavens; paparazzi took pictures of Miranda, who'd flown in from Italy, and of the high-level studio executives—the deal makers—who came to check out the film and to register their affection and admiration for their fallen comrade, Michael Gardiner, who had died in August. A handful of recognizable stars appeared too, stars whom Michael had directed over the years.

Zanni generated more publicity in absentia than if he'd been on the scene. The tabloids were full of the story of the government's refusal to grant him a visa.

The audience was enthusiastic and at the party afterward, at the new Ma Maison Sofitel, Esther schmoozed with everyone and accepted condolences on behalf of Beryl, who'd stayed in New York. She ate too many hors d'oeuvres and drank too much champagne, but she was clearheaded enough when Harry called her at the hotel to offer his congratulations. "You're gonna make some money," he said. "You're gonna do a lot of business."

"Thanks, Harry," she said. "It means a lot to me. I mean that you called."

He asked her if she wanted him to come to the hotel, but she said no. She was staying at the Beverly Wilshire, because she'd sold the house in Santa Monica. But it didn't matter. She'd buy another one. She was somebody again.

PIAZZA CALENDA

Beryl saw the uncut version of the film in her own private screening room in her apartment in New York. She hadn't gone to the opening in L.A., but she'd accepted a lifetime achievement award for Michael at the Golden Globes in January. Her children and their families arrived in the afternoon; the other guests came at seven for a light supper, which she prepared herself in the kitchen with two stoves and two refrigerators and two sinks, and served in the living room.

The screening room accommodated all her guests in comfortable chairs. It was the first time she'd used it. There'd been a problem with the modified Norelco projectors, and problems with the electronic focusing system, and the tech support people had been there all day and were still there, going over things with the projectionist, when the guests arrived.

What was she expecting? hoping for? afraid of? She was afraid it would be mediocre, "middling." Would her guests care? Would it matter?

Zanni was truly wonderful, but it wasn't Zanni Beryl was remembering; it wasn't Venice. It wasn't Florence. It was the time in Naples, when she was in the hospital bossing Michael around, sending him out to see this and that, Pompeii and Herculaneum, the mosaics at the Archeological Museum and the Spanish Quarter, and all the time he was drinking Frascati at a little trattoria in Piazza Calenda.

She tried to turn this revelation into something profound, but what she remembered was the food that he'd brought her from the restaurant, china plates covered with foil; what she remembered was Michael climbing into her hospital bed and holding her; what she remembered was the nurse pulling the sheet up over them. They'd never have gotten away with *that* in Sloan-Kettering.

THE SAME RIVER TWICE

Heracleitus of Ephesus says you can't step in the same river twice, but Woody wasn't so sure. He'd stepped back into his old life, taken up his former teaching duties—Horace, Catullus, Virgil, Homer, Classical Mythology, and Beginning Greek—moved back into a house just down the road from his old house, bordered by the same stream on the west and the same moraine to the east. If you floated a bottle on the stream, the way the girls used to do, it might just make it all the way to the Mississippi; and if you drove up to the little cemetery on the cusp of the moraine, where Cookie was buried, you could look down and see the light in his kitchen window.

Woody saw *The Italian Lover* the day after Christmas. His daughters had come to St. Clair for the holidays—Sara and her family, Ludi and her dogs. Woody didn't want to see it. It was too complicated. They'd have to get a sitter for the kids; they'd have to drive all the way to Peoria; it was snowing and the roads were slippery. But the girls wanted to go.

Woody wasn't sure why he was apprehensive. He didn't need to be. He hardly recognized the story. It would have been ten times better if they'd used the screenplay that he and Margot had written. He kept grousing about the differences. The girls shushed him, told him to hush, to relax and enjoy it for what it was—a romantic comedy. But when they caught a glimpse of their father in the piazza, with the dogs sniffing each other, they started whispering and Woody had to shush *them*.

They knew about Margot, and on the way home they kidded him about the love scenes. "Why did you come back?"

"*Naietao d' Ithakan eudeielon,*" Woody started to say, but they interrupted him. "Not in Greek, Papa. Don't hide behind Homer. What was your real reason?"

Woody couldn't answer the question. Florence was so beautiful in the film, more beautiful and interesting than he remembered it. The piazzas, Santa Croce, Fiesole, Settignano, the convent. Miranda was as beautiful as Margot. And Zanni. He and Zanni had hit it off. Zanni had been impressed with Woody's political role in Italy and had invited him to come back to Italy to go duck hunting up in the hill country around Padua. And then the happy ending. The lovers getting married. He pulled himself together. "The happy ending misses the whole point," he said.

The girls disagreed. They still wanted an answer. But he didn't find an answer till they'd left and he was alone, sitting at his desk, writing a letter to Margot. He sat in his study and wrote with the Montblanc pen she'd given him for Christmas, though he preferred the italic nib of his old Duofold.

"Dear Margot," he wrote. He didn't apologize for not writing, though it had been over six months since he left her at the Agip station at the lower edge of Settignano. He just told her what he could see in front of him, out his window. He could see the stream and the woods beyond the stream. He could see his own tracks in the snow, and the dog's tracks. He told her about the girls coming home for Christmas, and what they'd eaten and how the dogs had gotten along and how he pulled his grandchildren on the sled he'd bought for them on sale at Tractor Supply. He told her about his classes, how they were up to sixty lines a day in the Homer seminar, focusing on the Achilliad, and he told her about the young woman who'd replaced him when he was gone and who was now in a tenure-track position, a fire-breathing feminist who'd regarded him with suspicion at first. But he liked her because she'd fought tooth and nail to prevent the old dean, Woody's enemy, from folding the Classics department into something called "World Literature."

He told her how much he'd enjoyed her article in the November issue of the *National Geographic* on the twenty-fifth anniversary of the flood, and he told her about visiting his wife, Hannah, in the convent, before she died. "She wanted a favor. She wanted me to change the inscription on the tombstone, Cookie's epitaph. That's what we quarreled about originally. She'd wanted *la sua voluntadè è nostra pace,* God's will is our peace. That's what she had the monument company put on the stone in the first place, but I had them sand it down and put on a new epitaph: 'Against the strength of love, you will find no herb. Against the strength of love, no herb grows in the garden.' She hated it, but I couldn't see Cookie's death as part of God's plan. What kind of a plan could it be to let all those people be blown up? But what she wanted now was a line from Shakespeare: 'There's a special providence in the fall of a sparrow.' And the funny thing was, I could see it. 'Think about it, Woody,' she said. 'Do you think it didn't matter? That no one noticed? Look how *you* noticed, Woody. Look how you fought for her. I don't know the whole story, but I know you went to Bologna. You went to the trial. You fought for her, Woody. You loved her. It's not "just a man gone." Can't you work your way out from this, from your love, work your way out to God's love? Maybe not all the way. Just a little way. You can't say her death was meaningless. If it was, why did you care so much?'

"And I knew she was right. But she was having trouble talking. She was on a respirator and she started coughing. I told her I could go that far, and I tried to get her to stop coughing, to take it easy, and when she stopped coughing she asked me again, 'Will you do that for me, Woody? Then I'll rest easy. It's been on my mind so long.'

" 'I'll take care of it, Hannah,' I said, and I bent over to kiss her. I was thinking how happy we'd been, and I think she was thinking the same thing. 'I remember, Woody,' she said. 'I'll always remember. You'd better go now. I'm tired.'"

And he told her about stopping at the monument company on the way home to order a new tombstone and about the biography of Odysseus he'd started putting together. "Did you know that Odysseus had a sister?" he wrote. "Nobody knows that. She's mentioned only once, in Book X, but think of it. Odysseus grew up with a sister. Don't you have to wonder how she shaped his life, like all the other wonderful women he encounters in the poem? Arete and Nausikaa and Penelope and Kalypso and Circe. When I think of them, I think of all the wonderful women in my life, and especially you, Margot. Seeing the film last night brought it all back to me. I've been trying all morning to figure out how you've shaped my life, and the answer just came to me. I've thought of you as my temptation, like Kalypso or Circe, or even Nausikaa, but you weren't my temptation. You were my helper. You were my Athena. You came to me when I needed you, and you helped me on my way when I needed to go home."

And he told her that he read everything he wrote aloud to the dog, Biscotti. He told her about going duck hunting with Biscotti in the marshes down by the river, the Mississippi, and how she could swim under water and retrieve two ducks at a time, and how she could negotiate the thickest briars, and he told her that it was time for lunch, a salami sandwich for him and Science Diet for Biscotti, and that after lunch he and Biscotti were going to go to his office for a while to make up his syllabi for the new term.

And then he read the letter aloud to Biscotti, and then he signed it, "Love, Woody." He put it in an envelope and sealed it and addressed it and dropped it off in the mail room at the college.

A BROAD ROMAN ACCENT

Miranda spent a week in L.A. in December doing the interviews required by her contract, and she stayed for the premiere of the American version, which had been cut to get an R rating, but she left right after the premiere. She was two months' pregnant and wanted to go home. She was four months' pregnant when the film opened in Rome, dubbed into Italian. She was the only one who didn't enjoy it. She sat between her husband and her mother-in-law.

She'd turned down several offers from Gordon Talbot at Leviathan, and later on she turned down several job offers from Guido's father: she could be a secretary at the movie-supply house; she could be a salesperson; she could be a consultant; she could be whatever she wanted to be at Graziano Brothers Movie Supply Company. But what she wanted to be was a book conservator, and on the basis of a strong recommendation from Margot, who'd given her away at her wedding at the end of August, she had apprenticed herself to a conservator in Rome, working with her hands: folding, sewing, pressing, cutting. She gave her mother-in-law fits by riding Guido's Vespa 40X to work every morning, to Signor Melozzo's *studio* near the Piazza del Popolo. On Friday afternoons she volunteered at the cat shelter in Largo Torre Argentina.

She was embarrassed by the uncut sex scenes. Not because her bare butt was on display, but because there was no rhythm to them. No give and take. No long slow buildup, the way there was with Guido. But her mother-in-law leaned over and whispered in her ear, "How lucky, to be like that with Zanni, so intimate, even if he's from Venice."

"Mamma," she said, "you should be ashamed of yourself."

They watched the end crawl till they saw Guido's name listed with the principal *macchinisti*—and then they went to dinner at Casa Farnesina, which was only two streets away from the Graziano palazzo. They sat at a long table, and Miranda ordered the *risotto ai frutti di mare*. While they were eating bread and drinking wine and waiting for their *primi*, she tried to explain how Esther had ruined the story, but no one shared her indignation, and she soon forgot it herself. The risotto was so good. She'd eaten squid before, but had never realized what it's supposed to taste like. It was supposed to taste like this.

"It's just a movie," Guido's father said. "What do you expect?"

There were ten of them around the table, nine prominent Roman noses and Miranda's small button nose, ten opinions about happy endings. Guido's mother was the only one who agreed with Miranda. "In real life," she said, "you want a happy ending, but in a movie a sad ending would be nice."

In the morning, waiting for the light at Ponte Garibaldi on her way to work, Miranda saw a young man, who was leaning against the column at the head of the bridge, lift up his head, put his thumb under his cheekbone and twist it, and make kissy faces at her. *"Non me ne frega niente,"* she yelled in her broad Roman accent. She stroked the tops of her fingers under her chin. The light changed. She revved up the Vespa. She'd been living in Rome for over a year now. She still wasn't sure who she was, but she knew she was who she wanted to be.

A DARK WOOD

Margot didn't go to see the film when it opened at the Astra II in Florence in February. She walked by the theater in Piazza Beccaria several times. She'd wanted the film to validate her life in Italy, not to turn it into a comedy. But she stayed up late to watch

Esther, who'd come to Italy to plug the film on the Costanza show in Rome, and who was described in *La Repubblica* as *instancabile*, tireless.

Woody's letter was waiting for her one evening when she got home from her *studio*. She'd had a lot of trouble letting go of Woody. Eight months he'd been gone, and she was still uneasy. Finally, at the end of February, she drove to Severiano. To see Rabbi Kors. She wanted a *get*.

"Are you Jewish?" Rabbi Kors asked, his face registering surprise. "Were you married to a Jewish man? If it wasn't a Jewish ceremony, then you don't need a *get* if you want to get married again."

Margot explained. She still had her soul wrapped around a man, she said, the man who'd come with her when she brought Esther to the Seder, and she couldn't get it free. The man had been an irresistible force, but she'd been an immovable object. "It would be a real mitzvah," she said, remembering Esther's words, "if you would give me a *get*."

Legally, it was impossible, Rabbi Kors said. Nonetheless he thought he could let her do the last part of the ceremony — striking the floor five times with the willow branches; throwing the willow branches over the partition. That would be a good solution.

In his study the rabbi improvised a brief ceremony. "You shall be divorced from this man," he said, "from this very moment. And you are permissible to anyone. After ninety-two days. Now for the five sweetened severities." The rabbi handed her a bundle of willow switches that looked as if they'd been used before.

Margot got down on her knees and struck the floor five times; she threw the willow branches over the partition. She started to cry, and the rabbi comforted her, as if he were her father, and he asked the Lord to bless her, to open for her His bounteous treasures, the heavens, rain for her land in season, and to bless all the work of her hands.

It wasn't till the following November, when *The Sixteen Pleasures* was shown at the Casa del Popolo in Fiesole, where they showed a film every Thursday evening, that Margot broke down and went to see it. She still hadn't answered Woody's letter.

Her first reaction to the film, which had been dubbed into Italian, was, *what a lot of work went into this!* It was amazing. She hadn't really anticipated the beautiful shots of Florence. And Zanni was wonderful. He called her once to get Woody's phone number, which she didn't have, and then again to invite her to a performance of Machiavelli's *Mandragola* at the Teatro Goldoni in Venice in which he was going to play Callimaco. Miranda was beautiful and wonderful too, and now she had a baby—Margot was the godmother—and was still working for Luigi Melozzo in Rome. What Margot dreaded was the ending, when the lovers come together so that they can live happily ever after. She closed her eyes. But then she opened them. Sandro was waiting for Margot after the auction. Outside Sotheby's. Via Capponi dressed to look like Sotheby's on New Bond Street in London. She informs him that she's giving the money to the convent. He's happy. He proposes. They'll be poor but happy together.

And her heart melted. Margot's heart. All her resistance gave way, and she started to cry. This was the right ending after all. Esther's instincts had been right. Art heals the wound of individuality. After her cry, she was happy. Happy for the lovers. Happy their story ended this way. She didn't think she could have been happy in English, but she was happy in Italian, because everything is different in Italian.

She drank a glass of wine at the bar in the Casa del Popolo. People were talking about the movie. Mostly what they liked was to see Florence and Fiesole in the film. She was bursting at the seams. *That was me,* she wanted to shout. But she didn't, because it wasn't.

She thought she might go back to her *studio.* She'd put in five months of solid bench time to finish the Galileo codex, pressing the two-hundred-odd folios individually in a low-humidity environment to smooth out the cockling, scraping away the glue deposits left by the boy in the eighteenth century, mending tears, reconstructing the binding. But the codex had already been returned to the Biblioteca Nazionale, and she'd gone on to the next thing, and then the thing after that.

The treatment of the codex had ended as it had begun—with a flourish of trumpets. Sterling Pears liked publicity and the codex was news. A team from Harvard University wanted to reproduce the codex electronically. Old Professor Steckley from I Tatti had been at the press conference, along with reporters from *La Repubblica* and *Corriere della Sera.* Even *La Nazione* sent someone to cover the story. Not everyone was happy. "Why was it," Carlo Malagodi asked in *La Repubblica,* "that the restoration of one of Italy's national treasures had been entrusted to a woman from the American Middle West?"

Leaving the Casa del Popolo, the woman from the American Middle West headed toward the piazza to wait for the bus. But then she changed her mind and turned around and followed the road up toward Borgunto, past the Casa del Popolo, which was now closed. She followed the road till she got to the garbage containers and the Dumpster that sat at the beginning of the path to Settignano. She hesitated, but only for a moment, before setting off. In the middle of life's way—well, a little past the middle—she found herself in a dark wood. But the moon was full and she wasn't lost and she wasn't afraid. And she wasn't alone. Her mother was with her, at her side, and her father too. And Sandro and Francesca, and Esther. And Miranda. And Woody. She could hear their laughter, see their smiles, feel the warmth of the love they'd shared, as sure and familiar as the path beneath her feet.

ACKNOWLEDGMENTS

Thanks to my first three readers for their support and encouragement: my wife, Virginia; my agent, Henry Dunow; and my editor, Pat Strachan.

Thanks to Bob Misiorowski, for reading the manuscript and answering questions about everything from movie finances to production schedules. And to Amy Barnes and Duilio Ringressi, for movie help in Florence; to Julie Lindstrom and Ed Niehus, for movie help in Galesburg; and to Eric Graham, for solving a crane problem from Texas.

More thanks to John Mottishaw of Classic Fountain Pens, for help with the fountain-pen scene; to Rita Severi, Paolo Bolognesi, Janet Smith, Paola Polselli, and Luca Cataldi, for help with Italy; to Cheryl Porter and Jana Dambrogio, for help with book conservation; to Bill and Syd Brady, for their fund of general knowledge; to Dr. Thomas Patterson, for help with Michael's prostate cancer; and, to the Cipriani, Lodovici, and Broccoli families, for their hospitality in Florence and Bologna.

Robert Hellenga received his BA from the University of Michigan and studied at Queen's University in Belfast and at the University of North Carolina before completing a PhD in English Literature at Princeton University. He teaches at Knox College in Galesburg, Illinois, and is the author of four previous novels, *The Sixteen Pleasures, The Fall of a Sparrow, Blues Lessons,* and *Philosophy Made Simple.*